Finding
Eileen

Stephan Nebbia

Brandy Pond Publishing

Title: Finding Eileen / Stephan Nebbia

Author: Nebbia, Stephan P

ISBN (Paperback) : 979-8-99-54858-0-3
ISBN (e-book): 979-8-99-54858-1-0
ISBN (Hardcover): 979-8-99-54858-2-7

Cover Design: Amy Savoy

DEDICATION

For Eileen Markey, Brian Mikolajczyk, and Doug Noble; three extraordinary individuals and wonderful friends, who left this world a much better place for having passed through it. May they rest in peace.

TABLE OF CONTENTS

PROLOGUE

March 15, 1991

Darkness engulfed Mason Hollingsworth as his feet shuffled forward. With each rapid breath, the cloth sack covering his head was drawn to his nostrils, making it difficult to breathe. He was escorted by two lanky Irishmen who had picked him up from the cocktail lounge at the Boston Harbor Hotel. Derrick and Sean were the names he'd heard them call each other, his sense of hearing enhanced by his inability to see.

This wasn't part of the agreement, and he wondered if he'd made a terrible mistake. They walked beside him, gripping his arms above the elbows. Sweat poured down his brow, across his face, and onto the collar of his custom-tailored suit.

"Straight ahead," said Derrick on his left.

The air was cool and musty. With each step, Mason's heel plates clicked on the concrete floor, echoing in the periphery. A stale odor of cigar smoke percolated through the fabric covering his face.

They stopped walking, and he was spun forcefully by the hands gripping his arms. "Sit," said Sean from the right. Mason crouched reluctantly into a sitting position, unsure if there was a chair or stool behind him to prevent him from falling to the floor. He was relieved when something solid contacted the back of his leg, and he dropped down onto the seat of a wooden chair.

His eyes recoiled from the flood of fluorescent light as the sack was ripped off his head. He squinted, slowly regaining focus, at which point he saw Seamus Callanan seated directly across from him. The Irishman was slumped back in a wingback chair, a bourbon cupped in one hand and a cigar neatly dividing the fingers of the other. With his beige suit and Panama hat, he bore a passing resemblance to El Exigente from the vintage Savarin coffee ads.

Mason's pulse quickened, keeping pace with the profusion of sweat oozing from his pores. Looking around the room, he guessed that he was in some sort of warehouse. There were pallets of wooden crates stacked halfway to the ceiling. Small offices with desks and cabinets dotted the perimeter. A guard in a gray uniform, carrying a short-barreled rifle, paced an elevated second-floor walkway.

Callanan stared with humorless rigidity, then forced his mouth into a reluctant grin. "Good evening, Mason," he muttered in a lilting Irish brogue. "I hope you enjoyed the car ride." Then, leaning forward, "let's get straight to business, shall we? Have you brought the money?"

Derrick, the taller of Callanan's assistants, with light brown hair in a crew cut, slung Mason's leather briefcase onto the coffee table between them and popped open the two chrome clasps. He spun the briefcase toward Callanan and opened it. Packed neatly inside, filling the entirety of the case, were stacked bundles of crisp one-hundred-dollar bills.

"One hundred thousand dollars," Mason said. "It's all there. You can count it."

"We trust you, Mason," Callanan lied with feigned conviction. He looked at Derrick and nodded. On cue, Derrick closed the briefcase and set it down beside Callanan's chair.

Callanan spoke again. "That takes care of business item number one. What about number two? Where do we stand?"

Mason hadn't noticed until that moment the large plastic drop cloth on the floor adjacent to where they were sitting, secured at each corner with a brick. He swallowed hard and began to stutter as he spoke. "It's all taken care of, Seamus. Massport security will be staffed with the team you requested." His gaze darted back and forth between Callanan and the tarp.

"And..." Callanan prodded.

"And," Mason continued, "they'll be the sole security that evening in Terminal D at the Port of Boston."

"Good," said Callanan, tapping his thigh. "I'm a man of my word. You kept your part of the bargain. I'll keep mine." He motioned with a wave of his hand, and the shorter of the men, Sean, left the room. "You came to us asking if we might help persuade your opponent to drop out of the race."

Mason nodded. "Yes, that was the agreement."

"Well, I'm afraid our attempts at persuasion weren't heeded to our satisfaction." Callanan leaned forward in his chair, taking a puff of his cigar and slowly blowing out the smoke. "Not to worry," he said. "We've implemented plan B."

Sean returned, pushing a man in a suit, his hands bound with zip ties and a black cloth sack covering his head similar to the one Mason had worn. He limped along, favoring his right leg. Sean ripped the sack off his head.

The man stood for a second, blinking and squinting. He looked at Callanan, then at Mason. The blood drained from his face. "Hollingsworth? You filthy bastard." His eyes glared with incredulity. "What the hell is going on here? Are you out of your goddamned mind?"

Hollingsworth sat upright, grasping the back of his head with interlocking fingers, his eyes bulging. "Seamus, what the hell? You kidnapped him?" His eyes darted between the two men. "We'll be arrested!" He eyed the tarp, and a sudden realization seized him. "Oh my God." He stuttered. "Seamus! No! Please..."

Callanan looked at Derrick and gave a single nod. Derrick picked up the phone book from a shelf below the coffee table and held it next to the left side of the man's head. He then pulled out a silenced .22-caliber handgun, placed the canister directly against his right temple, and pulled the trigger.

Pffffft! A percussive blowing sound was followed by the thud of the bullet embedding in the phone book. The man's eyes rolled back, and he dropped with a thump onto the plastic tarp. Blood oozed out of the small exit wound in his skull, forming an enlarging crimson puddle.

Mason screamed as his calf muscles contracted involuntarily, pushing the legs of the chair backward, loudly scraping the concrete.

"Looks like you'll be running unopposed, Mason," said Callanan. "Or should I say Congressman Hollingsworth?"

"Jesus Christ, Seamus! What have you done?" Mason winced at the gurgling blood, choking back a churning wave of nausea. He started dry heaving.

"What have I done?" Callanan asked. "Don'tcha mean what have we done, Mason? We're in this together now. A conspiracy of sorts." Callanan stretched out the last words for effect. "Murder for hire," he added, patting the briefcase with a smug grin.

Mason pressed his forehead into his open palms. Fear gripped him like a bench vise. "This can't be happening!" Mason tried to catch his breath. He was hyperventilating, the words trickling out in fragments. "What happens when they find him?" His eyes darted back and forth. "It will be national news. I'll be the prime suspect."

"Find him?" Callanan laughed. "Aye, they won't be finding him, Mason. What the police will find is the record of a fishing boat being chartered earlier today by one state assemblyman, Richard Navagh." He leaned back in the chair, letting his arms fall to the rests. "A regrettable decision, what with the nasty weather brewing off the coast this evening. No, my friend, Mr. Navagh here, along with his boat rental, is going for a deep dive into Boston Harbor."

Mason stared up at Callanan through vacuous eyes.

Callanan shook his head in feigned pity. "It will be a terrible loss, and a shock to his constituents. God rest his soul." Then, to his assistants: "Now clean up this goddamned mess. The boat is waiting."

***

Crouched behind a stack of crates on the third-floor landing, Ellen McCarthy clapped her hand over her mouth. Her breathing stopped, water pooling in her eyes. Her other hand clutched Amanda's arm, her nails clawing the skin like an eagle's talons. Amanda's arm trembled, her eyes dilated in frantic panic as she stared back. They'd just witnessed a murder, and if they were discovered, they'd be next.

Amanda put a finger to her lips, silently mouthing, "shhhhh," exaggerating her facial expression.

Ellen choked back tears. "This was a stupid idea," she whispered. "Why did I listen to you." Her blond hair fell onto her face, as her head dropped in despair.

"Quiet, not now," Amanda pleaded with her eyes, shaking Ellen's arm.

Amanda Henderson was the first and only friend Ellen had made since starting high school At first, Ellen thought Amanda was crazy when she suggested sneaking into local businesses at night and taking cash from the registers. But she went along with it. How could she have been so stupid? "We have to get out of here!" Ellen looked back through the doorway to the room with the fire escape where, earlier, they had entered the building.

Amanda scanned the distance to the doorway, assessing their chance of making it out unseen. "They'll see us." She grabbed Ellen's collar and pulled her down. She mouthed the words, "We'll wait 'til they leave."

Outside, lightning flashed at the windows, followed by a booming crack of thunder. A storm had developed rapidly from the light drizzle they'd encountered when they arrived. Perhaps it would provide the cover they needed.

It was dark, and they hadn't noticed the clutter around them. As Amanda turned to assess their escape options, her foot inadvertently nudged the bottom of a fire extinguisher standing upright against a wall. It teetered on its base, then fell to the floor with a loud metallic clang.

"What the hell is that?" Seamus Callanan shouted, leaping from his chair looking to where the noise originated. "Someone's here." He drew a handgun from a shoulder holster and waved to his men. "Find them. Nobody leaves this building."

Amanda jumped first. She grabbed Ellen's shirt. "Run, Ellen, run!" She crawled through the doorway, then vaulted into a sprint toward the window exit to the fire escape. Stepping over the sill, the rain drenched her clothes. She took the stairs two steps at a time, her feet slipping on the wet iron steps.

Ellen had one leg through the window. Cold rain pelted her face and head. She looked around frantically, assessing her options, and spotted another building close by. Looking up the fire escape, she saw a flat roof two stories above.

"Not that way!" she shouted to Amanda, but it was too late. Amanda had already released her grip on the ladder at the base of the fire escape, splashing down into a puddle.

Ellen looked back through the window into the room. Nobody was there. She made a quick decision and climbed up the fire escape into the oncoming rain. Once atop the roof, she glanced over the wall. Still clear. Nobody would suspect she went up the fire escape. A bolt of lightning lit up the sky. Immediately she second-guessed herself. Now she was trapped.

Ellen darted across the roof through the torrential rain to the parapet wall beside the adjacent building. The other roof sat about five feet lower, with a gap of seven or eight feet between them . The height difference would work in her favor. Ellen went to the front of the building and peeked over the edge. Still, nobody on the fire escape. She could now see Amanda running through the downpour in the parking lot, scantily lit by a few scattered lamp posts and the moon filtering through the rain clouds.

She rushed back to the center of the rooftop giving herself plenty of space. She'd done this hundreds of times on her high school track team. Hurdles, long jump, 440, all of it. But never in a heavy rainstorm. And never with a risk of failure that included a potential five story plunge to her death.

With no time to think about it, she took a deep breath feeling the cool damp air expand her lungs. She leapt into a full sprint toward the other building, arms pumping furiously, flinging water. When she got to the wall, she lifted her right leg high, hurdling the edge and shoved off her left foot. But her left foot slipped backward on the wet rooftop, slowing her forward momentum. She gasped, frozen in midflight. Despite the bad footing, she sailed across the gap between the two buildings, just barely clearing the distance. She caught her trailing foot on the opposite wall, and with her foot as the fulcrum, her body was catapulted around, her head slamming onto the gravel. The pain was intense and immediate, and she lay motionless.

She could hear voices below.

"There she is," said one.

"Get that bitch," yelled the Irishman from the parking lot.

Run Amanda! Run! But the voices became increasingly faint and distant. A hazy veil blurred her vision, and then everything went black.

CHAPTER 1

Wednesday, May 13, 2020

Jack Monroe opened the driver's-side window of his BMW. The cool breeze enveloped his face and tossed the loose strands of hair on his forehead. He preferred the fresh air to the car's climate control system, especially on this beautiful spring day. However, with the smell of gasoline and idling engines tainting the air, *fresh* was probably an overly euphemistic depiction of the ambient air quality. But on that stretch of highway, in a bustling suburb of New York City, it was as fresh as it was ever going to get.

Jack sat distracted in thought, his palm kneading the soft leather knob of the stick shift, as he made his daily commute down State Highway Route 4 from Teaneck, New Jersey, to New York City. Teaneck was dotted with examples of seventeenth-century Dutch Colonial homes, one of which Jack had purchased a few years back. From there, he would travel the few miles of heavily congested highway to cross the

George Washington Bridge, and then a few blocks to Columbia Presbyterian Medical Center.

The mammoth gray steel suspension cables of the bridge baked in the sun, their western anchors appearing magnified through the windshield. Jack was happy that his commute took him over the bridge and not through the Holland Tunnel. That was the route he'd taken when he lived in a cramped apartment in Hoboken during his residency training. The tunnels were claustrophobic and filthy. The bridge, by contrast, provided panoramic views of the city and breathable air.

He passed through the town of Fort Lee, located on the rocky bluffs of the Palisades overlooking New York City. Washington's Army had retreated to this location when the British drove them from New York City during the Revolution. There were many historical sites in New Jersey, which Jack loved about the area. He'd always been a history buff.

As he approached the entrance to the bridge, his attention was drawn to a large bald eagle perched near the top of the westernmost bridge tower. He was mesmerized by its size and graceful stature. To be free as a bird, without a care in the world, he mused wistfully. No pretenses. No secrets to keep. How Jack envied that bird.

Thirty minutes later, Jack pulled into the parking ramp at the medical center. He waved his badge, contorting his arm and wrist in several directions before the boom gate opened. He parked in his usual spot.

***

Jack hurried his pace and entered the brown brick building that housed the Neurologic Institute of New York, the preeminent center in the world for the diagnosis and treatment of neurological disorders. Jack was proud to have landed a position there.

During his fourth year of medical school, he had done a rotation with the renowned pediatric neurologist Arnold Gold, whose inspirational manner had led Jack to choose neurosurgery as his career path.

On entering the building, he was greeted by Ned Hoffman, the security guard, who was nearly as old and in want of a facelift as the building itself. He'd probably been there since the Roosevelt administration. His uniform hung loosely on his cachectic frame.

"Good morning, Doc," he bellowed with a smile that elevated the tips of his bushy gray mustache.

"So you say, Ned," Jack joked, patting Ned's shoulder. Then he hustled through the open door of the elevator resting on the ground floor.

There were a few student nurses looking apprehensive, like baby bears who had lost sight of the mama bear. The mama bear, however, was right there beside them, figuratively speaking, in the form of Ruth Burgess. Ruth was one of the senior nursing supervisors, in every possible meaning of the word *senior*, who, behind Ned Hoffman, might have been the second-oldest employee at the medical center.

"Good morning, Dr. Monroe," she said in a rattling, raspy voice, which reminded Jack of the nuns at St. Anastasia. There, for various transgressions, he'd spent his formative years being cracked on the knuckles with the metal straightedge of a wooden ruler. It wasn't a fond memory.

"Hello, Ruth," he responded. "How have you been?" He wasn't really looking for an answer, but he got one, nonetheless.

"So-so, Doctor. You know how it is. You can't stop old age from creeping up on you."

Creeping? Jack nearly choked up a kidney. *More like a full-frontal assault,* he thought.

"But I'll be better next week," she continued, "sipping a rum drink on a beach in the Bahamas." Ruth laughed at her own comment, which evolved into a fit of coughing and wheezing.

Jack braced himself for having to perform the Heimlich, but fortunately it wasn't necessary. That started Jack thinking. He wondered when he'd last been on a tropical vacation, or any vacation for that matter.

"That actually sounds great, Ruth," he said as the elevator doors opened on the fourth floor. He jumped out, glad to escape the chitchat. "Enjoy your trip!"

He walked a short distance through the glass double doors of the Neurosurgery Department and into his office suite. It was nicely appointed after recent, long-overdue renovations, with a chic modern vibe in neutral gray tones.

"Good morning," he said, trying to sound cheerful, but sounding instead tired and monotone. Meghan, his office manager, was a short, stout woman with close-cropped black hair and large glasses that magnified her eyes. She sat at her desk holding the phone handset to her ear.

She put a finger up, finishing her phone conversation quickly. "We'll see you next Thursday at 10 a.m., Mrs. Hackney. Don't forget to bring the discs from your scan... okay... take care."

"Good morning, Doctor," she said.

Jack hung up his jacket on the Victorian coat tree by the door and started walking toward his office.

"Wait, Dr. Monroe..."

"Yes?" He paused.

Meghan lowered her voice and looked around conspiratorially. "There are three gentlemen here to see you. They don't have an appointment. I told them that they needed an appointment," she said, exasperated, "but they were quite insistent."

"Where are they?" he frowned.

"They're in the waiting room."

"What's it about? Did they say?"

"No, they didn't," Meghan replied. "Only that it's extremely urgent." She looked down at her notebook. "A Mr. Gigante."

Jack stopped, frozen in his tracks. He looked back at Meghan, the color draining from his face. "Jimmy Gigante?"

"Yes, that's him."

Jack ran his fingers through his hair. "Junior or Senior?"

"Hmm." She fumbled. "I'm not sure. He's maybe in his mid- to late sixties."

"That would be Jimmy Senior," Jack said, lost in thought. "Please." He waved his arms. "Bring them in."

A few minutes later, Meghan returned with three gentlemen who wore dark suits and no ties. Mr. Gigante towered over the others, a tall man about six foot three inches, solidly built, with salt-and-pepper hair slicked back with gel. The men accompanying him were also large and solid, one shorter and wider. They were younger than Gigante, early forties or thereabouts.

Jack stared for a moment at the three men and then reached out his right hand. "Mr. Gigante. Good to see you. It's been a while."

Jimmy Gigante stepped forward without taking Jack's outstretched hand, looking at it like it was radioactive. For a split second, Jack felt queasy. Then Gigante smiled, pushed the hand gently aside, and wrapped him in a tight bear hug. In a thick New York accent he said, "Jack! It has been a long time." Then, motioning toward the two men with him, "These are my associates, Fat Frank and Billy Beans."

Jack shook hands with the two gentlemen with comically childish nicknames.

"Frank and Beans," Jack said, smiling.

Nobody smiled back.

Jimmy Gigante walked forward, looking around the office at the diplomas on the wall and other framed accolades. "You've done well, Jack. You must be proud."

Jack, flustered and embarrassed, managed, "Thank you." Then, after a pause, "So how's Jimmy Jr.?"

"He's doing great, Jack. He's working for me at the printing company. I'll tell him you asked. You guys were close in the old days."

Jack didn't know how to address that. "And how are Connie and the rest of the family?"

Gigante's smile faded. "Well, that's why I'm here, Jack. I need your help." Jimmy Gigante started to tear up.

Jack was taken aback. He had never seen this man show even the remotest hint of emotional weakness when he used to hang around with his son in high school.

"Please, have a seat." Jack pointed to a comfortable leather sofa along the wall in his office. Jimmy sat. The other two men remained standing with their hands clasped in front of them like bookends. Jack closed the glass French doors.

"It's Connie," Mr. Gigante muttered.

"Connie?" Jack's ears perked up. "What's going on with Connie?"

Gigante looked at Jack pleadingly. "She's been having headaches and not feeling great. She went to Englewood Hospital, and they did a few scans." He choked up. "She's got a tumor, Jack. A brain tumor."

Jack felt like he had been punched in the gut. For a moment, he remained silent. "I'm so sorry, Mr. Gigante," Jack said, and he meant it sincerely. He remembered Connie, the younger sister of his friend Jimmy.

His mind drifted back through the years to the Jersey Shore: seagulls squawking overhead and a salty breeze blowing as he lay on a hammock with Connie. Her sun-warmed, bikini-clad body was pressed tightly against his, her head resting on his upper arm as his fingers playfully wound her silky black hair. That was the first time he had kissed her, and in the recesses of his memory he could still taste her tropical lip balm.

Gigante's baritone voice snapped him back to the present. "I asked around, Jack. I talked to a lot of people, and your name kept coming up. They say you're the best. I need your help. Will you do that for me? I mean, for Connie," Gigante pleaded.

Will you help? A simple interrogative which, if asked by any other person in normal conversation, would evoke a response. That response would be an answer: either yes or no, an affirmation or a negation. But in this case, no was not an option.

Forget, for the moment, that Connie Gigante was an acquaintance and a friend, and that doctors were typically discouraged, ethically speaking, from taking care of persons with whom they'd had an emotional connection.

Furthermore, Jack was more than just acquainted with Connie Gigante. A lifetime ago, they had dated. He'd spent many lazy summer days with her and Jimmy on the beach in Sea Girt. At first, she was just Jimmy's younger sister. But then she became a friend, and eventually, more than a friend.

But that was not the only reason. Jimmy Gigante Sr. was Jack's former boss during a summer job long ago, and the father of one of his best high school friends. He was the owner of a prominent New Jersey-based lithography company which, although a legitimate business, in truth served largely as a front and money-laundering operation for his primary occupation. Jimmy "Jugs" Gigante, as he was called because of the way his jugular veins would engorge when he became angry, was the boss of the Collazzo crime family. And *no* was definitely not an option.

Jack crouched down in front of the distraught Gigante and put his hand on his knee. "Of course I will."

Gigante laid his meaty paw over Jack's hand and nodded. Jack walked over and opened the glass doors to where Meghan was sitting. Meghan noticed the uncomfortable change in his demeanor. Jack tugged at his shirt collar, loosening it with his index finger. "Meghan, we need to set up an appointment for a Ms. Connie Gigante."

Meghan reached across her desk and pulled out a red appointment book. She flipped through it. "We're booking out three weeks into June."

Jack swallowed, contemplating this for a second, then turned back toward Mr. Gigante. "Would tomorrow morning work?"

Gigante nodded. "Yeah, sure, that would be great. She'll be here."

"Please have Englewood Hospital send us her workup and scans."

"Will do," Gigante said, flashing a smile and a nod of appreciation.

They shook hands with Jack and left.

CHAPTER 2

Wednesday, May 13, 2020

Jack shuffled slowly down the corridor of the neurosurgical ward, hands behind his back. He had a light schedule that day and was on morning ward rounds with his residents and fellows. Most of the patients on the service had been discharged, so there weren't many patients to see.

"Who's next?" he said to nobody in particular.

At that prompt, a diminutive female Chinese resident, with coke-bottle glasses and dyed blond hair, stepped forward.

"Wen Lee, what have you got?"

Wen Lee fumbled with the patient's chart as the others slumped, bored and half asleep. "We have the pontine astrocytoma in 816...."

"Stop!" Jack grimaced. He waved his hands, motioning for them to move down the hallway and out of earshot of the patient. Jack continued, pointing a finger toward the patient's room. "Wen Lee, I'm quite sure if I look into that room, I will not see a bloody lump of tissue tentatively diagnosed by pathology as a pontine astrocytoma."

Wen Lee dropped her head, knowing the cardinal sin she had just committed.

"I would, in fact, see Mr. Wilson," Jack continued, "a human being, with the distinct misfortune of having a tumor in a precarious location, with a bad prognosis. A retired college engineering professor, father of three teenaged girls, and an awfully nice guy, who deserves our help, and a significant measure of sympathy."

The other residents and fellows stirred from their trances, glad not to be the one on the chopping block. Wen Lee's arms hung down. "I'm sorry, Dr. Monroe."

"That's okay, Wen Lee." Jack eyed her sympathetically and said, "Years ago, I made that same mistake, rounding with Dr. Gold. Hopefully, he is looking down from above, pleased to have made a dent in this thick skull of mine." They all smiled, relieved that the tension had been broken.

After rounds, the group went to the surgical lounge, where there were trays of refreshments and a few pots of coffee. The coffee was never good. It had a burnt, barbecue flavor, as if licking an empty bourbon barrel. In truth, Jack had never licked an empty bourbon barrel, but that's how he imagined one would taste. Nevertheless, he was glad to have it. He always felt sleep-deprived and needed caffeine before starting his surgical schedule.

He had two cancellations that day, so he would get out reasonably early if all went well. There were two VP shunt revisions and a replacement of a skull fragment from a patient who had been in a motorcycle accident. The brain was swollen, and a portion of the skull had been removed for decompression. It had been sutured into the patient's abdomen for sterile safekeeping and, if one were to be perfectly honest, so that it could not possibly get lost. That would be embarrassing.

Sorry, sir, but we lost the top of your skull. For your trouble, at no charge, we will provide you with a complimentary helmet. Story on page two of The New York Times.

Now, with the swelling resolved, it was time for it to be returned to its proper location, protecting the cranial vault so that the patient could get back onto his motorcycle and do it all over again. For the life of him, Jack could not understand why anyone would get on one of those things. Donor cycles. That's what the transplant surgeons called them, and for good reason.

All told, it would be about six hours of surgery. Piece of cake. It worked out well because he had planned a dinner date with his girlfriend that evening, and it would be a nice change, for once, not to be late.

CHAPTER 3

Wednesday, May 13, 2020

The drive home was pleasant. It was rare for Jack to leave the hospital before 5:30 p.m. It was usually dark when he was driving home. Today, the sun shone brightly, and there was a cool breeze blowing off the Hudson River.

The traffic was light crossing the George Washington Bridge toward the New Jersey side. Looking westward, the sun hovered over the horizon, causing him to squint. He reached into his console for his Maui Jims and put them on.

The panoramic views from the bridge were a welcome contrast to the windowless, green-tiled operating rooms. One of the many regrets of his life was choosing a career that required him to be stuck in a windowless room for most of the day.

Jack's phone vibrated in his pant pocket. A second later, the ringtone sounded via Bluetooth from the display, and a photo icon of Leslie's face appeared next to her phone number. It was a beautiful face, with shoulder-length red hair and a light peach complexion, accentuated by piercing green eyes. A face made for television, which, if memory served correctly, was where he had first seen it before actually meeting her. That would have been when her network was doing a documentary on the medical center two years ago.

Jack pushed the button on his steering wheel, then spoke in a feigned Eastern European accent. "Monroe Muffler, can I help you?"

There was a pause on the other end. "I'm sorry. I must have dialed the wrong...."

Jack laughed. "It's me."

"Why do you always do that?"

"The better question is, why do you always fall for it?"

"You've got me there," she admitted. "Sometimes it's hard to believe that someone with your profound level of immaturity is a neurosurgeon." She sighed. "Are you out of work?"

"I am," Jack preened, enjoying the warm sun on his face and the cooling draft from the windows. "You?"

"Not yet. We're just wrapping up. Are we still on for dinner?" Leslie asked.

"Sure," Jack responded. "What about BV Tuscany on Cedar Lane?"

"The little Italian place near the railroad bridge?"

"Yeah, that one."

"Sure, sounds great."

"What about 6:30? Can I pick you up?" Jack offered.

"Timing-wise, it might make more sense if I just meet you there."

"Okay, I'll see you then."

"Yup, see you soon."

Jack clicked the button and ended the call. Fifteen minutes later, he turned onto his street, Vandelinda, beneath a dense cover of mature sycamore trees, and made a right turn into his driveway.

The home was impressive, not for its size or opulence, of which it had neither, but because the original stone structure dated back to the 1600s. It had been renovated many times throughout its long existence, retaining its Dutch Colonial charm, but with some modern conveniences added incrementally.

Jack sorted through his mail, mostly junk with a few bill invoices. Then he had a short nap on his couch, terminated by the shrill alarm on his iPhone clock. He showered and put on the requisite casual-but-neat attire, which would have satisfied each checkmark on a list from *The Official Preppy Handbook*. He quickly combed his dirty-blond hair and assessed his look in the mirror. He pointed both index fingers at his reflection. "Still looking good, Monroe."

Jack drove the three-quarters of a mile to the restaurant and found a parking space on the side of the road near the railway bridge.

He entered the restaurant and, as always, felt like he'd passed through a portal to a small village in Tuscany. The proprietor, an Italian gentleman with salt-and-pepper hair, greeted him with an enthusiastic handshake. "Welcome back, Doc."

Jack smiled and shook his hand. "Hello, Benny. I'm waiting for my girlfriend, so maybe I'll just sit at the bar until she gets here."

"Very well." Benny motioned with both hands toward the bar. "Salute!"

Jack took a seat and ordered a smoked Manhattan from the young barista dressed smartly in black and white. He did his best James Bond impersonation. "Shaken... not stirred." She shook her head and smiled without responding, the same way she did every previous time he had said it.

"Nice to see you, Doc," she said as she started making the drink.

"Likewise, Vic, always a pleasure."

Once served, he sipped his drink, enjoying the mellow overtones. The smoky bourbon flavor, while repugnant in coffee, is quite tasty in a Manhattan.

It wasn't long before Leslie made her entrance. *Entrance* was the appropriate term. The restaurant, which was small and cozy, seating about sixty, was filled to capacity. A number of patrons looked up as Leslie entered, some of the men no doubt because her appearance had that magnetic effect on them. The others likely recognized her as a prominent network news anchor. It was a classy establishment, however, so everyone quickly diverted their attention back to their own meals and conversations, so as not to be caught staring.

They were seated at a table near the window and placed an order for a bottle of Chianti, along with their dinner selections.

"You had an early day today," Leslie said.

"Yeah, not bad." Jack stared out the window. "I had an interesting visit from an old acquaintance."

"Anybody I know?"

Jack frowned. "Not likely. Do you know the name Jimmy Gigante?"

Leslie's attention perked up. She leaned forward, whispering, "Do you mean the mafia don?"

Jack put his hands up. "Alleged mafia don," he cautioned. He looked around and lowered his voice. "Okay, sure, possibly."

"What did he want?"

Jack folded his hands. "I was friends with his son in high school. We played football together. I used to do odd jobs for Mr. Gigante; I mowed his lawn, shoveled snow. You know, the sort of things kids do."

"Sure. If you mean male kids."

"Right. The summer after graduation, I worked as a delivery driver at his lithography company, delivering printing proofs, collecting checks, etc...."

"You never mentioned this before," Leslie said, her eyebrows rising.

"It never came up," Jack shrugged.

"So, what was he doing there?"

"His daughter has a brain tumor, and he wants me to take her on as a patient."

"Yikes! No pressure there." Leslie leaned back into the walnut chair, blowing a puff of air out through pursed lips.

"Yeah, no kidding. I know his daughter. Connie's her name. She was my friend Jimmy's younger sister. We hung out together in high school, and..." Jack caught himself and closed his mouth, omitting the part about previously dating her. "I'm gonna see her for a consult tomorrow. I'm not too thrilled, to be honest. She's almost like family. But I kind of owe him."

"Owe him?" Her eyes narrowed. "For what?"

Jack bit his lip, then said, "It's a long story, but he's helped me out with some stuff, long ago... anyway..."

Leslie cocked her neck. "You don't care to elaborate?"

"Like I said, it's a long story."

Leslie took the cue and sipped her wine.

The food arrived and was delicious. Leslie twirled her bucatini in the red sauce. "Have you given any thought to getting away for a weekend? Maybe up to Saratoga Springs, or Cape May?"

Jack paused to swallow what he was chewing. "Well, I do have some open weekends coming up. We could coordinate my free days with your schedule." Jack laughed. "You know, have my people call your people."

"You don't have people."

"No, I don't," he smiled, "but I have voicemail."

"We do have important things to discuss, you know."

"Sure, I know." Jack sighed, gazing out the window, hoping for something to change the direction of the conversation.

"We've been seeing each other for two years now, and we're not getting any younger."

Jack knew where the conversation was going. It wasn't that he was opposed to the idea of marriage. And Leslie was pretty much perfect. His gaze moved from the window to Leslie. He didn't know what it was, why he was dragging his feet. Or maybe he did know, and just tried to bury those thoughts deep in his subconscious, where they couldn't hurt him any longer. "I know, we'll talk for sure. I promise."

Mercifully, Leslie changed the subject. "Hey, don't you have a Bergen Catholic High School reunion coming up?"

"Yes, the twenty-fifth-year reunion. But I'm not sure if I'm going to go."

"What?" Leslie was incredulous. "You have to go. It will be fun to see your old friends. Won't it? Plus, I'd like to meet some of these characters you're always going on about."

"I guess." Jack gave it some thought. "Alright, we'll go."

"Great." Leslie seemed placated for the moment.

They finished their drinks. Jack paid the bill, and they left. Jack walked Leslie to her car, put both hands on her waist, and pulled her close. She always smelled nice, with a subtle floral-scented perfume, the name of which, *Eau de* something French, he could never remember. He kissed her soft lips, and then again.

"Do you want to stay over at my place?" Jack asked.

"I would love to, but I have to get up at 4 a.m. tomorrow, so I'd better not."

"Alright then, drive safely. Text me when you're home."

"I will." Leslie kissed him and left.

***

Jack got into his car and rolled down the windows. He started the engine but didn't move immediately. He stared into the rearview mirror, westward down Cedar Lane. The road went downhill for a few hundred feet and then leveled off into the central shopping district.

Not much had changed since Jack was a young boy riding his bicycle down Cedar Lane with his buddies. Sure, some of the businesses had come and gone. Restaurants had changed names. But, by and large, most of it remained remarkably familiar. As he sat there, the memories came flooding back like a fast-moving river, breaching the mental dam he'd erected years ago. Riding his metallic-blue Schwinn Stingray, long hair blowing in the breeze, and bouncing over the uneven slabs of concrete on the sidewalk. His mood turned sullen. Where had all the years gone?

The street was quiet at that time of night, with little traffic. Jack put the car into gear, made a U-turn, and headed down through the business district. He drove slowly, allowing the occasional car to pass him as he meandered.

On the right side was a pizza place. Now it was called Tony's Pizza, but when he was a kid, it was Angelo's. He and his friends would park their bikes on the sidewalk, with no need for locks, and go in for a slice or two.

And then, of course, on the left, was Bischoff's ice cream parlor, an iconic old-fashioned soda fountain dating back to the 1930s. Jack couldn't imagine how many ice cream sodas he'd downed while sitting on those rotating vinyl stools, bolted to a mosaic of tiny black-and-white tiles, but it had to number in the thousands.

Rolling slowly toward the Teaneck Theater, he pulled over to an open space at the curb and parked. The memories now seemed to be recruiting all of his senses simultaneously.

In his mind, he pictured the younger version of himself. A somewhat handsome... no, strike that... dashingly handsome eighteen-year-old high school athlete. He wore khakis and a light blue denim shirt on the first anniversary of the day he met the girl who would become his high school sweetheart, the girl he would, forever after, consider the love of his life, Eileen Delaney.

They were complete opposites. She was a free-spirited hippie, anachronistic for the mid-1990s. She wore a flowing sundress, with sunglasses and a headband corralling her braided blond hair. Whereas he was conservative, she was liberal. He was reserved and she was outgoing. They had no business being together. But she brought out the best in him and helped him overcome some of his shortcomings, as did he, for her. It was a true symbiotic relationship.

He struggled to remember which movie they had gone to see. His recollection for such things was not what it had once been. But then again, it was twenty-seven years ago. He thought, and it came to him. It was *The Bridges of Madison County*. What a great movie. Then again, was there ever a bad movie with Clint Eastwood in it? The movie really tugged at the heartstrings. Not that Jack was the sentimental kind of guy who had heartstrings. Nonetheless, it was ironic. The movie featured Meryl Streep, pining over a lost and forbidden love, Clint's character. A love that was brief, intense, all-enveloping, and then gone.

The irony wasn't lost on Jack. It described his relationship with Eileen perfectly. Jack stared out toward the theater as the youthful figments of his imagination faded, until all that was left was the present-day cityscape, coming back into focus. It left him with a hollow, empty feeling and a lingering sadness.

An idea came to him. He had another stop to make.

***

Jack put the car into gear and continued driving westward toward Hackensack. Once across the river, he made a right turn in front of the old Sears and Roebuck building and proceeded a few miles to the entrance of Hackensack Cemetery. It was more overgrown with tall trees and shrubs than he remembered.

He drove through the gates, down the narrow tree-covered lanes, making a right at the mausoleum building, to the easternmost section of the cemetery near Route 4. He parked the car and plodded between the stones to his destination. The cemetery was dimly lit by posted lamps, supplemented by the diffuse lighting in the sky from the nearby Riverside Shopping Mall. There, under a gigantic maple tree, was the stone with the name MONROE engraved on both sides and the inscription, "We only part to meet again." That was Jack's idea. It reflected a belief engendered by his Catholic school teaching. He hoped against odds that it was true.

He stood on the side where his grandparents were buried. He was fourteen when his grandfather died. Then, a few years later, his grandmother followed. He still felt the pain and emptiness of their absence. They were like surrogate parents to him. His parents had divorced when he was just three years old, and his mother had to work, so he and his sister would spend countless days and nights at their grandparents' home. He would give anything to be fourteen again, to see them one more time and tell them how much he loved them.

He went around to the other side of the gravestone where his mother was buried. Beneath her name was the same inscription. Tears moistened the corners of his eyes. He actually did have heartstrings, despite the facade he liked to erect. Growing up, they didn't have much, but they had enough. Even after his mother remarried to his stepfather. But given the chance, he would not have traded his mother for any other in the world. He was frumpy, overweight, and insecure as a young child. But she made him believe he could do, or be, anything. If not for her, he couldn't imagine how his life might have turned out.

He looked at the shrubs on either side of the stone. They were unkempt and in need of pruning. The bare dirt in front of the stone begged for flowers. A deep shame overcame him for letting it go, but life can sometimes get in the way of good intentions.

Tears wet the corner of his eye. All he could say was, "Sorry, Mom." He sniffed, sensing his sinuses filling up, and looked toward the moonlit sky. He promised her that he would be back with some flowers and gardening tools.

Jack got back into his car and drove farther west into the cemetery. He parked his car and wandered again through several rows of stones before finding the one that he was looking for.

He stood directly in front of it, then kneeled down. It was in an even worse state of neglect. Jack brushed ivy off the stone, revealing the inscription, DELANEY.

The emotion started to escalate, as if the vines that Jack had just brushed away had regrouped and wrapped themselves around his neck, winding and tightening. He felt like he was suffocating but was unable to move.

He took a deep breath and continued brushing off the stone. In smaller print, the names Mary and Daniel appeared. The birthdays were different, but the dates of death were the same.

Finally, he was able to get the words out. "I loved your daughter with all my heart, and I'm sorry for what happened."

CHAPTER 4

Saturday, May 16, 2020

Secluded off the beaten path near Warwick, New York, the McKinley rock quarry had lain dormant for the better part of fifty years. For the first half of the twentieth century, it supplied granite and cobblestones to builders in New York City. Over time, the abandoned quarry filled with water from underground springs.

Bob Windham, owner of the Deep Thoughts Dive Shop and Scuba School in Ringwood, New Jersey, had discovered the location several years back while hiking with friends, and kept it in mind as a place to bring students. This was his first outing to this location, and the late-spring weather was cooperating perfectly.

It was mid-morning, and the sun was bright in the eastern sky. Julie Dixon and the other divers sat on a small sandy beach wedged between a sheer wall of granite to their left and a rocky area, a few feet above the water's surface, to their right. Their tanks and equipment bags were strewn about on the sand.

Julie was relatively new to the sport of scuba diving, having only begun three years earlier. Her coworker, Marcie, a fellow teacher at Don Bosco High School in Ramsey, had regaled her with so many stories of diving adventures that Julie finally agreed to try the sport. She ended up loving it.

Bob Windham faced the group. He tapped a wrench against a scuba tank. "Can I have everyone's attention for a moment?" he said. The group paused their activities and looked his way. He cleared his throat. "You should all have copies of the maps and safety precautions which I printed. Does everyone have a copy?"

They all nodded. A few of them reached into their bags to pull theirs out.

Bob clapped his hands. "Alright then. Everyone gather around and follow along, as I go over the plan for the dive." He flipped through his notes.

Bob was in exceptional shape for a man in his late forties. His pectoral muscles and biceps had deflated slightly, compared to the photos in the dive shop from his days as a Navy diver. But he was still a hale figure who wore the sun-weathered face of an avid outdoorsman. His neatly trimmed beard and mustache sported a spattering of gray. He pointed to old train tracks, which passed through the right side of the sand on which they were standing and descended into the water.

"We'll follow those tracks," he said.

Tim Malone, a dentist with a paunchy belly, asked, "How far do they go, Bob?"

Bob turned and pointed to the opposite side of the quarry, about a quarter of a mile away. "According to these maps, all the way to that wall, and then they turn right and continue to the end of the quarry." He added, "We won't be going that far." A few of the group looked relieved.

"The water is deceptive," Bob cautioned. "Visibility is fifteen feet at best. I'll lead and carry a light. Jim?" Bob looked around, spotting the group of three young accountants from Price Waterhouse in Ringwood. They were athletic men in their late twenties. "Jim, there you are. I'm going to have you take the rear and carry a second light."

Jim nodded.

Bob pulled a long rope from his bag. "We're going to hold onto this rope as we make our way over to the northeast corner." He pointed in that direction. "You are each responsible for watching the person in front of you and the person behind you to make sure nobody goes astray. Jim, obviously there won't be anyone behind you, but you get the idea. If anyone has a problem, tug twice on the rope and we'll stop and sort it out." Bob looked at the group. "All clear?"

They all nodded.

"The water is cold. That's why we're wearing the four-three-thickness wetsuits and keeping the dive short." Bob raised his palms. "Okay, gear up."

They put on their wetsuits, set their dive computers, and selected the appropriate weights for their buoyancy compensation vests.

Out of the corner of her eye, Julie couldn't help but notice one of the accountants, Paul, staring at her backside as she wiggled her long, slender legs into the wetsuit. Her brown wavy hair flipped back and forth as she shimmied. She caught him and smiled. He blushed and quickly averted his gaze. Marcie leaned in. "Looks like you've got a not-so-secret admirer."

After a short period of time, everyone was ready. They had their tanks on their backs and were lining up, each taking hold of the rope. The dentist's shy teenage daughter, Taryn, stood in front of Julie and looked around sheepishly. There were eight divers in total, nine if you counted Bob Windham. Once assembled, they put their regulators in their mouths, pulled their masks down, and started to walk single file into the water, waddling awkwardly with their fins.

The water, in contrast to the warm air above, was cold. Julie shivered as her wetsuit filled with the frigid quarry water. A few minutes later, her body heat had warmed it. Once everyone was submerged, they started to slowly swim, each holding onto the tether. They followed the tracks illuminated by Bob's submersible lantern. Mud and silt covered much of the track, so there were gaps where they had to faithfully continue in the direction that it was going and pick it up where they could see it again.

The visibility was, just as Bob described, limited. As they slowly made their way along the tracks, they came across a collapsed gantry crane. It was rusted and broken in several places in about twenty feet of water. Further still, in about thirty feet of water, was a toppled front loader, its yellow paint largely intact and the Caterpillar logo semi-legible. Its massive tires protruded from its now-vertical underbelly.

The next twenty minutes were uneventful. There was an occasional tool or rail cart lying on the bottom. It appeared that the vast majority of equipment had been removed from the quarry when it was decommissioned. They reached the halfway point of their dive. Now, at about forty-five feet of depth, the water was noticeably colder, even with the thick wetsuits.

Julie slowed to purge water from her mask. The mask didn't have a purge valve, so she had to do it the old-fashioned way: by pressing the top of the mask to her forehead, lifting the bottom, and blowing forcefully. The cold water stung as it bathed her face.

They approached the steep vertical wall at the northern edge of the quarry. The wall rose some thirty feet above the surface of the water. Fifty yards beyond the upper edge of the wall was the single-lane country road that they had navigated to get to the entry gate. The gate itself had been removed or stolen, leaving no obstacle to getting into the property.

Once Julie replaced the mask on her face, she could see much better. The glass, which had been fogged, was now clear. Off to her left, she caught a glimpse of a shimmering bit of metal as Bob swung his light in a horizontal arc. Then darkness. She continued looking in that direction. A few seconds later, the lights Bob and Jim were carrying briefly converged on an object—the same object she had just seen. Only now she briefly saw the outline of what appeared to be an automobile. Then darkness again.

Julie stopped and tugged twice on the rope. The group stopped. Bob circled back, passing the other divers until he saw Julie waving her hand. She pointed in the direction of the object she had just seen. The group clustered tightly.

Bob shined his light in the direction indicated, and indeed there was something there, large and metallic. At that point, Jim pointed his light in the same direction. Bob began slowly moving the dive party toward the object.

It was now undeniable that it was an automobile. Furthermore, Julie could discern that it was a Ford Mustang, a vintage model from the 1970s. She knew this because she recognized the silhouette. As a young girl lying in her bedroom at night, she would look out the window between the sill and the bottom of the shade. In that gap of a few inches, she could see her brother's Ford Mustang parked in the driveway, its silhouette etched into her memory.

This was the same silhouette. As they got closer, her intuition was confirmed. In the light of the lanterns, it appeared to be rust-colored and was buried up to the wheels in mud. They were ten feet from the vehicle. Bob continued toward it, and the rest of the group followed closely behind, still holding the tether.

Bob reached the driver's side of the Mustang, which was in its normal upright position. Perhaps a quarry employee had simply abandoned it. Maybe it had become nonfunctional, or not worth repairing, and then simply left there. But a nagging intuition deep inside Julie told her that something was wrong.

The windows were covered with a thick residue of silt and algae. Bob took one of the fins off his foot and used its edge to scrape away the muck covering the window. It took several attempts to clear enough away to get a glimpse inside.

Julie and the others watched from a few feet away as Bob pressed his mask against the window and shined the light into the car. A sudden explosion of gas bubbles blasted out the side of Bob's mask. He'd forcefully exhaled his full lung volume while jerkily flapping his arms and legs to push himself away from the car. A shiver shot down Julie's spine. Bob looked back at the car. Julie could see Bob hyperventilating by the increased frequency of the air bubble release from his regulator. They watched and waited for what seemed like an eternity, but was more like a minute.

After regaining his composure, Bob again shined his light into the car. Julie and the others approached the car and gathered next to him. Curiosity may have killed the cat, but it is a powerful force in human beings, often more powerful than fear.

Death was the last thing Julie expected to see on this beautiful spring day in Warwick, New York, nor any other day, for that matter. Yet there, in the front seat of this Ford Mustang, was a human skeleton—or more precisely, a pile of bones that used to be a human skeleton, with the skull perched on top.

CHAPTER 5

Thursday, May 14, 2020

It was 7:40 a.m. on Thursday morning. Jack poured himself a cup of coffee in the physician's lounge, then walked to the elevator. He pushed the button for his floor, and the old, creaky elevator doors closed in a painstakingly slow fashion.

He lifted the plastic tab on the cup lid and took a sip. *Not bad,* he thought. But no sooner had that thought registered than the aftertaste followed. His face contorted, as though he had licked the scented disk from a gas station urinal. At least he had to give the hospital credit for consistency.

The elevator doors opened, and he walked down the hallway to his office reception area, unlocked the door, and went inside. He flicked on the lights, slipped into his office, and sat down in the leather desk chair.

He had just begun reviewing Connie Gigante's chart when Meghan came through the door, her purse over her shoulder, carrying a cardboard cup carrier from Dunkin' Donuts.

"Good morning, all," she bellowed.

"All? There are just the two of us," Jack laughed.

After putting the cups on her desktop, she examined the lids. "Black for me, death-by-sugar for you."

Meghan walked through the open glass door into Jack's office and handed him the cup. She picked up the one he had been nursing and frowned. "I'll get rid of this hazardous waste."

Jack smiled. "Thanks, Meghan, you're an angel of mercy."

"Yeah, yeah, yeah," Meghan smirked. "Let that be reflected in my Christmas bonus."

Jack considered it for a moment, then leaned sideways from his desk chair. "Duly noted," he shouted after her as she went back to her desk.

Jack sipped his upgraded coffee as he reviewed the chart. Overall, he was optimistic. Based on the scans he'd received from Englewood, Connie Gigante most likely had a meningioma. That was reassuring. If you had to have a brain tumor, that was probably one of the least aggressive ones to have.

This wasn't normally a day when Jack would have seen patients. He had a few meetings scheduled, which he canceled to get Connie in on short notice.

How long had it been since he'd seen her? Ten, maybe twelve years. In a way, he was looking forward to it. Although clearly, not under these circumstances.

Despite the coffee, he had nearly fallen back to sleep, daydreaming in his plush chair. He was awakened by the sound of the single chime as the office door opened, followed by Meghan's voice.

"Good morning," she said in a pleasant, welcoming tone. "You must be Ms. Gigante."

"Yes, I am," a soft, hesitant voice replied.

Jack rose from his chair, walked slowly to the doorway of his office, and stared at the girl he hadn't seen in so many years. He looked into Connie's brown eyes. She met his gaze and smiled. It was as though no time had passed. She was two years younger than Jack. Her black hair was set in a trendy French bob, offset by her light complexion and red lipstick. She had the same slim figure she had sported in high school, though her fashion sense was notably more con-servative. With her thick New Jersey accent, pale skin, and Italian good looks, she gave a distinct Mona Lisa Vito vibe from the movie *My Cousin Vinny*. Jack saw sadness in her eyes and a slight smudge in her mascara.

"Hey, Jack," she said demurely.

"Connie." Jack hesitated for a moment, then walked over to her and gave her a tight hug. "It's been such a long time."

"It has," she responded softly.

As Jack looked over Connie's shoulder, Meghan had cocked her head regarding the encounter with keen interest. She didn't have to say anything. After all these years, Jack could hear her thinking.

At that point, Jack realized that he was still holding Con-nie. He stepped back, looking at her, and said, "You look fantastic, Connie."

"So do you." She looked around the office. "I always knew you would be successful."

"Thanks. I wasn't so sure myself." He would have liked to smile, but the truth in his response weighed on him like an anchor.

Jack invited Connie into his office. "Please, come in," he said as he led the way, holding the door. Connie followed.

"It was good to see your dad," Jack smiled, "and now you, even better. Please have a seat."

"Thank you for getting me in so quickly, Jack. I've been sick over this thing." Her voice softened. "I'm scared."

"It's the least I can do, Connie. I'd do anything for you, you know that."

"Yeah," she said, seeing genuine concern in his eyes. "I do."

Jack picked up the chart on his desk. "Connie, this is good. I mean, not good as in, 'let's have a party,' but there's some relatively good news here. I agree with the doctors at Englewood that this is likely a benign meningioma. I've reviewed the MRI disc, and it looks like a small, noninvasive tumor."

He put down the chart and walked around the desk to where she was seated and put his finger on the back of her head to pinpoint the location. "Right here. It shouldn't be a difficult surgery. We'll need more information, but I feel good about this."

Connie reached up, putting her hand over Jack's hand. "I trust you, Jack." She smiled. "I remember how you used to put your hand on my head like that. Do you remember? Sea Girt, and the Parker House, all those crazy summer days? It feels like a lifetime ago."

"Oh, I remember," Jack replied, flustered. The feel of Connie's hair against his hand brought back pleasant memories. He hesitated, then gently withdrew his hand and went back to his chair.

He cleared his throat. "We would make a small burr hole, take a biopsy, and send a fresh specimen to pathology.

If it's a meningioma, as I expect, we'll make a larger opening and remove the tumor, then patch you back up."

Jack studied Connie's reaction. "Of course, if you'd like a second opinion, I could refer you to Dr. Elmer or Dr. Endl, both of whom I trust explicitly, and..."

Connie cut him off. "I don't need a second opinion, Jack. I trust you. You're the smartest guy I've ever known, and I..." She smiled and was about to say something more, but stopped herself.

"So, when would you like to get this done?" Jack asked.

"As soon as possible. I mean, why wait? Right?" Connie's eyes were becoming red. She clutched her hands in her lap, dropping her eyes.

"I agree," Jack said. "We can get you scheduled for next week. I have an opening if that works for you." Jack sensed Connie's mounting fear.

"Yeah, sure," she sniffled. "I mean, you know, I'm scared as hell..." Her voice broke. "But I want to get it over with." Her lip started to quiver, and a tear rolled down her cheek.

"Oh, Connie." Jack took his glasses off and came around the desk, kneeling next to her chair. He hugged her, resting his cheek against her head as he cradled it with his palm. "I'm going to take care of you. I would never let anything happen to you." He felt the gentle convulsions of her body as she sobbed quietly. They held the embrace, Jack gently stroking her hair, until it subsided.

Connie leaned back, wiping her eyes. "Thank you, Jack. I'm sorry for being a baby."

"Don't be sorry, Connie. It's perfectly normal to be afraid." Jack looked at his calendar. "We had a cancellation on Tuesday, May 19th. We could schedule you in the 8 a.m. slot. You'd have to be here around 6 a.m."

"Sure, that would be great. Thank you again."

Jack sat back in his chair and stared at Connie.

"What?" she said, regaining her composure.

"Nothing. I just can't believe I'm seeing you, after all these years. What's new? Are you still seeing that guy, Terry Sheridan?"

"God, no," she waved her hand. "That's ancient history. I'm in what I like to call a relationship intermission."

"I recall you were going to Rutgers for early childhood education?"

"You remembered. Well, miraculously, between all the partying, I managed to graduate." Connie's mind drifted. "And now, I'm teaching kindergarten at Saint Matthew's Elementary in Ridgefield." She let out a sigh. "Let the good times roll. Overall, I lead a pretty dull life." Connie looked at Jack. "Unlike you. Are you still dating that TV reporter? The redhead?"

Jack's eyebrows rose. "How did you know about that?"

"Oh, you know, the grapevine. Gossip travels at the speed of sound. Bessie's brother said he saw you guys somewhere."

"Ah, well, if Bessie's brother said it, then it must be true," Jack said, raising his hands in surrender.

"Hey, what ever happened with your girlfriend, Eileen?" Connie asked. "You know, the one that you started dating after you dumped me. Have you heard from her?" She regarded Jack's puzzled expression. "Oh, come on, I'm sorry, Jack. I'm only joking."

"Wait," Jack leaned back in his chair, holding up an index finger, "technically speaking, I never dumped you."

"Huh," Connie feigned indignation, looking sideways at him. "Well, it seemed to me, at the time, like a grain-elevator-to-train-car sort of dumping," she laughed.

"We weren't officially going out, right?" Jack said, making air quotes with his fingers, then started to feel bad about their conflicting perceptions of their relationship, as he saw the hurt in Connie's eyes. "And no"

"No what?"

"I mean, no, I haven't heard from Eileen since high school."

"I always wondered why she ran away. She always seemed upbeat."

Jack bowed his head and thought, and then looked at Connie. "Not a clue. In some ways, I feel responsible. She had a difficult relationship with her parents." Jack shook his head. "She was always on edge, distracted."

"How could you be responsible?"

Jack considered for a moment whether he should continue. "I don't like to talk about it, but one night, my parents found pot in my car and traced it back to Eileen."

"Seriously!" Connie's eyes widened. "They must have had a cow."

"Yeah, my car had a flat tire, so I borrowed my mother's car that night. And my stepfather, George, the detective, decided to change the tire. Afterward, he was snooping around my car. I was into sports and wasn't a pot smoker, so they knew it was hers. To make matters worse, he also found some latex products in the glove compartment." Jack rolled his eyes.

"Oh, no."

"Then they brought all of this to the attention of Eileen's parents, who were not amused. They had a powwow, the four of them, and made a joint decision, no pun intended, to ban us from seeing each other."

"I never knew any of this. So, what happened?" Connie listened intently.

"Eileen decided that we should run away. It was totally insane and impractical. But you know Eileen. We were both going off to different colleges. Anyway, I figured if it was meant to be then it would all work out. But when I told her I couldn't run away with her, I guess she decided to go alone."

Jack continued, "It was that night you guys had the party at your parents' lake house, the summer after we graduated. That's the last time I saw or heard from her."

Connie took it all in. "Wow, that's bizarre. What about her parents?"

Jack became more somber. "For a long time, her parents blamed me. There was nothing I could do. They wouldn't speak to me. Then one day, about fifteen years ago, I read in the newspaper that they had died in a car accident. I felt bad."

"I'm sorry."

"It's water under the bridge. I hope that, somewhere, she is happy. She was a kind person. I cared about her. We had even planned our future. Marriage, kids, the whole she-bang." Jack shook his head, lost in thought. "We were just stupid teenagers."

Connie started to speak, but stopped herself. She tightened her lips and stood, bending to pick up her purse from the floor. "I'd better get going. I've got things to take care of." She shrugged. "I guess I'll see you next week. I wish I could say I was looking forward to it."

"It's gonna be okay, Connie." Jack walked her into the reception area.

"Promise?"

"What?"

"That it's gonna be okay?" She stared at him.

"Yes, I promise."

Connie gave Jack a hug and went to kiss him on the cheek, but her lips overlapped the corner of his mouth, lingering for a moment, as they looked into each other's eyes. He felt her soft, moist lips against his, and he pressed back, holding the contact. She slowly backed away.

Jack caught Meghan's inquisitive gaze as she moved some things on her desk, pretending not to be watching.

As Connie stepped backward, she looked again into Jack's eyes, mouthing the words *thank you*, and then left.

Jack looked at Meghan, raising his arms. "What?"

Meghan continued to push things around on the top of her desk. "Oh, nothing at all." Her eyebrows raised. Then, with emphasis and a pause between each word, "Nothing... at... all."

"Okay," Jack sighed. "Just say it."

Meghan stopped what she was doing and leaned against the desk. "Well, not that it's any business of mine..."

Jack shrugged, laughing. "When has that ever stopped you?"

"I'm just wondering about the ethics of you operating on that girl. I mean, she's not hard to look at." She twisted her head, puckering her lips. "No sir... not hard at... all..."

"What does that have to do with...?"

Meghan interrupted. "And she's clearly got the hots for you. That was as plain as day from the conversation."

"Ugh," Jack closed his eyes and held his forehead, "a private conversation that you weren't supposed to be eavesdropping on."

"She was on you like maple syrup on a pancake."

Jack put his index fingers into his ears. "I'm sorry, I can't hear you," and turned to walk back to his office.

"Well, I guess it's none of my business," Meghan conceded.

Jack continued walking into his office. "And on that, we completely agree," he replied.

CHAPTER 6

Thursday, May 14, 2020

Jack had no surgical block time on Thursdays. So generally, except for emergencies and urgent cases, he did not operate on Thursdays. Typically, Thursdays were for office work.

Meghan opened the door to his office. "The calendar has you scheduled for lunch today, with Mr. Sherlock and Mr...." She looked down at the calendar. "Some name I can't pronounce."

Jack squinted and leaned back in his chair. "Oh, right. Those are my high school friends. We've been trying to get together, but haven't been able to coordinate schedules."

"Well," Meghan put her hands on her hips, "chop, chop."

"What time is it scheduled for?" Jack asked.

"Noon." She tapped on her watch. "It's 11:40, Lord Tardy." She bowed and rolled her hand in a circular motion.

Jack looked at the watch. "I better get a move on."

Sherlock and Mikolajczyk were two of his best friends. They were co-captains of their high school football team. Ben Sherlock played defensive end, and Brendan Mikolajczyk, middle linebacker. After graduation, they played college football together at Michigan State.

Mik was a private investigator and owned his own security firm in midtown Manhattan. It was his idea to meet at the Blarney Stone, an Irish pub in the theater district.

At 11:50 a.m., Jack walked outside and found a yellow cab idling. He opened the door and jumped into the back seat.

The Pakistani cab driver, Prashant according to the name tag, didn't turn around but eyed him in the rearview mirror. "Where to, mate?" he asked in a British accent, catching Jack off guard.

"Blarney Stone, on Forty-fifth and Eighth, near the Shubert Theatre."

"Yes, sir," he replied. Then he stepped on the gas pedal and, for a few harrowing miles, did a bang-on impersonation of a Formula One driver at Monaco.

Jack paid the fare and exited the cab, dizzy and grateful to be alive.

Inside, the pub was authentically Irish. It was dimly lit, with most of the lighting coming from Tiffany-style fixtures above the booths. There was a long, ornate mahogany bar with a bronze rail and coat hooks. On the walls hung an eclectic collection of everything Irish: Gaelic writing, shamrocks, pictures of Dublin, and an assortment of green stuff.

It was crowded, and a din of voices competed over a soft background of melodic Irish music. Jack looked around and spotted Mik at the bar. Mik raised his hand, and Jack walked toward the empty barstool next to him. As he closed the distance, they did a fist bump, followed by a handshake.

"Iceman, good to see you. How's it going?"

Apparently, you are doomed to spend the rest of your earthly life answering to your high school nickname. Jack had earned his one evening at a party, where the host had run out of ice. The stores were closed at that hour. So Jack, thinking out of the box, took Quentin, Biff, and a couple of plastic bags in his Camaro to the Hilton along the highway and raided the ice machines.

Thinking back on it, maybe he should be ashamed, as technically it was theft, but it was only frozen water, so was it really? The party would go on, and the nickname, bestowed on him that evening, stuck.

"Status quo," Jack replied. "You?"

"Ah, you know." Mik shifted his weight on his legs, hands in his pockets. "Business is a bit slow this time of year. There's a lot of competition, but I'm doing Okay."

Jack patted Mik's shoulder. "It'll pick up. Things are cyclical."

Mik straightened his back. "How's work for you?"

"Oh, you know." Jack shrugged. "Never a shortage of head injuries, bullets, and tumors." He looked around the bar. "Where's Sherlock?"

Mik pointed his thumb over his shoulder. "He's taking a piss."

As if on cue, Ben Sherlock came from around the side of the bar and let out his trademark jocular laugh. "Iceman!" he bellowed.

"Hey, Ben, long time."

"It has been," he said as he shook Jack's hand.

The bartender, in his mid-thirties, with a crew cut, reddish beard, and mustache, leaned his Popeye-like forearms on the bar top. His name tag said Kelly. In a thick Irish accent he asked, "What'll it be, fellas?"

They all ordered Guinness and took seats in a nearby booth, a quieter location for talking. After a few minutes of catching up, they reminisced about their high school days and various exploits. But mostly, the conversation revolved around football.

"Remember that day at Patterson Kennedy?" Sherlock laughed.

"Hard to forget," Jack replied. "Tommy G. picked a fight with that defensive tackle who looked like a kitchen appliance."

"Hang on," said Mik. "It wasn't Tom's fault. That jerk was taking cheap shots the whole game."

"Tom lost it," Sherlock added. "Remember how he charged the guy, then tripped, so the punch struck his balls?" He laughed. "Then after the guy squealed and collapsed, he got up and hoisted Tom off the ground by his shoulder pads."

Mik nearly choked, laughing. "Tom would have been a human piñata if we didn't swarm the guy. We were lucky to get out of that stadium alive."

Jack added, "I got hit with a bottle and a rock."

Mik said, "I got hit with a yo-yo."

They both went silent, looking at Mik with blank stares.

"Who throws a freaking yo-yo?" Sherlock asked.

Mik shrugged. "Maybe someone who wants his projectile back."

Jack rolled his eyes.

The waitress, Riley, came by. She had jet-black hair pulled back in a ponytail and a green shamrock tattoo on her forearm. She took their order.

"I should be thankful I made it here alive," Jack commented. "I think the cab driver had Mr. Thomas for driver's ed."

"Good God," Mik chimed in. "Remember he would take us down the block from the school to practice parallel parking in front of Grimstead's Tavern?"

Sherlock perked up. "Then he'd go in for a pint while you were left idling the car and reading some lame pamphlet that he gave you to buy time. That would never fly today!"

"I don't know how it flew then," Mik said. "Hey, that reminds me, are you guys going to the reunion?"

"When is it?" Sherlock asked.

"A week from Saturday. I guess you missed the memo."

Sherlock conceded, "I miss all the memos."

Jack piped up, "I wasn't going to go." He folded his hands and stared off across the room. "There are some things about high school that I'd just rather forget." Neither of them responded. The silence became uncomfortable, and he turned back to face them. "But I'm going. My girlfriend wants to meet you knuckleheads, so why don't you both come?"

"Who, the TV babe?" Mik smirked.

"Yeah, her," Jack shrugged it off.

"Can I still get tickets?" Sherlock asked.

"Sure," Jack said. "Just call the alumni office and ask for Marge."

"Okay," Sherlock pounded the table, "I'm in."

"Like Flynn," Jack added, holding up his glass.

"Who's Flynn?" Sherlock asked.

"Errol Flynn," Jack explained. They looked at him as though he were speaking Chinese. "The actor. Dashing, playboy sort of a guy in the 1930s and '40s."

The blank stares continued.

"Oh, come on. Do you guys live in a cave?" Jack went on. "He played pirates and action heroes. Thin mustache, handsome guy."

"Well then," Sherlock raised a fist, "I'm in like Flynn."

Their meals came, and they wolfed them down. They all needed to get back to work, so they agreed to meet at the reunion and left.

Jack stood on the curb, not knowing whether he wanted to catch the subway back or take a chance hailing a cab and risk, against all odds, getting Prashant again.

CHAPTER 7

Tuesday, May 19, 2020

The days passed quickly leading up to Connie's surgery. Jack got plenty of sleep. He didn't need it. His body was accustomed to functioning on little sleep, but he didn't want to take any chances.

On arrival to the medical center, Jack stopped briefly in the lounge to get a coffee and continued on to the Milstein Pavilion. He changed into scrubs, grabbed his loupes, and headed toward the visitor waiting room. It was filled with yawning people sipping coffee. As he expected, there was a large contingent there for Connie. He spotted the elder Gigante and, beside him, his wife, Joan. Also present was Gigante's associate, Billy Beans, and a few others whom Jack did not recognize. They paced back and forth, chewing their lips, their faces frozen with apprehension, which was understandable.

As Jack approached the group, Joan stepped forward and hugged him. She was dressed in the manner he had always been accustomed to seeing her. That is, very nicely, with a lot of expensive jewelry. Tears bled into her mascara, smudging the skin under bloodshot eyes. "She'll be alright, Jack, won't she?" Her lips quivered.

Jack knew he couldn't make any guarantees, so he equivocated. "We have no reason to believe otherwise, Mrs. Gigante," he said, holding the embrace as she sobbed, tears falling onto his scrub shirt. Jimmy Gigante approached and gave his wife a handkerchief, then escorted her to a chair.

Jack had expected to see his old pal, the younger Jimmy Gigante, and was surprised that he wasn't with the group. As if on cue, the door to the men's restroom opened and out walked Jimmy, still fidgeting with his zipper. He was wearing a dark suit and was thinner than Jack remembered him, his black hair now peppered with streaks of gray. Gone was the thin mustache he sported throughout their high school days.

They slowly walked toward one another. When they were face to face, Jimmy said, "This is crazy, man. It's good to see you. I wish it was under different circumstances."

"Good to see you too, Jimmy."

"It's been a while, buddy." He smiled. "I know how busy you must be, but we should get together when this is over."

"Yeah, for sure," Jack responded. "I'd like that." They shook hands.

The two walked back to the group. The room was starting to fill up with the families and friends of other patients.

Gigante put his hand on Jack's shoulder. He maintained his composure, but the puffy dark circles around his eyes betrayed his anxiety. "We've said our prayers, Jack. She's in your hands now."

Jack said, "We have a good team, Mr. Gigante. We'll take great care of her."

"I trust you, Jack." He gave Jack a few pats on the shoulder and asked, "Will we see her before you start?"

"I'll make sure of it," Jack said. "They're prepping her for the OR, but I'll have the nurses bring you back to see her before she goes in."

Jack went through the door and down the cluttered hallway toward the preoperative holding area. He looked at the chalkboard and saw the name Connie Gigante in slot number nine. He grabbed the chart and walked down toward bay number nine, where the nurse had just finished securing the IV.

Connie was sitting on the gurney, wearing the blue-and-white hospital gown, her bare legs sticking out. She wore no makeup, and her black hair was uncombed, which made her look younger and more like she had looked in high school. She was surprisingly calm, or maybe it was just a protective facade.

"Hey, Jack."

"Hi, Connie, are you alright?"

"A little hungry, and my stomach is in knots, but I'm alright."

Jack sat down in the bedside chair and held her hand. "Do you have any questions?"

"No. Your fellow was here. She explained everything."

"Great. I talked to Jimmy. When this is over, we'll get together for dinner or something."

Connie smiled and squeezed his hand. "That'd be great, Jack. I'm gonna hold you to it."

"It's a date." Jack's face flushed. "I mean... not a date date... a dinner date."

Connie pulled Jack's hand to her chest and grasped it with both hands, rubbing it rhythmically with her fingers. She rested her chin on his hand. "I'm scared, Jack. Really scared." She swallowed. "In case something happens... I, um... I need you to know something."

"Yeah, sure, Connie... I'm listening," he said, looking into her eyes. "You can tell me anything."

"I still..." She looked away. "I know you have an amazing girlfriend, and I'm just being stupid, but... I..."

They were interrupted by a double rap of knuckles on the glass sliding door. It was the anesthesiologist. Jack stood and shook his hand. "Doug, thank you."

He looked at Connie. "Connie, this is my friend, Dr. Noble. I asked if he could be assigned to your case, and he arranged it."

"Good morning, Ms. Gigante." Doug Noble stepped forward and shook hands with Connie. He was the same age as Jack, tall and lean, with a square jaw and Roman nose. He was of Italian heritage, yet his skin tone was light, his family being from Northern Italy near the Alps. He wore his wavy black hair in a stylish cut. Jack mentioned that Doug cycled competitively as a hobby and liked to go on bicycling trips throughout Europe and South America.

Connie noticed his empathetic and engaging dark eyes. "Good morning, Doctor."

"I'd just like to ask you a few questions, if I may," Dr. Noble said. Then he turned to Jack. "But first, what position are you going to want for this, Jack?"

"She'll be seated, in pins."

Dr. Noble nodded his head. "Okay, we'll put in a multi-lumen central line."

Jack nodded. "Yeah, good. Better safe than sorry."

Jack patted Dr. Noble on the arm and said, "Okay, do your thing." Then, turning to Connie, "Connie, when Dr. Noble is done talking to you, we'll get your family back to see you."

"Okay," she smiled, looking around, "I'll wait here."

Jack went to the operating room to hang the MRI images and adjust the microscope.

***

Connie hugged her parents tightly, as the gravity of the situation dawned on her. Their faces, rigid as marble, belied their assurances that all would go well. This wasn't like her tonsillectomy. This was brain surgery. Major, potentially life-threatening surgery.

Dr. Noble and the operating-room nurse stood aside as her family gave her kisses and said a prayer. Her mother wept as she hugged her. "Good luck, baby. God will be watching over you."

Twenty minutes had passed since Jack left, but time seemed to stand still. Dr. Noble connected syringes of Versed and fentanyl to the stopcocks on her IV and pushed the plungers. Warmth and euphoria traveled up her arm and throughout her body. Time and space morphed into a single dimension. The tiles on the ceiling rushed by one after the other, then the gurney bumped through the metal doors and into a cavernous room with bright halogen lights.

Connie felt completely relaxed, as if in a drunken stupor. Her sense of smell, in contrast, heightened, with scents of iodine and alcohol filling her nostrils. People wearing blue masks and scrubs surrounded her, then pulled the sheet under her body, causing her to slide sideways onto the operating table. She felt weightless. Bright lights shone down upon her.

Jack walked over to the table and put his hand on her forehead. He leaned down and whispered, "We'll see you in a little bit, Connie." She struggled to speak, as if her tongue was disconnected. The drugs had ablated all inhibition. She had to tell him, now, how she felt. What if she didn't make it through the operation, and he would never know?

The room started to get fuzzier as lines blurred. Connie listened, in a fog, as the circulating nurse went through the safety check, the words racing from her mouth at breakneck speed. The nurse's voice was becoming more distant as Dr. Noble put the clear plastic oxygen mask on her face. She stared through glazed eyes at Jack, struggling to get the words out. He leaned closer.

"Jack," she reached for him, mumbling, "I... I... still..."

The last thing she remembered was Jack's tenuous smile, and his hand holding hers, just like old times. Everything seemed right at that moment. Then oblivion.

***

It was an hour into surgery. Country music played softly from the Bluetooth speaker. Doug Noble sat in his high-back chair, cocooned in by the surgical drapes and his anesthesia machine. He studied the waveforms on his monitors at regular intervals, listening to the mesmerizing beep of the heart tones on the pulse oximeter. He noticed that the blood pressure had dropped slightly, and he reached for the vaporizer to dial down the sevoflurane. It was time to check the eyes, so he reached under the drape using his flashlight. The patient was in a seated position, with her head flexed slightly forward. Pins from the fixation halo punctured her scalp and skull in three separate places, through small patches of dried blood. Her eyes remained taped and padded.

He settled back into his chair, continuing to read the headlines from the Fox News app on his iPhone. His foot tapped along as Toby Keith's *I Should Have Been a Cowboy* played through the Bluetooth speaker.

Over the drape he could see the neurosurgical fellow, Dr. Kim Reynolds, who looked like Cameron Diaz in scrubs, her blond hair braided and tucked into her surgical cap. She was tall and slim, with a serious affect. The halogen surgical lamps were hot, and sweat collected on her brow as she intermittently suctioned the surgical field. As he was drawing up some muscle relaxant, he heard Jack's voice.

"How's it going, Doug?" he asked.

Doug stood up, peering over the drape. "Good, she's been stable."

"Great. We've got the specimen out, and we're sending it to pathology. As soon as we hear back, we'll start the resection." He folded his arms. "Have we got blood in the room?"

"Four units of packed cells in the fridge, and two units of fresh frozen plasma."

"Good."

Fifteen minutes later, the pathologist called into the OR on speakerphone, confirming the suspected diagnosis.

"Thank you," Jack said. "We'll send you the complete specimen later."

The operation continued uneventfully until the four-hour mark. As Doug was entering information into the electronic record, he heard a few ectopic beats on the monitor. He looked at the arterial-line waveform, and the blood pressure was 110/75. Suddenly, the end-tidal CO2 dropped precipitously and the nitrogen rose. The ectopic beats increased in frequency, and the next blood pressure read 52/24. The shrill alarm on the anesthesia monitor sounded.

Doug looked at the monitor, then yelled, "Shit, Jack! It's an air embolism!"

Jack shoved the microscope out of the way and yelled to the scrub tech for a basin of saline. "Trendelenburg position."

Doug had already pressed the Trendelenburg button, and the bed was rotating to a head-down position.

Jack took the basin and flooded the field with saline. Doug screwed a sixty-cc syringe onto the stopcock of the central line and began suctioning, pulling back frothy blood and air.

As Connie's heart rate continued to decelerate, Jack's brow beaded with sweat. The last numeric blood pressure reading displayed was 22/12, just before the arterial line went flat. Additional alarms on the machine blared.

"She's arresting," Doug shouted.

Jack pulled the drape off Connie's chest and began chest compressions. The circulating nurse hit the code button and called out the clock time; the dreaded countdown to ceasing resuscitation began. Harder and harder, he pressed. "Come on, Connie, come on." His eyes were red, glistening with suppressed tears. Emotion started to cloud his judgment. He was angry at himself. This is why a surgeon shouldn't operate on someone he loves. *Love?* Jack paused. It was like the word itself slapped him in the face, urging him on.

The circulator called out the time. "Twelve minutes."

"Shut the goddamned clock off," Jack yelled, out of character. "We're not stopping!" They all stared, and he immediately regretted losing his cool. "I'm sorry... keep going, please."

Doug continued pulling air from Connie's heart, with each syringe containing more blood and less froth. Jack paused the chest compressions, and the waveform continued increasing in amplitude. The blood pressure read 83/46. Doug gave 20 mg of ephedrine through the IV and squeezed the fluid bag.

"Good call on the central line, Doug," Jack said, between catching breaths.

After three minutes and an additional liter of fluid, the blood pressure stabilized. The monitor alarms went silent, and everyone breathed a collective sigh of relief. Jack crouched down in a corner of the OR, covering and wiping his eyes. The team prepped and re-draped to continue the operation.

Two hours later, they rolled into the surgical ICU. The ICU staff gathered around the bedside, and Jack gave the report. Afterward, he told the ICU attending, "I'd like to keep her intubated and sedated overnight. I'm worried about cerebral edema."

The ICU attending nodded and instructed the ICU nurses to set up remifentanil and propofol infusions. Jack turned to Doug.

"Doug, thank you. You saved her life." He gave him a fist bump and pointed a finger at him. "Call me next time you're going on the bike trails."

Doug nodded. "Absolutely."

Jack felt tired. He headed to the surgical waiting room.

There, he found the Gigantes, wide-eyed and pacing circles. They rushed him, and he gave them a rundown of what they'd done.

Jimmy Gigante spoke first. "Were you able to get it all?"

"I'm confident that we did."

Jimmy arched his back and let out a sigh of relief. "Thank God! Thank you, Jack!"

The rest of the family were all smiles, hugging each other and Jack.

"There was a complication," Jack interjected.

They paused their celebration and listened as Jack told them about the air embolism and the cardiac arrest.

Joan Gigante grabbed her cheeks, her face pale. "Dear God, will she be alright?"

"Yes," Jack explained, "the arrest was brief and we were able to resuscitate her immediately. She should be fine."

"I don't know what I would do if something happened to her," Joan Gigante said. "She's everything to me."

Jack nodded, swallowing, lost in his own thoughts. "I know how you feel, Mrs. Gigante."

"You guys are miracle workers," Gigante added.

Jack put his hands up, deflecting the praise. "Dr. Noble deserves the credit. He diagnosed the embolism quickly."

"Is that so?" Gigante responded.

"Just so you are aware," Jack continued, "we will be keeping her intubated and sedated overnight."

They all seemed content knowing that Connie had made it through the surgery. Jack encouraged them to go home and unwind. They agreed, thanked Jack once again, and then left for their home in Englewood.

They invited Jack to join them for dinner at the Crab Shack restaurant in Edgewater, but he politely declined. After the day's events, he just wanted to go home and pour himself a drink.

CHAPTER 8

Wednesday, May 20, 2020

Jack arrived at the office just after 6 a.m. His surgical case-load didn't start until 7:30, but he wanted to check on Connie before he got tied up in surgery. He walked at a brisk pace to the Milstein Pavilion and took the elevator to the surgical ICU. He passed the nurses at the desk and exchanged pleasantries before coming upon Dr. Winston Spaulding.

Dr. Spaulding, the well-respected director of the surgical ICU, was in his early fifties, yet still retained a natural, jet-black head of hair, mustache, and goatee. He was brilliant and wouldn't hesitate to tell you so himself if you asked. Nonetheless, he was well liked and had a calm, non-perturbable demeanor.

"Good morning, Win. I was hoping to find you," Jack said, catching Spaulding off guard.

He looked up, balancing some files in his hand. "Oh, hello, Jack. I guess you're here for the Gigante gal."

"Yes," Jack replied.

"Come on, let's go have a look."

They walked to room 915. Dr. Spaulding grabbed a chart from the cubby. The nurse, Molly—cute, with long brown hair in a ponytail—came out of the room and put her hand up. "Don't hit me again, Dr. Monroe."

Dr. Spaulding looked up, narrowing his eyes.

"Dr. Monroe throws a mean elbow," Molly continued.

Jack grimaced and held his head down.

Now Spaulding was really confused. "What's this all about, Jack?"

Jack explained, "One day Molly was bending down to detach the oxygen from the tank while I was reaching up to grab the IV bag, and my elbow came down on her head."

"He nearly put me into a coma! I think he was trying to drum up business," Molly said.

"Oh, I've got plenty of business, Molly, don't worry."

"I'm just messing with you, Dr. Monroe."

"That's fair. How did Ms. Gigante do last night?"

"Great, no problems."

Jack looked at Connie. She was unconscious, with an endotracheal tube protruding from her mouth. The ventilator bellows dropped with a rhythmic whooshing sound every four seconds, followed by the rise and fall of her chest. The EKG beeped in a regular pattern as the wave traced across the monitor.

Jack had seen Connie asleep before, but not like this. In the past, it was on a lounge chair at the beach after a good happy hour at Key Largo. Jack started to feel nostalgic. He walked over to the bed, picked up Connie's hand, and held it. With the other hand, he brushed the hair off her face. He started to choke up.

Dr. Spaulding examined the chart. "I agree, Jack."

"That's good," Jack managed. "Why don't we wean the sedation and try to get her extubated later today?"

Spaulding nodded. "Let's turn off the propofol, Molly, and the remi, and see how she does. I'll put the orders in."

Molly shook her head. "Will do, Dr. Spaulding." Then, as Jack moved to pass her, Molly smiled and held up two crossed index fingers.

"Oh God," Jack said. "I'm never going to live that down."

Molly replied, "No, you will not."

CHAPTER 9

Saturday, May 23, 2020

Jack downshifted to first gear, coming to a slow roll under a canopy of maple trees shading Ridgewood Avenue. He turned into the parking lot of the Bacari Grill. His engine whirred as he pulled up to the valet.

"Good evening, sir," said the young man, smartly attired in black and white. "Are you folks here for the reunion?"

"Yes," Jack replied, as a second valet opened the passenger door for Leslie.

Jack jumped out of the car and handed the valet the keys.

"Enjoy your evening, guys," he said, smiling.

"Thank you," Jack replied. He pulled a navy sport jacket from his back seat and put it on.

In her long red dress, Leslie exuded class and elegance. Jack sauntered around the car, wrapped his arm around her waist, and they went inside.

Passing through the door, they were greeted by the rhythmic pulsations of Blondie's *Hanging on the Telephone* and a cacophony of animated voices. People milled about, holding cocktails, engaged in lively conversations.

A large paw gripped Jack's shoulder, followed by Mik's voice. "Iceman, glad you made it."

"Iceman?" Leslie cocked her head. But before she could ask the obvious question, Mik stepped forward, hand extended. "I'm Brendan, but everyone calls me Mik. You must be Leslie."

"Hello, Mik. I've heard a lot about you. It's good to finally put a face to the name." She shook his hand.

Jack scratched his head, looking around. "Who's here?"

Mik responded, "Everyone. Keeney, Tommy G., Rice, Sherlock... I saw Shalhoub with Quentin and Heyer at the bar. They're all spread out."

Jack took in the ambiance as he scanned the restaurant. It hadn't changed much over the years. The scent of fresh pasta sauce and garlic filled the room. The dark plank floors complemented the white tray ceilings and decorative moldings. Outside, landscape lighting illuminated the shrubs.

Walking through the room, Jack greeted his former classmates, most of whom he hadn't seen since high school. The usual conversations ensued: "How are you? What have you been up to? How's your family?" Then there were the obligatory introductions to spouses. Some of them were fresh new faces, and some were older versions of familiar faces.

Leslie remained close in tow. She didn't know anyone, yet many of the attendees recognized her from her news show and were keen to engage her in conversation.

They made their way through the room to the large circular mahogany bar in the back. Three bartenders—two older gentlemen and a young blonde woman—methodically went about fulfilling drink orders. Ben Sherlock was holding his cocktail with two hands, trying to avoid spillage as he erupted into his familiar laugh, which sounded like a goose being strangled.

"Mik, Jack," he shouted to them, "I made it."

"You don't say, Captain Obvious," Mik smirked.

Jack put a hand on Leslie's shoulder. "This is my girlfriend, Leslie."

Sherlock stepped forward. "Nice to meet you, Leslie."

Mik pulled a few beers from an ice bucket on the bar and handed them out.

Jack frowned. "What, no craft beer?"

"I'm trying to recreate our high school experience. Don't be such a snob, Doctor," Mik joked.

"Yeah. Don't be a snob, Monroe."

The voice came from behind Sherlock. The muscles in Jack's neck and spine tensed at the discordant, grating sound of the voice. The only voice he'd hoped he wouldn't hear that evening.

Eric Buchalter's soulless eyes stared at him over the same angry scowl he'd worn throughout high school.

"Booky," Jack managed in a calm and pleasant cadence, trying to remain cordial. "How's it going?"

Buchalter took a swig of his beer. His bloodshot eyes and disheveled appearance betrayed the fact that he'd already had too many. "Can't complain," he blurted, in a tone that sounded much like a complaint. "Still on top of the turf," he snorted.

"Glad to hear," Jack said. Then, lost for words, he turned his attention toward Mik and Leslie.

Buchalter had held a grudge since junior year, when Jack beat him out for the starting wide receiver position. He blamed Jack for the fact that he didn't receive a college football scholarship. Whether or not he would have gotten one, had he been given the starting position, is a matter for debate. He was very good, but Jack was better. The coach, Tony Karcich, made the decision, and none of the assistants disagreed.

To Jack's dismay, Booky pressed the conversation. "Looks like you're doing alright though, Monroe." There was a faint hint of resentment in his slurred words. "That's a sweet ride..."

Thinking Buchalter was formulating a crass comment about Leslie, Jack turned toward him, fists starting to clench.

Then Booky continued, "Beamer, M8, right?"

Jack relaxed the tension in his fingers and calmly inhaled.

"Thanks, Booky... uh, yeah, it's an M8."

Having sensed tempers flaring, Mik raised his glass above his head and said, "A toast to staying above the turf."

Booky, having accomplished his goal of ruining Jack's evening, wandered off to spread his version of anti-cheer elsewhere.

"Jack," a deep voice muttered from behind, as a hand clamped onto his shoulder. He turned to see his old friend Santora, their team's formidable tight end, lumbering toward him. Santora's long, thick nose dropped straight down from his forehead, like the metallic nose guard on a legionnaire's helmet. His dark eyes peered out from deep in their sockets.

"Hey, buddy." Jack gave him a one-armed bear hug and they clanked bottles. They started to catch up, reminiscing about the old days.

Somewhere during the conversation, Santora's eyes widened, fixating on something behind the bar. His face turned a shade of gray. "Holy crap!"

Jack saw the transformation and asked, "Hey, man, are you okay?" His breathing had paused, and for a moment Jack thought he might be choking.

Santora put his left hand on Jack's shoulder and, with his right hand holding a beer, pointed to the television above the bar.

Jack glanced over his shoulder, not understanding what the fuss was about. Several other people had stopped talking, their attention vacillating between the TV and Jack. Mik asked the bartender to turn up the volume.

Jack turned around again. This time, there was no mistaking what he saw.

It was an old FBI photo of his high school girlfriend occupying one side of a split screen. On the other side, a female reporter in a raincoat spoke:

"Days ago, in Warwick, New York, divers discovered the body of a Bergen County teen runaway, Eileen Delaney, who was last seen in the summer of 1995. New York State police and FBI agents are on location investigating. Full story at 11 p.m."

It was as if all of the muscles on Jack's face went slack simultaneously. The room began to swirl, as though he were being drugged from within by the bile and stomach acid rising up his esophagus.

He walked, slowly at first, then faster, toward the door, covering his mouth with his hand.

Outside, he draped himself over a white rail fence and vomited. His abdominal muscles convulsed in forceful spasms, and when everything within him had been expelled, he buried his eyes in his crossed forearms and wept.

CHAPTER 10

Saturday, May 23, 2020

A few minutes had passed when Mik walked out and leaned his back against the fence next to Jack. He held a glass in each hand. "I thought you could use one of these."

"Thanks." Jack took one of the glasses and downed it.

Mik looked at Jack, his brow furrowed. "Are you alright, man? That was some whacked-out news, and the timing, during the reunion..." Mik shook his head.

Jack stared off into the wooded brush beyond the parking lot. A squirrel holding a nut stared back. Jack's eyes dropped to the ground. "It's a shock, you know." His eyes started to water. "It's been a long time, but I loved her." He grabbed Mik's shoulder. "I should get back inside. Leslie doesn't know anyone."

"Don't worry. Sherlock and his wife are with her. We told her what happened. I asked her to give us a few minutes."

"Thanks," Jack said. "You're a good friend, Mik."

Mik slapped Jack on the shoulder. "We've been through a lot. That's what friends are for."

They started to walk back into the restaurant, but slowed when Jack's phone rang. He pressed the answer button and put the phone to his ear.

"Dr. Monroe?"

"Yes."

"It's Mandy," she spoke rapidly, "the evening nursing supervisor in the ICU at Presbyterian."

"Yes?" Jack stopped walking.

"Dr. Spaulding asked me to call you. Your patient, Gigante, may have had an intracranial bleed. Dr. Reynolds ordered an MRI, and they are preparing the cath lab."

"Jesus!" Jack's eyes widened and the words came quickly as he spoke. "Tell them to get everything ready. I'm on my way. Tell Reynolds to stay with the patient." He hung up the phone. "Shit. Damn it!"

Mik overheard the conversation and saw Jack's urgency. "Go, buddy. We've got things covered. Sherlock or I will give Leslie a ride home."

"She lives in Manhattan, Mik... in SoHo."

"Okay, then... Sherlock will give her a ride. Go on."

Mik put his hand on Jack's back and pushed him forward. "Get going."

Jack hurdled a log that separated the lawn from the parking lot and sprinted toward the valet.

Mik yelled a suggestion, fully knowing it to be futile. "Drive safely!"

***

Jack was out of breath as he slapped the metal disk on the wall, opening the door to the ICU. Winston Spaulding stood at the desk, looking no worse for wear despite the late hour, his bow tie perfectly knotted and symmetrical.

"Jack, thanks for coming."

"Win," he said, still out of breath, "what's going on?"

"Relax, Jack." Spaulding waved his hands. "She's stabilized. She's back from MRI, in her room."

"How are the pressures?" Jack said.

"Good. We gave mannitol and Decadron, and started a nicardipine infusion."

"The MRI?"

Spaulding said, "Come on, I'll pull it up." They walked over to the computer at the nursing station desk. Spaulding waved his badge over the electronic pad to log in. After a few mouse clicks, the MRI images appeared.

"May I?" said Jack.

"Of course." Spaulding pushed the mouse over, and Jack took control of it. He scrolled through the images, going back and forth several times. He moved closer to the screen, squinting. "Looks like a small intraparenchymal hemorrhage."

"Exactly," Spaulding said. "That's the report we got from radiology."

"Which room is she in?"

"Twelve, come on," Spaulding led the way.

They entered the room. Connie's nurse was on a computer, charting. A respiratory therapist adjusted the ventilator settings as Connie's chest rose in synchrony with the bellows. Multicolored waves danced across the LCD screen, each in a monotonous pattern, none of which caused any alarm in either of the men.

"So, what now?" Spaulding asked.

Jack shrugged. "I assumed that I'd be taking her back to the OR." He scanned the monitor again. "But I guess we can hold off and see how she does."

Spaulding nodded. "That's what I was thinking. By tomorrow morning we should have a better idea of how this will play out." He pulled out his phone. "I've got your number, Jack. I'll call you if anything changes."

"I'm not going anywhere, Win," Jack said, pulling a pillow and blanket from the closet and throwing them on the recliner. He moved to the bedside and put his hand on Connie's cheek. A tear rolled down the side of his nose and stopped at his lip. He bent down and kissed her on the forehead.

Spaulding's eye's narrowed, "Oh, I see." He cleared his throat, and left the room.

CHAPTER 11

Sunday, May 24, 2020

Out at the nurse's station, shoes clapped against the linoleum floor as the drone of multiple conversations filtered into Connie's room. Jack's eyes met resistance as he struggled to open them. He'd fallen asleep with his contacts in, and they felt glued shut. He yawned, remembering where he was, and then checked the monitor. Everything looked good.

Jack's spine protested, pain shooting in all directions as he tried to free himself from the clutches of the industrial vinyl recliner. Playing football had left him with a few bulging discs, which acted up periodically.

Jack hobbled to the bed and looked at Connie's face. Her wavy black hair was matted and sweaty. The endotracheal tube protruding from her mouth tugged at her lip. She had no makeup on, but even in this condition, she was beautiful.

Jack put the back of his fingers against Connie's cheek. Her skin was soft and warm. He let his mind drift back to the days of his youth. He longed to be a teen again, back on that hammock in Sea Girt. He could almost smell the salty ocean breeze carrying the scent of French fries from the boardwalk, beckoning back to a carefree time, before everything had changed.

Jack looked at the girl he once cared for so deeply and realized how much he still did. Feelings of that nature have an inherent tenacity. They may change over time or hibernate in our subconscious, but they remain.

"Wake up, Connie. Please, wake up," he whispered.

***

It was Sunday, so there was no traffic on the drive home. Jack's mind was preoccupied with Connie as he struggled to sort out the feelings which had been reawakened. But he had invited Mik and Sherlock over for a cookout and to watch the baseball game, so he needed to get ready.

Among the renovations Jack had made to his home was a stamped concrete patio with an outdoor kitchen, where he sat under an umbrella at his table. The colorful garden could have tumbled from an impressionist painting, the scent of lilac filling the air.

He sipped an IPA and snacked on garlic-stuffed olives as he read from a novel that had been collecting dust on his bookshelf.

Jack's iPhone rang. He answered it.

Leslie's voice came through the speaker. "Jack, I haven't heard from you. How are you doing?"

Jack folded the page of his book. "Good, thanks. The guys are coming over, and we're going to watch a baseball game. Want to join us?"

"I'd rather chew gravel," she said. "You know watching sports isn't my thing. I was worried about you. The news last night had to be disturbing."

"It was a lot to take in."

"And then getting called back to work. Were you operating all night?" Leslie asked.

"No, by the time I arrived, everything had resolved."

"Oh." Leslie's tone changed. "So, what were you doing all night?"

Jack took a sip of his beer. "I was worried the situation might change, so I decided to stay in the hospital."

"Well, I know how you hate those call room beds. Your back must be a mess."

Then came the forced error, baseball pun unintended. "I didn't sleep in the call room," he said, "I slept on the..."

But it was too late. He couldn't extricate himself from his verbal faux pas. He continued, "on the, um... recliner in the patient's room."

"The patient?" Leslie said in a decidedly cooler tone. "You mean, Connie Gigante?"

"Yeah," Jack's shoulders slumped, "that patient."

Leslie exhaled forcefully into the receiver.

Jack held the phone away from his ear as Leslie's voice became louder. "One of your ex-girlfriends is found dead in a quarry, so you decided to sleep in a room with another one of your ex-girlfriends? Is that what you're telling me?"

"Admittedly, that does sound bad when you say it out loud." Jack stood up and let out a nervous laugh. "You aren't jealous, are you?"

He waited. Silence.

"Oh, come on! It wasn't like we were in a hot tub." He paused, waiting for a reprieve which didn't come. "She's in a medically induced coma, for God's sake. I didn't want to have to rush back if things took a turn."

"Please, Jack. I've never seen you so invested in one particular patient. I know she's an old friend, but is there something going on between you two that you're not telling me?"

Jack hesitated, resting his iPhone against his lip. "No," he said, not even convincing himself. "We're just old friends, and I wanted to make sure she was okay."

It was one o'clock when Mik and Sherlock arrived. They came around the corner of the house under the old silver maple tree.

"The guys just arrived," Jack said into the phone. "Can I call you later?"

"Whatever," Leslie's tone was sharp.

"I'm sorry," Jack said. "I'll talk to you later then. I promise, there's nothing going on. okay?"

"If you say so," Leslie said in a calmer tone, then hung up.

Jack addressed his friends. "There's beer in the fridge, help yourselves."

Sherlock opened the refrigerator, pulled out two "Hopsecutioners," and tossed one to Mik. They sat down at the table.

"Quite the scene last night, eh?" Sherlock asked. "Who were all those wrinkled geezers masquerading as our classmates?"

Mik smirked. "Can you have that little self-awareness? We're all the same age."

Sherlock retracted his hands in mock surrender. "I may be biased, but I think the three of us were the best-preserved fossils at that archaeological dig." He pulled the tab off his beer can. "So, Jack... what happened with Connie?"

"She had a setback, but she's okay. And thanks for taking Leslie home. I know it's a hellish drive."

"Mik didn't tell me where she lived until after I offered to drive her." He glanced sideways at Mik. "Putz!"

Jack placed some burgers and hot dogs on the grill. He pointed the remote toward the television above him and turned on the game. The Yankees were hosting the Red Sox at Yankee Stadium. It was scoreless at the top of the third inning.

"When did you build this outdoor kitchen thing?" Mik asked.

"Last fall."

"Wow, I haven't been here since then?"

"I guess not," Jack said. "Time flies."

Mik turned his chair to face the television. A rocket off the bat of Tanaka bounced between the center and right fielders, bringing in three runs for the Yanks. A short time later, a pop fly to center field was caught, which brought the inning to a close.

Jack pressed the burgers with the spatula. The flames shot up as the grease hit the charcoal, sending the aroma of seared beef into the air. Sherlock's mouth watered. "I'm starving. Those burgers smell good."

The TV station went to a commercial break. Jack stirred the baked beans on the burner. They loaded their plates. Nobody paid any attention as a few musical notes ushered in a news story.

A tall blonde woman in a teal dress holding a microphone spoke. "After a surge in popularity following his lead role in the Senate impeachment trial, Massachusetts Senator Mason Hollingsworth is considered by many to be high on the list of potential Democratic VP candidates. The fact that he is not among the presidential candidates may give him an edge."

Mik leaned forward from his seat. "Hey Sherlock, pass the mustard."

Sherlock passed the mustard to Mik.

Behind them on the television, the camera jumped to a portly male newscaster with neatly trimmed gray hair and a sport jacket that was too tight on him. "Quite right, Rebecca. With the way the candidates have been attacking each other, it wouldn't surprise me if the winner looked outside that group for a running mate."

The camera panned back to the woman in the teal dress. "Back to the game, Jim."

Ketchup and cheese spilled from the corner of Mik's mouth, which he wiped with a napkin. "These are good burgers. Are they Wagyu?"

"No," Jack said, "just plain old burgers. I got them from Gertie's Deli on Queen Anne Road."

Sherlock nodded as he swallowed. "I've gotta start going there."

Jack's ears perked up. "Wait, what did she just say?"

"Who?"

Jack turned his head toward the TV. The game was back on, and the Yankees had taken the field.

CHAPTER 12

Tuesday, May 26, 2020

Jack slapped the metal disk on the wall, and the glass door to the ICU slid open. A symphony of sounds from the patient monitors and the noise of human commotion spilled through the doorway. Heading toward him was Winston Spaulding, his face deep in a chart.

"Winston," Jack nodded as he passed by.

Spaulding took a bite out of an apple, still looking at the chart. He didn't look up, but with his mouth chewing the apple said, "You're welcome."

Jack raised his eyebrows as he looked back at Spaulding. "You're welcome? For what?" Jack noticed three of the nurses at the desk smiling in his direction.

Jack was used to smiles. He was genuinely well liked, but something was up. He said, "Good morning, ladies."

"Good morning, Dr. Monroe," they responded in near unison, still watching him. He felt self-conscious, peeking over his shoulder as he glanced at the board.

Connie was still in the same room. He walked past the nurse's station and made a right turn into room twelve. The ventilator was silent in the corner, and Connie sat with crossed legs in her bed. The endotracheal tube was gone, replaced with nasal prong oxygen.

Connie's nurse, Morgan, smiled. "Good morning, Dr. Monroe."

Jack's weary eyes were now wide open. "Good morning."

"Hey Jack," Connie said, her voice hoarse.

"Connie! When did this happen?" Jack turned to Morgan. "Why didn't anyone tell me?"

Spaulding reappeared behind him in the room. "That's on me, Jack. We wanted to give her a few hours off the vent to be sure she'd tolerate it before we called you."

"No problem. I'm just thrilled that the tube's out."

Jack walked over to the bedside. Connie's hair was a mess, but she'd managed to apply her red lipstick. "It's good to have you back, Connie," he smiled.

He took a step back and held a finger in front of her nose. "I want you to follow my finger with your eyes." He then moved it up, down, and from side to side. Her brown eyes tracked the movements of his finger.

"Put your arms straight out. I'm going to push, and I want you to resist." Jack pushed her outstretched arms up, then down. Then he moved down to her feet and tested them in a similar manner.

"What day is it?"

Connie shrugged. "I don't have a freakin' clue." The Jersey accent was unambiguous.

"Demeanor intact," Jack responded, smiling.

"What's your name?"

"Connie Gigante."

"Where'd you go to high school?"

"You know where I went to high school."

"Connie, please."

She huffed. "Holy Angels Academy."

Jack scratched his chin. He bent down and gave Connie an awkward hug while leaning over her bed, his cheek resting on top of her head. Her hair smelled of coconut conditioner.

"Is smelling my hair part of the neurological exam?" she laughed.

"Um, no. It's not." Jack snapped back, his face flushed, looking at the nursing station. He backed up abruptly, aware of their scrutinizing gazes, and cleared his throat. "Okay then. This is good progress."

"Don't forget," Connie pointed her finger at Jack. Her ID bracelet dangled from her thin wrist.

"Forget?"

"Dinner, remember? You, me, and Jimmy... you promised. Ahh... forget about Jimmy." She smiled, her pearly teeth gleaming under the hospital lighting.

"Yes, I did promise." He pointed back at her. "Let's get you recovered first. We'll get you down to physical therapy today. I'll put the order in."

"It's a date then." Connie pulled up the covers on her bed.

"Yeah," Jack folded his arms, his eyes locked onto hers, "it's a date."

***

The suction tip made a slurping sound as small quantities of blood crept up the tubing into the canister. Jack looked over the drape at the monitor. "What's our blood loss, Leo?" Jack asked the anesthesiologist. Leo looked at his computer, then at the blood-soaked sponges hanging in plastic pockets.

"I'd say about 400 cc."

"That's not bad. How long have we been in here?"

The circulating nurse scrolled back through the chart. "We got in the room at 08:37 a.m. Going on about three and a half hours."

Jack stood with his arms folded, looking over his loupes at the clock. Dr. Reynolds held the Yankauer tip and periodically suctioned the wound. "When did we send the specimen down to pathology?"

"Twenty-eight minutes ago," the circulator answered.

"Can we give them a call and see what's going on?"

"I'll call them," the circulator responded.

Jack's cell phone started to play the marimba ringtone from his pocket. He looked back at the circulator. "Dawn, would you mind getting this? Maybe it's pathology."

"Sure thing." She walked over and lifted the back of Jack's surgical gown. She grabbed his phone from his back pocket, pressed the answer button, and then held the phone to his ear.

"Hello?" Jack said. "Pathology?"

"No," the deep masculine voice on the phone responded. "Is this Dr. Monroe? Dr. Jack Monroe?"

"Yes, it is. But I'm sorry, I'm in surgery. I can't talk..."

"Oh," the voice continued. "I apologize. This is Special Agent Gerry Spath with the FBI. Please call us back as soon as possible."

Jack's eyes darted around the room. A chill ran up his spine. "Can I ask what this is in reference to?" he asked.

"We just need to speak with you, Doctor."

Jack's teeth clenched, and he pressed his lips together. "Am I in some kind of trouble?"

There was a pause before the agent responded tersely. "We just need to speak with you. Here, at our office."

Jack swallowed, keenly aware that everyone was watching him. The words came slowly as he responded. "I'm free tomorrow around 4 p.m. Would that work?"

"Yes, that would be fine. We're at the Claremont Tower, 11 Centre Place, Newark. When you arrive, ask for me, Agent Spath."

"I'll be there."

"Good. We'll see you tomorrow," Spath said, then hung up the phone.

Jack took a breath. "Thanks, Dawn."

"I'll put your phone with your loupes box," Dawn said.

"Thanks," Jack responded, absorbed in thought.

Dr. Reynolds tilted her forehead, shining her headlight into the corners of the wound. "It looks dry," she said. The phone on the wall rang, jolting Jack out of his trance. Dawn picked up the phone. "It's Dr. Li from pathology."

"Put him on speaker," Jack said.

"Jack? Ji-Hong here. This is a glioblastoma. Superior margins are clean. Inferior and right anterolateral margins still showing tumor."

"Thanks, Ji-Hong," Jack shouted back from across the room. He looked at Dr. Reynolds and shook his head. "Not good."

CHAPTER 13

Wednesday, May 27, 2020

Jack parked his BMW in the parking ramp at the FBI's Newark branch office and made his way down to street level, where large concrete bollards surrounded the building. He entered through bulletproof glass doors into a foyer manned by several uniformed guards.

"Name?" said the guard with one lazy eye, seated behind the desk. He pecked away at his computer keys with disinterest.

"Jack Monroe."

Another guard with a crew cut, and sleeves struggling to contain his biceps, waved a wand up and down Jack's body as he held his arms outstretched.

"Purpose?" said the seated guard.

Jack cleared his throat, taking in the stark utilitarian decor. "I'm here to see Special Agent Spath."

The seated guard picked up the phone and dialed a number. After a few seconds he spoke. "We've got a Jack Monroe here for Agent Spath." He looked up at Jack as he continued. "Uh huh, yeah, uh huh." He turned his eyes upward at "Crew Cut" and nodded.

The burly guard handed Jack a plastic basket. "Everything out of your pockets. Keys, cell phone, wallet..."

Jack complied.

The items passed through the scanner. Jack went to collect them, but a third guard stepped in front of him. The guard handed Jack the wallet. "We'll hang on to your phone and keys. You can pick them up on your way out."

Jack frowned. He didn't like the idea, but he wasn't about to question their protocol.

The seated guard gave Jack directions. "Up the escalator, make a right through the gray metal door, and check in with the receptionist."

Jack followed the directions. He entered a small room with rows of chairs. The receptionist was a fifty-something woman with too much makeup, chewing a large wad of gum like a goat in tall grass. She didn't look up. "Have a seat," the words came out of her nasal passages, "we'll be with you shortly."

As Jack sat down, a camera near the ceiling rotated downward so that it pointed toward him. Its green LED light flashed on.

Shortly, it turned out, equated to forty-five minutes. Finally, a male and female agent, both dressed in government-issue black suits, entered the room. The woman carried a heavy file held together with elastic bands. The male, who was of medium height and build, with handsome, sharp features, extended his hand. "Dr. Monroe, I'm Special Agent Gerry Spath, and this is Special Agent Katie Creighton."

Agent Creighton was a tall attractive woman with platinum-blond, shoulder-length hair. Her lips were thin and devoid of emotion. She nodded without speaking.

Spath peeked through the window and asked the receptionist, "Which room?"

"Take him to interrogation room six," she said.

Jack froze. "Whoa.... Interrogation room? Do I need a lawyer?"

Agent Creighton stepped forward. "Do you feel that you need a lawyer, Doctor?"

"Well, no..." Jack answered too quickly. "I mean, I haven't done anything wrong."

"It's entirely up to you, Dr. Monroe. You are free at any time to call a lawyer."

Jack's eyes wavered between the two of them. "No, it's fine."

Agent Creighton led the way down a hallway to a room marked number six. The room looked like the stereotypical interrogation room in every crime drama ever produced, with an industrial-quality metal table surrounded by six chairs. One wall was completely occupied by what appeared to be a one-way mirror. The agents sat down on one side of the table, and Jack took a seat facing them and the mirror. There were two cameras positioned in opposite corners near the ceiling, their LED indicators lit.

The room was warm. The back of Jack's shirt was moist with sweat. "I assume this has something to do with the body found in the quarry."

Spath turned quickly to his partner, then back toward Jack. "Yes. How did you know that?"

"I didn't," Jack answered, "I just can't think of any other reason that I'd be here."

Agent Creighton spoke next. "We've begun a preliminary investigation, and it appears that you may have been one of the last persons to see Ms. Delaney before her disappearance." She put on her glasses and read from the file. "Late in the summer of 1995."

"Yes, I suppose that's true." Jack leaned back, staring at the ceiling and trying to remember. "But I'm confused." His eyes met Agent Creighton's light blue eyes. "Why is the FBI involved?"

The agents glanced at each other. "We're not at liberty to discuss that at this time," Spath said. "Suffice it to say, there are factors in this case which require our involvement." He pulled out a yellow notepad and a pen. "So, Dr. Monroe, when did you last see Ms. Delaney?"

Jack didn't have to think about his answer. The date was ingrained in his memory. "August 22, 1995."

"That's very specific. You're sure of that date?"

"Yes, I'm sure."

"Can you tell us what happened on that date?" Agent Creighton asked.

"We were at a party. The family of one of our friends had a house on Lake Hopatcong. It was the end of the summer. One of the last chances to get together before we all left for college."

"You were dating Ms. Delaney at the time?"

"That's correct," Jack said.

"And who drove there, you or Ms. Delaney?" Spath asked.

"We drove separately."

"You were a couple, yet you drove separately to a party. Had you been having some sort of quarrel?" Spath asked.

Jack stiffened up. "No," he said with emphasis. "I had to work that day. People arrived early for swimming and boating. But I got there later, after work."

"Yes, about that," Agent Creighton struggled to lift the four-inch-thick, elastic-bound file from the chair next to her. The cover sheet was labeled *Jack Monroe.*

Jack leaned forward. His jaw dropped. "Is that file all about me? Why is there a huge file on me?" his voice breaking.

Spath rested his elbows on the table. "Relax, Doctor, we have files on everybody."

"Not everybody," said Agent Creighton, tilting her head.

Spath looked at Creighton. "Not everybody. A lot, anyway." He looked at Jack. "We have a lot of files."

The intercom on the wall next to the door buzzed and lit up. Agent Creighton got up and pressed the button. "Yes?"

The receptionist responded, "Sheriff Townsend is here."

"Send him in," said Creighton.

Jack's heart rate accelerated. *Why is a sheriff here?*

A moment later the door opened. A man wearing a white shirt and navy-blue uniform entered. "Sorry I'm late." He was a beefy man in his late fifties with a ruddy complexion.

Agent Spath stood and made the introduction. "Dr. Monroe, this is Sheriff Justin Townsend of the Bergen County Sheriff's Department."

"We've met," the sheriff said, extending his hand toward Jack.

Jack stared blankly while extending his hand. "We have?"

"That's alright. You probably don't remember. It was a long time ago. After Ms. Delaney left home. Ran away, or at least so we assumed. We questioned a number of people, yourself included."

Jack nodded. "I vaguely remember. I'm sorry I didn't recognize you. It's been a long time. You were..."

"Younger and thinner?" the sheriff finished Jack's sentence. "Don't I know it."

They took their seats, the sheriff joining the agents on the opposite side of the table. Agent Creighton got right back to business. Jack's file was marked with dozens of tabs sticking out the side. She said, "You mentioned you were coming from work that day."

"Yes, that's right."

"And you worked at Spectrum Color Graphics, owned by James Gigante, the father of a friend?"

Jack fidgeted in his seat. "Yes."

"Were you aware at the time, Doctor, that Mr. Gigante was under federal investigation for violations of the RICO Act?"

Jack looked around nervously, then shook his head. "We'd heard rumors. We didn't know what to believe."

"What were your specific duties at Spectrum?" Agent Creighton asked.

"Umm, well..." I drove a van and delivered printing proofs. All over Manhattan and the five boroughs."

"Printing proofs?" She raised an eyebrow as she looked at Spath and Townsend. "Did you make any other deliveries?"

The room felt warm, and sweat started to drip from Jack's forehead. "Look. I never did anything illegal, if that's what you're asking. I took envelopes, about two feet square," Jack used his hands to show the size, "and delivered them to businesses in the city."

"How can you be sure what was in the envelopes?" Agent Creighton asked.

"I can't." Jack put both palms up. "The Amazon driver doesn't open your package before he delivers it." He looked at the agents. "I just made the deliveries. I didn't inspect them."

"Fair enough," Spath said, placing his chin on his knuckles. "Let's get back to the party. We have records from the 1995 investigation of Ms. Delaney's disappearance. One of your classmates at that time reported seeing you arguing with Ms. Delaney prior to her departure from the party."

Jack leaned forward. "Who said that?"

"We have to maintain confidentiality, you understand."

"We weren't arguing." Jack closed his eyes, the events long ago still vivid in his mind. "Eileen was having a rough time at home. She seemed agitated throughout that summer. She got this idea in her mind that we should run away together."

Jack paused, grasped the back of his head, and stretched his neck. "It was crazy. We didn't have any money, or anywhere to go. We both had scholarships to college."

"Go on," Agent Creighton prodded.

"When I told her that I couldn't go, she slapped me and left in her car."

"Had you any physical altercations prior to that?" Creighton asked.

"No," Jack shouted. Then, "No," he repeated in a softer tone. "There was no altercation." He waved his hand dismissively. "She just slapped me once and left."

"What did you do next?" Spath said.

"Nothing." Jack swallowed, disgusted with himself. "I let her go."

"We have learned from the same individual that, a short while later, you left in the Spectrum company van. Where did you go?"

"I tried to go after her. I thought she would go to her friend's house in Sea Girt. She spent a lot of time there."

"Did you find her?" Agent Creighton seemed engaged in the story.

"No. I stopped halfway. I realized that I didn't have anything more to say that would change anything. We were on different trajectories. She had her plans and I had mine, and they weren't compatible."

Jack's head hung down. He clasped his hands. He had put this loss behind him long ago, but the sadness which had receded with time was again weighing heavily on him. Through bloodshot eyes, he looked at each of them. "It hurt losing her. But all this time, I believed that she was somewhere, happily living her life. And now, to think that all this time she's been..." He started tearing; his words trailed off. Agent Creighton bit her lip and looked down at the table.

The sheriff, who had been quiet up until that point, broke the silence. "Jack, the files from the original investigation noted that you, yourself, disappeared for a few days after that night. Can you tell us where you went?"

"Honestly, no," Jack lied. He knew that lying to the FBI was a serious crime, and he started to feel sick. "It's a bit of a blur. The breakup was hard. I didn't want to be around people, so I just kept to myself."

"The former classmate, who we interviewed, recalled seeing you two days after the party with a black eye and facial contusions," Sheriff Townsend continued. "Do you recall how you got those?"

They were all staring directly at him. He swallowed, starting to feel ill. "It's warm. May I please have some water?"

Agent Creighton left the room and brought back some bottles of water. She handed one to Jack, who drank half the bottle in one gulp.

"We were talking about the bruises, Doctor Monroe," she said. "Please tell us how you got those."

"As I recall, I was in Key Largo, a bar in Belmar. I drank too much and acted like a jerk. I don't recall the details, just waking up with a scuffed-up face on a boardwalk bench."

Agent Spath asked, "Would you say that you have a bad temper? Do you get into fights often?"

"No." Jack said, shaking his head for emphasis. "It's not like that. I was young and stupid, feeling down after a breakup, that's all." Jack grabbed his knee to stop it from shaking. The inquiry seemed to be going in an ominous direction. He wondered if he should have had a lawyer present, but he feared if he asked now, it would give the appearance of guilt.

Agent Spath whispered to Sheriff Townsend. "A word, please." The two men went out into the hallway and shut the door.

Jack and Agent Creighton sat looking at each other. Maybe it was his imagination, but the room temperature seemed to drop twenty degrees. The silence was awkward. Jack looked at the annotated tome with his name on it. "You guys must do a lot of reading."

"Part of the job," she said curtly.

Jack clenched his teeth, dropping his eyes. *A guy could get frostbite holding this one's hand.* He pursed his lips and exhaled.

"Of course." Jack looked around the room. More silence. He tried again. "You know how it is when a relationship ends?"

She bowed her head and bit her lower lip. "Not really... I don't date."

"Ever?"

"Not since my fiancé passed away. Two weeks before our wedding. Colon cancer."

Nice one, Jack. What's your encore? Strangling her puppy?

Jack met her eyes as she looked up. "I'm sorry." He saw the tough facade melt away, exposing the woman inside. She nodded her head slowly. Jack looked around the room, and then at his watch, praying that Spath and the sheriff would come back.

The door opened. The two men returned. Sheriff Townsend placed an aluminum briefcase on the desk. They sat down. "We have a few items we'd like you to identify, Jack."

"Items? What sort of items?" He tensed up.

The men looked at each other. The sheriff popped the clasps on the briefcase. He reached in and pulled out a ziplock bag, pouring the contents onto the table. It was a ring. He held it up and rotated it in his hand. It was bronze in color with the letters BC on one side. On the other side, the numbers '95. He handed it to Jack. "Do you recognize this ring?"

Jack rolled it around in his hand and studied it. He froze when he saw his first initial and last name etched inside.

He choked up. "It's my high school ring." He looked at Townsend. "I haven't seen this in twenty-five years." He slid it onto his finger. "Where did you...." His voice trailed off, suddenly realizing the only place they could have found it.

The sheriff's face softened, and he drew in his lips. He looked at the agents and then back toward Jack. "We found the ring on a finger of the skeleton in the quarry."

Jack abruptly ripped the ring off his finger. He took off his glasses and put them on the table. He put his elbows on the table and buried his face in his palms, pressing on his eyes to prevent them from watering, as the memory came back. He spoke softly. "When I gave it to her, I promised her that someday I'd replace it with an engagement ring."

"I'm sorry," said Agent Creighton. She reached across the table and touched Jack's hand.

"You know... you have so many dreams and plans for the future when you are young," Jack said. "But that's all they are, dreams."

"There's more, I'm afraid," Sheriff Townsend said.

"More?" Jack looked up, afraid of what else there was.

The sheriff pulled a larger zip-lock bag out of the brief-case. Inside was a rusty, narrow-bladed knife.

Jack saw the walnut and bronze handle, and knew immediately that it was his. The sheriff removed the knife from the bag. On the side of the handle was a brass plate inscribed with the initials JPM. "For the record, Doctor, your name is Jack Patrick Monroe, is that correct?"

"Yes," Jack nodded, "and yes, it's my knife," he said, anticipating the next question. "It was a gift from my grandfather. He used to take me fishing when I was a kid." A spark of momentary happiness returned as Jack savored the memory.

Agent Spath leaned forward. "Can you explain how it might have ended up in Ms. Delaney's car?"

"Yes," Jack said, "I think I can. Two weeks before the party, we were at the Jersey Shore and went fishing in the Barnegat Bay on a friend's boat. I must have left it in her car."

"And that was the last time you saw this knife?" Spath asked.

"I guess so. I thought I'd lost it." Jack looked at the sheriff. "It has sentimental value. May I have it back?"

Spath's eyes met those of Sheriff Townsend. Townsend looked at Jack and responded. "I'm afraid not, Dr. Monroe. This knife has been entered into the file as evidence." He hesitated. "It's been determined, based on marks found on the ribs of the skeleton, to be the murder weapon."

The color drained from Jack's face, and he felt dizzy. He scanned the room, and all eyes were glued to him. "I think I'd like to speak to a lawyer."

CHAPTER 14

Wednesday, May 27, 2020

Agent Spath turned and whispered something to Agent Creighton. She whispered back. Spath turned toward Jack. "Actually, Doctor, I think we are finished for now." Then he repeated, "for now."

Jack looked up, surprised. "That's it? I'm free to go?"

"You're free to go," said Spath.

Agent Creighton chimed in, "You are certainly within your rights to retain a lawyer, in the event that any further developments arise."

Sheriff Townsend added, "I'd take that advice, Jack, and I'd do it soon." He pushed his chair back and gathered the items he'd brought. "Do you have a lawyer?"

Jack bowed his head and squeezed his eyes shut. "Oh yeah. I have a lawyer, all right." He looked up at the ceiling and then back at the sheriff. "A great lawyer. Top of her class at Georgetown." He flung open his fingers. "She loves to remind me of that." Then he mumbled under his breath, "I'm just not sure if we're on speaking terms."

The sheriff looked at the two agents with a confused expression, then back at Jack. "We'll let you sort that out."

"You're not planning any trips, are you, Doctor?" asked Agent Creighton, looking over the top of her glasses.

"Am I prohibited from traveling?"

"There are no restrictions," she said, "but you should probably stay in the area for the next week or two."

"I have no trips planned," Jack said.

"Good. We'll be in touch."

They picked up their files and briefcases, then escorted Jack back to the stairway. They shook hands, and Jack descended the stairs to the lobby. The agent with the crew cut removed Jack's keys from a numbered hook behind the desk and handed them to him. "Your car is parked out this door to the right, slot number twenty-eight."

"Oh," Jack said, surprise in his voice, "you moved it. How did you know where...? Never mind." He shook his head.

Another agent with thick horn-rimmed glasses and a pocket protector came from a door behind the staircase. He was putting the case back on Jack's cell phone and handed it to "Crew Cut", who then handed it back to Jack. "Your phone, Doctor."

Jack looked at them, then rotated the phone in his hand.

"Thanks," he said with a tinge of sarcasm. He put the phone in his pocket and left the building.

He found his car and walked around it, looking for signs of tampering. He bent down, looking under the chassis. Through the glass door "Crew Cut" watched his every move.

Who was he kidding? If the FBI bugged his car, he wasn't going to find it. Maybe he was being paranoid. But as a precaution, he'd assume that every conversation he had, from that moment forward, would be monitored.

***

It was 6:30 p.m. when Jack arrived home. The neighbor's son and his friend were tossing a football back and forth on a freshly mowed lawn. Jack could smell the sweet, zesty scent of grass. He waved, and they waved back. The neighborhood was quiet except for the rhythmic slap of the football against the boys' hands.

Jack went through the side door into the kitchen and tossed his mail onto the countertop. He grabbed a beer from the refrigerator and then collapsed on the recliner in his family room.

He dialed Leslie's phone number. It rang five times before she answered. "Hey, how's it going?"

"Oh, just peachy," he replied. "I'm worn out from my meeting today."

"What did they want?"

"They were asking questions about my ex-girlfriend, Eileen."

"But you haven't seen her in twenty years."

"Twenty-five."

Leslie, the consummate journalist, continued with questions. Finally, "Do they have any suspects?"

You mean besides me? Jack wanted to say. "I don't know," he said. He tried to change the subject. "Did you want to get dinner?"

"I'm sorry," she said. "It's late, I already ate."

Jack heaved a sigh of relief. He didn't want to leave his La-Z-Boy.

He asked, "Tomorrow?"

"I'll have to get back to you. We've got some big stories that we're working on."

"That's alright. We'll figure it out."

"I'll talk to you tomorrow then. I love you. Have a better evening."

"Love you too." Jack hung up.

He really should call his lawyer, he thought. But he procrastinated, making the excuse that it was dinner time. He'd call later, although he looked forward to it with ever so slightly more enthusiasm than a broken-glass enema.

He sat back, sipping his beer. His gaze drifted toward the walnut bookcase, the bottom row of which contained photo albums.

He walked over, opened the glass doors, and selected the album labeled *High School 1991-1995*, then returned to the recliner.

He paged through it. The early part of the album had pictures of himself as a freshman with long curly hair and ridiculous sideburns. How could he have gone out in public looking like that? One could have made an argument for a criminal negligence charge against his parents for allowing it.

Further along in the album were photos at the football games, taken by his stepfather George, who fancied himself a sports photographer. And to be honest, there were some pretty good shots.

There was one of him being yelled at by Coach Karcich. Jack smiled and shook his head. That was such a regular occurrence that it came as no surprise that at least one such photo should make it to the album.

It wasn't until junior year that the photos of Eileen started to appear. She had transferred from somewhere in Massachusetts to Holy Angels Academy in Demarest.

It was at one of Jimmy's parties, at his family's estate in Englewood, that they met. Her father worked for Jimmy's dad as a lithographer. There was something about her that caught Jack's attention.

He recalled sitting with a bunch of people around the fire pit. She had slid over, creating a space for him.

They sat listening to music from the seventies and eighties, drinking beer. It was a perfect night, the sky full of stars and a big harvest moon. His right hand was on the ground next to her left hand. At some point they touched. It was awkward at first, but he didn't want to be rude and pull it away abruptly. At the same time, he didn't want to seem presumptuous, crowding her space. He couldn't be sure if it was intentional on her part or accidental. While he contemplated this, that question was answered. Without looking his way or saying anything, she looped her left pinky over his right pinky. It remained there for several minutes. At some point she slid her entire hand over his, and gripped it, her fingers sliding between his own. That's when they looked at each other.

She had light blond hair, long and straight, with strands hanging in her face. She was beautiful. Her eyes were like narrow almonds tilting upward from her Celtic cheekbones, exotic in an ill-defined way. Her complexion was pale, and she wore a light peach-colored lip gloss. She looked at him with magnetic blue eyes.

Jack thumbed through the pages until he found pictures from that party. His memory of that evening was as clear and detailed as the photos that he held before him.

He kept turning the pages, but stopped and returned to a previous page. There was a group photo, and he could see a very young Connie Gigante sitting across the fire pit from him. She was looking at him with a sullen, forlorn look on her face. A few frames later, she was no longer there, an empty space where she had been sitting.

Jack closed his eyes and let his thoughts drift back to that night. Eileen leaned over and whispered into his ear, "Come with me." As they got up, she took hold of his hand and they walked down the grassy hill, along the bicycle path and past the tennis courts. They reached a secluded area out of view of the other party guests and sat on a wooden bench.

"My name is Jack."

"I know," she said, staring straight ahead.

"What's your name?"

She hesitated, then said, "You can call me Eileen."

Jack started to speak, but she leaned over and put her hand behind his head, gently pulling it toward her. She closed her eyes and their lips met. She pulled him in tighter, her tongue touching his teeth. He could taste her peach-flavored lip gloss. A pleasant floral scent from her hair filled his nostrils. She was stunning. They wrapped their arms tightly around each other, alternately kissing and pausing to breathe.

Abruptly she stood up and pulled him by his hands.

"What's wrong?" he said, confused.

"Nothing. Let's go back to the party."

"Wait," he said, "can I call you?"

She pulled him in again, looked into his eyes, and kissed him. "You'd better!" she said.

Back on his La-Z-Boy, Jack opened his eyes and the fond memories of that day melted into a looming feeling of grief. For all of those years, he believed that someday, they might meet again and rekindle that spark. In truth, that idea had probably doomed most of his subsequent relationships. But all that time, while he dreamed those thoughts, she had been decomposing in a cold, dark, watery grave.

He closed the photo album and returned it to the bookcase. Perhaps at a later date he would go through the photos. He would reminisce about the good times and be appreciative of those precious memories that they had made in their youth. But today was not that day.

Jack looked at the clock on his phone. It was 7:45 p.m. The dinner hour was over. He dreaded making the call to his lawyer, but any further procrastination was pointless.

He pulled up his contacts application and found the entry. She worked long hours and would still be at work. She had an annoying habit of not answering her cell phone, preferring to filter her disturbances through the switchboard. He dialed the number for the law offices of Berkshire Benderson in Washington, DC.

Her secretary answered the phone. "This is Jack Monroe," he said, "is Erin available?"

"One moment, sir," she said. "I'll connect you."

A minute later the familiar voice answered the phone. Lest he worry that he'd have to wait for the sarcasm, it came straight away.

"Well, it's too early for Christmas, and it's not my birthday, so that must mean you're in trouble."

"Hey, sis!" Jack replied. "Nice to speak with you too."

***

"I'll take that as a yes," Erin Monroe said. "Let's hear it."

Jack wasn't sure where to begin. "Do you still follow the North Jersey news?"

"I get electronic delivery of *The Bergen Record*, if that's what you mean." She shouted something to her secretary. "I'll call them back, hold my calls." Then back to Jack. "But honestly, I've been swamped with work, so I've been out of the loop. Why do you ask?"

"Do you remember Eileen, who I dated in high school?"

"Oh... yeah." Erin let the words dribble out as though she were gearing up for an awake colonoscopy. "May I be blunt?"

Jack laughed. "Do you have any other temperament that I'm not familiar with?"

"I never liked that girl. I didn't trust her. I've got pretty good intuition, and she always rubbed me the wrong way."

"That's so unfair," Jack said. "She was always nice to you. She liked you. I don't know why you were mean to her."

"I wasn't mean to her. I just didn't trust her. She was always elusive, like she was hiding something." Erin sighed. "So, what are you going to tell me? She robbed a bank? She embezzled funds from an old folks' home? Or, maybe plain old identity theft? My guess is number three. And now she needs a lawyer? Am I close?"

"No," Jack buried his forehead into his palm and closed his eyes, "she's dead."

"Oh," Erin said, her tone more sympathetic, "I'm sorry."

Jack quickly recounted the news story about Eileen being found in her car in an abandoned rock quarry. He then filled Erin in on being called in to the FBI office, giving a detailed account of their questions and his responses.

"That's horrible. Obviously, she didn't put herself in the quarry. But why was the FBI involved?"

"I asked that same question. They wouldn't tell me."

"Hmm," Erin said, "there's something fishy about all of this." She caught herself. "Oh, sorry. Bad choice of words."

Jack continued, "I wasn't worried until they pulled out that old fishing knife that Grandpa gave me. That freaked me out, to think that somehow..." He trailed off, not finishing the sentence.

"Whoa, whoa, whoa!" She made a long irritating sound like a game show buzzer going off. "You left out that little item," she spit the words out. "Okay. Number one: you're an idiot," Erin blurted. "But that's established fact, so we'll accept that, and move on. Number two: why, on God's green Earth, would you go and answer their questions without calling me?"

"You're right, as usual, I should have called you."

"Alright. Let's not panic. You haven't been charged with anything. Yet. So let's just see how this plays out. And don't do anything foolish, contrary to your inclinations, though that might be." She paused and then continued. "You're in luck. I'm going to be working out of our New York office for most of the next three months, so I'll be available if you need help. I also have a fair amount of vacation accrued because, as we are all painfully aware, I have no social life."

"Thank you."

"Keep me posted."

Jack hung up the phone. "Well, that went better than expected."

CHAPTER 15

Thursday, May 28, 2020

Jack was eager to get back to his routine and forget recent events. Thursday started as a typical day. He busied himself taking care of paperwork and clearing a backlog of emails. Around 8:30 a.m., the office door chimed.

"Good morning, Meghan."

Meghan strolled in with an armful of stuff. "Good morning, Doctor."

Jack talked too much. It was a character flaw. He filled Meghan in on the meeting with the FBI and the call to his sister.

"So let me try to understand," Meghan said. "What is this feud about between you and your sister?"

"It's not so much a feud as a unilateral distaste on her part for everything me. I irritate the crap out of her."

"Do tell," Meghan rolled her eyes and pulled up a chair.

Jack began, "She was always the smart one in the family, always playing by the rules. And I was the Ferris Bueller who always managed to tip the balance in my favor. Sports came easy to me. I was good at everything, and she struggled."

Meghan said, "So, she was the smart one and you, being of lesser intellect, had to settle for becoming a neurosurgeon? Is that the sob story you're telling me?" She closed her eyes and rubbed her thumb against her forefinger. "Let me pull out the world's smallest violin and play a sad, sad song for your family."

"Fair enough," Jack raised his hands. "But when you don't have big problems, small problems loom large."

After clearing his desk, Jack decided to check on Connie. She'd been moved from the ICU to a regular room on Eight Hudson South. On his way, Jack spotted Ruth Burgess down the hallway, heading toward him. She hadn't seen him yet. He stopped walking, fretting that she would ensnare him in her vortex of verbosity, narrating the minute details of her recent tropical vacation.

Thinking quickly, he seized the next doorknob, opened the door, and ducked inside. He immediately felt like an idiot, standing in pitch darkness inside a janitorial closet. His foot kicked a mop bucket and some water splashed out onto his shoe. He contemplated the situation, wondering how long it would take the arthritic Ruth to walk down the hallway and pass the space where he now stood. Before he could complete his calculations, the mop water had wicked through his sock, bathing his toes in dirty water. "Well, that's just great," he whispered.

But what if she stopped some other poor sap and started telling her story? How long might that take? What a mess?

Just then Jack heard Ruth's voice. Was she talking to herself? The voice became louder, and then softer, as it receded in the opposite direction. He waited. All clear.

He opened the door and put his head out. There stood one of the radiology techs. "Good morning, Dr. Monroe," she shifted her eyes to the lettering on the door, which read *Utility Closet.*

He cleared his throat and stepped out of the closet. "Good morning, Kelly." His face turned red. "Everything seems to be in order in here." He patted the door, dropped his gaze to the floor, and kept walking.

Kelly shrugged.

Jack arrived at the Eight Hudson South nursing station and asked, of no one in particular, "Gigante? Anyone know which room Gigante is in?"

A nurse with short hair and pink glasses stepped up. "She's in room twenty-four, Doctor," she said, "but she's not there."

"Oh. Where is she?" Jack asked.

"She's in occupational therapy. Fourth floor satellite room."

"Thank you," Jack said, trudging off toward the elevators.

On the fourth floor, he found the room. Connie was in the back corner of the rehab gym with the therapist. She had on black, form-fitting Lululemon workout pants and top. She'd lost weight while in the hospital, not that she needed to. Jack eyed the curves of her body. He shouldn't be looking at her in that way, but he couldn't help it.

The occupational therapist was testing her reflexes, throwing a beanbag to her. Connie threw it back, softball style, with pinpoint accuracy.

Jack walked over to them. Connie's face beamed when she saw him. "Jack, good morning."

"Good morning, Connie." He turned to the therapist. "How's she coming along?"

The therapist, a fit-looking fifty-year-old woman with white hair and glasses, said, "Great, couldn't be better." She looked at Connie and waved her hand. "Take a break, Connie," and then started to type a note.

Connie sat on one of the therapy tables, her hands under her thighs. "So?"

"So what?"

"So, when am I getting out of this place?" she asked.

Jack smiled. "I see no reason why you can't go home today."

She leapt off the table and flung her arms around his neck. He felt her breasts compress against his chest through her thin poly top. "Thank you." She kissed him on the cheek and then looked into his eyes. "And thanks for, ya know, saving my life," she said as she flipped her curls off her face.

"Finish the therapy session and I'll go write the discharge orders." He turned to the therapist. "We're going to send her home. Could you please give her the home exercise instructions?"

"Sure, Doc." She looked over her glasses at the two of them.

Jack realized his hands were still on Connie's waist, and her hands on top of his shoulders. He stepped back. "Do you have someone to drive you home?"

"I guess I can call my dad or brother."

Jack looked at his watch. He didn't have much going on that day. He was on a budgeting committee and had a meeting with the COO starting in twenty-five minutes. After that, he was free.

"I could drive you, in about an hour and a half. It will take that long for the discharge to go through anyway."

"Yeah," Connie said, "I'd like that. I'll just wait for you in my bedroom." Another female patient looked up, wide-eyed, from the machine she was working on. Connie blushed and looked away. "I mean, my hospital room."

"I'll come and get you when my meeting is finished." Jack waved as he left.

*****

"Your chariot awaits, my lady," Jack said with one hand on the wheelchair and the other making a flourishing motion as he bowed.

Connie grabbed her bag, walked over, and sat down in the wheelchair.

"Should I call for transport, Doctor?" Connie's nurse asked.

"Nah," Jack waved his hand. "I'm going that way anyway, and I can still push a wheelchair." That was true, though he hadn't done it since he was an intern.

Jack pushed the wheelchair out of the room and down the hallway.

"I could get used to this," Connie said. "Maybe I'll sell my car."

"Yeah, well, don't." Jack laughed. They navigated through the Milstein Pavilion into the Neurological Institute over the connecting bridge.

When they got down to the lobby, Ned Hoffman was standing guard at the door, metaphorically speaking. More precisely, he was slouched in a chair, head tilted to the side, snoozing.

"Ned," Jack whispered as he squeezed Ned's shoulder. Jack looked around the room. Nobody seemed to notice Ned napping.

Ned's eyes opened, and his jowls shook. Suddenly realizing he was still at work, he stood up. "Good morning," he looked at his watch, "um, good afternoon, Doctor. What can I do for you?"

"Ned, I'd like to leave Ms. Gigante here with you while I go get my car and bring it around."

"Certainly, my pleasure," he said as he tipped his cap to Connie. "Good day, young lady."

A few minutes later Jack returned with the car. He got out and opened the door. Ned and Connie were having an animated conversation.

"Oh, he's here," she said. "Have a great day, Ned."

"Likewise." Ned smiled like a kid on a seesaw.

Jack held the door for Connie and then repeated the process for the car's passenger door as she got in. He went around and jumped into the driver's seat, shifted into gear, and drove toward the bridge.

The George Washington Bridge was congested, and they moved slowly across it. Connie looked at Jack. "Those are cute glasses! You look suave."

"They are not cute." Jack took them off and looked at them. "They're... manly."

Connie rolled her eyes and drew the corner of her mouth up. "If you say so." She looked at him again. "Put 'em back on, ya look like a movie star," the Jersey accent coming out again.

Jack smiled at her.

"Hey, it's early," Connie said, "wanna take a walk around Fort Lee Park? We can get some fresh air. I could use it after being cooped up in that hospital."

Jack thought about it, nodding his head. "Sure, why not?"

They got off at exit 73 for Fort Lee and US 9W. Jack parked on Terrace Street. They walked up and down the length of the park, catching up on the events of their lives, wondering why they hadn't kept in touch over the years. Neither of them could think of a good reason.

They passed a hot dog vendor with *Hiram's* written in red script around its yellow umbrella. Connie asked the vendor, "Are you from the same Hiram's across the street from where Palisades Amusement Park used to be?"

"Yes, that's right," he said.

She looked at Jack and grabbed his shoulders. "Jack, we have to."

She addressed the vendor again. "Do you still sell Yoo-hoos?"

"We sure do," he said.

"I think I died and went to heaven, Jack." Connie smiled, flashing her perfect teeth.

Jack paid and walked away with a box full of food and drinks.

They found a grassy spot under a tree on a hill, giving them a perfect vantage point to view the New York skyline.

"What could be better?" Connie said, in between voracious bites of her hot dog. It was char-grilled perfectly, with spicy mustard and relish.

She finished it quickly and washed it down with her Yoo-hoo. She closed her eyes and turned her head toward the sun.

Jack stared at her profile. She had soft features and a nicely shaped nose. Her thin dark brows and red gloss lipstick contrasted with her light complexion.

"That was fast," he said.

"You try eating hospital food for two weeks."

"You were asleep for half of it."

"Well, now I'm awake."

She got up, faced him, and knelt down, straddling his legs as he was taking a bite of his hot dog. She laughed and put her fingers on the ground on either side of him, leaned forward, and slowly bit the other end of his hot dog. She smiled as she chewed, staring into his eyes. "You better hurry," she said with her mouth full.

They continued eating until she grabbed the last small piece with her thumb and index finger and shoved it into her mouth.

They looked at each other for a moment as she swallowed the last bit, neither knowing what to do. Connie paused, then rolled to her side and lay on the grass next to Jack.

"You look like you're deep in thought," she said. "Are you worried about this FBI stuff?"

"Sure, I'm worried. Who wouldn't be?"

She put her elbow down, resting her head on her hand, and looked at Jack.

He looked back at her. "You asked me why I haven't kept in touch all these years. I guess it's because of that night. I've never forgiven myself." He swallowed and looked away. "I guess you, and anyone else associated with that night, remind me too much of what a screw-up I am."

She looked away. "We all have things we'd like to forget, Jack. You have to move on. It was a long time ago."

"I have. I try to focus on work, which distracts me for a while. But when I'm alone, and the memories resurface inside my head, it haunts me." He looked back at her. "Sometimes it gets to be too much. I don't know why I can't let it go. There have been times when I have thought about climbing to the top of the Empire State Building," he pointed at the building across the Hudson River, "and jumping." He stared, his hand still outstretched, "oh, who am I kidding? I'd be too worried I'd land on someone walking their dog." He laughed and lay his head back on the grass. "I'd probably just inject myself with some propofol and rocuronium." He snapped his fingers. "Poof, no more worries."

In a flash, Connie rolled over onto Jack, straddling his abdomen once again and pinning him down. This time her hands clutched each side of his face. The smile was gone.

"Jack Monroe! Don't you ever say that again." She shook him. "Do you hear me? Promise me."

Jack saw fear in her wide eyes, and something else. He looked into them. "Okay, sure. I promise."

She stared into his eyes for a few moments, assessing his sincerity, then dropped her focus to his lips. Jack felt her pelvis lower onto his abdomen. He put his hands on her waist. She inched forward slowly until their lips touched gently, testing his reaction. She kept her eyes open, holding Jack's gaze. She pressed harder, still holding his cheeks in her hands. He closed his eyes, in tacit approval, as an ember of passion from the distant past reignited.

Jack enjoyed the familiarity of it all and found it difficult to resist. But he turned his head and said, "Connie. I can't do this. I have a girlfriend. I shouldn't be doing this. I'm sorry."

Connie lay back on the grass facing Jack. "No, I'm sorry, Jack. I was out of line."

"You know how much I care about you, right?" Jack said. "I've always considered you one of my best friends."

Connie shook her head. "Yeah." She rested her head on his shoulder and sighed. "Friends."

CHAPTER 16

Thursday, May 28, 2020

Jack dropped Connie off at her apartment in Ridgefield. It was cozy and nice in its own way. But there was a loneliness about it, tucked away in a shaded corner of her residential neighborhood. She invited Jack in for coffee, but he declined. As Connie had let her feelings for Jack become apparent, Jack found it harder to keep his own feelings for her in check.

Jack struggled to understand what was happening. He and Leslie made a perfect couple, didn't they? His mind pondered the question. Why was he letting these feelings resurface? Sure, Connie was beautiful, and kind, and fun to be with. But she was part of his past, privy to things he had to forget, for his own sanity. She was, through no fault of her own, a reminder of the glaring flaws in his character. Perhaps the fact that she still held him in such high esteem was the reason Jack loved Connie. On his drive home, Mik called.

"Hey Jack, where are you?"

"Driving through Leonia, why?"

"I'm with Sherlock at the Yorkie," Mik said. "Why don't you join us? I have information that may be of interest to you."

The Yorkie was the Yorkshire Inn, a British pub on Kinderkamac Road in River Edge. It was a place they used to frequent in high school, back when nobody checked IDs.

Jack thought for a moment. "Okay, I haven't eaten yet. I can be there in twenty minutes."

"See you then," Mik said.

Jack arrived and slid into the booth where Mik and Sherlock were seated. It was dimly lit inside, with dark wood furnishings. Outside, dusk had come, and the parking lot glowed with flickering lanterns.

Jack recounted all that had transpired since they'd last met at the reunion. He told them about the FBI, Connie's release from the hospital, and about calling Erin.

"How is your sister anyway?" Mik asked.

"She's fine," Jack said. "She'll be working out of New York for a few months."

"Really?" Mik scratched his chin. "She was always cute, in a spectacle-wearing, librarian sort of way."

"Don't even think about it," Jack said. "She may look cute, but so does a black mamba."

"Well, it's a good thing she's on your side, because I think you're going to need her."

"What do you mean?" Jack asked.

Mik folded his hands and tightened his lips. "I've got a friend in the Bergen County Sheriff's Office."

"Okay..." Jack said. "I'm listening."

"There's this DA, Gavin Schictman. He's a complete asshole. Word has it, he's looking for his party's endorsement to run for state attorney general next election cycle. He needs a signature win, and he's eyeing this Delaney story, since it's gotten a lot of public interest."

"And you think I should be worried?"

"Well, my friend tells me that this guy is looking for someone to take the fall," Mik leaned in, "and from what we know so far, I wouldn't be surprised if that someone was you."

"Not what I wanted to hear." Jack put his hand on his forehead and brushed back his dark blond hair.

The waitress came by, and Sherlock ordered another beer. She was twenty-something, with black hair in a ponytail and a nice smile. "Would you like one too, sir?" she asked Jack.

"Better make it a double shot of Basil Hayden, please."

Sherlock looked at Mik. "Did you bring any good news?"

"Um, no, not really." He shook his head. "But I do have some additional information."

"I'm not sure I want to hear any more," Jack said.

"This is actually interesting. The car has been positively identified as Eileen's. The driver's license, jewelry, and other belongings are also Eileen's. But they are having trouble making a definitive identification. It's just a formality. Nobody has any doubt that it's her in the car."

"Can't they just use DNA?" Sherlock asked.

"Apparently not," Mik said, "After twenty-five years in that chemical swill-water, there's nothing left. Not that it would matter. They have nothing to compare it to. Her parents are dead, and there are no other known relatives."

Jack's stomach churned.

"What about dental records?" Sherlock asked.

"Ah," Mik said, "here's where things start to get interesting. There are no records from Eileen's childhood. No vaccinations, no medical records. No records of visits to a dentist. It's like she just appeared out of nowhere in the fall of 1993."

"She came from Boston," Jack said, snapping out of his trance. "Her records are probably up there."

"Nope, no records in Boston either." Mik steepled his fingers. "There were two medical encounters after 1993, one a routine gynecology visit and the other some sort of skiing injury."

Jack's eyes lit up. "I remember that. We were night skiing, on a school trip to Vernon Valley/Great Gorge. Eileen broke her wrist. She missed a turn and wiped out. They took her to Hackensack Hospital. I went with her. The next day she had surgery."

Mik continued, "Her Holy Angels transcript shows that she transferred from Henley Academy in Boston. It's a private girls' school. The county investigators went to Boston to find information, and sure enough, there was a record of an Eileen Delaney attending Henley Academy."

"I don't remember her ever talking much about Boston," Jack said, "but I did know that's where she came from."

"Here's the strange part," Mik said. "Nobody there at Henley knew her, or had ever heard of her. Not any of the teachers, the administrators, or any of the students who would have been classmates."

"She must have had recommendation letters to get into Holy Angels," Jack said.

"She did," Mik continued. "Three letters. Two from teachers who don't exist and never taught at Henley. And the third was from the headmaster, who does actually exist, but claims that she never composed the letter, and doesn't remember an Eileen Delaney."

Jack folded his arms. "What does it mean?"

"People don't just materialize out of thin air," Mik said, "unless..."

"Unless what?" Sherlock jumped in.

"Are you guys familiar with WITSEC?" Mik said.

"You mean the witness protection program?" Jack asked. "For criminals?"

"Not just for criminals," Mik said. "It's also for ordinary people who witness crimes and face retribution for testifying."

Mik shook his head. "Can you imagine giving up your identity, your entire life, your friends, and sometimes your family?" He looked at Jack. "I don't think I could do it."

Jack's eyes sank to the table. "So, you are saying Eileen Delaney may not have been Eileen Delaney?"

"Oh no," Mik said. "She was Eileen Delaney. The question is, who was she before that?"

***

The chaotic parade of thoughts coursing through Jack's mind started to organize. The Basil Hayden was having its intended effect, calming his nerves, and Jack's subconscious began to formulate a plan.

"This is your line of work, Mik," Jack said. "I'd like to hire you. I want to get ahead of things if this DA comes after me."

"I'll do whatever I can to help."

"And I'll pay you."

"We're friends, Jack. I'm not going to charge you for my services. But there will be some costs to cover expenses. If you can take care of those, then we're good."

"Thank you." They shook hands.

"I've got this Chinese guy, Henry Wan. He's a freaking genius. Started life as a computer hacker, but now he's on our side," Mik said. "I'll send him to Boston to dig around."

Sherlock watched the two of them over the rim of his pint glass. "This is getting interesting."

"I used to complain that my life was dull," Jack said. He dropped his head, slowly shaking it back and forth. "I need to be more careful what I wish for." He slapped his hands on the table. "Alright guys, I'm going to get going. I need some sleep."

He threw a few twenties on the table. As he stood up, his head began to spin. He felt light-headed. It came on like a seizure. A scene flashed through his mind. It was dark, and he was in the middle of nowhere. The Blues Traveler song, *Hook*, played on a loop, lulling him into a tranquil state. There was a loud bang. Then a dreadful silence. Blood everywhere. It lasted a few seconds, then it was gone. He sat back down.

"Are you alright?" Sherlock asked.

"You're white as a ghost, man," Mik said.

Jack was sweating, his heart pounded in his chest. He struggled to speak over a deep sense of foreboding. "Yeah," he swallowed, "I'm alright." He wiped his forehead with his napkin. "Maybe I better have some coffee."

"Good idea," Mik said. "You don't want a DWI."

The words sank in, as Jack stared blankly across the table. "No, I don't."

They sat and had coffee and carrot cake, to try to counter the alcohol. After half an hour Jack felt much better. "Okay guys, this time I'm going for real." He stood up.

He got into his car and headed home. A short distance down Kinderkamac Road, he pulled into the parking lot of the River Edge Post Office. He opened his console, pulled out a pair of rubber gloves, and put them on. Then he opened the glove compartment and pulled out a preprinted, addressed envelope from a box. He found the bank envelope, withdrew ten one-hundred-dollar bills, and stuffed them inside the addressed envelope. He poured a small bit of water from his water bottle onto his gloved index finger and used that to moisten the glue strip on the envelope, which he sealed closed.

Jack got out of his car, walked into the post office, and pushed the envelope into the outgoing mail slot.

CHAPTER 17

Friday, May 29, 2020

The sun dipped low in the western sky, casting an orange opalescence upon the horizon. Anna sat in her screened porch, gazing out at the peaks of New Hampshire's White Mountains. She leaned back on her cushioned Adirondack chair and sipped from a glass of chardonnay.

Has it been another year? She glanced with teary eyes at the framed photo of her daughter in her high school rowing uniform. A second-place silver medal hung from a crimson and navy lanyard around her neck. Next to the photo on the wicker table sat a ceramic vase filled with white roses, Elsa's favorite flowers.

"Happy birthday, Elsa," she said aloud as she let the tears fall. In the glass of the sliding French doors, her reflection stared back at her with unforgiving candor. Her loosely tied white hair perched like a mop above her wrinkled forehead. Her jowls sagged, accentuating her melancholy appearance.

Twenty-five years. *Is it really possible? Can it have been that long since she last hugged her daughter?* Anna looked out again over the beautiful New Hampshire countryside, its quiet serenity a stark contrast to the pain tormenting her.

"Come home, Elsa. We love you. Please come back." She buried her face in her hands and quietly sobbed. She didn't notice the door slide open. Lars Johansson stood in the doorframe. He had an angular jaw and a weathered complexion, and like his wife, the years had not been kind to him. His exposure to Agent Orange during his tours Vietnam had left in him with mild neurologic damage. He stood in silence, looking at his wife.

He stepped down onto the porch and sat in the chair next to her. He reached out and took her hand. They sat quietly for a few moments. Lars broke the silence.

"I'm worried about you, Anna."

"No need to worry. You know how this day is always hard for me," she said.

"Yes, I know." He swallowed. "I'm wondering if maybe we shouldn't be doing this every year. It just gets you so upset."

"And what?" She squeezed his hand and looked into his eyes. "Do we just forget about her? Forget that we had a beautiful little girl..." She started crying again, throwing her arms out toward the mountains, "who is out there... somewhere." She tugged on his hand. "I'll never give up hope, Lars. Never."

"You're right," he said. "Forget I said anything."

"Do you ever wonder if maybe we didn't do enough? When she was going through her depression, and her grades started to slump?" She looked into his eyes. "Could we have done more?"

"I don't think we should start assigning blame, dear." Lars leaned forward, taking Anna's both hands in his. "We took her to psychologists. We got her tutors for the subjects she struggled with." He let out a sigh. "And the bullying," he shrugged his shoulders, "well, that's something that all kids deal with, at one time or another. I think we did the best we could."

Anna nodded. "I suppose," she said, not entirely convinced. She changed the subject. "Did you talk to the kids?"

"Yes, I just spoke to Niles. He picked up Lisa, so they're coming together. They should be here soon."

"I'll set the table," Anna said. She grabbed her lower back as she got up from the chair and winced. She bent backward to stretch before stepping into the house.

A short time later the doorbell rang, and Lars greeted his children with hugs and kisses.

"Hey, guys," Anna said from the kitchen.

"Hey, Mom," Lisa said, as she walked into the kitchen and kissed her mother. She smiled broadly, her blond hair resting on her shoulders.

Niles walked into the kitchen with a pout on his face. "Hello," he said, lacking enthusiasm.

"Can I get you guys something to drink?" Lars asked.

"Yeah," Niles replied, leaning his frame against the counter, "anything with alcohol."

Anna gave him a look. "Please, Niles, you could at least try."

"I am trying, Mom," he said. "I'm here, aren't I?"

Lisa said, "Iced tea for me if you've got it."

"Dinner is almost ready," Anna said, "if you want to take seats at the table."

There were five place settings. The setting at the head of the table was placed symbolically for Elsa. Her favorite pink sweater, with the cartoon moose logo, draped over the back of the chair.

Niles and Lisa sat, while Lars poured the drinks. Lisa sat down facing the portrait of Elsa hanging on the family room wall in a beautiful maple frame. She studied the features of the sister she hadn't seen since their youth. Sadness replaced the smile she'd walked in with.

Anna put the food platters on the table and sat. "Lars, would you do the honors?" They all held hands as Lars recited the blessing before meals.

Anna added, "And please, Lord, keep our daughter and sister safe in your care, until she's back with us again. Amen."

Niles rolled his eyes.

When dinner was over, they moved to the family room. The room was cluttered with an array of family photos, mostly of Elsa. There were some more recent photos of Niles and Lisa, but Elsa's stood permanently frozen in childhood.

It was a ritual which they repeated each year on Elsa's birthday. After dinner they would watch home movies. Lars had recorded so many of them throughout the children's early years, first with the old analog video cameras using Hi8 and MiniDV cassettes, and later using digital cameras. There was a treasure trove of exploits, preserved forever in digital form.

The current feature was of the family at their lake house on Brandy Pond in Naples, Maine. They were with their neighbors, the Clavettes, who had set up an inflatable jungle gym in the lake in front of their house. All the kids were having a great time, climbing it and jumping into the water. Elsa, the youngest, sat atop the thing with the biggest smile on her face. As Anna watched, she wished she could turn the clock back to that day, or any other day before Elsa left them.

The next segment of the annual *Elsa birthday ritual* was for each family member to recount a story about Elsa that had meaning to them. Lisa went first. Her recollection was of the long walks that she and Elsa used to take from their lake home in Naples Bay Colony, over the causeway between Long Lake and Brandy Pond, to the ice cream shop. Elsa always got moose tracks in a cone. Lars remembered teaching Elsa how to ride a bike.

It was Niles's turn. He thought for a moment and then spoke. "Look, I loved Elsa every bit as much as any of you did. And I have a lot of great memories of the times we had together. But I just think this isn't helpful. We sit and pretend that Elsa was a saint. But we all know that's not true. Elsa was a very troubled kid. When she ran away, it cast a dark cloud over this family which affected all of our lives. It was like Lisa and I didn't matter anymore. All your attention was focused on Elsa."

"Niles!" Anna barked. "Please don't do this on your sister's birthday."

"But it's true, Mom, you know it as well as I do," Niles said, "she's not coming back."

"What did you just say?" Her mouth hung open and her face turned flaming red. "Don't you ever say that again."

"It's true, Mom. We all know the statistics. If somebody goes missing and they haven't been found in a few days..." Niles choked up, "it's time we stopped pretending."

Anna started to cry. "You've ruined everything, Niles. Please just go." She pointed toward the door.

"Are you throwing me out?" Niles asked.

"Well, I'm staying," Lisa said. "Dad can give me a ride home tomorrow."

Lars said, "Sure, I can do that."

"You better go, Niles," Lars said, "you're just upsetting your mother."

"Fine. I'll go," Niles shouted. He put on his shoes and left.

"I'll sleep in the guest bedroom, Dad," Lisa said. "I'll go make up the bed."

Anna went to the master bathroom and locked the door. She clenched her teeth as the tears rolled down her face. She looked in the mirror. Staring back, she saw a haggard shell of the person she had once been. She used to be a vibrant, happy woman, blessed in life with so many good things, and so many wonderful friends. But they no longer came around. Anna couldn't blame them. She knew she wasn't much fun to be with.

She shut her eyes and grimaced. The pain in her back was throbbing. She opened the medicine cabinet and pulled out the bottles of methotrexate and hydrocodone. The cancer had spread to her bones, and it was only a matter of time now. Her greatest fear was going to her grave without finding her youngest daughter.

CHAPTER 18

Saturday, May 30, 2020

Dusk descended on Englewood, New Jersey, like a blanket smothering a campfire. Gray cloud formations divided the sky into horizontal slivers. Below, New Jersey Route 4 stood in sharp contrast, brightly lit by the overhead street lamps. They got off at the Jones Road exit and headed north.

Jack drove with his left hand on the wheel and his right arm resting on the center console. Electric Light Orchestra's *Telephone Line* playing on the oldies station, pulsated rhythmically from the Bose speakers.

Leslie leaned forward in the passenger seat. She folded down the vanity mirror and used it to apply her lipstick. "I still don't feel good about going to a Mafia boss's house," she said. "How would it look if the other networks found out?"

"Just give them a chance," Jack implored. "They're a nice family and I've known them for a very long time. Besides... there will be a lot of people there and we can blend into the crowd."

"I suppose," she said. "I just wish we'd been given more notice."

"To be fair, I just discharged Connie from the hospital two days ago, without much warning," Jack said. "Her family wanted to celebrate, and it was thrown together last minute, but it should be nice. Trust me."

Leslie looked out the window. Glitzy mansions lined both sides of the road. They seemed to be growing larger the farther they drove into the suburban enclave. "Nice neighborhood."

"Oh yeah," Jack said, "there's big money here."

They turned a corner and started to drive up a hill. Thick maple trees towered over each side of the road. Cars were parked alongside them. Jack had to park a full block down from the house. The property was surrounded by a seven-foot-tall wrought-iron fence, divided into segments by square brick columns with capstones. Through the fence, the decoratively lit home and grounds looked like the Hotel California.

Approaching the gates, Jack said, "Remember, they are just a normal family."

Leslie stopped walking and laughed. "Oh really." She tipped her head toward the gate and spoke in a hushed tone. "Normal families don't have armed guards in suits patrolling their driveways."

"Shhhh," Jack put his index finger to his mouth, "we're almost there, so let's stop talking about it."

They approached a podium with the guest list splayed open on top. Jack recognized the large man behind it. He had a pockmarked face and a serious expression bordering on a scowl. It was Fat Frank, from the initial meeting with Gigante. "Hello, Frank," Jack said, extending his hand. Leslie's brows arched, surprised that Jack knew this man.

Frank's scowl morphed into a wide grin. He gripped Jack's hand and squeezed it like he was trying to turn coal into a diamond. He turned to two beefy men with handguns tucked into their suit pants. "Hey, fellas, this is the doc who took care of Connie." The men nodded and shook Jack's hand.

Frank looked at Jack. "I guess that makes you a guest of honor, Doc." Frank turned to Leslie and shook her hand. "Welcome, Ms. Miller." He pointed in the direction of the path leading toward the house. "Please, go right in, guys."

As they took a few steps, Leslie leaned in and whispered, "Guest of honor? Oh yeah, we'll blend right in."

They continued up the walk to the house. The air was crisp, with a breeze carrying the scent of pine and mulch.

A doorman in a tuxedo tugged at the oversized, and overly decorated, mahogany door, ushering them in. They stepped into a massive Gatsby-esque atrium with white marble floors and a large marble fountain in the center. It contained a statue of a female figure holding a pitcher, from which water cascaded into a travertine-tiled basin. Classical music filtered into the room. The walls had floor-to-ceiling mirrors with gilded golden frames, and the ceilings high above bore ornate plaster moldings, corbels, and medallions with fleur-de-lis patterns. Pleasing aromas from the Italian cooking wafted in from the serving areas.

Connie suddenly appeared at the far end of the room, as if a Disney princess taking the stage. Her heels clicked on the marble floor as she approached. She looked stunning in a sleek white dress, cinched at the waist with a dark green leather belt. Her wavy black hair, with hints of walnut, was pulled back with a green elastic band, while a few strands dangled near her cheeks.

Though Leslie hoped she was mistaken, she suspected this was the woman the party was being held for. Connie's moist, red-glossed lips seemed to part in slow motion as she spoke. "Hello, Jack, I'm so glad you're here." She turned and extended a hand toward Leslie, her arm shaking. "Leslie, um... nice to meet you. I'm Connie." She averted her eyes from Leslie's. "I um... love your news show."

"Nice to meet you," Leslie said with all the sincerity she could muster. As she shook hands, her eyes performed a not-so-subtle full-body scan of Jack's favorite patient. Her smile faded. In her mind, she had pictured her to be so much less... beautiful.

Leslie cleared her throat. "Jack tells me you've known each other since high school."

Connie glanced at Jack. "Oh yeah, we go way back," she said. "After Jack and my brother became friends, they used to hang out here a lot, swimming and playing tennis. And then there were weekend trips to the shore, or to our lake house. Jack was one of the family."

"Oh," Leslie said, nodding, hands folded, "one of the family." She gave Jack a look, then turned toward Connie with a forced smile. "How nice."

"Come on," Connie said, "let's go get some drinks and hors d'oeuvres."

She turned to lead the way. Leslie frowned, tilting her head. If she had hoped to see oversized buttocks or some other detracting physical feature, she was sorely disappointed. The view of Connie from the rear offered no contradiction to the view from the front. She was drop-dead gorgeous. Leslie's eyes were glued to her backside as she sashayed across the floor. No way in hell was Jack going to spend another minute with this girl.

They followed her into a large parlor where people were holding cocktails and engaged in lively conversations. The walls, paneled in mahogany, dated to when the house was built in the 1920s. The home exuded elegance and money. The silver-haired bartender named Tony, manning the bar in the corner, fulfilled their cocktail requests.

They took their drinks and headed outside. The Italian marble terrace, which wrapped around the entire back of the house, had three levels. A string quartet in the corner of the upper level played the classical music of Bach. Surrounding the terrace on all sides, meticulous landscape lighting illuminated the shrubbery. The pool was lit by an underwater, turquoise-colored light and was situated directly in front of the marble staircase, which descended down the center of the terrace. The tennis courts sat off to the right.

"This is amazing," Leslie said.

"Thank you, Leslie. We're very fortunate," Connie replied.

Smartly dressed people mingled. There were at least a hundred guests. Among them, Leslie recognized a state senator, a prominent injury attorney whose billboards were particularly nauseating, and a handsome older actor who played a character on an ABC soap opera.

Young girls dressed in black-and-white outfits served hors d'oeuvres from silver platters. "Crab cakes, ma'am?" said one to Leslie.

Leslie tightened her lips and shook her head. Another came by with a platter of shrimp.

"You have to try the coconut shrimp, Leslie," Connie said. "They're delicious."

She answered curtly, "I'm a vegetarian."

"Oh," Connie said. She looked at Jack. "Sorry." She put her palms up. "Come with me, Leslie, we have an antipasto bar inside with cheeses, and lots of veggie options." She took Leslie by the arm. Leslie followed reluctantly, looking back at Jack.

Jack stood looking out over the property. Jimmy Jr. sauntered up next to him and clanked his glass with Jack's.

"Cheers, buddy. Just like old times."

Jack smiled. "Thanks for the invite, Jimmy. This place brings back a lot of memories."

"It sure does," Jimmy said.

"So, fill me in. What's new?"

"Well, you know, it's all downhill after your twenties." Jimmy laughed. He took a sip of his drink. "I shouldn't complain. I've got a good job working for my dad."

"Oh," Jack said, staring out toward the pool, "that's great."

"Oh no, it's not like that." Jimmy waved his hand, smiling. "I know what you're thinking. I'm just running the operations at the printing company. That's all. None of the, you know, other stuff."

"Oh no," Jack lied, "I wasn't thinking anything..." His voice trailed off.

Jimmy leaned back on the marble railing. "I didn't really have the same sort of options as you did, coming out of high school. My grades were pretty average. Not all of us are freaking geniuses." He gave Jack a pretend punch on the shoulder.

"I'm no genius, Jimmy. You of all people know that." Jack turned around and leaned against the marble next to his friend. "I've got a freakishly good memory, that's all." Jack tipped his glass back, taking a large gulp. "But sometimes memory can be your worst enemy."

"Some things are best forgotten," Jimmy said. "But it's pretty cool, you being a doctor and all. That's what you always wanted, right?"

Jack shook his head. "Not really."

"What?" Jimmy's eyebrows rose. "I thought you did."

"No, remember?" Jack said. "I wanted to be a pilot, but my vision was crap, so I couldn't do that."

"Right. Now that you say it, I do remember. So, what happened?"

"Well, my mom was a nurse, she suggested medicine." Jack's eyes glazed over as he stared out into the garden. "Anyway, I did it more to make her happy than anything else."

"Wow, that's a bummer. So, you don't like your job?"

"I wouldn't say that. I feel good about helping people. Like Connie. Don't get me wrong. That's a great feeling. And there are a lot worse things I could be doing. I just don't have a passion for it, like some of my colleagues do."

"Makes sense," Jimmy said. He spun around to face Jack. "So, what would you do instead?"

"Ahh. Don't laugh," Jack said, "but if I could go back to high school and do it over again, I'd like to be a writer.

I've always loved reading books and getting lost in their pretend worlds."

"You could still do it. Not going back to high school, of course. That would be weird," he laughed, "but you could be a writer."

"I suppose," Jack said. "I just need to find the time."

Jimmy clanked his glass with Jack's again. "Come on. You're empty. Let's go get a refill."

On the way, they ran into Connie and Leslie.

"What happened?" Jack said, staring at the stain on the front of Leslie's dress.

"It was a stuffed pepper," Connie said, clenching her teeth. "The stuffing just squirted out." She demonstrated, throwing her fingers in the air and making a raspberry sound with her mouth.

Leslie stood silently, a pained facial expression like she'd sat on a tack. "I tried to wash it off, but it just made it worse." Leslie pointed over her shoulder back toward the bathroom, narrowing her eyes. "Was that an actual Picasso in that bathroom?"

"I forgot about that," Jack said, looking at Jimmy, "you guys still have that?"

"Yeah, it is," Jimmy answered Leslie, "but it's not one of his good ones, so it wasn't super expensive."

"I'll go get you some club soda and a sponge," Jimmy offered. He ran off to grab the items.

Jimmy Gigante Sr. stepped out onto the terrace near the archway leading back into the house, so he could be seen by everyone, indoors and out. He banged on his martini glass with the handle of a knife. People paused their conversations. The string quartet held the music, and the place became quiet.

"We are happy that each of you could join us on this special occasion," Jimmy said. "As you all know, our beautiful daughter had a serious medical problem. But by the grace of God, she's been cured, and we owe it all to our friend, a wonderful doctor," he stretched his arm out toward Jack, "Dr. Jack Monroe."

Gigante started the clapping, and everyone joined in. Jack's face turned red. He put his hand up, in a half-hearted gesture, to wave off the applause. Connie walked over and hugged Jack and gave him a peck on the cheek.

"Thank you," Jack said.

Leslie stood there with her arms folded, her eyes laser-focused on the red-gloss lipstick on Jack's cheek. She looked down at the splotch of pepper stuffing on her fancy dress. The spicy pepper had caused her eyes to water, and she could now taste her mascara running down her face. She wanted to scream.

Jimmy Jr. returned with the sponge and club soda and gave it to Leslie. Leslie sat down at a nearby table and started to work on the stain. Jimmy Gigante Sr. walked over and put his arm around Jack.

"A word, Jack?"

They took a few steps away from the others to a more private spot on the terrace.

"This is a nice party, Mr. Gigante. Thanks for inviting us."

"Don't be silly, Jack, we couldn't have had it without you." He looked back to make sure their conversation was private. "Listen, Jack, I've heard some things. I've got contacts, and well, I don't know how to say this, so I'll just come out and say it. That douche-bag prosecutor has filed charges against you with the grand jury. It's possible that an indictment could be coming."

Jack's eyes closed and he put his hand on his forehead. "I can't believe this. I didn't do it," he said, louder than he'd intended. Then, in a whisper, "how can he get away with this? It's ridiculous."

"Of course it is." Gigante looked around. "After what you did for Connie, you're family now." He looked around again, and then lowered his voice. "Just try to stay calm, and don't let it get to you."

"How can I stay calm, Mr. Gigante?" Jack hung his head and clasped his hands behind it. "I'm petrified. Innocent people go to jail all the time."

"I told you, you're family now." Gigante put his hand on Jack's shoulder. "In a family, you look out for one another. Try not to worry. I can't explain why, because I've made promises to other people. But this won't stick. I won't let it. *Capisce?*"

Adrenaline was coursing through Jack's veins, and he started to feel queasy. A knot formed in his stomach. He nodded. "I understand."

CHAPTER 19

Monday, June 1, 2020

Jack's caseload on Monday was busier than he had planned. In addition to his two scheduled cases, he had two add-ons, one a revision of a VP shunt, and the other an emergency subdural hematoma in a five-year-old boy who'd been walking down a sidewalk with his grandfather when someone's lawnmower shot a rock into the side of his head. Still, Jack was able to finish by 4:45 p.m.

He was enjoying his drive home with nothing planned for the evening, except maybe sitting on his patio and reading the novel he was halfway through.

Those plans were about to change.

As he turned the wheel to make a right turn into his driveway, a police cruiser with its emergency lights flashing approached from the opposite direction. It stopped at the curb in front of his house. Two other police cars, lights flashing, advanced from behind. Notably, there were no sirens, so it all occurred in an eerily quiet manner.

As Jack got out of his car, two officers in navy blue uniforms with high-brimmed, Gestapo-styled hats approached him, their right hands on their unbuckled holsters.

"Jack Monroe?" one of the officers barked. A few of the neighbors watched from their front lawns.

"Yes," Jack answered, "I'm Jack Monroe."

"Turn around. Keep your hands where we can see them." Jack did as they asked. The other officers moved closer from behind. "You are under arrest for the murder of Eileen Delaney," said the tall, stone-faced officer. He pulled out an official-looking document on parchment. "We have a warrant to search the premises."

Binnie Benson, the neighborhood busybody who owned the home next to his on the north side, cupped her hand over her mouth as she looked on. She grabbed her granddaughter by the shoulder and pulled her close.

Jack looked at her and shouted, "It's all a mistake, Mrs. Benson. Nothing to see."

The officer grabbed his hands and handcuffed them behind his back. He began, "You have the right to remain silent. Anything you say can and will be used against you in a court of law. You have the right to an attorney. If you cannot afford an attorney, one will be appointed for you. Do you understand these rights?"

The events were unfolding fast, and Jack felt dizzy.

The second officer, looking at the house and the BMW, smirked. "Looks like he can afford an attorney, Dean."

A knot formed in Jack's stomach, and he started to feel nauseous. They walked him down to the street and put him in the back seat of the police cruiser. He sat there behind the metal mesh divider. The car smelled of donuts and coffee. Jack began heaving, and the officer flung open the door and pulled him out.

"Don't you dare puke in my car," he said.

The crowd of neighbors who'd gathered to watch the spectacle grew by the minute. A white cargo van pulled up. Block letters on the side read: BERGEN COUNTY CRIME SCENE INVESTIGATIVE UNIT.

Jack vomited, and when he stopped, they put him back in the car.

Jack leaned back into the seat, the taste of vomit in his mouth, and closed his eyes.

***

Two police officers returned to the car. The tall, stone-faced one named Dean drove. His partner, a short pudgy officer with light brown hair and a five o'clock shadow, picked up the remaining half donut from the dashboard and stuffed it into his mouth.

"Where are you taking me?" Jack asked.

Officer Dean looked into the rearview mirror, making eye contact. "Bergen County Jail."

"I need to make a phone call," Jack said.

"You'll have that opportunity once you are processed."

The route to the Bergen County Jail took them down Cedar Lane. What a difference two and a half weeks can make. On his previous jaunt down memory lane, he was on this very street, fondly remembering his date with Eileen. Now he was in a police car charged with her murder. Jack closed his eyes and took a deep breath. He didn't want to look out the window. He'd rather preserve the previous drive in his memory than supplant it with this new version.

It wasn't a long drive. They arrived at the Bergen County Jail, or as it was officially called, the *Corrections and Rehabilitation Center.* It was a brown block building with a strange little rotunda jutting out from the front. With alternating horizontal rows of gray and beige block, the rotunda looked like it was wearing stripes. The architect must have had a sense of humor.

The ordeal that they described as processing was a slow, tedious affair. There were reams of paperwork, the confiscation of his keys, cell phone, and clothing, and lastly, changing into the orange outfit, which was basically a sturdier, uglier version of the blue scrubs he wore at work every day.

After the processing was done, he was allowed to make a phone call. He knew exactly who he had to call, but he was not looking forward to the derisive comments he would get from his sister. He stood at the bank of telephones, leaning on the wall as a guard watched him. He made the call.

"Well, well. What a surprise?" Erin said. "I was expecting this call. Not quite this quickly, I must say." Jack could hear some papers shuffling in the background. "The number coming up is reading Bergen County Correctional Facility, so at least I know where you are."

"Just tell me what to do."

It sounded like she was biting into a sandwich. She spoke with her mouth full. "First let's do a grammar check. That sentence should have started with, or ended with, the word please."

Jack huffed. "Okay then, please tell me what to do."

"Better," Erin said. "Nothing. Do absolutely nothing. Don't speak to anyone. Don't sign anything. You can breathe and use the toilet until I get there. Got it?"

"Yes."

"Grammar check."

Jack clenched his molars tightly, trying to calm himself. "Yes... thank you, sis."

"Ahh, just when I thought you were untrainable, you surprise me," she hung up.

The phone's speaker must have been loud enough for the guard to hear the conversation. He grinned as he led Jack into an office.

"The DA would like a word with you," he said.

Don't speak to anyone, he told himself. *Follow directions, Jack.*

The guard stepped out and returned with the DA. He was as pompous-looking a turd as Jack had ever seen, with all the arrogance of an Ivy League frat boy. His salt-and-pepper hair was greased back on the top and sides into what could only be described as a fifties-inspired duck-ass hairdo. His lower lip was plump, whereas his upper lip was a thin line, giving him a Hitchcockian look, without the British charm.

"Dr. Monroe. I'm the district attorney, Gavin Schictman." He didn't extend his hand, and Jack wouldn't have shaken it anyway. "You've been charged with a serious crime, but I'm here to offer you a time-limited opportunity."

Jack leaned back, arms folded. He didn't speak.

Schictman sat down in a chair and pulled it forward, his face, showing a dusting of facial makeup, much too close to Jack's. His breath smelled of vinegar and oil. "Since you have been a productive member of the community for many years, and were a youth at the time of the infraction, I'm prepared to offer you a sweetheart plea deal. Fifteen years, with the possibility of parole, for a full confession."

He leaned back and smiled. "Of course, that assumes that we don't come across any other bodies in the quarry."

Fifteen years! Jack felt nauseous again, the gravity of the situation weighing on him like an anvil. He crossed his arms on his chest, stuttering as he spoke. "My lawyer has advised me not to speak to anyone without her being present."

Schictman stood up abruptly, pointing his finger at Jack's face. "You're making a mistake, Dr. Monroe." He turned to leave, then stopped. He turned back toward Jack.

"And who is your lawyer?"

"Erin Monroe."

"A relation?"

"She's my sister."

"I'm not familiar with the name," Schictman said dismissively.

Jack's fear morphed into anger. "No, you wouldn't be. She works in DC, at a high-powered litigation firm handling very wealthy clients and politicians. She's extremely well known there. And when this is over, you'll wish you'd never met her. I won't plead guilty to a crime I didn't commit."

Schictman cast a blank stare at Jack and then turned to leave.

"Oh, and Gavin," Jack said.

Schictman turned his head back toward Jack.

"Better buckle up!"

***

The guard took Jack to his cell. Due to the high census, there were two other inmates in the cell with him. The iron door slammed shut. The electronic lock engaged with a *cha-ching*. The sour smell of body odor filled his nostrils. Jack stood and assessed his new companions.

Lying on the single bed to his right was a filthy, jaundiced, thirty-something man with greasy hair. Track marks lined his arms between tattoos of a bleeding skull and a Confederate flag.

"What the hell are you looking at, shithead," he said, saliva drooling from the corner of his mouth.

Jack didn't answer. He turned away toward the bunk bed on the left. Lying on the bottom bunk, hidden in the shadow, was a very large Black man. His bright white eyes peered at Jack. He was clean-shaven with a short haircut.

"Don't pay no mind to that worthless druggie," he said. "I oughta beat his ass for that Klan tattoo he got on his back. What's your name?"

"Jack."

"I'm Marvin. What they got you in here for?"

Jack hesitated, shrugging. "Murder," he said, the full weight of it starting to sink in.

"Man," Marvin whistled, "that's some serious shit."

"I'm innocent," Jack said, throwing his arms up.

Marvin laughed. "Yeah, ain't we all innocent." He rolled from his side onto his back. "Don't matter one way or the other."

Jack climbed up the ladder to the upper bunk. The sheets and pillow smelled dank and musty. The ceiling was a popcorn-style plaster with paint flaking. The mattress, just slightly more comfortable than a morgue slab.

"Hey, Marvin."

"Yo."

"What are you here for?" Jack asked.

"Man... I was set up. There's a cop I had some run-ins wit'. Name's Dudley. That mo' fo' hate my ass. One day he pull me over, and drop this bag o' shit on my back seat. Next thing, I'm in here."

Jack listened and shook his head. "You hear about that kind of thing, but you don't want to believe it actually happens."

"Well... it do." Marvin put his hands behind his head. "I ain't no saint. Don't get me wrong. But this ain't right."

"Quit bitchin', you two, I got a splittin' headache," the druggie chimed in.

"Shut yo' mouth," Marvin said, "before I pop you one." Marvin doubled his pillow up under his head. "That guard called you Doc. You a doctor or something?"

"Yeah," Jack answered, "I am."

"What kind o' doctor?"

"I'm a neurosurgeon."

"Damn!" Marvin said. He thought, as he scratched his chin. "Hey, where do you work at?"

"Columbia. In New York City."

"No way," Marvin said. "My nephew was there. A few years ago. He got shot in the head. Wrong place, wrong time, I guess. He was fourteen years old. Just walking home and some other guys goin' at it. He got hit with a stray. Andre Jackson's his name."

Jack sat up. "Dre?" he said.

"Yeah, Dre," Marvin leaned his head out the side of the bunk. "That's what they call him. You know him then?"

"Sure do," Jack said. "I operated on him. Took the bullet out. Nice kid. Nice family. It was a sad situation. How is he doing?"

"He doing great, Doc. Good as new. He just started college at St. John's last year. Man, what a coincidence running into you here."

"That's great," Jack said. "I'm glad to hear that."

Suddenly something dawned on him. In all the confusion he'd been completely distracted. What about his job? What about his patients scheduled for surgery? How would they know he wouldn't be able to be there tomorrow?

Surely Erin would have thought to reach out and notify his office. What was he thinking? Of course she would. She thinks of everything. If she was on the Titanic, she would have thought to bring her own inflatable raft, and a spare, in case the first one got a hole.

Gurgling noises came from the other side of the cell. Jack looked down. The druggie's face was rigid. Sweat drenched his clothing and his eyes stared blankly from their sockets. Slowly at first, his stiff outstretched arms and legs began to twitch. The twitches gained in amplitude and soon he was bouncing up and down on his bed, drooling.

Jack jumped down off the bunk and yelled for help. He turned the druggie on his side and used the sheet to clear his mouth. One of the guards, appearing outside the cell, used his walkie-talkie to call a code. A minute later two more guards came with their guns drawn, followed by two medics in white uniforms carrying a code box.

"Step back," the first medic yelled.

"I'm a doctor," Jack said.

"Thank you, we'll take it from here." The medic pulled a bottle of Narcan out of the box and started to draw it up into a syringe.

"Wait," Jack said, "he's having opioid withdrawal. That could kill him."

The medics looked at each other.

"He's having a grand mal seizure. Look at his arms, trust me," Jack said. "He needs Valium or midazolam."

They looked at each other, uncertain what they should do. Then the second medic looked in the box. "We have Valium."

"Great. Give him 5 mg IV," Jack said.

The second medic drew the drug up in a syringe, as the first one started an IV. They administered the drug, and within thirty seconds the seizure stopped. Marvin sat curled up on his bed watching the whole thing unfold. "Damn," he said.

The guards brought a stretcher around, loaded up the druggie, and took him to the infirmary. After they'd gone, Marvin said, "You a good man to have around, Doc." He crawled back into his bunk and said, "Goodnight, Doc, better get some sleep."

Jack climbed up to the top bunk and laid his head on the pillow. But sleep wouldn't come.

CHAPTER 20

Tuesday, June 2, 2020

E rin Monroe enjoyed those occasions when work would take her to New York City. It wasn't always that way. Early in her career, when she was a new associate with the firm, they would put her up in accommodations that were marginal at best. But with one win after another, she'd risen to partner faster than anyone in Berkshire Benderson's long and storied history. Now when she traveled to New York for company business, they put her up at the New York Palace Hotel on Madison Avenue. The iconic landmark had portions constructed during the Gilded Age, retaining all of the opulence of that period.

Her driver awaited as she strode past the doorman in her dark-gray business suit, French-style beret, and Ray-Bans. Her briefcase dangled from one hand as she balanced her chai latte in the other. The driver, Louis, opened the door for her.

"Good morning, Ms. Monroe." Louis tipped his hat.

"Good morning, Louis," Erin said. She got in and he closed the door after her.

Once back in the car, Louis asked, "Where to, Ms. Monroe?"

"Bergen County Prosecutor's Office, Two Bergen County Plaza, Hackensack." Erin leaned forward. "And if you wouldn't mind, Louis, until we get there, no more 'Ms. Monroe.' I'd like you to speak to me in a derogatory manner, using a foul tone of voice."

Louis stared into the rearview mirror. "Pardon, ma'am?"

"You heard me, Louis. I want to be in a lousy mood by the time I meet Mr. Schictman."

Louis's eyebrows raised, not sure how to respond. "As you like, Ms. Mon..." he caught himself, "I mean... you miserable, crusty bitch."

Erin folded her arms, a smug, satisfied grin on her face. "Thank you, Louis."

The drive wasn't bad. Most of the rush-hour traffic in the morning headed into Manhattan, opposite the direction in which they were traveling. Thirty-five minutes later Louis pulled up to the front of the massive stone building, with a central rotunda and rectangular sides. A large bronze Statue of Liberty capped the building's dome.

Erin climbed the marble staircase, passed through security, and followed the guard's directions to get to the prosecutor's office.

She found the office marked BERGEN COUNTY DISTRICT ATTORNEY, GAVIN SCHICTMAN, ESQ. and opened the frosted glass door. Schictman's secretary was a middle-aged woman with a bouffant hairdo and heavily applied mascara. She sat behind her desk filing her nails.

Erin walked up to the desk and removed her sunglasses. "Ahem!" she said.

"One moment," said the secretary as she put down her file. For the next thirty seconds she appeared to be doing absolutely nothing.

Erin rolled her fingers, sequentially tapping the desktop. Finally, the woman asked, "Can I help you?"

"Good question," Erin said, "but the bar is low, so let's give it a try. I have a 9:30 a.m. appointment with Mr. Schictman."

The secretary lowered her glasses. "And you are?"

"Punctual, and on a tight schedule," she rested her knuckles on the desk, "I'm Erin Monroe, of Berkshire Benderson."

"Have a seat, I'll notify Mr. Schictman that you are here," she said, clearly annoyed.

At 9:50 a.m. Schictman skulked through the doorway. The description Jack had given her was accurate: arrogant, visually irritating, and immediately unlikeable. "Good morning. Ms. Monroe?"

Erin made a point of fully extending her arm, then bending it at the elbow to look at her watch. "I am," was all she said.

"Please step into my office."

Erin followed as he led the way. The office was large and sterile. Yet somehow, he'd managed to turn it into a cluttered pigsty. The walls were devoid of artwork and boxes sat piled in the room. They took seats in two armchairs which faced each other in front of the desk.

Schictman spoke as if the words were trying to squeeze through a puckered rectum. "This is somewhat awkward, Ms. Monroe, as the defendant in this matter is your brother.

I hope that won't affect your ability to rationally consider the plea deal that I had outlined. I think it's a fair deal."

Erin gripped the armrests on her chair. "Not at all. I'd reject your offer for any innocent client."

Schictman leaned back in his chair. "Surely, as his sister, I would expect you to say that. But the evidence says otherwise."

Erin laughed. "Ah, the evidence. Surely, you're not basing your entire case on a rusty fishing knife and a school ring. The deceased was my brother's girlfriend. And much to my consternation, he actually loved her. There are any number of good reasons why those items might have been in her car."

"Well, I'm not at liberty to go into the details of our evidence against Dr. Monroe. Suffice it to say that we feel good about our case."

Erin briefly saw the lack of confidence in his eyes and pounced.

"Uh huh." Erin leaned forward. "As good as you felt in *Bergen County v. Phlegging?*"

Schictman started fidgeting in his chair. He opened his mouth to speak.

"Or maybe *Bergen County v. McVeigh*, or possibly *Bergen County v. Campbell?*" She looked up and pinched her chin in her thumb and forefinger. "And what was that last one? Oh yes, *Bergen County v. Mejia.*"

Schictman's eyes opened widely. He stood and started pacing. "Human beings, and our judicial system, are not infallible, Ms. Monroe." It was clear from his expression that he knew she'd done her homework. "Do you think we don't feel terrible about those cases? I regret every day those men spent in prison. But our job is to keep the public safe, and we use whatever evidence presents itself. And sometimes, we get it wrong."

Erin crossed her legs and leaned back into her chair. "Excuse me. Not infallible? That's all you have to say? Four innocent men, that you sent to prison, spent a cumulative total of thirty-one years incarcerated for crimes they didn't commit!" The trace hint of cordiality evaporated from Erin's face, replaced by an ice-cold stare. "I'll be damned if I'll allow my brother to be your fifth victim."

Schictman's neck turned red. He thumped his fist on his desk. "We're not here to relitigate past cases, Ms. Monroe. None of which have anything to do with your brother's case."

"Oh, but you will, Mr. Schictman. I promise you that all of those cases will come out during this litigation. Frankly, I'm surprised and appalled that you still have a law license, much less this job."

Schictman's eyes narrowed and his brow began to furrow. Before he could respond she changed the subject, pointing to the diploma on the wall behind his head.

"Columbia Law School. Very impressive."

He calmed himself, falling into her trap. "Thank you," he mumbled cautiously.

"Very difficult to get into," Erin said. "I had a friend in college who was rejected from Columbia with an LSAT score of 170 and a 3.7 GPA in mechanical engineering."

Schictman puffed out his chest, momentarily caught off guard. "It's very competitive. Thousands of applicants apply for a limited number of slots."

"Exactly." Erin flicked her wrist and pointed her index finger at Schictman. "Which is why I'm curious, Mr.

Schictman, as to how you made that cut with an LSAT score of 157 and a GPA which was, let's be honest, less than stellar."

Schictman swallowed and loosened his collar with his fingertip. "There are many factors which go into the law school admissions process, Ms. Monroe. I don't pretend to know them all."

Erin pulled some papers from her folder. "Your father's investment firm made a sizeable donation to the school two weeks prior to your being put on a wait list. And a second larger donation immediately before your acceptance. Those sort of factors?"

Schictman stood up abruptly, nearly knocking his chair backward. "Well, I'm afraid that's none of your business, Ms. Monroe." He began to stutter. "How did you get that information, anyway?" He waved his hands frenetically. "That's personal, non-public information."

"I have an outstanding research team," Erin said, "and they're just warming up."

"Is that some sort of a threat?"

"Threat? No. I don't make threats. Unless facts threaten you."

"I think we're finished here, Ms. Monroe. I will see you at the arraignment tomorrow."

"Great. I'll look forward to your office providing our team with all of your files related to this case." Erin stood and grabbed her bag.

"In all candor, Ms. Monroe, I find your manner abrasive and off-putting."

"On the flip side, Mr. Schictman, I feel reassured after meeting you," Erin said. She took a step toward the door and looked back at Schictman's greased-back hair. "Oh, and thank you for your service."

"I'm not a veteran."

"I meant for doing your small part to maintain our strategic petroleum reserve."

Schictman looked with a blank stare. A sudden realization struck him, and he reflexively brushed his hair back with his hand. "You can show yourself out, Ms. Monroe."

Erin threw her bag over her shoulder. "See you in court, Schictman."

✳✳✳

Erin exited the building and found Louis waiting outside with the car. She got in and let out a huff of air. "Is it warm out, or is it just me?" Erin asked.

"It's a little warm, ma'am, I'll turn up the AC. Where to?"

"The Bergen County Jail. It's a few blocks from here."

"We passed it earlier," Louis said.

They drove a few blocks through a drab section of Hackensack, devoid of greenery, before arriving at the correctional facility.

Erin checked her watch. She was on time. Once inside the building she met with one of the corrections officers, who verified her appointment and checked her identification.

He pulled out his phone and dialed a number. "José? It's Robert. Would you bring Dr. Monroe down? His attorney is here. We'll be in consult room number four, thanks."

He guided Erin into a nearby consult room. "He should be down shortly."

"Thank you."

Erin did some busywork on her laptop. After a short while José appeared. He was a young Hispanic officer with black hair combed back behind his ears. He held the door for Jack. Jack wore a wrinkled orange jumpsuit and looked like hell.

"You look like hell," Erin said.

"Yeah well, it's not exactly the Waldorf Astoria. I didn't get much sleep."

"Well, you're going to have to suck it up for at least one more day. Your arraignment is tomorrow." She looked at him and softened up. "Are you okay?"

Jack nodded without speaking.

José said, "I'll be right outside if you need anything." He left and closed the door.

"The judge has a reputation for being tough, but fair. So, we'll see what happens," Erin said.

Jack's shoulders sank. "Okay."

"Have you heard anything from Mik, or his guy in Boston?"

"Not yet," Jack shrugged.

"How are you holding up?"

"As well as can be expected, I guess. I just want out of here."

"I'm working on it."

"Speaking of which," Jack said, "I've got this cell mate, Marvin Jackson. He claims he was set up by a police officer named Dudley. For some reason, I believe him."

Erin let out a laugh and took off her glasses. "So now we're making friends. In the county pen of all places, with a convict in the unique position of claiming that he is innocent. You never cease to astound me." She shook her head.

"Seriously, Erin, this guy can't afford a lawyer. I know his family. He's a decent guy and he stepped in when another guy was hassling me."

"Okay," she shook her head, "I'll take a look."

"Thanks, sis."

CHAPTER 21

Tuesday, June 2, 2020

Henry Wan arrived early for his meeting with the headmistress at the Henley Academy, in the historic Beacon Hill district of Boston. He sipped an espresso in a boutique coffee shop across the street from the school's campus and the large wrought-iron gates bearing the school's name and crest. His table wobbled on the colonial brick sidewalk as he tapped on his laptop's keys. The sweet scent of almond paste in freshly baked bear-claw pastries wafted toward him. He looked at his watch. It was 9:45 a.m. Time to go. He picked up his computer and put it back into its case.

He walked across the street, through the gates, and down the tree-lined path toward the administration building. It was a brick edifice in the Georgian architectural style. A bronze plaque marked the school's founding in 1847. He entered and stopped at the receptionist's desk. She was a young brunette about thirty years old, with her hair in a bun, wearing a light floral dress.

"Good morning, sir, may I help you?" she said.

"My name is Henry Wan. I have a ten o'clock appointment with the headmistress, Ms. Elizabeth Hancock."

"One moment, sir." She got on her computer and after several mouse clicks she responded. "Yes, here it is. Please follow me." She led the way down walnut-paneled hallways to the headmistress's office.

Ms. Hancock stood on a step stool, returning a book to the bookshelf on the wall behind her desk. She was about fifty, with short-cropped silver and black hair. Wire-rimmed glasses rested loosely on her nasal bridge.

"Ma'am, this is Mr. Wan, your ten o'clock appointment," said the receptionist.

Ms. Hancock stepped down off the stool and smiled. "Good morning, Mr. Wan." She shook his hand. "Please, have a seat." Then to the receptionist, "Thank you, Ann."

Henry sat in one of the chairs in front of the desk.

Ms. Hancock pulled a folder from her desk drawer and opened it. She pushed her glasses up on her nose with her index finger and looked at Henry. "Mr. Wan, I have reviewed the files on Ms. Delaney. Investigators from a sheriff's department in New Jersey recently visited us with a similar inquiry, so the information is fresh in my memory."

"Thank you," Henry said, "I appreciate your time. Ms. Delaney would have attended Henley from 1991 to 1993, before transferring to Holy Angels Academy in Demarest, New Jersey, in the summer of 1993." Henry pulled a photo of Eileen from his jacket pocket. "This is a photo of her taken in 1995."

"Yes, I've seen that photo, Mr. Wan. It's the same one that the investigators brought with them."

Henry wasn't surprised. "To be honest, there weren't many photos that we could locate."

"That would seem to be the case. It's the darndest thing. We have two years of transcripts for Ms. Delaney. But there were no photos of her in the yearbook. Now, sometimes students miss school on the day that class photos are taken, so that is not unusual. But you would expect that she would have been involved in some clubs or sports teams and had her photo appear as a participant in one of those activities."

"Yes," Henry scratched his chin, "you would think."

"Most of the teachers who were here at that time are gone. Except for three. The others have retired or moved on. I questioned those three teachers and none of them could remember Ms. Delaney. I even showed them the photo I was given. But, of course, it was a long time ago."

Henry continued, "We also learned that there was something amiss with the recommendation letters on file at Holy Angels Academy."

"That's correct, Mr. Wan. We don't have any record of two of those teachers ever having worked here. There was also a letter from Ms. Alice Rhodes, my predecessor. We contacted Ms. Rhodes, who currently resides at the West-minster Estate Senior Living Facility in Cambridge. She claims that she did not write the letter which bore her signature." Ms. Hancock rolled her eyes. "It was twenty-five years ago, and Ms. Rhodes is in her nineties. She has a touch of dementia, so you can take that for what it's worth."

Henry sat forward in his chair, elbows resting on his knees, his hands folded in front of his chest. "Ms. Hancock, may I have a look at the yearbooks from those years when Ms. Delaney attended the school?"

"Of course. I'll show you to our library. Our librarian, Mrs. Emerson, can help you."

"That would be great."

"Come along then." She motioned for him to follow her.

They followed a labyrinth of hallways with beautiful woodwork and portraits of past heads of school. They arrived at the library. Modern glass doors, a later addition, marked the entrance. It was a cavernous room, with beautiful architecture, that looked like it belonged in an Ivy League college. It was overflowing with books, the clutter creating a warm and cozy atmosphere. A few girls, in blue and gray plaid uniforms, quietly studied at desks or upholstered armchairs.

They approached the librarian, who was an elderly woman neatly dressed in pants and a cardigan sweater. "Mrs. Emerson," Ms. Hancock said in a hushed tone, "this is Mr. Wan. He is interested in examining our yearbooks from the years 1991 to 1993. Would you be so kind as to help him?"

"Certainly," she responded, extending her hand. "We have a complete collection from the school's founding, over there by the fireplace. Each shelf contains two decades' worth. The dates are labeled on the edge of each shelf. Can I offer you coffee or tea, Mr. Wan?"

"Thank you, you are very kind, but I've already had my morning coffee."

"Well, I'll leave you to it then. Please make yourself comfortable." She winked. "I, myself, am partial to that leather wingback chair beside the fireplace. It's so comfortable you might just fall asleep in it," she whispered.

Mrs. Hancock said, "I'll be back in my office, Mr. Wan, should you need anything else."

"Thank you very much. I appreciate your hospitality." Henry bowed, in customary Chinese fashion. But who was he kidding? He was born in New York City. He'd seen the bow in a Bruce Lee movie and liked the look.

He stood up and walked over to the yearbook section. He found the 1990s on a shelf just above head level and took out the three volumes of interest.

He sat down in the chair which Mrs. Emerson recommended, next to the antique lamp and end table. She wasn't kidding. It was as if the MyPillow guy had branched out into the armchair business. Good thing he'd had that espresso.

Henry placed the photo of Eileen on the armrest of his chair and pored over the volumes. He stopped at each photo of a blond girl with almond eyes. A thought crossed his mind that she could have dyed her hair, so he started looking at all of the photos. He'd brought a jeweler's loupe to examine them under magnification if necessary. But each one turned out to be a dead end. The saving grace was that it was an expensive, prestigious school, with small class sizes. It took him just two hours to completely review the three volumes.

Think, Henry. He leaned back into the chair and closed his eyes. *Imagine being a girl in her situation. You'd have to provide evidence of having attended school, in order to transfer. But assuming there were people searching for you, you wouldn't use the actual school that you attended.*

What would one logically do? he thought. *You'd probably pick a school, similar to your own, in the same city, to facilitate answering questions about your past.* Now, he just needed to find all the private girls' schools in the Boston metropolitan area and go through their yearbooks. Henry covered his face with the palm of his hand. That would take weeks.

The dilemma highlighted one other area where Henry failed to conform to the stereotype of his ancestors. The Chinese pride themselves on hard work and industriousness. Henry worked hard to avoid hard work. That led him to his career as a hacker, diverting funds earned by others into his numbered offshore account. Until he was caught, and traded service to the government for a suspended sentence. Afterward, Mik was the only one who would trust him with a job. Henry would never forget that, so the exception to the rule was that he did work hard for Mik.

Henry thought. *I've got my computer.* A smile started to grow on his face, like the Grinch when he thought his plot to steal Christmas might work. Henry knew Python, JavaScript, and C++, and several lesser programming languages. He could tap AI to conduct a reverse image search.

Henry pulled out a pen and notebook to outline his plan. First, he'd use age-editing software to create multiple images from the photo. Then he'd code a program to search the internet for photos with identical facial geometry. He'd have to set the parameters tight to avoid inundation with false positives. It just might work. It would take him all day to create the program, but he had run a similar search a few months ago and could reuse most of the code. It was a long shot, but a lot better than physically going to schools and looking through their yearbooks.

An hour later, Mrs. Emerson tapped him on the shoulder. "Mr. Wan." Henry opened his eyes. Mrs. Emerson was staring into them. "The chair got you. I warned you." She laughed. Henry was curled in a fetal position around one of the frilly pillows.

He yawned, looking around the room, getting his bearings, then he looked at his watch. "Thank you, Mrs. Emerson. I should be on my way now." He stood up and replaced the yearbooks on the shelves. She gave Henry directions to get back to the front door. On the way, he passed Ms. Hancock's office and stopped to thank her again. He said goodbye and left the building.

Ms. Hancock watched him leave through her window. Her eyes followed him as he walked down the long brick path to the street. She picked up her phone, opened her contacts list, and found the entry for the US Department of Justice. She pressed dial. After several rings a woman with a stern voice answered. "US Department of Justice. How may I direct your call?"

"US Marshals Service, please."

***

Henry returned to his hotel, the historic Omni Parker House in downtown Boston. Part of his arrangement with Brendan Mikolajczyk was that he wouldn't stay in any flea-bitten dumps while traveling for business. He'd gotten used to the finer accommodations during his previous life as a high-tech swindler.

Seated at the foot of Beacon Hill near the Boston Common, the Omni Parker House showcased a combination of historic splendor and modern comfort. Built in 1855, it remains the longest continuously operating hotel in the United States. The list of celebrities, politicians, and other notable members of society who have stayed within its walls could fill volumes. Add Henry Wan to that list.

Henry decided to start right away. All he needed was his laptop and a comfortable place to sit, with food and beverage at the ready. He chose the Parker Bar, a venerable whiskey bar within the hotel. The room was an homage to dark wood, with rustic planks on the floor and inlaid mahogany-paneled walls, dimly lit by wall sconces.

There was a pleasant aroma of beef with peppercorns coming from one of the tables.

"Good afternoon, sir," said the hostess, "will you be joining us for dinner?"

"Dinner, cocktails, and work," Henry held up his laptop. "Could I please have that corner table?" He pointed at it.

"Certainly, sir." She grabbed a leather-bound menu. "Follow me, please."

Shortly after he sat down, the waitress arrived. She was a middle-aged woman, with red curly hair and freckles, thickly proportioned. She spoke with a heavy Boston accent. "What can I get you, sir?"

"For starters, a glass of water and a Manhattan. Whistle-Pig bourbon and a single ice cube, please. And the assorted cheese platter."

"Certainly, sir, I'll be right back with your cocktail."

"Thank you," Henry said. "You can leave the menu. I'll be here for a while."

"As you wish, sir."

Henry pulled out his laptop and got to work. He cropped the photo of Eileen. Then he opened his digital aging software and applied the filters, creating multiple images of Eileen as she would have looked at various ages. That was the easy part, which took less than twenty minutes.

The waitress returned with his Manhattan. "The cheese platter will be up shortly," she said.

"Thank you." Henry held up the Manhattan. "And if you would be so kind, madam, please just refill them as they empty. I fear they may evaporate quickly with the dry air." He smiled.

"Yes, sir."

Henry thought about the famous writers who had met in that room. Emerson, Thoreau, Hawthorne, and Longfellow. He too was a writer in a way, but instead of writing prose he would be writing computer code. He opened his text editor. He chose C++ for its rapid app-development and code-compilation ability. Once he got into a groove, the code flowed from his brain like water from the tap. He did the hard part first, creating digital markers for female photos. He used calipers to measure the facial geometry of the photo, measuring distances between eyes, chin to brow, width of the nasal alae, etc. He scaled them to account for different-sized photos and digitalized the data. That took a while. Long enough for him to polish off the cheese platter and a lobster dinner.

He set upon creating the engine to search the internet for newspaper archives, digitized files from academic and government institutions, Google Images, and anything else that contained photos matching the parameters he'd created. Those files would be compared to the photo images of Eileen.

He would focus on the period from 1990 through 1993. Then, if necessary, he could always expand the search.

He was going to be there for a while. Fortunately, his chair was comfortable. There were certainly worse places he could be. Prison came to mind. He looked around at his posh surroundings, took a sip of his Manhattan, and muttered to himself, *I love my job.*

CHAPTER 22

Wednesday, June 3, 2020

"All rise! Court is now in session," the bailiff proclaimed. "The Honorable Judge Harlan Moody presiding." There were not many people in the courtroom, but all in attendance stood as the judge entered.

Judge Moody was a tall man with a long face and deep-set eyes. "You may proceed, Mr. Schictman," the judge said in a deep baritone voice with a faintly perceptible southern accent.

"Your Honor, we have obtained an indictment from the grand jury for second-degree murder committed in 1995. We intend to prove that Mr. Monroe..."

"Doctor Monroe," Erin interjected.

"Please wait your turn, Ms. Monroe," Judge Moody cautioned. Erin rested her knuckles on the table and pursed her lips.

Schictman regarded Erin with a wry smile. "Excuse me, Your Honor. The state intends to prove that on, or about, August 22, 1995," he looked at Erin, "Doctor Jack Monroe did murder his then girlfriend Eileen Delaney, a minor, and dispose of her body in a rock quarry in Warwick, New York."

"How do you plead, Dr. Monroe?" Judge Moody asked.

"Not guilty, Your Honor."

Schictman spoke up. "Your Honor, we ask that bail be set at one million dollars."

"Your Honor," Erin said, "the defense requests that Dr. Monroe be released on his own recognizance. He is a respected member of the community, a prominent neurosurgeon, with no prior criminal arrests..." She looked down at Jack seated next to her, as he tugged on her jacket and shook his head subtly. She cleared her throat and continued. "That is to say, no recent prior arrests, Your Honor. There were a few misdemeanor infractions for disorderly conduct at the Jersey Shore during his youth."

Schictman rolled his eyes in dramatic fashion.

Erin went on. "Further, Your Honor, my client has strong community connections and is a member of several charitable organizations, including the ASPCA and Children's Cancer Society. He is certainly not a danger to public safety and has lived his life as a law-abiding citizen." She shuffled some papers on the table. "We intend to show that Mr. Schictman has steamrolled this case through the grand jury, with the flimsiest of circumstantial evidence, and that my client is entirely innocent of these charges."

The judge addressed Mr. Schictman. "I am inclined to agree with much of what Ms. Monroe has argued. It doesn't appear that Dr. Monroe is a flight risk, or an imminent threat to public safety."

Judge Moody leaned back in his chair. He shuffled through some documents on his desk and then put his index finger to his chin. "I am going to set bail at a quarter of a million dollars."

He looked at Jack. "Dr. Monroe, it is further stipulated that, should you post bail, you are enjoined from leaving the contiguous United States until resolution of this case. Furthermore, you shall be expected to be present when required for any and all proceedings of this court. Is that understood?"

"Yes, Your Honor."

"Ms. Monroe," Judge Moody asked, "is it your client's intention to post bail, and if so, what will be the intended funding source?"

From the back of the courtroom a deep and familiar voice spoke. "I'm the funding source, Your Honor."

All eyes turned toward the back of the courtroom. Jimmy Gigante stood in the center aisle wearing a sharp navy-blue suit and tie. With him were Frank and Billy.

Judge Moody was caught off guard. His wide eyes peered over the top of his bifocals. "Well, we meet again, Mr. Gigante," he said. He looked down at Jack. "You travel in an interesting circle, Dr. Monroe. Very interesting indeed." He turned to the bailiff. "Harold, see to it that Mr. Gigante is instructed on posting the required funds."

"No need, Your Honor," Gigante said, "I've done this before."

"Yes. I suppose you have, Mr. Gigante." He turned back toward the bailiff. "See to it that Dr. Monroe is taken back to the correctional facility and processed for release as soon as the funding goes through." He looked at his calendar. "The preliminary hearing will be set for one week from today. Mark it. Court is adjourned." He banged the gavel on the sounding block.

***

Back at the Bergen County Jail, Jack awaited the processing of his release. The guard allowed him to wait in a communal sitting room. It was a featureless room with glass-block windows. There were tables with industrial-grade wooden chairs, a few low-quality vinyl armchairs, and a wall-mounted television. One of the other inmates was flipping channels. A news station came on, and a female reporter stood outside Columbia Presbyterian Medical Center. Jack's medical staff photo appeared on the screen.

"Wait, leave it there," he said to the other inmate.

The reporter was holding a microphone. "We have just learned that Dr. Jack Monroe, a prominent local neurosurgeon, has been indicted for the murder of his high school girlfriend, Eileen Delaney, twenty-five years ago. Dr. Monroe is known in New York social circles to be romantically involved with prominent news personality Leslie Miller, who has a prime time show on one of our competitor's stations. Dr. Monroe has pleaded not guilty to the charges."

A split screen appeared, showing Leslie attempting to dodge reporters as they chased her down in Rockefeller Center. They cornered her along the wall of shrubbery above the sunken ice rink, which in summer transforms into a mixed arts and food venue.

"Ms. Miller, can you comment on the arrest and indictment of your boyfriend Dr. Monroe?" one asked.

"Turn it up," Jack said as he moved closer to the television. The inmate turned up the volume.

"I wouldn't necessarily call him my boyfriend," Leslie said, still walking. "We've dated, but nothing serious."

"Huh?" Jack stared at the television. "What happened to 'we've been dating two years, and we're not getting any younger'?" He folded his arms and bowed his head.

The other inmate, a middle-aged African American male with an uncombed afro, looked bug-eyed at Jack. His eyes darted back and forth between Jack and the television. "Damn! The bitch is ghostin' you, Doc."

Jack shook his head and sat down at one of the tables.

A guard opened the door to the room. "Monroe?" He looked at Jack. "You're all set. Get your things, you're free to go."

After he changed into his own clothes, Jack walked out of the building and sat outside on the concrete steps. He tried calling Leslie several times, but each time it went to voicemail. Was she actually ghosting him? He was still annoyed that she had disowned him on national television.

Jack made a few other calls. Sherlock was free and available to pick him up. When he arrived, Jack filled him in on recent events.

"Have you heard anything from Mik?" Sherlock asked.

"No. I'll call him tonight and see if Wan has made any progress."

Sherlock nodded. "That guy Wan is a genius. If anyone can help, it would be him. We all know you're innocent."

Jack stared with glazed eyes out the car window as the scenery sped by. "Yeah... innocent."

Sherlock dropped Jack off at his house. "Wanna grab lunch?"

Jack leaned his elbows on the car door. "Thanks, but I need to check in at the hospital."

"Okay," Sherlock made a thumbs-up gesture.

Jack planned to stop in at the hospital and see what accommodations they had made in his absence, and to let them know he was available for work. His message box was probably inundated with charts for completion. Work would take his mind off things.

It was mid-afternoon, so the traffic into the city was light. Jack arrived at the medical center, parked, and walked into the building.

He rode the elevator up to his floor, got off, and stopped in front of his office. The lights were off. Meghan was nowhere to be found. Jack waved his badge at the scanner next to the door, but a red light came on. He tried several times, but it wouldn't work.

"God damn it," Jack said.

He pulled out his phone and called security. When a woman answered he said, "Hello, this is Dr. Monroe from neurosurgery. Something's wrong with my badge. It's not working."

"Let me check, Doctor. What is your badge number?"

Jack looked at the back of his badge. "It's NS-46130."

A few minutes passed while she checked the system. Jack remained on hold. She came back on. "I'm sorry, sir, but that badge has been deactivated. It can only be reactivated by the chairman of your department, Dr. Hagen."

"Thank you." Jack hung up the phone. *What the hell is going on?* he thought.

Jack strode briskly down the hall to Dr. Hagen's office.

Hagen's secretary looked startled to see Jack. "Dr. Monroe, please have a seat. I'll let Dr. Hagen know that you're here." She tapped some keys on her phone and sent out a text message.

A few minutes later Dr. Hagen opened the door, a sullen look replacing his customary smile.

"Ronald, what the hell is going on?"

"You tell me, Jack. Come into my office."

They both went into his office, and Dr. Hagen closed the door. "We were all very surprised and upset to hear about your arrest, and the serious allegations being leveled against you."

"I'm innocent, Ron." Jack pounded on the desk.

"Be that as it may, the board of directors has decided that you are to be given a leave of absence, and a temporary suspension of privileges."

"What the hell happened to innocent until proven guilty?"

"These aren't the good old days, Jack, when we controlled things. Medical centers now are owned and operated by large corporations. All that matters to them is the profit line. And right now, they feel that the publicity from your case is a liability."

"Come on, Ron. That's completely unfair."

"It's out of my hands, Jack. I'm sorry. Believe me, we're going to miss you. We're short-staffed as it is. Take the time off. Clear your head, and clear your name. We're all rooting for you, and we'll see you back when it's over." Hagen patted Jack's shoulder.

Jack shook his head. "I guess I have no choice in the matter."

"Take care of yourself, Jack."

Jack trudged through the hallways. Some of the nurses and doctors said hello, the ones who had been too busy to follow the news. Others, who had heard the news, just stared at him uneasily, or walked in another direction to avoid an encounter. Jack suddenly felt like a stranger in a place that he once lorded over. He just wanted to get out of the building.

Outside, Jack found a bench and sat down. A homeless man was asleep at the other end, curled up in a ratty blanket. Next to him was a grocery cart containing his worldly possessions, nothing of any value.

Jack dialed Leslie's number again. To his surprise, she answered.

"I saw you on the news. What was that about?" Jack said, his tone cool and detached.

"I'm sorry, Jack, it's all just a bit much."

"What is?"

"Well first, you have us cavorting with mafia sorts. And then, I find out that you've been closely associated with them since high school…"

"Leslie," Jack interrupted, "I haven't seen them in years. Gigante's daughter had a brain tumor. He asked for my help."

"Yeah, that's the other thing, Jack. You seem to have developed an unusually strong interest in that daughter, staying over in her hospital room. Hugging and kissing. I've seen the way you look at each other. I'm not blind."

Jack wanted to make a denial, but it would have fallen flat.

"And now, being indicted for the murder of your high school girlfriend…" she choked up, "It's just… I don't feel like I know you the way that I thought I did."

"Come on, Leslie! Do you actually believe that I'm a murderer?"

Her failure to answer was, in fact, an answer. Jack let the phone drop down to his thigh. Leslie was still talking. He stared at a graffitied cinder-block wall. He could hear her muted voice coming from the phone. "I think we need to take a break. You need to focus on your legal defense, and I need to get my head clear, and decide what I want to do...."

Jack tapped the button to hang up. He sat there with his eyes closed, thinking. How could things have gotten to this point? It had to be karma. God was punishing him for what he had done, that day long ago. The day that changed his life, and replayed itself in his mind, over and over, consuming his self-respect over the last twenty-five years.

Jack stood up and looked at the sleeping homeless man. He pulled out his wallet and searched inside. Two hundred and forty-two dollars. He removed the bills and rolled them up. He lifted the man's dirty blanket and stuffed the wad of bills into his flannel shirt pocket.

He used his iPhone to call an Uber. It would be easier to take an Uber than to try to park his car in midtown. The Uber driver arrived in a Tesla. He was an older Asian man. He looked at the app on his touch screen. "West 34th Street?" he asked.

"Yes," Jack answered. "The Empire State Building."

***

Jack entered the lobby of the Empire State Building and was struck by the opulence of a bygone era. In 2009 the lobby had undergone a major restoration project. All of the original art deco motifs and architectural features were recreated exactly as they had appeared when the building first opened in 1931. On the far wall was a beautiful floor-to-ceiling rendition of the building itself, with rays of light radiating from its spire. The ceiling high above was covered in gold-colored metallic sheets, decorated with depictions of the sun and machine components.

Jack closed his eyes and opened them again, taking it all in. He stood for several minutes, marveling at the ingenuity and boldness of mankind in the twentieth century. *Nothing this beautiful could ever be built again,* he thought. *The artistry and craftsmanship just don't exist anymore. And the cost would be prohibitive. Now we build featureless concrete, or glass and metal, structures with not a shred of redeeming architectural value. Perhaps man's best days were behind us, lost somewhere between the Gilded Age and the Roaring Twenties. The world was not going to get better and perhaps now was as good a time as any to leave it.*

Jack wandered around and located the ticket sales booth. The woman behind the counter was an older, white-haired lady with granny glasses.

"Can I help you?" she said.

"I'd like one ticket to the open observation deck on the eighty-sixth floor."

"There's a better view from the 102nd floor," the lady replied.

"But that deck is enclosed, isn't it?"

"Yes, that's true," she said, "but the view is amazing."

"Thank you," Jack said, dropping his eyes, "I'd prefer the fresh air."

"Very well. That will be $48, please."

Jack paid the woman with his credit card, and, with an arthritic hand, she passed him the ticket. "The express elevator is in the back." She pointed. "You take that elevator to the eightieth floor. Then you will need to get on a second elevator to get to the eighty-sixth floor."

"Thank you," Jack said.

Jack strolled through the lobby again, gazing one last time at its magnificence. There was a scent of cinnamon and coffee in the hallway. He boarded the first elevator. When it started abruptly upward, he could feel his weight increase against the floor. The elevator traveled at a surprisingly fast speed up its shaft. As instructed, he got off on the eightieth floor, his legs wobbly. He located a stairway and chose to take that for the last six flights. Perhaps it was a form of procrastination.

Jack went through the steel door on the eighty-sixth floor, turned a corner, and saw the glass doors leading to the observation deck. As he went out onto the deck, filled with tourists holding their cameras and phones, he was at once deflated. It was something he hadn't considered, but which he should have known. Surrounding the deck entirely, above the waist-high concrete wall, was steel fencing. It was composed of small rectangles on the bottom, with candy-cane-shaped uprights above, coming to sharp points where they hooked inward. They were, for all practical purposes, unclimbable.

Jack ambled to the western side of the building. He slid his arms through the metal fencing and grabbed it from the outside. The feeling was not unlike being back in prison. He looked off to the left and saw the Statue of Liberty. How small it looked from that vantage point. He could see Ellis Island and imagined his ancestors reaching America for the first time and disembarking their steamship there. The sun, making its descent in the western sky, cast a golden glow over the New Jersey side of the Hudson River. A refreshing cool breeze brought relief from the sun.

Jack looked northwest toward the George Washington Bridge. His life flashed quickly before him. He thought of his childhood and the days he had spent with his grandparents at Palisades Amusement Park. How disappointed they would be, seeing him here now, knowing what he intended. He thought of his days at St. Anastasia and all of his earliest friends, a few of whom had already passed away. His thoughts traveled back to high school and to his teammates there, many of whom he still saw on occasion. Would they miss him? And he thought of his mother. She had always made him feel like he had worth. That he could overcome any obstacle as long as he put his mind to it. She would be so upset to see him fail like this. But most of all there was Eileen. Of all the memories, bouncing like pinballs through his subconscious, the ones which dominated his thoughts were of Eileen.

Jack's eyes started to water. He thanked God for the metal fencing which his hands were now gripping as tightly as a shipwrecked mariner might cling to a life raft. This was his life raft. Had it not been there, he might have dashed impetuously to the wall and jumped before sanity could intervene. He vowed, with God as his witness, to change his life going forward and do the right thing. Twenty-five years was long enough to keep a secret.

***

Jack took an Uber back to the hospital to get his car. Once he got into his car, he turned on the air conditioning and caught his breath. His clothing was damp with perspiration, retaining some of the fried-food odor from the Uber driver's car.

He pulled out his iPhone and did a Google search for nearby Catholic churches. Several popped up. Then he selected a few of the closest ones and pulled up their websites. He checked schedules for the Sacrament of Penance for each of the churches. He was in luck. The Church of the Incarnation at 1290 St. Nicholas Avenue was a short fifteen-minute walk from the hospital. They offered confession starting at 5:00 p.m. on Wednesdays.

It would be difficult to park there, so he got out of his car and set out on foot to find the church. He walked down 165th Street to Broadway and turned north. The walk was mostly uphill, and Jack started to feel it in his calves. Twenty minutes later, he arrived.

The church was a massive gray stone building in the Gothic architectural style. Multipaneled windows with pointed arches adorned the sides of the building. Ornate concrete mullions separated the glass. Another relic of a bygone era.

Jack entered through the front door, which was of sturdy oak with bronze hardware. He found himself in a marble anteroom, and proceeded to enter the main part of the church. It was dimly lit inside, with a stifling scent of burning candles and incense.

Conveniently, there was a metal pole holding a sign which simply said *confession* on a handwritten card, with an arrow pointing to the left. Jack followed the arrow behind the back row of pews and along the left side of the church toward the front. Midway, there was an arched concrete vestibule housing the confessional. There were two wooden doors in the same pointed-arch shape as the windows above. One door for the priest, and the other for the penitent. There was a small rectangular wooden toggle near the doorknob on the penitent's door which indicated either *vacant* in green, or *occupied* in red. Currently it was green.

Jack stood frozen. He had come all this way, but suddenly he was having second thoughts. His stomach was in knots with acid refluxing into his esophagus. His heart rate had accelerated, and he could sense the pounding in his chest.

Minutes passed. He stood frozen. He thought of how close he had come at the Empire State Building. There was no way he could turn back now. This day had been twenty-five years in the making. He was angry at himself for his lack of resolve. "Not one more day, Jack," he said to himself, finally. And with that, he turned the knob and entered the confessional chamber. It was dark inside, save for a tiny nightlight in the upper corner. There was a black metal grill over an opaque black cloth filter, protecting the anonymity of the penitent. He pulled the door closed and kneeled on the cushioned block.

The priest spoke first. *"En el nombre de padre, y del hijo, y del espiritu santo, amen."*

Jack looked up, his eyes opening widely, and then he buried his face in the palm of his hand, smiling at the irony. *You couldn't make this up.* He chastised himself. *Dumbass, you had to pick a church in Spanish Harlem.* Now what? He struggled to recall what little he retained of his high school Spanish. *"Habla inglés... Padre?"*

The priest began speaking in broken English with a thick accent. "Yes. I speak English," he said. "In the name of the father, and of the son, and the holy spirit, amen. How long has it been since your last confession?"

Jack hesitated. He was embarrassed to give the answer. "It's been twenty-six years, Father."

The priest let out a whistle. *"Ay, caramba.* That is very long."

Jack stared at the black metal grill, clenching his lips. *Are priests supposed to editorialize?*

He stumbled over his words. "Yes... it has been a long time." Jack stared at the black grill. "The truth is, I've been reluctant to come in, Father."

"You are always welcome in the Lord's house."

"I've done something terrible, very long ago, and it's been weighing on my conscience."

The priest cleared his throat. "The Lord is merciful; his capacity for forgiveness unlimited, like that of a father for his children."

"Yes, I hope so," said Jack.

"To be absolved of your sins, you must be truly sorry, and commit to repentance. You must make a promise to God and to yourself, to sin no more."

Jack was choking up. Tears filled his eyes and his voice was strained. "I do, Father."

"Then tell me what it is that bothers you."

"Forgive me, Father, for I have sinned." Jack closed his eyes, his lips quivered. "I killed a woman."

CHAPTER 23

Wednesday, June 3, 2020

Henry sat on a bench in the Boston Common, an oasis of tranquility in the center of the city, with flowering shrubbery canopied by lush green trees. He had nearly completed the code for his search program the previous day. All that remained was some final debugging and compiling. But he badly needed to get outside for some fresh air. He arrived at nine o'clock in the morning and sat near Bagheera Fountain, looking out over the lagoon and the swan boats. The scent of coffee and breakfast sandwiches from a nearby vendor blended harmoniously with that of the flowers and fresh-cut grass. The cool breeze felt good on his cheeks as he pecked away on his laptop keys.

It was almost noon, his work nearly complete. He would head back to the hotel and launch the compiler. Then he could grab a quick lunch and afterward, hopefully, begin the search. He packed his laptop into its case and slung it over his shoulder. He took Lagoon Path up to Beacon Street, passing the bronze ducklings. He passed by the Bull and Finch Pub, whose exterior facade was used for the sitcom *Cheers*. The familiar *Cheers* logo hung from a wooden plaque. The roads were congested with traffic, and the car exhaust mixed with the smells coming from food vendors and piled garbage. He headed south on Park and then made a left on Tremont.

There was a short stone wall topped by a black wrought-iron fence. Henry stopped at the old Granary Burying Ground, which was sandwiched between a horseshoe-shaped configuration of midsized brick buildings. On the fence hung a greened copper plaque commemorating Paul Revere, who was buried there. The stones were all ancient thin slabs of marble, many with ghoulish renditions of skull and crossbones at the top. Tributes in writing covered the stones with a verbosity no longer seen on modern memorials.

Henry was captivated. He was a nerd, and he loved history. A tingle of adventure flowed down his spine. *Why not?* he thought. He could spare a few minutes to explore, so he entered through the gate of the cemetery. He wandered the narrow, shaded paths and found the headstones of notable historical figures; he found Sam Adams, Paul Revere, and John Hancock. His excitement grew. Further along, he located the graves of Benjamin Franklin's parents as well as the victims of the Boston Massacre. *Fascinating,* Henry thought. *What stories these ghosts could tell.*

Henry was on his way out of the burial ground when he sensed, through his peripheral vision, that he was being followed. He scanned his surroundings for anything that might come in handy. There were other people in the area, mostly tourists, older people, and small children. In front of him was a cart containing gardening tools, likely left by one of the caretakers on a lunch break.

Henry glanced over his shoulder to see three Eastern Europeans in their mid-twenties. They were rough-looking with scraggly facial hair. One had a scar across his left cheek. Henry slowly turned to head out when one of them spoke in a Russian accent.

"We'll take the laptop."

Henry turned back to face them. "Excuse me?"

"Your laptop. We'll take it," the Russian said. The one on the far right pressed a button and a knife blade flipped open from the handle in his grip.

Henry carefully assessed the situation, as he took slow, imperceptible steps backward toward the gardener's cart. When Henry was seven his family had moved to Buffalo, New York, where his father enrolled him in the Mandarin Kung Fu Society. At first Henry had no interest in the rigorous training, but he grew to love it as his skills improved. Twelve years later he earned his black sash. Sifu Mandarino lauded him as one of his most accomplished students. That was a proud day. He had never used it in a real fight, but he was about to find out if all the hard work would pay off.

"Ordinarily, I'd just let you have it," Henry said.

"But unfortunately, it contains work that I need, so I cannot."

"Unfortunate for you," the first Russian said, laughing. "Get his bag."

The three of them walked toward Henry as he backed up to the gardener's cart. He pulled out a six-foot-long hoe and began spinning it in a figure-eight pattern. His hands moved quickly in front of his chest; the hoe accelerated, spinning invisibly like a plane's propeller.

The Russians laughed. "Are you going to plant some vegetables, Chinaman?" one said. They started to surround him in a ring. Henry addressed the one with the knife first. He spun the hoe over his head so that the working end went behind him and then lunged forward, jabbing the tip of the handle into the knife-holder's eye. Henry started to sweat as the adrenaline kicked in. As the man stumbled backward, Henry swung the hoe over his head, crashing the blade down onto his wrist. The wrist cracked with a loud snap and the knife fell to the brick walk. The blade cut the artery, and blood was pumping under pressure.

Henry's heart was now pounding and he felt jittery. Another approached Henry from behind. Henry jumped toward him, planting his right foot and then, using his momentum, delivered a crushing side kick with his left foot to the abdomen. As the guy bent forward with an agonized grunt, Henry retracted his left foot without putting it down, swung it upward in an arc, and delivered a roundhouse kick to the head. Several teeth shot out and tinkled as they fell to the brick walk. Henry swung the hoe around in a complete circle, smashing it down on the guy's head. He collapsed unconscious. Henry turned to the third one. The Russian's mouth hung open, looking at his two wounded comrades. He put up his fists and then, thinking better of it, took off running.

Henry pulled the belt from the pants of the one who had passed out, then walked over to the guy who had pulled the knife. "If you want to live, you better put pressure on that artery, and keep it there." Henry used the belt to make a tourniquet around the knife-wielder's arm. He put the hoe back neatly into the gardener's cart. "I'd love to stick around and have you morons arrested, but I've got better things to do." He bent down and picked up the switchblade, rotating it in his hand. "Nice. I'll hang on to this."

Visitors throughout the cemetery had stopped to watch the melee, as though it were entertainment provided by the chamber of commerce. Henry brushed off and straightened up his clothing. *Why not?* he thought. He turned toward the crowd and bowed, then walked out the gate toward Tremont Street and his hotel.

***

Back at the Omni, Henry went to his room, still wired from his encounter. He set his computer to run the compiler and then hung the do-not-disturb sign on the room's door handle. He cleaned up and went downstairs to the restaurant. He ordered lobster rolls, washing them down with a few Bloody Marys to calm his nerves. He took his time eating lunch since there were numerous hefty databases to compile. He picked up the local edition of the *Where* magazine to scout out potential dinner restaurants. Maybe Italian in the North End.

Henry returned to his room and was pleased to see that the program was ready to go. He had paid the extra fee for the higher data transfer speed offered by the hotel. He fed the program the digitally aged photos of Eileen and clicked on the start button. All that he had to do now was wait.

Henry set the alarm clock on his phone to 5:00 p.m. and then crawled under the blanket to have a nap. He was snoring in minutes.

At 5:00 p.m. the alarm went off. Henry got up, went to the bathroom, and splashed cold water onto his face. The room was stuffy, so he decided to go down to the whiskey bar. The moment of truth had arrived where Henry would examine the results of the search. Henry, a creature of habit, asked the hostess for the same table in the back corner, which she was happy to accommodate.

In preparation, Henry opened an identification program which compared facial geometry between different photos to determine if the subjects matched. Then he checked the results of his search, neatly organized in a folder labeled *output*. In the left upper corner of his screen, he had the digitized photo of Eileen. He pulled up the first photo in the folder. Abigail Simpson was her name. She had dirty blond hair and green eyes and the same basic head shape, but Henry could tell immediately that the faces didn't match. The same thing occurred with the next three girls' photos. The fifth photo got Henry's attention. *That could be her,* he thought. Maggie McGuire. Henry looked at the two photos. To his naked eye it could very well have been Eileen. He loaded the two photos into the facial comparison program. The program examined facial features, skin and hair coloring, skull shape, and other markers, comparing five hundred separate metrics for a match. A greater than ninety-five percent score was required in order to verify that the photos were of the same person. Maggie McGuire scored seventy-four percent.

And so the process went. Henry had gone through thirty-four different girls' photos. The highest match percentage he had gotten was eighty percent. Not good enough. Henry started to worry. A knot formed in his stomach. What if all this work was for nothing? What if there was no match? He didn't want to think about it.

The waitress came around and refilled his empty glass.

Henry pulled the forty-seventh photo out of the output box. He had stopped examining the photos for comparison with his own eyes. Too many times, he thought he had found a match and was proved wrong. It was demoralizing. His enthusiasm was waning as he continued the process by rote.

He looked at the name. Ellen McCarthy. He dragged the two photos into the facial comparison program. One minute later a green light flashed on the program. The word **MATCH** in capital letters appeared in the evaluation box. The score read 100 percent.

Henry, who had been lulled into somnolence, sat straight upright and put his face close to the screen. "Holy cow," Henry whispered to himself. He pulled the jeweler's loupe out of his pocket and swung out the lens. He went back and forth over the two photos. A wide smile exposed Henry's crooked teeth. He made a fist and held it up. "Bingo!"

***

The steel bar pressed heavily on Mik's chest. His hair and the sweatband around his forehead were soaked. He let out a groan as he pushed the bar up until his arms were fully extended. Three hundred and fifteen pounds, including the bar.

"Four," said the young spotter standing behind him. "Come on, one more. You've got this."

Mik let the bar drop down to his chest with a thud as it smacked his pectorals. He growled loudly as he pushed the bar up to full extension once again and let it fall backward onto the rests. It slammed down with a loud metallic clang. Mik sat up out of breath.

"Man, you rock, pops," said the young spotter. "I hope I can do that when I'm as old as you."

Mik laughed. "You can't do it now. What are you talking about?"

"I'm working on it," the young man frowned.

"Thanks for the spot," Mik said. With the loud music pulsating in the gym, he didn't hear his phone ring at first. When he realized it was ringing, he picked it up from the floor under the bench. He pressed the answer button. Henry Wan's voice was animated.

"Hey Mik."

"Henry, what's up?"

"You were right. Eileen Delaney's real name is Ellen McCarthy. I'm going to pull up everything I can find on the McCarthy girl."

Mik wiped his face with a towel and stood up. "That's fantastic, Henry. Get anything you can get, and then come back. We should set up a meeting with Jack and Erin to fill them in."

"Will do, Boss. I've booked the first flight out in the morning."

***

"Father?" Jack said, "you haven't said anything." He leaned his ear against the metal grill in the confessional. There was silence. The cloth privacy filter gave off a musty, stale odor of incense. "Father, are you still there?" He pressed his ear tighter and he could hear a muffled wheezing. Jack had a moment of indecision. He wasn't sure what to do. Once again, he shouted, "Father, are you okay?" He listened again and now heard gasping and wheezing, and a faintly audible high-pitched plea.

"Help."

Jack opened the door and jumped out of the confessional. There were a few other people present in the church. An old woman at the front was lighting a votive candle in front of the statue of Mary. A monsignor, in a purple-trimmed cassock, was near the altar speaking to another woman.

"Help," Jack yelled. He opened the door to the priest's side of the confessional and found a young Hispanic priest, in a black frock, slumped over. His skin was blue and he'd lost consciousness. Jack grabbed his wrist and put the priest's arm over his shoulder and dragged him out. He laid him down on the marble floor.

The monsignor who was standing near the altar said something to the woman, who went running into the vestibule. He was elderly and hobbled as best he could to where Jack and the unconscious priest were located.

"Father Perez..." Monsignor said. "Donald!" He looked at Jack. "Our youth counselor is calling 911. We have some emergency medical supplies. I asked her to bring them."

Jack turned the priest onto his side and did a jaw thrust. He coughed and resumed breathing. He was loudly wheezing from an obstructed airway.

"I'm a doctor, Monsignor. Is Father Perez an asthmatic?"

"Yes, as a matter of fact, he is," the monsignor answered.

A minute later the woman returned. She was pulling a cart toward them while holding a phone to her ear, talking to the 911 operator. "Yes. Church of the Incarnation. St. Nicholas. Please hurry!"

The cart had an oxygen tank strapped to the side. "Is there a mask in there?" Jack asked. The woman pulled open the drawers and found a green plastic oxygen mask and tubing. She plugged it into the regulator on the oxygen tank and turned the dial. Jack put the mask on Father Perez. "I need your help, Monsignor." The monsignor, with some difficulty, knelt down beside them. "Here," Jack said, "hold his jaw, just like I'm doing."

The monsignor took over holding Father Perez's jaw. "Like this? Am I doing it right?"

"Yes, that's exactly right, Monsignor, just keep holding steady," Jack answered. He pulled open a drawer and found some syringes and needles. The drawer below it was filled with an assortment of drugs in labeled compartments. Jack scanned the labels and found epinephrine. He broke open the ampule and drew up 200 micrograms into a tuberculin syringe and injected it under the skin of Father Perez's neck. He looked again in the drug drawer for albuterol, but it wasn't there. He pulled open the other drawers and inside one he found drugs in boxes, too large to fit in the upper drawer. One of the boxes contained the albuterol metered-dose inhaler. He pulled it out, took the cap off, and sprayed ten puffs under the plastic oxygen mask and then pulled it tight to Father Perez's face.

Father Perez's breathing gradually became less labored. The wheezing decreased in amplitude and the color of his face went from purple to blue to pink. Jack took over the jaw thrusting again, freeing up the monsignor.

The monsignor stood and looked at the crucifix above the altar and made the sign of the cross. He put his hands together to pray. "Thank you, Lord, for bringing this doctor to our parish in our hour of need." He looked down at Jack. "Doctor, I thank you sincerely."

Jack smiled. He started to feel pretty good about himself. Perhaps it was divine intervention that brought him to this place where he arguably just saved a man's life, when only hours earlier he was atop the Empire State Building contemplating ending his own. Maybe God did have a master plan for him. His bubble of contentment quickly burst, however, when he remembered that it was his confession that triggered Father Perez's asthmatic attack in the first place. Perez appeared to be fairly young and perhaps hadn't, prior to this day, heard such a malevolent revelation in a confessional. Jack's eyes darted around, as panic set in. Hopefully, Father Perez wouldn't accidentally reveal his confession, as he recovered to semi-consciousness.

The sound of a siren outside grew louder until it stopped just outside the main entrance. Two paramedics in blue jumpsuits burst through the glass doors between the anteroom and the church proper. Once Father Perez was loaded onto the gurney and taken to the ambulance, Jack began his slow walk back to the hospital garage to get his car.

On the way, his iPhone vibrated in his pocket and the marimba ringtone sounded. He stopped walking and leaned his back against the steel traffic signal pole, which was warm from the sun. He pulled his phone out of his pocket and put it to his ear. "Hello," he said.

"Hey buddy," Mik responded. "I heard from Erin that you're out on bail."

"I am."

"That's great. Where are you now?"

Jack's eyes tracked up the pole nearby to the green street signs. "Corner of Broadway and 168th Street."

"Okay, I'm not even going to ask what the hell you're doing there," Mik said. "Listen, we've made progress. Henry has uncovered some interesting background on Eileen. We need to get together. Henry will be back tomorrow and we're going to dig deeper. I've got a whole team working on it. I was thinking maybe Friday evening. Will that work for you?"

"Sure," Jack looked up at the sky, "my, um, work schedule has been... cleared."

"Great. We'll get you, me, Henry, and Erin together. Where should we meet?"

"We can do it at my house if you want."

"Good. Let's say around 5 p.m. I'll tell you everything then."

CHAPTER 24

Thursday, June 11, 2020

Judge Harlan Moody held a document in his hand. His eyes moved back and forth behind his bifocals as he skimmed it. He looked at the bailiff and motioned with his hand.

"Bring in Mr. Jackson please."

The bailiff nodded. "Yes, Your Honor." He left the room and returned a few minutes later, escorting Marvin Jackson, who was wearing his orange prison jumpsuit. His hands and ankles were shackled. The corrections officer accompanied him, gripping his upper arm as he shuffled toward the front of the courtroom. Marvin's hair was a mess, and he looked like he'd just rolled out of bed.

The judge looked down at the prosecutor. "Mr. Schictman?"

Schictman stood and cleared his throat. "Your Honor, Mr. Marvin Jackson is charged with felony possession of cocaine with intent to distribute. The arresting officer, Officer Mark Dudley of the Hackensack PD, is present in the courtroom."

Schictman turned and smiled at Dudley. Officer Dudley sat a few rows behind Schictman. He wore his police uniform in a disheveled manner with his tie askew. He leaned back on the wooden bench with his legs crossed, his shirt straining to contain his large belly. He raised his hand, a smug expression on his face, as he nibbled on a toothpick.

The judge frowned, then looked at Marvin. "Mr. Jackson, do you have an attorney? If you do not, or cannot afford one, one will be appointed to represent you."

Marvin stuttered. "Um, no, Your Honor, I don't have...."

"Need for an attorney." A voice from the back of the room cut him off mid-sentence. Erin Monroe walked in holding her briefcase. "I'm his attorney."

Marvin looked back, a puzzled expression on his face.

Schictman's skin blanched like a kid in a school play whose pants just fell down. He raised a hand. "What's going on here?"

Erin walked briskly to the front of the room and stood next to Marvin. She handed him her card and whispered, "Erin Monroe, Jack Monroe's sister."

Judge Moody looked over his glasses. "Ms. Monroe, we meet again. Your practice in our jurisdiction seems to be expanding."

"Idle hands are the Devil's workshop, Your Honor. That's what the nuns used to tell me."

"How does your client plead, Ms. Monroe?"

"Innocent, Your Honor." Erin gritted her teeth and flashed a frosty look at Schictman. "Further, we will show that Officer Dudley has exhibited a pattern of behavior which has led to repeated reprimands by his superiors for questionable conduct. There have been three previous occasions in which suspects have argued that Officer Dudley planted evidence."

She placed her briefcase on the table and popped it open. She held up a stack of case reports, each with its own cellophane cover. Dudley sat up and gripped the bench in front of him. He snarled and his eyes narrowed. Erin looked back at him. "Coincidence? I don't think so."

Schictman shot back. "This is outrageous conduct! She is impugning the integrity of a law enforcement officer with no proof whatsoever."

Erin shouted back, "He's a corrupt bum who shouldn't have a badge. I intend to file a formal complaint to have him investigated for criminal misconduct, and hopefully thrown off the force."

Judge Moody banged his gavel multiple times. "Ms. Monroe, these are incredibly serious accusations which you are making. Making unsubstantiated allegations of this sort could result in libel charges against you, or even referral for disbarment."

"Point taken, Your Honor." Erin held up her index finger. "Let's move on to the substantiation." She reached into her briefcase, pulled out two DVD discs, and held them up. "These discs contain video footage from two separate Ring doorbell cameras from the street on which Mr. Jackson was arrested, at the time of his arrest. They show two distinct angles of Officer Dudley removing a Ziploc bag containing white powder from his pocket, and tossing it in the back seat of Mr. Jackson's car. Will that suffice, Your Honor?"

Dudley's jaw dropped. He looked down at his feet and then at Schictman, who had closed his eyes and folded his arms. Judge Moody looked at the two of them. He glared at Officer Dudley. "What have you got to say for yourself, Officer?"

Dudley wiped sweat from his forehead. "I, um..." he stuttered. "I'd like to speak to an attorney, Your Honor."

"Mr. Schictman?"

Schictman started to do a nervous dance around the desk. He threw his arms up into the air. "I am appalled, Your Honor. You must believe, I had no prior knowledge of any of this. Had I known, we never would have brought these charges."

Erin stood there with her arms folded in front of her, a smug grin on her face. Her mouth was closed as she moved air back and forth between her two cheeks. Finally, she put her hands together and spoke. "Your Honor, I'd like to make a motion to have all charges dismissed."

"Mr. Schictman?" The judge turned his eyes toward the prosecutor. Gavin Schictman opened his mouth without speaking. He nodded his head.

The judge slammed the gavel down hard. "Case dismissed." He looked at the corrections officer and waved his hand toward Marvin. "Please release Mr. Jackson from those shackles. Mr. Jackson, you will be taken back to the correctional facility to collect your belongings and then you are free to go, with this court's sincere apology."

Then his eyes narrowed and he scowled at Officer Dudley, who was catatonic on his bench seat. "You'd better get that lawyer, Officer Dudley. I expect I'll be seeing you back here in another capacity, very soon."

Erin walked over to Marvin and put her hand on his shoulder. He had tears in his eyes.

"Nobody ever did anything like that for me before. I don't know how to thank you." He instinctively went to give her a hug, but his hands were still chained to each other and to his ankles, so he stutter-stepped before regaining his balance.

"Don't mention it, Marvin. It's on the house. I may have enjoyed this more than you did." She smiled, which required muscles that she hadn't used in a while.

"How did you get those videos?" Marvin asked.

"Oh, these?" she held up the two discs, whispering, "these are a couple of movies I was going to watch after dinner tonight. I don't get out much." She laughed, then put a hand on his shoulder. "Good luck, Marvin."

"Thank you, Ms. Monroe. And please... thank your brother. He's a good man."

"Yeah. He is. But don't you ever tell him that I said that."

***

A woman pulled her light-blue wheeled carry-on through the crowded security line at Dublin Airport. Her chestnut brown hair was tied back under a floppy beret, a few stray strands poking out the sides. Near her was a woman holding the hands of two young girls, both with blond hair in pigtails, wearing matching floral dresses. She gazed wistfully at the family as the two girls laughed and played with each other, oblivious to the world around them. There was still a chance that she could have children, though she was past that golden age when most women give birth. She had been in love once. But that was a long time ago.

For travel, she'd chosen a comfortable pair of dark blue jeans and a plaid cardigan sweater over a white collared shirt. It would be comfortable for a long flight, and inconspicuous so as not to attract attention.

"Next," the security officer called out.

She pulled her bag and walked up to the officer, who stared at her heavily tinted glasses. "Passport and boarding pass," he said.

She dug into her handbag, pulled out the documents, and handed them over. He held up the passport, looking at the photo. "Take your glasses off, please."

She removed her glasses and stared straight ahead at him. His gaze went back and forth several times between the photo and her face. She tried to hold still, as sweat formed on her brow. Her pulse raced. He looked closer at the photo and then once more at her face. She swallowed hard, trying to maintain a smile to conceal her anxiety. Finally, the security officer handed her documents back, looked at the gentleman behind her in the queue, and waved. "Next."

She let out a sigh of relief and walked forward.

Once she'd passed through the scanner and retrieved her bag from the conveyor belt, she stopped at the departures board. She looked up and found her flight information. Aer Lingus flight 3402 to JFK, on time, terminal seven, gate eleven. She proceeded toward the gate, keeping her head down as she passed the throngs of people moving in either direction.

She was early and had time to kill, so she stopped in a pub called The Slaney. It was lively with people engaged in conversation, drinking cocktails as they awaited their flights.

A woman in a business suit approached her sheepishly. "Ms Hennessey, is that you?"

She nodded, nervously looking around. "Yes, that's me." She smiled.

The woman held up a book. "I just love your books," she said flustered. I've read them all. I'm so sorry, could I trouble you for..."

"Of course. What's your name?"

"Mary O'Leary."

"Lovely to meet you, Mary. And thank you for being a loyal reader." She signed the book, handed it back and smiled. The delighted woman took the book and left.

She moved to a dimly lit area, at the far corner of the bar, and ordered a Cosmopolitan. On her computer, she thumbed through the online edition of *The New York Times*. On page seven, she found the article she was looking for, about the surgeon at Columbia Presbyterian who'd been in-dicted for murder. There was a photo accompanying the ar-ticle. She brought her face closer to the screen. She raised her glasses and stared at it, her focus blurring as her mind wan-dered a long-dormant labyrinth of emotions.

CHAPTER 25

Friday, June 5, 2020

It was 4:45 p.m. when Mik arrived with Henry. Jack said, "I thought we could sit on the patio."

"That'll work," Mik said, "I can use your TV to mirror my laptop."

"Have at it."

They moved outside and Mik started to set up. Henry laid a cardboard file box on a patio chair. A gentle breeze carried the scent of wisteria from the pergola over the flagstone walk.

"Drinks are in the fridge, help yourselves," Jack said, "I ordered pizza and mussels from Jimmy's."

Mik closed his eyes and grinned, drawing his thin lips back under his long narrow nose. "Jimmy's is the best. They've got that molten mozzarella, drenched in olive oil. I feel like whenever I leave the New York area, I'm in a black hole for pizza."

"I'll say," said Henry. "I had pizza in Toronto, and it was like I was on another planet."

Jack texted Erin and let her know that they were out back. They sat at a patio table under an umbrella patterned after Van Gogh's *Starry Night*. Soon after, Erin came around the side of the house under the maple tree. She carried her bag and was still wearing her gray jacket-and-skirt combination that she wore to work. She put her bag down on a chair. "Gentlemen," she tipped her head, then to Jack, "your friend Marvin says hello."

"Thanks for doing that. I owe you."

"Yes, you do," Erin slowly nodded. She interlocked her fingers and then stretched her arms above her head, leaning back, and then from side to side. "Alright, enough idle chit-chat. Let's get to work."

They huddled around the patio table. Mik clicked a few laptop keys. His home screen appeared on the sixty-inch LCD panel on the wall of the outdoor kitchen.

"As you know, we sent Henry up to Boston to see what he could dig up on Eileen." He turned to Henry. "Henry, tell us what you found."

Henry cleared his throat and pulled the laptop over to him. "Well, I paid a visit to the Henley Academy, which Eileen supposedly attended." "Other than her transcripts..." Henry clicked a few keys and the transcripts appeared, all A's and A-'s. He looked at each of them. "There was no other corroborating evidence that she attended the school."

Henry detailed creating the search engine. They all listened intently.

"Very impressive, Henry," Erin said. "Mik tells us you found something."

"Yes, indeed." Henry clicked a few keys on the computer and two photos came up, juxtaposed side by side. "The one on the left is a headshot of Eileen Delaney from her high school yearbook at Holy Angels Academy." On the right was a photo labeled *Ellen McCarthy*. "The other photo was found in a yearbook from St. Agnes Seminary in Boston." They all stared at the photos. "In case it's not obvious to everyone," Henry pointed at the screen, "these are photos of the same girl."

"Well, that explains a lot," Erin said. "I knew she was hiding something."

Jack sipped his beer as he stared at the photos. Memories came flooding back. He remembered the sights and sounds, and even smells, of those days he'd spent with Eileen. The salty air, and the tangy scent of barbecued shrimp at Beach Haven. Sipping hot chocolate, flavored with cinnamon and nutmeg, in the ski lodge at Vernon Valley. And the sweet floral fragrance of her Silkience shampoo.

"Earth to Jack," Mik said, snapping his fingers.

Jack shook his head and blinked his eyes. "Sorry." He cleared his throat. "So, Eileen Delaney was Ellen McCarthy. But how does this help me? Regardless of whether she was Eileen or Ellen, or Bertha for that matter, she's still dead, and I'm still accused of her murder."

Henry put his hand up and looked around the table. "There's more. After uncovering Eileen's birth name and identity, we came up with some other information." Henry moved his finger on the laptop's mousepad and opened a file. He clicked on one of the items within the folder. A newspaper article filled the entire screen. It was the *Boston Globe*, from March 17, 1991. The headline read: **Teen Girls Witness Murder in Warehouse, Seamus Callanan Arrested.**

Erin squinted, trying to read the small print. The story detailed how Ellen McCarthy claimed to have witnessed a murder. Seamus Callanan was arrested for the trafficking of heroin, which was found at the warehouse. However, according to the article, police could find no evidence that a murder had been committed.

Henry rolled his finger over the trackpad, scrolling through subsequent articles from the *Globe* as he summarized them for the group. "Both girls disappeared for a day, causing their parents to report them missing. The next day both girls reappeared, but told the police conflicting stories."

Henry switched to a PowerPoint document, pulling up side-by-side bullet-pointed lists showing the discrepancies in the stories. Henry continued, "Eileen claimed that they had witnessed a murder from the third floor of the warehouse. They couldn't hear the conversation because of noise from a thunderstorm at the time."

"Boston gets some wicked storms," Mik said, feigning a Boston accent.

"They do," Henry continued. "Anyway, the McCarthy girl had no idea who the alleged victim was. Their presence was discovered, and they fled, becoming separated from each other."

"Eileen claims that she suffered a head injury when she fell trying to escape. She woke up soaking wet and shivering the next day, made her way back home, and her parents took her to the police station. At the police station, she told the story of having witnessed a murder."

"What about the other girl, Amanda?" Erin asked.

"I'll get to that in a moment," Henry replied, interlacing his fingers.

"The Boston Police Department conducted a search of the warehouse, finding no evidence of a murder having been committed. There was evidence, however, that there had been large-scale movement of crates out of the warehouse. Eileen had described the interior as filled to capacity with crates. When the police arrived, the room was sparsely filled. However, police canine units were able to sniff their way to enough heroin to put Seamus Callanan in prison for twenty years."

"So, what did the other girl say?" Erin asked.

"Amanda Henderson reappeared later that day and told a markedly different story. She said that they had snuck into the warehouse to smoke pot and drink alcohol, but claimed that there were no other people there. She said at some point, Eileen tripped, hit her head, and lost consciousness. Amanda tried her best to wake her up, and then attempted to carry her out, but was unable."

Jack's mind flashed back to that day when his detective stepfather had found the pot seeds in his Camaro.

"Amanda said she panicked. Eileen was breathing, and didn't appear to be in any danger, so Amanda decided to leave her there to sleep it off. She was terrified that if she called the police they would be charged with breaking and entering, underage drinking, and possession of marijuana. She knew it was a lousy thing to do, but she had to leave her friend there, hoping that Eileen would wake and find her way home."

Mik said, "Something doesn't add up. In high school, your friends are everything to you. You would never abandon them. Would you?"

"Well, we wouldn't," Jack said. "I don't pretend to understand the female mind, but wouldn't you at least try to call a friend, to come and help?"

"Remember, this was 1991," Henry said, "they wouldn't have had cell phones."

"No," Mik said, "but the warehouse would have had land lines."

"Henry," Erin interjected, "were you able to get any of the police reports, of the interrogation of the girls, specifically Amanda?"

"Well, it wasn't easy," Henry smiled, rubbing his hands together, "but hey, it's me we're talking about." He shuffled through his file box. "Here it is." He handed the pages to Erin, who scanned through them, her eyes darting back and forth.

"Listen to the verbiage and descriptions in this report," Erin said, reading. "Trembling, averting her gaze, sweating, stumbling with her words, evasive, fidgeting in her chair. To me, that describes someone who's hiding something. Someone who isn't telling the truth. The officer, named at the bottom of the report, also questions the veracity of her statement."

"Maybe they got to her," Mik said, "Callanan's crew. Maybe they threatened her, or her family, if she testified against them."

Henry chimed in, "Mik could be right. In Ellen's testimony, she reported that just prior to falling and hitting her head on the rooftop, she saw Amanda in the parking lot, being chased by Callanan's goons. It's unlikely that a young girl would be able to escape several fit adult males, in close pursuit."

"I see where this is going," Erin said, "I'd bet my next month's salary that the defense argued at trial that Ellen's testimony about a supposed murder was a figment of her pot-stoked imagination, after suffering a fall and, I presume, a severe concussion."

"Luckily, health care privacy was lax back then," Henry said, "so we were able to get the medical reports. Ellen was evaluated at Mass General the day after the event, and found to have suffered a severe concussion. And yes, Erin, your salary is secure, that's exactly what the defense argued."

Mik leaned back in his chair, putting his hands behind his head. "Well, I guess my WITSEC theory is looking pretty good," he said, stretching out the last two words.

Just then a young man, who looked like he fell out of the cast of *Fast Times at Ridgemont High*, came around the corner under the maple tree. He had long scraggly blond hair and a mustache, and carried two Jimmy's pizza boxes with paper bags on top. Jack took the boxes and placed them on the table and paid the delivery guy with a generous tip included.

"Thanks, man," his head bobbed excitedly. "Enjoy the pizza," he said, as he waved and sauntered around the corner.

Mik opened the top pizza box. He closed his eyes and waved his hands in a circular motion, fanning the aroma toward his nostrils. "Oh yeah," he said. "That's what I'm talkin' about."

Jack opened the trays of mussels. Even Erin had a smile on her face. "I haven't had Jimmy's in years. I forgot what I was missing."

"Well then you're really going to love dessert," Jack said. "I stopped and picked up Italian pastries at Rispoli's."

Mik's mouth was full of pizza, but he quickly jumped in. "Sfogliatelle?"

"What do you think? I'm not an amateur. Of course."

"What about cannoli?" Henry asked.

"Relax, Henry, I got the large assortment box."

They sat there in near reverential silence, as they enjoyed the rapture of Jimmy's pizza, and the promise of Rispoli's pastries to come.

They sat stuffed and bloated, trying to find one last cubic millimeter of space in their stomachs for the remaining morsels of pastry. Jack broke the silence. "I guess the next question is, how did Eileen, or Ellen, end up in New Jersey?" Jack asked.

"I thought you'd never ask," said Henry, using his napkin to wipe cannoli filling from the corner of his mouth. He picked up the laptop from the chair and opened it, scrolling through the files. He found what he was looking for. Several photos appeared on the TV screen. A few individual photos from a grade school yearbook, and a few photos of two children together. One boy had black hair and olive skin, and the other a fair complexion and red hair. There was a photo of the two of them, about six years old, in identical Little League baseball uniforms with *Astros* scrolled across the front of the shirts.

"Who are those boys?" Erin asked.

Henry folded his arms and looked at each of them, pausing for dramatic effect. "Those two boys are Jimmy Gigante and Danny McCarthy. Lifelong friends. They attended Saint Joseph's Catholic Grade School in West New York. They played on the same Little League team together. They were inseparable, which in itself was an enigma, since in those days the Italians and the Irish usually kept to themselves. Maybe they found a common bond in that both of those communities were generally shunned by polite society. Jimmy was devastated when Danny's parents moved the family to Boston, to be closer to Danny's mother's family. Danny McCarthy, of course, was Ellen's father. Jimmy Gigante became godfather," Henry peered over his glasses, "no pun intended, to Ellen McCarthy. Eileen."

"So that would explain how Danny McCarthy came to work at the Gigantes' lithography company," Jack said.

"Exactly," said Henry. "We've gone through real estate transaction records and found that shortly after Callanan's trial, the McCarthys sold their home."

Erin stood and put her hands behind her back. She started walking circles around the table in deep thought. "This is fantastic. Now we have someone who had a very strong motive for killing Eileen." She pinched her lower lip. "All we need is evidence that Callanan or his associates were able to track her down in New Jersey, and commit this crime. Anything to cast reasonable doubt that Jack was the killer."

"We'll get our team on that," Mik said.

"Then I suggest we adjourn and meet back in a few days," Erin said. "Any questions?"

"One," Henry looked sheepishly at the others, "is anyone going to eat that last cannoli?"

CHAPTER 26

Saturday, June 6, 2020

The phone rang in Erin's hotel room. She answered, "Erin Monroe."

"Hello, Ms. Monroe, this is Nigel, concierge at the Palace. There's a gentleman here with a delivery for you, which he claims must be delivered to you directly. Shall I send him up?"

Erin wasn't expecting anyone and was a bit wary. "No, that's alright, Nigel. I'll come down."

"As you wish, madam."

Erin was casually attired. She hadn't had time to put on makeup, and didn't care. She took the elevator to the white marble lobby and found the concierge desk. The concierge had a thin black mustache and wore a black tuxedo with a bow tie. With him was a man in a gray business suit, in his mid-thirties, carrying a box full of documents. A second younger man, possibly an assistant, carried a second box.

"Ms. Monroe," the older of the two introduced himself, "I'm Deke Samuels from the Bergen County prosecutor's office, and this is Harold, one of our interns. We work with Gavin Schictman."

Erin folded her arms. "My condolences."

The two looked at each other. "Yes, well," Samuels raised his eyebrows, "we've brought you the discovery documents that Mr. Schictman has released."

"That was fast. Frankly, I expected to have to fight for them."

Samuels looked around and leaned forward. "Just between us, Ms. Monroe, I think Mr. Schictman was impressed with your courtroom performance the other day. He's not inclined to take any chances on procedural technicalities." He set the box down and pulled out a pen and envelope. "This is a release form, itemizing the contents of these boxes and acknowledging that you have received them. We'll just need your signature, please."

"Certainly," Erin said. She took the pen, removed the document from the envelope, and scanned through it. She signed her name at the bottom. "Thank you, gentlemen."

"You're quite welcome," Samuels said. They turned and left.

Erin bent to lift the boxes and grimaced at their weight.

The concierge looked at one of the porters near the entrance and snapped his finger. The porter pushed a cart over toward them.

"Please accompany Ms. Monroe, and take these boxes to her room," the concierge said.

"Of course," the porter replied.

A few minutes later they were on the twenty-second floor. The porter deposited the boxes inside Erin's room. She tipped him with cash.

He pinched the brim of his hat. "Thank you, ma'am."

Erin closed the door and unpacked the boxes. One large manila envelope contained X-ray films and photographs of the bones found in the quarry. She went over to the window and drew the curtains. Far below, she could see the roofline of St. Patrick's Cathedral, which was in the shape of a gigantic crucifix occupying the entire city block, its green copper surface lit by many adjacent lights. She wasn't a particularly religious person, but it occurred to her that she might need some help from above to get Jack out of this mess.

She moved the boxes close to the bed. She piled up a few pillows and sat upright in the bed, poring over the documents. There were transcripts from the meeting with the FBI, and records from 1995 when Eileen went missing. One particular interview with an Eric Buchalter seemed particularly unfriendly to Jack's cause.

She'd gone through a number of documents, none of which appeared useful to their defense. Then something caught her eye. It was a record of financial transactions dating back two decades, detailing electronic transfers from Jack's bank account to a numbered account in the Cayman Islands.

"Jesus Christ," she muttered. *What the hell was that all about?* Whatever it was, this was going to be a problem. Schictman obviously considered it pertinent to the case or else she wouldn't have it in her possession. She clenched her fists, pounding the bed. "God damn it, Jack. What the hell are you up to?"

***

Erin's phone rang. She got up and went to the dresser where her purse sat. She pulled out her phone and answered. "Hello, Erin Monroe speaking."

"Erin, it's Brendan Mikolajczyk. Is this a good time?"

Erin brushed her light brown hair back. "Sure, Mik, what's up?"

"We've got more information that may or may not be helpful. We wanted to keep you up to date."

"Okay, I'm listening." Erin pulled out the desk chair and turned on the lamp.

Mik continued, "I had Henry do a search for any news articles in Boston relating to WITSEC or the U.S. Marshals Service. And he found something. In the spring of 1995, a U.S. marshal by the name of Vitai Lee was found dead, floating in Boston Harbor. An autopsy revealed that he had been beaten prior to his death."

Erin's eyes widened. "Go on."

"He had a shackle around his ankle with a broken, rusted piece of chain attached. It appears that someone wanted him to stay at the bottom of the harbor. But the anchor, or whatever they used to weigh him down, broke and he floated to the surface. He was found by the crew of a lobster boat."

"And you believe this marshal was in some way connected to Ellen McCarthy?"

"Better than that," Mik said. "We don't just believe it. We can prove it."

"How so?"

"Hang on," Mik said.

Erin's phone played a ringtone signifying an incoming text. She clicked on her message application and there was a photo. It was a black-and-white photo from a newspaper, taken in a courtroom. Ellen McCarthy was in the center, and standing next to her was a U.S. marshal.

"Let me guess. The U.S. marshal is Vitai Lee."

"Correct," Mik said, the satisfaction evident in his voice.

Erin paced the room, piecing together the information. "So, we have Ellen McCarthy, who would have been living under her assumed identity in New Jersey," Erin said. "The U.S. marshal who handled her case is found beaten and murdered, and this is reported in the news."

"Exactly," Mik said.

"Soon after that, Eileen Delaney, as she was now known, starts to behave erratically, and then in August of 1995, disappears."

"So, you are starting to see what I see," Mik said.

"I think so. Eileen feared that the U.S. marshal had been brutally interrogated in an attempt to get him to reveal her whereabouts. Shortly after that, she decided she had to run, and possibly assume a new identity. But she wasn't sure if she could trust the Marshals Service again. She tried to get Jack to go with her. But Jack, not being privy to any of this, thought it was just crazy talk, and declined. So, Eileen made an escape. But before she could get away, Callanan's men found her."

"That's exactly what I see," Mik said.

"Mik, this is huge. This presents a plausible scenario. There is motive, and there is means." Erin looked at the documents spread out on the bed. "Hey, you mentioned something about a skiing accident involving Eileen when she was on a school ski trip with Jack, where she broke her arm."

"Yeah, what about it?"

"Would your team be able to look into obtaining any reports or X-rays that might be available from that hospital visit?"

"We already did," Mik said. "Those were the days before electronic medical records. Hospitals are only required to retain X-ray films for five years, at least in New Jersey. It varies from state to state."

Erin sighed. "That's too bad."

"Yeah," Mik replied. "They would usually give copies to the patient if they requested them, but that won't help us."

"No, it won't." She stood up and looked out the window again at the roof of St. Patrick's and the shimmering lights of midtown Manhattan. "Please thank Henry."

"Will do," said Mik. "I'll call Jack, but I wanted to get this information to you first, in case it might help prepare your defense."

Jack, Erin thought. "Right, Jack," she said, shaking her head. "That boy's got some explaining to do."

"Huh?" Mik said.

"Never mind. I'll fill you in when I see you."

CHAPTER 27

Sunday, June 7, 2020

J ack drove up the tree-lined street and coasted to a stop near the iron gates of the Gigante home. A gentle breeze ruffled the leaves on the trees, carrying a sweet, woodsy scent. The guard at the gate watched apprehensively, his right hand brushing back the fabric of his suit jacket, until recognition set in.

"Oh, hey, Doc." It was Billy Beans. "What brings you out tonight?"

"I was hoping to speak to Mr. Gigante," Jack said.

"Is he expecting you?"

"No. I was in the area. I have some things I wanted to talk to him about."

"I'll check if he's available." Billy turned and walked a few feet away. He pulled out his phone and dialed. He spoke quietly on the phone for a moment, and then hung up, turning back toward Jack. "Mr. Gigante said to come on back. He's on the terrace if you wanted to go around."

"Thank you," Jack replied. "I know the way."

He walked along the winding brick walk, with patches of moss growing between the bricks. He paused at the bench that he sat on with Eileen that summer twenty-seven years ago. His shoulders slumped and his arms hung at his sides. A profound feeling of sadness came over him. How he wished he could go back in time and relive that moment. You never appreciate the good things in your life until they are gone.

He walked to the back near the pool. Jimmy Gigante sat on the upper terrace at a patio table under an umbrella. He wore shorts and a linen shirt. His legs were crossed on an adjacent chair, and he waved for Jack to come up.

Jack walked up the steps and stood next to the table, his hands in his pockets. A bottle of Amaro sat uncorked on the table next to a small sipping glass. Gigante's Colombian housekeeper, Rosalita, strode out from the kitchen. "May I get anything for your guest, Mr. Jimmy?"

"A drink, Jack?"

"No, thank you."

"No thanks, Rosalita," Jimmy said. "Have a seat." He motioned to the chair next to him. Jack sat down, his hands still in his pockets.

He looked at Jack. "How are you doing?"

"Pretty good," Jack said.

"Look, Jack, I know you're not just passing by. We live off the beaten path, tucked away in a cul-de-sac, for a reason," he smiled. "So, what's on your mind?"

Jack swiveled his head, looking around the yard, and spoke without looking at Gigante. "We know that Eileen

Delaney was born Ellen McCarthy. And we know about Callanan and the trial in Boston. We're pretty sure she was in the federal witness protection program, but you knew all this already, didn't you?"

Jimmy took a sip of his Amaro and looked down at the table. "Yes. I'm sorry, Jack. It was a secret. One that I made a vow to keep."

"More secrets." Jack shook his head. "Danny McCarthy was your best friend."

Jimmy choked up and nodded. "He was like a brother. It was really hard when his family moved away."

"But you stayed in touch," Jack said.

Jimmy nodded. "As best we could. When the shit hit the fan with his daughter, and they had to disappear, I offered him a job. The U.S. Marshals were reluctant, at first, to have a man like me privy to their new identities, but Danny convinced them. I was sworn to secrecy. Nobody else knew. Not even Jimmy Jr., or Connie, or my wife. And I've kept that promise."

"What happened to Eileen, Mr. Gigante?"

"If you've gotten this far, I assume you also figured out that Callanan got to the marshal who relocated the family. Eileen learned about his death, and decided she had to run again." He took his feet off the chair and leaned forward toward Jack. "We got her a forged passport, cash, and an airline ticket, and waited for her to come in. But..." He turned his palms up. "I guess they found her first."

Jack folded his arms. "I guess so."

"I'm sorry, Jack. I know you loved her. Eileen was like a second daughter to me, so I get it. And well... I also knew that Connie had a thing for you, and maybe I had hoped..." He waved his hand. "Never mind."

"Connie's a wonderful girl."

"Thank you. She's here actually, inside with her mother. You're welcome to stay for dinner if you'd like."

No sooner had he said that than Connie came walking out the door wearing jeans and a black tube top. She was holding a glass of white wine. Her face lit up when she saw Jack.

"Jack. What are you doing here?" Her lip gloss glistened in the fading sunlight.

Gigante looked at Jack. "I, um, invited him for dinner."

"Oh," Connie tilted her head and smiled. "That's great." She walked over and sat down at the table.

"There's something else," Jack continued. "It involves you too, Connie, so you may as well hear this." Jack looked down and bit his lower lip. "It's about the accident. Erin has been all over me, asking questions about those days following the party at the lake house. Asking where I was, and how I got the bruises." He sighed. "Now she's asking about my bank account in the Caymans. I keep putting her off, but frankly, I'm tired of keeping up this lie."

"It wasn't your fault, Jack," Connie said, putting her hand on his arm.

"I was plastered, Connie. I never should have been behind the wheel."

"You were chasing your girlfriend. And who knows, if you had reached her, then maybe..." she looked down as her voice trailed off.

"I left the scene of an accident, where a woman died! What kind of horrible person does that?"

Jimmy put his hand on Jack's arm. "A frightened young man, with his life ahead of him. One who understood that his acceptance, and scholarship to college, would have gone up in smoke with a DWI conviction."

"A woman died, Mr. Gigante. A mother of two young girls. And it was my fault."

"No, Jack," Connie grabbed his other hand, "she hit you. I was there, remember? When you left the party, I was worried about you. I tried to catch you before you left but I couldn't. I knew where you were headed, so I followed and caught up to you, just in time to see the accident." Connie closed her eyes. "That's when I called my dad and brother. And they got you and the van out of there."

"It was a mistake to run. So many times, I've thought of turning myself in, but I didn't want to implicate any of you."

"The statute of limitations has passed, Jack," Jimmy waved his hand. "Do what you have to do to ease your conscience. Even if it hadn't, being charged with abetting a hit-and-run would be low on my list of worries."

"Jack," Connie grabbed his shoulders, "you're a good man. You've done everything you could. The anonymous checks you've been sending have provided a good life for those girls. My dad felt just as bad as you did. He's kept tabs on them through the years, sending additional money when necessary. And despite the tragedy, they've had good productive lives, being raised by their aunt and uncle."

"It's time I put this behind me," Jack said. "I'm going to tell Erin the truth, and inform the police."

Jack stayed for dinner. It was a delicious homemade lasagna. Jimmy had a very fine collection of Brunello di Montalcino, and Jack overindulged.

"After our discussion earlier, there's no way I'm letting you drive home," Connie said. "I'll drive you, and we can get your car tomorrow."

Jack was in no position to argue. It was still early when they arrived at Jack's house. They sat in Jack's family room and turned on the television. A sappy Family Network movie was just starting about a woman revisiting her small hometown in Vermont, where she runs into her ex-boyfriend.

"I think I've seen this one before," Jack said.

"How can you tell?" Connie laughed. "The plots are all the same. The girl meets a prince from some phony, made-up country, yet he always has a British accent. A girl has to save her family farm. The high school sweethearts get back together. They cycle through a few well-worn plots, using the same actors and actresses."

"True," Jack said, "but they have happy endings. I wish life was like that."

"Yeah," Connie said, staring at Jack, blushing, "I do too." She brushed her hair back with her hand. "Got any wine or snacks?"

"Nothing as good as your dad's, but I have some Chianti." Jack looked in his refrigerator. "Garlic-stuffed olives, and a block of Asiago cheese."

"Mmm," Connie licked her lips.

They sat and watched the movie, sipping wine and eating snacks, laughing at the corny parts. At some point Connie took Jack's hand and held it on her thigh. His fingers gently stroked the denim on her jeans. To nobody's surprise, the girl in the movie did in fact reunite with her ex-boyfriend and save the family vineyard. The credits rolled.

Jack looked into Connie's eyes and she stared back at him. His fingers were still stroking her thigh, and he was thinking thoughts that he shouldn't be thinking. There was an awkward moment, neither knowing what to say. Finally,

Jack pulled his hand back. "I guess we should call it a night." As Jack continued to look at Connie, he noticed that her eyes were glassy and her smile askew. "Now, I'm the one who has to object to you driving."

"I'm okay." She got up and took a step, stumbling into the side of the coffee table and falling back onto the couch on top of Jack. She put her hand on his chest and giggled.

"Okay, no way am I letting you drive."

"Well," Connie ran her finger across Jack's shirt, "if you insist."

"Hang on, I'll get you some sleeping clothes." Jack went to his bedroom and put on gym shorts and a T-shirt. He came out and handed Connie one of his long T-shirts. "There are three bedrooms, Connie. They all have clean sheets, so whenever you're tired, you can just pick one."

"Any one?"

"Sure," Jack looked at her, "have a good night, Connie, and thanks for everything. I really enjoyed tonight. It was nice." He stood looking at her, wanting to say more but hesitating. "Anyway, good night."

Jack closed the door to his bedroom. He washed up in the bathroom, brushed his teeth, and got into bed, staring at the ceiling. He enjoyed watching the sappy movie with Connie. It was one of the few lighthearted moments he'd had in recent days. He was learning to appreciate those moments. Twenty minutes went by. He still wasn't asleep. The room was dimly lit by a small night-light in the corner. It cast a large triangular shadow of the walnut dresser onto the ceiling.

The door slowly creaked open, and Connie slipped in. She was still wearing her jeans and tube top. She closed the door behind her and quietly walked over to the other side of the bed. Jack remained silent as he watched her take off her earrings and put them on the night table.

Their eyes met. Connie crossed her arms over her head and slowly pulled off her tube top, allowing her breasts to drop down. She watched as his eyes scanned her body. She undid the buttons on her pants, one by one, and let them drop to the floor along with her panties. Jack swallowed, as Connie stepped out of her pant legs. Her nude body shimmered in the dim light. She lifted the covers and crawled into bed. She lay looking at the ceiling for a moment while Jack stared at her profile.

"You are so beautiful," he said, touching her shoulder.

She looked back and slid over toward him. She put her head on his shoulder and her soft, supple breasts pressed against the side of his chest. She drew her knee up, laying her silky thigh across his lower abdomen. Her body was warm, and Jack could feel ringlets of hair bristle against his hip.

"I like this room," she said, smiling coyly as she looked into his eyes. "But I'll go to one of the others if you want me to."

Jack stared, mesmerized by the beautiful gold, brown, and beige patterns in her irises. Their lips were close enough to feel the warmth of each other's breath. Jack's left arm was under Connie, his hand resting on her lower back. He cupped the curvature of her back, pulling her against him. "I don't want you to go," Jack said, as he wrapped his arms tightly around her, their lips coming together in the darkness.

CHAPTER 28

Monday, June 8, 2020

It was just past 8 a.m. when the ringtone sounded on Jack's iPhone. He was slow to wake. As he gained consciousness, a floral scent bathed his nostrils. Curled strands of sweaty black hair tickled his nose and mouth. He turned his head to look at the clock, then turned back to assess his situation. Connie's nude body was warm against his skin, her arms and legs intertwined with his own. The saltiness of her skin lingered on his lips.

With his free arm, Jack reached to grab the phone and pressed the answer key. "Hello, Jack Monroe," he whispered.

"Jack, it's Erin," she spoke quickly. "I've been going over these documents, and I think we need to get together."

"What, you mean now?" Jack blurted, in a high-pitched tone.

"No. Not now. But before the hearing on Wednesday. And I need you to cut the bullshit and start telling me the truth. Are we clear?"

The noise from their conversation caused Connie to stir from her sleep. "Jack," she smiled without opening her eyes, "kiss me."

"Um... am I interrupting something?" Erin asked. "What the hell is going on there?"

"Nothing." Jack covered the phone. "Maybe it's the TV."

"I thought I heard a woman's voice."

Jack changed the subject. "Look, you're right. When we get together, I'll tell you everything that happened that night. I swear to you."

Connie was still semi-conscious and nuzzled her nose into Jack's neck. She flexed her leg up over Jack's leg, inadvertently kneeing him in the groin.

"Ahhh... Connie," Jack winced. He clenched his teeth and closed his eyes, realizing his blunder.

There was a moment of silence, and then recognition. The words came out one at a time, each preceded by a pause. "Oh... my... God."

"Wait. It's not what you think."

"Really? Because what I think is that you're in the happy sack with Connie Gigante. Jesus, Jack!"

"Okay... okay..." Jack stuttered, "maybe... it might be what you think."

"Jack!" Erin shouted into the phone. "You've been indicted for murder. There's a lot going on. You might want to focus." She sighed loudly. "Now I'm going to be busy all day with my actual job. Remember that merger I told you about? The reason I'm in New York?"

"Yes," Jack answered, "I remember."

"Why don't you plan on meeting me here, at the Palace Hotel, this evening. Say around 6 p.m. Alright?"

"Yeah. 6 p.m. I'll be there."

"Check if Mik can join us. He said he was working in the city today."

"I'll call him."

"Goodbye," Erin said.

"Goodbye," Jack responded.

There was a pause.

"Goodbye, Connie," Erin shouted into the phone.

Connie lifted her head off Jack's chest and rubbed her eyes. "Bye, Erin."

***

The Villard House, built in the late nineteenth century for railroad magnate Henry Villard, is one of the last remnants of Gilded Age mansions in New York City. The neo-Italian Renaissance-style building was subsequently incorporated into the plan of the Palace Hotel and now functions as its upscale cocktail lounge, called the Gold Room.

That was where Jack's team were to have their meeting that evening, since both Erin and Mik had late business in the city.

Jack held Connie's hand as they walked down Madison Avenue. After the last night, he could no longer deny his feelings for her. "Thanks for coming with me tonight."

"No problem," Connie replied. "Thank you for dinner. How did you find that place? I've been to some great Italian restaurants, but that was amazing."

"I didn't. Sherlock found it. Sometimes the best restaurants are the dives that only the locals know about." Jack laughed. "Sherlock's like a truffle pig when it comes to finding them. The man loves his pasta."

As they turned to walk through the recessed plaza in front of the hotel, they saw Mik arrive from the opposite direction.

"Hey, Mik," Jack said.

Mik walked with his head down, carrying his briefcase in one hand and his suit jacket slung over his shoulder in the other. He looked up. "Oh, hey, Jack." His gaze dropped to Jack's hand, which was holding Connie's. His eyebrows peaked as he looked at Jack.

Jack said, "You remember Connie Gigante."

"Connie?" Recognition set in. "Oh my God, of course." Mik's eyes shifted to Connie. "You're Jimmy's little sister. It's been a long time. How's it going?" Mik put down his briefcase and gave Connie a hug.

"Nice to see you, Mik," Connie said, with a broad smile, her teeth gleaming in the city lights.

Mik looked at Jack. Confusion registered on his face. Jack read Mik's expression. "Connie's here because I thought she might be able to help fill in some details. I need to tell you guys things that I've not discussed before about the night Eileen disappeared."

"Great," Mik nodded, "first, let's go find this Gold Room."

They passed through the shimmering marble lobby with grand staircases rising up on either side and navigated their way to the Gold Room. When they arrived at the hostess's podium, they gave Erin's name to the smartly dressed woman wearing Gucci glasses and a black dress. She led them to a table in the back corner, secluded from the crowd, where Erin had already been seated.

Erin looked up from the drink menu. She saw Connie and the corners of her mouth dropped. "Jack. This was supposed to be a business meeting, and you've brought a guest." She stood up and extended her hand. "Connie." She looked her up and down. "You look fantastic. Looks like Father Time has somehow given you a pass."

"Thanks, Erin. Likewise."

"I wanted Connie to come," Jack said. "It will all make sense shortly."

They sat down. The drink selection included exotic concoctions, some dating back over a century, with names evocative of their eras. They each ordered a different one from the enthusiastic server.

The room was magnificent. Gold was everywhere. There was a cylindrical ceiling with gilded rectangular sections and ornate octagonal inlays. John La Farge lunette paintings hung above the north and south arches, and there were enough Renaissance-style carvings and statues to fill a museum.

Once the young waitress returned with their drinks, they got down to business. There was lively chatter from the other patrons, along with classical music playing in the background. That, and the fact that their table was sufficiently separated from the nearest occupied table, gave them adequate privacy.

"Okay, Jack," Erin began, "I want to know what happened the night of that party. And where you went afterward."

Jack cleared his throat. "You all know the background. Eileen was agitated and had been acting strange that summer.

She asked me to run away with her, and I told her that I couldn't. We argued back and forth, and it got heated." Jack closed his eyes, lost in the memory. "She slapped me." He shook his head. "I can thank Booky Buchalter for blabbing that detail to the FBI. I'd like to slap him."

"Wouldn't we all," said Mik, balling a fist, staring off in the distance. "Oh, sorry. Continue."

"Go on," Erin said.

"I'd had a lot to drink. I wasn't thinking properly, but after Eileen left in her car, the reality hit me. Though neither of us had said the words, it was a de facto breakup. I still loved her. I couldn't let it end like that. So, I went after her."

"How did you know where she was going?" Mik asked.

"I didn't," Jack said, "but I suspected she would go to her friend's house in Sea Girt." He narrowed his eyes and tapped his fingers on the table trying to remember her name. "Laura Stevens. One of her close friends. Eileen spent a lot of time down there."

"Got it," Mik said.

"But you turned around and came back," Erin said.

Jack sat silently, staring at the floral piece in the center of the table.

"Jack," Erin prodded, "you turned around and..."

"No," Jack shook his head, "that's the lie I've been telling everyone for twenty-five years." He closed his eyes tightly and exhaled. After a moment he reopened them. They were tearful and red.

"Then tell us the truth, Jack," Erin said.

Connie put her arm around him and pressed her forehead against his. "Go ahead, Jack."

Jack looked around the room and lowered his voice. "I got into an accident. A woman died, and I..." he swallowed hard and closed his eyes. "I left. It was a hit and run. I left the scene. It was the worst thing I've ever done, and I've never been able to forgive myself."

"No, Jack," Connie said, "that's not true." She shifted her eyes between Erin and Mik. "I followed him. When I saw him get into the van, I tried to stop him. He'd had way too much to drink, but he wouldn't listen. So, I followed him."

"What did you mean when you said, it's not true?" Erin asked. "Was there an accident?"

"Yes," Connie said, "that part was true. But it wasn't Jack's fault. I saw the whole thing. Jack went through an intersection. He had the right of way. The other driver ran a stop sign and plowed straight into the side of the van. The van spun around and the other car veered off the road, down an embankment, and hit a concrete wall in a drainage culvert."

"Holy crap," Mik said, "then what?"

"Jack was stunned. He was banged up and bruised but not seriously injured. We got him out of the car and went to check on the driver of the other car. When we got down the embankment, we saw that she was dead. Her neck was broken, and flexed at a right angle to her body." Connie closed her eyes as the memories from that night came flooding back.

Erin took Connie's hands into her own. "It's okay, Connie, take your time."

"We checked her pulse. There was nothing. She wasn't breathing. Her eyes were open and sightless, like glass. We knew she was gone."

"Were there any other people around?" Mik asked.

"No, that's the thing. We took Route 206. We were maybe half an hour away from the lake house, somewhere south of Chester. It was rural. Well... as rural as it gets in New Jersey. Jack had gotten off the highway. I presumed to get gas."

"So, what happened next?" Erin said.

"The accident wasn't Jack's fault." Connie's eyes darted between them. "But he was drunk. His scholarship to college and his plans of going to medical school would have vanished with a DWI conviction, especially one involving a fatality. There was nothing we could do for the other woman. She was already gone. How would it have helped if Jack's life was also destroyed?"

Erin and Mik looked at each other. Neither spoke.

Connie continued. "The van was still drivable. I drove it down the road, on a dirt path, into a wooded area. I walked back and got my car, where I had told Jack to wait. He was still in a daze. We drove down the street to a convenience store, which was closed, and used the pay phone outside to call my father. I told him the story, and where the van was. He sent his guys to get it. I drove Jack to our beach house in Sea Girt, and we stayed there for a couple days."

Connie held out her hands. "The next day the van was in a chop shop, and eventually on a garbage barge, headed out to sea. My father advised Jack to lay low for a few days to let the bruises heal. We came up with the story about getting into a bar fight at the shore to explain the bruises."

"But why would you do all this, and implicate yourself in a crime, Connie? I don't understand," Erin said.

Connie looked at Jack, and hesitated. She dropped her eyes down to the table. "Because I loved him." She folded her hands and fidgeted with her fingers. "I knew he was in love with her, but I couldn't help it. I loved him."

Jack slowly lifted his eyes from the table and looked at Connie. He took her hand and rubbed it with his thumb.

She tilted her head and sucked in her lips. Her eyes watered. "I still do."

Jack looked at her, then spoke up. "I'm going to turn myself in. This lie has been eating away at me long enough. My conscience won't rest until this is resolved."

Mik tapped the table with his fingers. "You know, that may not be the worst idea. It would at least account for your whereabouts that evening, and for the bruises."

Erin nodded. "Mik's right. The statute of limitations has expired, so criminal charges would be off the table. However, it could affect your medical license."

"Oh," Jack said, "about that. Now's probably as good a time as any to tell you that my hospital privileges have been suspended."

"What? Jack, seriously?" Erin said.

"The strange thing is..." Jack let out a nervous laugh. "I don't even care."

"What about income?"

Jack leaned forward, resting his elbows on the table. "There may be something else I've been keeping to myself. Remember that financial advisor that Sherlock set me up with? Jeremy Armstrong?"

"What about him?" Mik asked.

"The guy was the worst. I was getting four percent returns when the market was roaring. He always said, 'Diversify. Don't put all your eggs in one basket.' And I figured, if this guy is so bad at his job, I should probably do the exact opposite of everything he tells me. So, I did. I picked one promising company and funneled all of my free cash into its stock. That was back in 2005."

"Oh no," Erin buried her face in her hands, "that is the single dumbest thing I have ever heard."

Mik leaned forward and narrowed his eyes. "Which company?" he asked.

Jack shrugged. "Nvidia."

Mik pulled out his phone and googled Nvidia. He looked at the returns over the last twenty years. His eyes popped open, and his jaw hung slack. "Holy shit, Jack." He pulled up his calculator app and pushed a few keys. "That's an annualized return of 42.7%." They all stared at Jack.

"So how much is in the account?" Erin asked.

Jack bit his lip and looked around the table. He pulled out his phone and clicked a few keys. "As of the market closing today: seventeen million, four hundred and fifty-three thousand, and forty-seven dollars... and fifty-two cents."

The three of them stared blankly back at him. They were silent, their mouths hanging open.

Jack shrugged. "I don't need to work. I just do it out of boredom. Maybe that's why I'm good at it. It doesn't feel like work."

"Wait," Erin said. "Is that what the numbered account in the Cayman Islands is all about? Damn it, Jack. The Feds will nail you for tax evasion."

"I paid every penny of tax on that money. Every year."

"I don't understand. Then why is it down there?" Erin asked.

Jack put his elbow on the table and rested his forehead in his palm. "The woman that died in the accident was the mother of two little girls, aged four and two. We found that out through news articles. I thought of those girls every day, growing up without their mother. I felt guilt and shame. I've been sending anonymous checks every month for the last twenty-five years to help the family."

The waitress returned to the table. "Would anyone like refills on their cocktails?"

"Oh yes!" Erin blurted, much too quickly.

CHAPTER 29

Wednesday, June 10, 2020

J ack's mountain bike rolled to a stop. He unbuckled his helmet and removed it. Sweat beaded on his forehead as he struggled to catch his breath. Doug Noble was already seated on the wooden park bench overlooking the waterfall in Saddle River County Park. Jack got off his bike and flopped down next to Doug. Downstream, a couple of fishermen in chest-high waders were casting flies. Jack took a gulp from his water bottle. The wooded acreage went as far as the eye could see, with a strong scent of pine filling the air.

"This place is really nice," Jack spit the words out between panting.

"It's one of my favorite places to ride," Doug said.

"How far did we go?"

Doug pressed a button on his watch. "Twenty-five miles."

"What are they fishing for?" Jack asked, pointing his water bottle toward the anglers.

"The county stocks the river with trout and bass."

"Nice," Jack said. "Hey, thanks for inviting me, I needed this."

"Ready for more?" Doug asked.

"I can go a few more miles," Jack said, huffing. "I just have to be back in time for my preliminary hearing today. Erin will kill me if I'm late."

"Right," Doug said. He leaned forward, sucking in his lower lip. "Good luck with all of that. I feel bad for you, man."

The ringtone from Jack's cell phone sounded. He removed it from his bike shorts' pocket and answered. "Hello?"

Meghan's voice came through the phone. "Hey, Doc. How are you doing?"

"Meghan," Jack smiled, "thanks for asking. Nice to hear your voice. I'm good. What about you?"

"Ahh. Alright." She let out a sigh. "I've been temporarily reassigned to Dr. Posner's office. His office manager went into early labor and now she's out on leave."

"Posner, the bariatric surgeon?"

"Yeah, that's the one."

"He was two years ahead of me in med school. Good guy. How's that going?"

"It's good," Meghan said, "just not the same. Everyone wants you back."

"I appreciate that. It means a lot."

Meghan paused. "Do you know how many times I've watched you catch a spider, or a ladybug, on a piece of paper, and open the window to let it out?"

Jack smiled. "I like to consider the spider's point of view."

"No way in hell you're a murderer, we all know that. If you need a character witness, I'll be there in a heartbeat. I just wanted to wish you luck today."

"Thanks, Meghan, I appreciate that. You take care." Jack hung up.

"It was my office manager," Jack said.

Doug nodded. He leaned back on the bench. "Hey, I've been meaning to ask you something."

Jack turned to face Doug. "Sure, what is it?"

"That Gigante girl that you operated on; she seemed nice, and she's pretty cute."

"Yes, she is." Jack thought about it.

Doug leaned forward. "Do you know if she's single, or seeing anyone?"

"Seeing anyone?" Jack puffed out his cheeks and raised his eyebrows. "Umm... well... sort of."

Doug looked at him. "Sort of?"

Jack leaned his elbows on his knees. "You know my girl-friend Leslie... I guess ex-girlfriend..."

"The TV girl," Doug interjected.

"Yeah, well, she dumped me over this whole..." Jack made quotation marks with his fingers, "murder thing. And you know, Connie and I briefly dated in high school."

"Oh, I didn't know that," Doug said.

"Anyway, we just recently started up again..."

"Oh, hey, I'm sorry," Doug raised his hand, "I had no idea."

"No problem," Jack said. They both stared straight ahead for a moment.

Then Doug jumped up and said, "Ready?"

Jack put his helmet back on. "Ready as I'll ever be."

***

Jack arrived at his house at 11 o'clock. The hearing was scheduled for noon. He pulled into his driveway and noticed his front storm door ajar, with a square yellow envelope partially sticking out. He parked, and went in through the front door so he could grab the envelope.

He went inside, put the envelope on the table, and ran up to have a shower. Once out of the shower, he searched for a suit. His navy-blue suit was still at the dry cleaners. He found his gray suit and started to put it on, but he'd forgotten that the gray suit was an athletic cut. He had bought it when he was in crazy-good physical condition a few years back. He wasn't overweight now, but the suit was uncomfortably tight. He had other suits stored in the attic, but had no time to dig them out.

He looked sadly upon his only other option. Reluctantly, he put it on. It was a light blue tuxedo that he might have worn to his senior prom. If so, he had repressed all memory of it. He left off the cummerbund. It had a three-button jacket with a high and wide lapel. It was snug but wearable. The pant legs barely reached his ankles, no farther. He looked at the clock, and it was nearing 11:30 a.m. There was no time to think about it.

He ran down the stairs, remembering the envelope. It had no address or any sender identification on it. He quickly opened it and looked inside. The envelope contained X-ray films. He pulled them out and looked at the markings on them. A shiver ran down his spine. His head spun around, looking in every direction. He ran to the front window, pinched the curtain, and looked outside, then went back to the counter where he'd laid the X-rays, looking at the markings. Eileen Delaney, January 13, 1995, Hackensack Hospital.

Stuffing the X-rays back into the envelope, he ran outside, got into his car, and sped off for the courthouse.

***

"The prosecution calls Mr. Eric Buchalter, Your Honor," Gavin Schictman said, holding up his notes.

"Please take the stand, Mr. Buchalter," Judge Harlan Moody directed. "Raise your hand. Do you swear to tell the truth, the whole truth, and nothing but the truth, so help you God?"

"I do," Eric Buchalter answered. His greasy hair was uncombed. Loose strands fell onto his face which he periodically blew off with a puff of air from his protruding lower lip.

Schictman approached the witness stand. "Mr. Buchalter, please recount for us your testimony on the altercation that you witnessed between Ms. Delaney and the defendant on the night that she disappeared."

Buchalter smiled with delight as he retold his story. "She smacked him hard. Left a red welt on his face you could see from ten yards away." His body rocking as he nodded his head.

"And how did Jack Monroe respond," Schictman asked.

"Oh, he was angry. His eyes were demonic."

"Angry enough to kill, would you say?" Schictman said.

"Objection, Your Honor," Erin shouted, "leading."

"Sustained. Be careful, Mr. Schictman," the judge admonished.

The door of the courtroom flung open, and Jack rushed in carrying the envelope.

Judge Moody looked at his watch, 12:19. "Nice of you to join us, Dr. Monroe. Was there somewhere more important you had to be?"

"No, Your Honor. I apologize. It won't happen again."

"Let's hope not."

Jack walked toward the defense table. Erin's mouth hung agape as she watched him walk toward her and sit down. He dropped the envelope on the table.

"Where were you?" she glared at him. She looked him up and down, mouth hanging open, aghast at his attire. "And what, in Dante's lowest corner of Hell, is that costume you're wearing? You look like a pimp," she whispered. "Never mind," she put a hand up, "I don't want to know."

Schictman finished his questioning of Booky Buchalter.

"Ms. Monroe," Judge Moody extended his arm toward the witness.

Erin pulled her suit jacket taut as she walked to the witness stand. "Mr. Buchalter, you just testified that in response to being slapped, Jack Monroe's eyes became demonic. That's the word you used."

"Yes."

"Well," Erin shook her head, "your eyesight must be fantastic, Mr. Buchalter. I mean, to be able to see Jack's eyes through the back of his skull. Are you Superman? Do you have X-ray vision?"

"What?" Buchalter's eyes danced around the room, confused.

Erin continued, "In your deposition, you stated that Jack came out of the house and walked past you toward Eileen who was coming toward you. Then they stopped and got into an argument. So, Jack had to have been facing away from you as he spoke to Eileen."

Booky began stuttering, with unintelligible sounds coming out of his mouth, along with drops of saliva.

Erin pounced like a leopard. "So, are you Superman, Mr. Buchalter? I don't think you are, because if you were Superman, you probably wouldn't have lost that starting wide receiver position to Jack Monroe in high school. Isn't that right?"

Booky took the bait. His face became red and he started to grit his teeth. His breathing morphed into a snarl.

"You hated Jack Monroe!" Erin continued, "with every cell in your body, because he stole your chances of getting a college football scholarship. Isn't that right, Mr. Buchalter, and I remind you that you are still under oath." Erin pointed her finger at Booky's face, shouting, "You hated him, didn't you? Didn't you?"

"Yes," he spit the words out, "I hated him."

"No more questions, Your Honor."

Erin strode confidently to the defense table. She looked at the envelope Jack had brought. "What's that?" she asked.

"Someone left it in my front door." Jack leaned closer. "They're X-rays from when Eileen had the ski injury. Freaked me out."

Erin peeked into the envelope and saw that it contained film, then closed it. "I can't read an X-ray. We can take a look at these later. Do you think Mik or Henry left them?"

"I don't think so. Mik would have told me."

Erin looked to the back of the courtroom where Mik was seated with Henry. "We can ask them during the recess."

Schictman called his other witnesses. Sheriff Townsend got on the stand and told of the recovery of Jack's high school ring and fishing knife from the car. A pathologist for the prosecution testified that the slash marks on the ribs of the skeleton found in the quarry were consistent in size and shape with the serrations on the fishing knife. Schictman even went so far as to introduce records of Jack's arrest for drunk and disorderly conduct, and getting involved in several bar fights during his early twenties in Belmar, at the Jersey Shore. Jack held his folded arms across his abdomen. The acid in his stomach was multiplying, churning.

When it was time for the defense to present their rebuttal, Erin called Henry Wan to the stand. "Mr. Wan, we previously learned through Sheriff Townsend, that no evidence of Eileen Delaney's life, prior to high school, could be found. Please tell us what relevance this had concerning your trip to Boston."

"Yes," Henry answered, "I work for Mr. Mikolajczyk's security firm as an investigator. We suspected that Ms. Delaney may previously have had an alternate identity, and I was sent to Boston to see what I could find."

"Your Honor," Erin said, "with your permission we'd like to present photographic evidence of Mr. Wan's findings." There was a large LCD screen to the left of the bench.

"Proceed," the judge said, waving his hand.

Mik brought a laptop to the front of the courtroom and connected an HDMI cord from the computer to the LCD.

"Mr. Wan," Erin said, "what was the result of your search?"

Henry cleared his throat. "We discovered that Eileen Delaney was an alias used by a woman whose birth name was Ellen McCarthy." Mik pressed a button and the screen lit up with the juxtaposed photos of Eileen Delaney and Ellen

McCarthy. There was audible whispering throughout the courtroom.

"And how certain are you of this, Mr. Wan?"

"Our analysis of the two photos shows that they are identical."

"What else did you learn?"

Henry continued, "We learned that Ellen McCarthy had been witness for the prosecution of an Irish mobster, Seamus Callanan, for heroin trafficking." The LCD screen changed to a news article showing a photo of Ellen testifying at the trial. "After the trial, Ellen McCarthy disappeared. And soon after, Eileen Delaney appeared in Oradell, New Jersey. We assume, but can only speculate, that she was put into the Federal Witness Protection Program."

Schictman sat in his chair, elbows resting on the table and his chin perched on folded hands.

"Your Honor, I'd like to make a motion to dismiss this case against my client," Erin said. "We have shown that the deceased was in fear for her life, having testified against an Irish mobster, who had a very strong motivation to kill her. We will further prove that on the night that the decedent vanished, my client was involved in an accident, in which he fled the scene. He is willing to admit to leaving the scene of an accident resulting in a fatality, but for which he was not at fault. This explains the bruising that was seen on my client in the days following the party at the lake house. We can also account for his whereabouts in the days following."

The noise in the courtroom became louder. The judge banged his gavel on the sounding block. "Order in the court," he shouted.

"Your Honor," Schictman said as he approached the bench, "I see no relevance to any of this. Whether her name was Ellen McCarthy or Eileen Delaney is immaterial. She's still dead, and she was killed with his knife." He pointed at Jack, "and furthermore, I'd like the opportunity to explore this hit-and-run claim, which if true, would further demonstrate moral depravity on the part of the defendant."

"Your motion is denied, Ms. Monroe," the judge said. "We'll take a forty-five-minute recess and return back at that time." He tapped the gavel once again.

Erin picked up her leather tote, with all of her materials, and took the folded manila envelope that Jack had brought and stuffed it in. She walked to the back of the courtroom with Jack and met Mik and Henry.

"I loved the way you handled Buchalter, Erin," Mik said. "That was a master class in humiliation."

"Thanks," Erin responded. "Hey, did you or Henry leave a manila envelope containing X-rays at Jack's house today?"

Mik looked at Henry. Henry shrugged. "Not me."

Mik turned to Erin. "It wasn't us."

"That's strange," Erin looked off in deep thought. "Okay, never mind. There's a gourmet coffee shop down the hall. Let's get some coffee."

They walked out the back of the courtroom into a cavernous marble atrium. Along one of the walls under a decorative arch was a marble statue of Justicia, blindfolded and holding the scales of justice in one hand and a sword in the other. Jack focused on the sword, the Roman mythological symbol of punishment.

The Cafe Le Mans was a French-style coffee shop and boulangerie that served specialized coffee, croissants, and pastries. They sat at an iron bistro table, on cushioned seats. The waitress, an Asian girl with long black hair and glasses, looked to be in her late teens. She took the coffee orders. Jack and Mik ordered the regular coffee, and Henry, the French press. Erin ordered one of the frilly special lattes with oat milk and various spices.

"Can I see the envelope Jack received?" Mik asked.

Erin handed it to him. He pulled out the films, looked at them, tilted his head, and then shrugged. He put them back in the envelope. "We'll have our tech team take a look at them."

The waitress returned a few minutes later with the coffees. Jack's stress level was slowly escalating. The real possibility of going to prison started to consume him. His hands felt clammy and his muscles tensed. The waitress set the coffee down. "Would anyone like any croissants or pastries?" she asked.

They shook their heads. "No, thank you," Erin said.

Jack stared into the distance down the long hallway as he sipped his coffee. From Erin's cup an aromatic blend of spice wafted through the air to his nostrils. He drifted into a trance-like state. An olfactory memory, long dormant, resurfaced. The aromas of cinnamon and nutmeg took him back. But to where? he thought. It struck him like a smack to the head. His eyes popped open. It was the smell of those spiced hot chocolates at the ski lodge at Vernon Valley. He pictured himself there, in front of the stone fireplace, in a rustic log chair. And Eileen with that beautiful smile. Her blond hair dangling from under her ski hat onto her wool sweater, holding her steaming cup, with that same familiar combination of spices. That was an hour before being taken down the hill, by ski patrol, with a broken arm.

Jack's eyes came into focus. "Let me see those," he said with urgency in his voice, pointing at the yellow envelope.

Mik passed him the envelope and Jack pulled the X-rays out, spreading them on the table.

"Erin," Jack rushed the words out, "do you have those skeletal photos from the quarry?"

Erin dug into her tote bag. Everything was arranged into folders labeled with Post-it stickers. She found the one Jack wanted. "Here it is," she handed it to Jack.

Jack held the folder upside down and dumped the contents onto the table. There were several 8x10 inch photos. He picked one up. Then another, and a smile stretched across his face. "It's not her," he said. His eyes watered. He took off his glasses, and wiped his eyes with his shirt sleeve. "It's not her," he repeated, his voice cracking. He buried his forehead into his hands.

"Not who?" Mik asked.

"What is it, Jack?" Erin asked. "Spit it out."

"Look," Jack held up the X-ray from Hackensack Hospital. It showed the left radius bone with a titanium plate and screws across a mid-shaft fracture.

"I'm not following," Henry said.

Jack picked up a composite photo which showed the skeletal bones from the quarry laid out as they would have been in life. Then he held up a second photo which was an isolated photo of the arm.

"There's no plate," Mik said. They looked at each other with blank stares.

"Which means..." Henry said.

Erin smiled, her eyes lit up. "Which means... the girl in the quarry is not Eileen Delaney, or Ellen McCarthy." Erin looked around the table, "it's someone else."

They re-entered the courtroom before the allotted time. Henry and Mik took their seats in the rear. Erin and Jack strode confidently to the defense table. Erin's grin was nearly sinister as she looked at Schictman. Schictman looked back and did a double take, confused by her apparent confidence.

The bailiff shouted, "All rise, court is now in session, Judge Harlan Moody presiding." Everyone stood and then took their seats. All except Erin, who remained standing.

"Your Honor, I'd like to reintroduce the motion to dismiss," she said.

Schictman threw his papers down onto his table and shook his head.

Judge Moody slapped his hand on the bench and addressed Erin. "Ms. Monroe, I have already ruled on the motion to dismiss, so unless you have some earth-shattering new evidence to present I..."

Erin cut him off, "we do, Your Honor. Evidence which has just come to light; evidence which would make it legally impossible for this case to go forward."

Schictman raised his arms. "Please, Your Honor, this is a shameless waste of the court's time."

"Well, I would love to hear this, Ms. Monroe. And I caution you, it better be good, or I will hold you in contempt."

Erin walked toward the bench and blurted it out. "The girl in the quarry is not Eileen Delaney. Or Ellen McCarthy, if you prefer. It is a person, as yet, unknown." She turned toward Schictman who stood motionless, stunned by the revelation. "And, as the grand jury has issued an indictment for the murder of Eileen Delaney, and not any other person or persons, this case must be dismissed."

"We've not seen any such evidence, Your Honor," Schictman shouted.

Erin proceeded to present the X-ray and photographic evidence, after which Schictman appeared defeated. His shoulders slumped and his arms hung limp at his sides. His head seemed too heavy for his neck to support.

The judge looked at Erin. He pursed his lips and scratched his jowls between his thumb and index finger. "Ms. Monroe, your legal argument is admittedly sound." He looked at Schictman. "Mr. Schictman, this begs the question, does the prosecution have any irrefutable evidence that the body found in the quarry was, in fact, Eileen Delaney?"

Schictman started to squirm, his words dribbling out seemingly at random. "No, Your Honor, as we have previously mentioned, the DNA was too degraded, we um..."

"So, the answer I'm hearing is no. I have no choice, then, but to dismiss this case." He banged his gavel, and the sonorous crack filled the room.

Erin walked back to the defense table. Jack stood up and hugged her. For one moment in time, their sibling rivalry vanished, replaced by relief and joy. But it would be short-lived.

Schictman's eyes narrowed and his mouth twisted as he spoke, his greased-back hair bobbing like a turkey. "This isn't over. We still have a dead girl, in a car that Jack Monroe had access to. We have his possessions in that car including the murder weapon. I intend to reconvene the grand jury to return a murder indictment for whoever the deceased may have been."

"Tread carefully, Mr. Schictman," the judge admonished as he slowly rose from his chair. "You are walking a thin line, bordering on harassment."

They gathered with Mik and Henry in the atrium outside the courtroom. Henry said, "We still don't know who sent those X-rays."

Mik asked, "Jack, do you have a Ring doorbell, or any video surveillance at your home?"

"No," Jack shook his head, "it's a safe neighborhood. I've never bothered."

"Too bad," Mik said.

Jack thought. It was an unusual size for a manila envelope, but there was something distinctly familiar about it. He just couldn't put his finger on it. And then suddenly it dawned on him, recognition of where he'd seen those envelopes before. He kept a straight face. He would explore this on his own. "I have to go, guys, I'll catch you later," he said abruptly and then left.

CHAPTER 30

Wednesday, June 10, 2020

Jack drove to the Gigante house and parked his car near the gate. The gate attendant was one of the men Jack had met on the night of Connie's party.

He recognized Jack. "Hey, Doc, what's up?"

"Is Mr. Gigante around?"

He shook his head. "Nah, I'm sorry, he ain't here."

"Any idea where I might find him?" Jack asked.

"Yeah, he's at the Trinacria. It's a social club in Little Ferry, on the Hackensack River. Used to be a restaurant called Tracy's Nine Mile House." He brought the fingertips of his left hand together, touched them to his mouth, and closed his eyes. "Madone, the best steak sandwiches. What a shame that it closed." He scribbled an address on a piece of paper and handed it to Jack. "Knock on the door. When the wood slat slides open, you say this: *Non fare il citrullo*. Got it?"

"Got it," Jack repeated the phrase.

"Okay, and listen, if nobody answers, don't go snooping around the back. That could get you shot, *capisce?*"

"Understood," Jack nodded. "Thank you."

Jack had been to Tracy's many times with his family, so he knew the location. His drive took him through the township of Bogota, through the business district on Main Street with its quaint brick storefronts dating to the early part of the twentieth century. Tall, thick maple trees lined the street. In his rearview mirror, he saw a black Lincoln Town Car—the same one that had been following him since he left Englewood.

Jack pulled over and parked in front of the Jersey Brothers Bagel shop. The smell of fresh bagels coming out of the oven was delightful as he entered the shop. He walked down a corridor, past the restrooms, through a back door that led to a parking lot. The fetid, acrid odor of trash coming from the dumpsters was a rude departure from the smells inside. He crossed the parking lot to the street parallel to Main Street, made a right turn and walked one block under tall elms, then made another right turn which brought him back onto Main Street. He saw the Lincoln parked halfway down the block.

Jack blended in with the shoppers and restaurant patrons strolling the sidewalk. He walked up to the open passenger-side window of the Lincoln and bent down. "Good evening, Agent Creighton," Jack said, smiling at her. "Fancy meeting you here."

Agent Creighton's face blushed. She put her fingers up to her forehead and brushed a loose strand of hair. "Good evening, Dr. Monroe."

"You know," Jack said, "if you wanted to know where I was going, you could have just asked." He shrugged. "But I'll save you the trouble. I'm going to a social club in Little Ferry called Trinacria. But enough about me, you guys might want to redirect your effort to figuring out the identity of that girl in the quarry."

The driver was a younger male agent, twenty-five or so, with close-cropped brown hair and narrowly spaced eyes. They looked at each other, confusion on their faces. Then Agent Creighton said, "I'm not following."

Jack handed her Erin's business card. "You can call my sister. She's my attorney. She'll fill you in on what happened today. Oh, and no offense, Agent Creighton, but I don't think you're cut out for this clandestine surveillance work. Your looks don't exactly blend into a crowd," Jack raised his eyebrows and shrugged.

Creighton's face reddened further, and though she tried to conceal it, the compliment broke the rigid line separating her thin lips.

Jack walked back to his car.

Twenty minutes later, he arrived at the address to find a featureless building, unadorned with any pleasing architectural accoutrements. It was not as he remembered, looking more like a Soviet-bloc rectangle tucked between industrial buildings along the Hackensack River. The only living things present, aside from Jack, were three flowering plants in blue ceramic pots. Within view was a WWII submarine, permanently moored as a naval museum, and a seaplane marina, partially visible behind the building.

Jack walked along a nautical-themed path with pine planks and a handrail made of thick rope draped through wooden posts. He arrived at the door and knocked on it. There was a small opening at eye level, closed off with a sliding wooden slat on the inside. The board slid open and Jack saw an eyeball peering out, looking left and right.

A gruff voice said, "Password."

"Password?" Jack stood confused. "Oh, right..." He had written the phrase down. He pulled the piece of paper from his pocket. "*Non fare il citrullo.*"

Three distinct *ka-ching* sounds could be heard as bolts were thrown before the door swung open. Jack stepped cautiously through the doorway. Everyone looked to see who had entered. The room reeked of cigar smoke, coffee, and garlic.

Two men in khakis and T-shirts chalked pool cues next to a billiard table.

A couple of guys in ties and white shirts sat at the bar drinking bourbon, their sport jackets hanging from the backs of the chairs. One wore a black pork pie hat. Toward the back, Jimmy Gigante was playing poker with three men. He looked up as Jack entered the building and placed his cards face down on the table. He waved for Jack to follow him and then walked out the back door.

Jack followed him onto a worn wooden deck, whose gray paint was peeled and curling. The deck overlooked a dock which had seen better days, and the river. A marsh full of tall reeds surrounded the dock. A dead fish floated in the water, which was iridescent with oil and gasoline residue.

Jimmy sat down at a table and motioned for Jack to do the same.

"What's on your mind, Jack?"

Jack stared off across the river, watching seagulls circling overhead. "The judge dismissed my case today."

"That's great news," Gigante said, a smile erupting on his face.

"Thank you for the X-rays."

"Oh," Jimmy folded his hands, looking down at the table. "How did you know?"

"I didn't at first. Then I noticed the manila envelope. I haven't seen one with that square, non-standard size for many years. Not since I worked at your printing company."

Gigante pressed his lips together and stared up at the seagulls, their squawking punctuating the background drone of automobile traffic.

"Is she alive?"

"Jack," he turned away.

Jack spoke louder, his voice emboldened. "Please, Mr. Gigante. I have to know."

Gigante stood and walked over to the white wooden railing surrounding the deck. He leaned over and rested his forearms on the rail. "Jack, you're asking questions that I just can't answer."

"Can't, or won't?" Jack said, in a tone which he immediately regretted.

Gigante turned around and put his hands in his pockets. "Maybe both, Jack." He started walking around the deck. "We like to believe that we control our lives, but we don't. God has a plan, and we are all pawns in His game. We have no more control over what happens to us than that fish." He pointed to the dead fish bobbing up and down as the ripples of water splashed against the bank.

"The DA is not quitting," Jack said. "He's planning to re-indict me for the murder of whoever the girl was, in Eileen's car." Jack looked at Jimmy. "You wouldn't happen to know the answer to that question, would you?"

"No, Jack," he sighed. "I swear on my children's lives, I have no idea." He waved his hand. "Don't worry about Schictman, we'll deal with him."

Jack nodded.

"Listen, Jack. I made a promise long ago to a good friend. A promise that I cannot break. But I'll do my best, okay? You saved Connie's life, and I won't forget that. I'll do everything I can to help you get the answers you deserve. It may take some time. You need to be patient, alright?" Jimmy put his hand on Jack's shoulder.

***

The day's activities left Jack mentally exhausted. When he got home, he put on shorts and a T-shirt and popped open a bottle of beer. He sprawled on his couch with a bag of chips and flipped through the channels on his streaming app. He stopped on the NBC affiliate's local news programming.

A pretty woman with dirty blond hair stepped in front of a camera holding a microphone. Jack recognized the Bergen County Courthouse in the background. He sat up, leaning forward, and raised the volume.

The reporter announced, "We are bringing viewers an update on the story we've been covering about the local girl found deceased in a rock quarry in Warwick, NY. According to our sources, there is now compelling evidence that the body found is not that of missing teen Eileen Delaney, but rather another young woman whose identity remains unknown."

"Well, that was fast," Jack said aloud, just before his doorbell rang. His pulse quickened. He wasn't expecting anyone.

He got up and pushed aside the curtain covering his front window. He looked outside and saw the Bergen County Sheriff's car parked in front of his house. The muscles in his neck tensed. His shoulders sagged. Was he being arrested again? Sheriff Justin Townsend stood on his front stoop with his palms on his hips.

Jack closed his eyes and leaned his head back. "What now?" He hesitated for a moment, then opened the door. He stepped out onto the landing. "Sheriff, what brings you here tonight?"

Jack looked to his right and saw Binny Benson standing on her porch watering her potted plants. She looked at Jack, then at the sheriff's car, and scampered back into her house.

"Jack, relax," the sheriff said. "This isn't an official visit. May I come in, please?"

Jack hesitated, then nodded. "Sure." He motioned for the sheriff to come in.

They walked into the house. "Can I get you anything, Sheriff?"

"Maybe just some water, if you don't mind."

Jack grabbed a bottle of water from the fridge and handed it to the sheriff. "Please have a seat." They both sat down on the sofa.

"Jack, I want to apologize," the sheriff said. "Schictman had me convinced you were guilty. But now, I'm sure we had it all wrong. And, for whatever it's worth, I don't support his plan to pursue further charges against you. But keep that between us."

Jack exhaled, relieved. "Thank you, Sheriff. I appreciate that. But why are you doing this?"

"I knew your stepfather, Jack. George was a good man, and a damn good detective. We went to the academy together. We both started out on the Teaneck Police Force. Later, I had an opportunity to join the Sheriff's Department for a small increase in pay, so I took it."

"I didn't know that."

"You were probably too young to remember, but I remember all of you kids at the police picnics at Votee Park. It was fun to watch you all together, like one big family. And it was a family, Jack. We all looked out for one another."

"I remember those picnics," Jack laughed. "I looked forward to them. Detective Finn had a cute daughter, Stacy, who I had a major crush on."

"Anyway, I can't tell you how relieved I am that we were wrong about you."

"Not as relieved as I am," Jack said.

"But that's not why I'm here." The sheriff folded his hands and looked at Jack. "There's more."

"Ahh." Jack's smile dissipated. "There's always more."

"We got hold of police records from Sommerset County, from August 22, 1995, detailing a report of a hit-and-run accident with a fatality. One Marilyn Anderson, thirty-one years of age, was found deceased at the scene. The investigators determined that the collision involved a large, heavy vehicle with white paint, but that vehicle was never recovered."

Jack hung his head down. "I was the driver of that vehicle, Sheriff. I should have come forward long ago." Jack looked at the sheriff. "I'm responsible, and I'm willing to answer for that."

"I knew that, Jack. I have the coroner's autopsy report, which was never released publicly." He reached into his shirt pocket and pulled out a folded document. He put on his reading glasses and skimmed through it. "The conclusion was as follows: Ms. Anderson succumbed to a ruptured intracranial aneurysm prior to the collision, which caused her to lose control of her vehicle and go through the stop sign. The immediate cause of death was an aneurysm, not the collision. You're not responsible, Jack." He folded his glasses and put them back into his pocket.

Jack leaned forward and buried his face in his hands. The emotion hit him hard. His lips started to quiver, and his palms became wet with tears. He felt embarrassed as he sobbed in front of the sheriff.

"Leaving the scene of a fatal accident was an error in judgment, Jack. But you were just a kid. One momentary lapse in judgment, twenty-five years ago, doesn't make you a bad person. You've had a good, productive life."

The sheriff stood up and patted Jack on the back. "You've had a long day. I'd better be on my way." Jack walked the sheriff to the door and said goodbye.

Within ten minutes, Jack was sound asleep in his bed. It would be the best sleep he'd had in two and a half decades.

CHAPTER 31

Thursday, June 11, 2020

In slip number sixty-one at the Boston Harbor Shipyard and Marina, the Fleming 75 luxury yacht *Finnegans Wake* bobbed up and down with the tide. Each undulation of the surf caused it to tug against its moorings, the tension on the deck cleats emitting an eerie report of creaks and groans. Though people always assume the boat was named after James Joyce's novel, in fact, Seamus Callanan named the boat after his friend and mentor, Riley Finnegan. Finnegan's Irish wake was the best damned party Callanan had ever attended. Never mind that it was Callanan himself who put Finnegan in the grave with a single shot from a silenced Walther PPK, to take control of the Clan Kilkenny, the faction of the Irish mob that ran South Boston.

Callanan sat in a chair on the rear deck, a black patch covering his right eye, as he took in the sun and the views of Boston's skyline. His cane rested at a lazy angle, hooked to the armrest. A salty breeze blew steadily across the harbor as Callanan popped the cap off his third Guinness. In his line of sight, approaching him on the dock, was his long-time associate, Derrick. Derrick ambled with the stalling gait of a man with little desire to reach his destination. That procrastination wasn't lost on Callanan. When Derrick was within earshot, Callanan shouted to him, "Either you shite yer britches and want no part o' spillin' the load, or you're bringin' some bad news, so which'll it be?"

Derrick walked across the gangplank and jumped down onto the deck. His lips tensed. In his hand he held a copy of the *Boston Globe*. Without speaking, he handed the paper to Callanan.

Callanan took it and opened it. He tilted his head from side to side, perusing the article headings until he came upon the one of interest. His eyes scrolled left to right, over and over, as he read the article. The smile left his face, which started to glow a reddish purple. He clenched his teeth and banged his fists down with such force on the arms of the chair that the aluminum bent. The scream could be heard across the marina.

"Shit!" He stomped his good foot on the deck. "Jesus, Mary and Joseph. How could this happen?" He got up, yanked his cane from the arm of the chair as if pulling a sword from its sheath, and hobbled around in circles.

"Fifteen years, I spent in that God-forsaken hellhole. I lost an eye to a fork." The radius of his circles grew larger. "Those filthy animals crushed my leg with a concrete block."

Callanan snatched the newspaper from the table and jabbed his finger at the photo of Ellen McCarthy. "And she put me there. I was assured that she was dead."

Derrick had been carefully skirting Callanan's path as he vented his rage, retreating into a corner. Callanan turned toward him with fire in his eyes. "How did this happen? I want to know who's responsible, Derrick." He rolled up the paper and threw it down onto the deck.

"I'll find out, Seamus," Derrick said. He turned to step up to the gangplank to leave the boat.

"Wait," Callanan shouted, "that little bitch who ruined my life is still walking and breathing. Both of those activities need to end."

"Aye," said Derrick, "understood." He left the boat.

Dusk fell over the harbor, and the lights of the city illuminated the evening sky.

Callanan hobbled his way into the cabin and leaned against the wet bar, fixing himself a drink. He sat down on the teak-trimmed vinyl couch and pulled out his cell phone. The phone rang three times before a voice answered, "Hello?"

"Senator Hollingsworth?" Callanan said.

The voice on the other end dropped to a whisper. "I'm at a conference, can I call you back?"

"No, Mason, you cannot. We need to talk."

"One moment." There was a shuffling sound on the other end of the phone, and then the sound of a door closing. "What is it, Seamus?"

"Have you seen the article in the *Globe*?"

"What article?"

"She's alive, Mason."

"Who is?" Mason asked.

"The McCarthy girl. The one in the warehouse who put me in prison for fifteen years. Remember her, Mason?"

"I can't really talk now," his voice sounded strained.

"Do you remember the location where we last met?"

"Yes."

"Be there. Midnight tonight," Callanan snarled, "and don't disappoint me."

***

Detective Lieutenant John Carter was a square-jawed man of medium build in his early fifties with a small gray mustache and marine-blue eyes. He wore a gray suit and tie, with a matching fedora. He rapped on the glass door of Sheriff Townsend's office at the Bergen County Sheriff's Department.

"Come in, John," said Sheriff Townsend, "how did you make out?"

"Very good, Justin, we've come up with some promising leads." The detective sat in the chair facing the sheriff's desk and opened his briefcase on his lap. "As we discussed, I scoured cold case files of missing girls, sixteen to eighteen years old, who went missing in the mid-1990s."

"I'm guessing that wasn't a small number."

"No," Detective Carter lowered his eyes and shook his head, "sadly not. However, we narrowed it down to girls from the Northeast. Then we sorted them, looking for girls matching Eileen Delaney's height, weight, and physical attributes."

The sheriff folded his arms. "What did you find?"

The detective pulled out a few files from his briefcase. Each one contained a photo of a girl with her identifying information in a clear plastic folder, each representing some family's worst nightmare. "We found these five solid leads, but I've got my money on this one." He pulled out one of the files and laid it on the sheriff's desk.

The sheriff picked up the folder and stared at the yearbook photo of a young girl from rural New Hampshire, Elsa Johansson.

"Following her disappearance, her mother was relentless in getting the word out to local news organizations and organizing searches. In the late summer of 1995, there were reported sightings of the girl in Springfield, Massachusetts; Waterbury, Connecticut; and Paramus, New Jersey. And then they stopped. The case went cold."

The sheriff's eyebrows raised. "And you believe this is the girl in the quarry?"

"Well, we can't be sure, but there's a chance. We reached out to the police department in New Hampshire and got in touch with the detective who worked the case back in 1995. His name is Nate Foster. He's retired now, but he still does consulting work. He seemed interested when I contacted him. He became close with the family, and it took a toll on him when the case went cold. He considered it a personal failure. He agreed to facilitate getting the local police to provide materials that would allow us to either definitively identify this girl or rule her out, as the case may be."

"And where do we stand on that?"

"We're waiting for them to get back to us," the detective responded.

"Good work, John. Keep me informed."

"Will do." The detective stuffed the files into his briefcase, shook hands with the sheriff, and left.

✳✳✳

Gavin Schictman paced the floor of the grand jury room, one hand gripping the other wrist behind his back. His hair was coiffed and pasted to the side of his head with mousse. That, and the near-uniform appearance of his skin tone, rendered by some cosmetic base product, gave him a cadaveric appearance.

Twenty-three pairs of eyes watched as he delivered his opening monologue.

"Ladies and gentlemen, I have reconvened this grand jury in the case of the State of New Jersey vs. Jack Monroe. You are aware of the technicality which required Judge Moody to dismiss the charges." Schictman paused to take measure of the jurors and make sure they were paying attention.

He pointed his finger to the ceiling and raised the volume of his voice. "Rather than providing resolution of this case, we are presented with more questions, and the possibility of criminal activity more sinister than originally conceived." He picked up a glass of water from the table and took a drink. As he did so, his mouse-like eyes peered over the glass at the jurors. "It is our contention that Jack Monroe is not only a murderer, but perhaps a double murderer. Consider the facts of the case. Eileen Delaney, Jack Monroe's girlfriend, disappears after having a witnessed altercation with Mr. Monroe. He admitted such in his own words. For several days afterward he was not seen. Then he returned, bearing multiple scratches and bruises."

Schictman turned to face the jurors whose attention he had captivated. All but two seemed riveted by what he was saying.

Schictman continued. "Now, years later, Ms. Delaney's automobile is found submerged in a rock quarry with an as-yet unknown female decedent. But who would have had access to her car? Consider this possibility. Jack Monroe caught up with Ms. Delaney as she sought refuge from him. He became enraged, and at some point, murdered her and disposed of her body. Perhaps the other girl was witness to the murder, and Monroe felt the need to get rid of her, along with Eileen Delaney's vintage Ford Mustang. Or perhaps Jack Monroe is just a murderous psychopath. We still have the fact that Jack Monroe's fishing knife was determined definitively to be the weapon used to murder the girl found in the quarry. His high school ring was found on her finger."

Schictman, ever the showman, removed his suit jacket and sat on the table facing the jurors. He crossed his legs like Mr. Rogers sitting down for storytime in the neighborhood. "In summary, I ask you all to search your hearts and minds, and determine whether the new developments in this case make Jack Monroe less dangerous to society or more so. Remember, he will have every opportunity to prove his innocence. All we ask of you is to return an indictment so that we can get to the bottom of this sordid mess."

***

It was 11:50 p.m. Seamus Callanan walked along the cobblestones of Hull Street, using his cane for balance. The gas lanterns flickered against the midnight blue sky, casting ghastly shadows in ever-changing patterns. Down the block, directly in front of him, the steeple of the Old North Church towered above. Gone were the lanterns which guided Paul Revere on his midnight ride, the only light coming from the ground-mounted spot lamps illuminating the building's exterior.

Callanan ascended the brick steps and passed through the wrought-iron gates into the Copp's Hill Burying Ground. He passed the thin, arched stones of long-deceased patriots keeping ghostly vigil over Boston's North End. There was a dank, stale smell of dew and moss. The stones, worn by centuries of wind and rain, were barely legible. Some were worn completely flat, the names of those buried below long erased. They were adorned with carvings of skulls and crossed bones, angel wings, and other gothic ornamentation.

Callanan walked to the southeastern corner of the graveyard. A rectangular brick crypt sat above ground, topped by a capstone with an embedded bronze plaque. Individual stones marked the graves of Increase and Cotton Mather, the Puritan ministers who presided over the horrors of the witch trials in Salem.

Callanan checked his watch. It was 11:58 p.m. A quiet solitude blanketed the grounds. The only sound, slowly gaining in amplitude, was the clicking of heels on the brick walk. A man approached from the opposite direction, wearing a long dark slicker, his head down, covered with a hood. He walked up and stood next to Callanan.

"Good evening, Mason," Callanan said.

Mason nodded. "Seamus."

"Were you followed?"

"No."

"Anyone know you're here?"

"No."

"Good."

"There's a shit storm brewing, Mason, and I want to make sure that when it hits the fan, we're not standing in front of it. Do you follow me?"

"I think so."

"Good. You and I have had a good thing going these many years. We've gotten rich from our joint enterprise." Callanan looked at Mason. "I couldn't begin to guess how many kilos of fentanyl have come through the Port of Boston, tucked inside your ceramic Chinese lamps. I've got to hand it to you, Mason, that was a stroke of genius, sealing the powder inside the ceramic, where no dog's nose can sniff it."

Mason shifted back and forth on his feet. "Yes, you're right, Seamus. It's been good for both of us." He paused, fumbling with the words. "Perhaps we've made enough money." Mason paced frenetically, his pulse quickening. "Now, as a United States senator, everything I do is carefully scrutinized. I was thinking maybe we should get out, while the getting's good."

Seamus let out a deep belly laugh. "Bollocks! Enough and money are two words never to be uttered in the same sentence, Mason."

"Senior members of my party are lobbying, behind closed doors, to position me as the likely VP choice. I can't risk a scandal."

Callanan turned toward Hollingsworth and grabbed his upper arm, digging his nails into the flesh. His smile evaporated and he clenched his teeth. "Let's not forget who put you there, Mason. While you were enjoying the sweet, hoity-toity trappings of privilege, I was rotting away in a cold, dank cell in Hazelton." Callanan spit the words out, foaming at the mouth. He tugged on Mason's shoulder.

Mason flinched, turning his face away from the spittle spraying from Callanan's mouth. His chest was pounding as he leaned away, cowering.

"I lost my goddamned eye, and the use of my leg. I could have gotten a lighter sentence if I'd given up your name," he tugged again at Mason's coat, "but I didn't. I suspect it's not too late. Now, I expect some loyalty, my friend. Do we understand each other?"

Mason nodded. "Yes, take it easy, Seamus. I'm sorry. Forget I said it. We'll just have to tread carefully."

"Good," Callanan released his grip on Mason's arm and gave him a single pat on the shoulder. "Our first order of business is to find this McCarthy girl, and get rid of her."

Mason winced. "Is that necessary, Seamus? It's been twenty-five years, and she hasn't said anything. We don't know for sure she's alive. Why would she be a threat to us now?"

"Because, Mason, as long as we thought she was dead, she had nothing to worry about. But with all of the publicity, she will know that we know that she didn't die in that quarry. That knowledge will make her desperate, and desperate people do desperate things. Her only chance at security would be if we were to die, or go to prison, and I intend to make damned sure that neither of those things happen."

"Twenty-five years ago, in that warehouse, you were a state senator. She had no clue who you were. But that's changed now. You're a U.S. senator and possibly, soon to be vice president. Your face is going to get a lot of airtime. She may put two and two together. And we can't afford for that to happen."

Callanan moved forward until he was nose to nose with Hollingsworth. "We are in this together, Mason. Thick as thieves, we are. The girl must die."

Mason swallowed, a lump in his throat. "How will you find her?"

"You just leave that to me. All you need to worry about is keeping that flow of Chinese lamps coming."

CHAPTER 32

Friday, June 12, 2020

Jack drove his car through the stone-arched gateway into the Hackensack Cemetery. He navigated to his family's marker under the dense canopy of maple trees and parked. Connie leaned over toward him. She wore no lipstick, and her unadorned lips were a dusty rose color. She put her hand on Jack's cheek and pressed those lips to his, which sent an electric tingle up his spine.

"Thanks, Connie," Jack said.

"You don't have to thank me for kissing you."

"No, I meant for coming with me to plant flowers."

"Oh," she laughed, "I'm happy to." She moved back to her original position on the seat. "So, when do you think you'll go back to work?"

"I haven't given it much thought. I have to reapply for privileges."

"Because I was thinking," Connie took his hand, "since I'm off on summer break, we can spend some time together. Maybe go to the shore, or the lake house."

Jack's mind drifted back through the years to those days in Sea Girt on the hammock together. He imagined Connie in her bikini, the smell of coconut on her skin. "That's a great idea," he said, nodding.

They got out of the car, retrieving their supplies from the trunk. Jack filled a bucket of water from a faucet near the car path. He went back to the stone and started scrubbing the pollen and green moss off using a brush. Connie, with gloved hands, pulled weeds from the beds in front of the stones.

"Your mom was a nice lady," Connie said.

"She liked you too."

"You're just saying that."

"No. It's true." He stopped scrubbing and looked at her. "She told me one time she thought you and I were good together."

Connie looked at the stone and smiled. "She was right."

Connie finished pulling the weeds and began planting the flowers. Jack used hand shears to trim down the evergreen shrubs on either side of the stone. When they had finished, they stood side by side and admired their work. Connie put her arm around Jack's waist.

"It looks nice," Connie said.

"Yeah," Jack nodded, "it does. Thank you."

Connie spun around to face Jack, putting both arms around his waist and pulling him close. "What's my reward?"

Jack rested his chin on top of her head. "Why don't we get away for the weekend, to the shore?"

"Could we?" Connie's face lit up. "I would love that, Jack. When can we go?"

"Right now. We'll stop and grab our things."

They loaded their equipment and garbage bag into the car's trunk. Jack drove around the circular path to exit the cemetery. He looked over his right shoulder where Eileen's parents' stone was located. He caught a glimpse of it, then jammed his foot on the brake. The seat belts locked as their torsos slammed against them.

"I'm sorry." Jack jumped out of the car and rushed with a long stride toward the stone. He stopped a few feet in front of it. Connie came running up behind him.

"What's wrong, Jack?"

The stone was clean. The vines and the green moss were gone. On top of the stone sat a single, white, long-stemmed rose.

"Nothing." Jack shook his head, gulping. "It's Eileen's parents' stone." He put his arm around her. He twisted his head, scanning the cemetery. "I thought we might tidy it up, but it looks like somebody's already done that."

"You're so thoughtful, Jack. That's one of the things I admire about you."

Jack stared off into the distance.

***

Detective John Carter leaned against a pillar near Gate 6, Terminal C, at Newark Liberty International Airport. United Flight 3407 from Manchester had just landed. The passengers were slowly filing out of the jetway, bags and strollers in tow. A thin man in a gray suit, bald on top with narrow-set eyes, walked forward carrying a briefcase and pulling a small suitcase.

Detective Carter recognized the man from the photo he'd received. As the man approached, he extended his hand.

"Nate Foster?"

"I am," he said. "You must be John Carter."

"Yes, sir, pleased to meet you. Thank you for making the trip," Carter said.

"I didn't want to chance the items getting lost, so I thought it best to hand-deliver them."

"Probably a wise decision."

"I've got my car in the short-term lot," Carter said, "we can go straight to the Medical Examiner's office."

Nate Foster extended his arm. "Lead the way."

They exited the airport and took Route 78 West toward the Garden State Parkway.

"So, you were the original detective on this Johansson case?" Carter asked.

"That's correct. It's a sad story, but unfortunately not unique. Elsa Johansson was a girl who struggled in school, didn't really have a lot of friends, and was bullied."

"Seems to be a common thread with runaways," Carter said.

"Sadly so," Nate Foster continued. "She came from a wonderful family. It didn't make any sense. For twenty years I searched for her. It was like she became part of my own family."

"Did you ever get close to finding her?"

"Initially we tracked her through sightings in Connecticut, New York, and New Jersey, but then the case went cold."

John Carter shook his head. "It must be heart-wrenching to watch a family go through that. Watching the years of your own life go by without that family member, and thinking of all the things she missed out on."

"Oh, it's horrible. Just horrible. It tore the family apart." Nate Foster stared out the window.

They exited the parkway onto Oradell Avenue and shortly thereafter pulled into the parking lot off East Ridgewood Road. The Bergen County Medical Examiner's office was perhaps the least impressive government building ever built. It was a small, one-story, featureless brick building with a flat roof and multiple air-handling units on top, slightly larger than a Dairy Queen.

But Dairy Queen it was not. That was evident the moment one's nose crossed the threshold into the building, and was assaulted by the stench of formaldehyde and chemical cleansers. They checked in at the desk and the receptionist called the Medical Examiner.

A few minutes later they were greeted by Dr. Robert Perry, who had tousled brown hair, downturned eyes, and an infectious smile. His mustache, of medium size, was well trimmed. He looked like a cross between Edgar Allan Poe and Gomez Addams, to such extent that you almost expected him to lunge at you with a foil.

"Welcome, gentlemen," he said. "What have you brought, Detective Foster?"

"A few things." Foster placed his briefcase onto a table and opened it. "We have dental records on CD discs, with a written report. We have DNA samples from three family members, and for good measure, we threw in chest X-rays from when she was twelve and caught pneumonia."

"So far, we've had no luck in extracting DNA from the skeleton in the quarry," Perry said, "but follow me, we can take a look at the other items." He led them back into the autopsy suite.

Detective Foster wasn't ready for what he would see. On a slab was a barely recognizable body of a woman burned in a house fire, with a fetid musky stench of decaying flesh and pseudomonas. Foster heaved and covered his mouth, the sour taste of stomach acid regurgitating up his throat. He turned away.

In the far corner, a table labeled *Girl in the quarry* had a human skeleton laid out upon it.

"May I see those dental X-rays, Detective Foster?"

"Certainly." Nate Foster slowly regained his composure and pulled a CD out of his briefcase. He handed it to Dr. Perry, who removed the sleeve and popped it into his computer. The mirrored images appeared on the LCD screen on the wall.

"Eureka!" Perry said, his perpetual smile growing larger.

"What is it, Doc?" Detective Carter asked.

"Look there," he pointed to the screen on the wall. "You see those bright white areas on the teeth?"

"Yes."

"Those are silver fillings. I won't bore you with the standard numbering system for teeth used by dentists, but there are fillings in the teeth numbered two, eighteen, and thirty." Dr. Perry walked over to the autopsy table and opened the jaw on the skull. "Look here," he pointed with his pencil. "I previously noted in my report that there are fillings in teeth two and eighteen. And in tooth thirty, we see a hole where a filling used to be. It must have fallen out."

"Incredible," Carter said.

"Detective Foster, can I see that chest X-ray?"

"Of course." He dug through the items in his briefcase and pulled out a manila envelope.

Dr. Perry removed the X-ray from the envelope and stuck it into the clip of the illuminated reading box. "Ah-ha!" He clenched his fist and swung it in front of his chest. He pointed to the base of the neck. "Do you see this small extra rib here?"

The detectives gathered closer. Nate Foster squinted, looking at the image.

"That's abnormal. It's called a cervical rib, and is found in 0.5-1.0 percent of the population." He moved to the skeleton on the table and pointed. "And voila, here it is."

The detectives stood impressed by what they had just learned. Carter spoke first. "This sounds convincing to me."

"Indeed, Detective," Perry said. "We will do some in-depth metric testing of the sizes and geometric configurations of the ribs, scapula, vertebrae, and other bony structures, for confirmation. But it is my opinion that, without a shadow of doubt, you are looking at the skeletal remains of Elsa Johansson." Foster bowed his head and removed his glasses, wiping a tear from his eye.

***

Jack left the Hackensack Cemetery and passed the ramp for Route 4 East. Connie watched as they passed the exit and asked, "Hey, Jack, where are we going?"

"Sorry, just one more stop. Mik wanted me to stop by so he could check my car."

"What's he, a mechanic now?"

"No," Jack laughed, "he thinks the FBI may be tracking my car."

Connie looked out the window and closed her eyes as the breeze blew onto her face. "How come you didn't get a convertible?"

"What do you mean?"

"A car where you can put the roof down."

Jack grinned. "I know what a convertible is, Connie. I meant, why do you ask?"

"I don't know. It would be nice."

"I suppose. I never thought about it."

"Well, you should. With those cute sunglasses and a convertible, you'd be a chick magnet."

Jack winced. "They're not cute, they're..." his voice trailed off, "manly." He took the glasses off and looked at them. "And besides..." He took her hand. "What do I need with a magnet when I've got you?"

Mik lived on Second Street, in Oradell, in a beautiful brick specimen of upscale suburban housing. He was waiting in a lawn chair in his front yard sipping a coffee.

Jack pulled into the driveway, and they got out.

"Hey, Mik," Connie waved.

"Hi, Connie."

"You guys want coffee?"

"Nah, thanks anyway," Jack said, "we're gonna head down to the shore for the weekend."

"Awesome. That should be fun," Mik said. "This won't take long. Pop the hood and trunk."

Jack did as Mik asked.

Mik looked under the hood, and into the engine compartment. He reached his hand down into the crevices.

"Nothing there."

He walked around to the trunk and ran his hand in the recesses along the sides. He lifted the compartment where the spare wheel was stored. He closed the hood and trunk. "Give me your keys, Jack." He took the keys and drove Jack's car onto two metal ramps in his garage. Then he grabbed a flashlight and used a creeper to slide under the car. Mik shined his flashlight. "There it is."

Jack bent down. "What is it?"

"Gimme your phone."

Jack unlocked his phone and handed it to Mik. The phone's flash went off four times under the car. Mik slid out and handed the phone to Jack. They looked at the photos.

"What is it?" Connie asked.

"It's a GPS tracker." Mik pointed to the components. "This is the tracker, and this is the transmitter, and here is the battery pack."

"Can you remove it?" Jack asked.

"Yes," Mik said, "but that might not be wise. I'm familiar with this device. It has built-in tamper detection. Are you planning on doing anything illegal?"

"No," Jack answered.

Mik shrugged. "So, leave it. They'll get tired of tracking you, and eventually take it off. If you remove it, they'll just replace it."

"Thanks, Mik," Jack said, patting him on the shoulder, "I appreciate it." He looked at Connie. "Ready to go?"

"I'm ready," Connie replied, "see you later, Mik."

***

The waitress, a bubbly young college girl with auburn hair, wide eyes, and two dangling Kokopelli earrings, refilled Connie's glass with white wine.

"Can I bring you guys coffee, or dessert?"

"Not for me, thank you," Connie said. She looked at Jack.

"Just the bill whenever you get a chance," Jack smiled.

"This is so romantic, Jack." They sat on the porch of the Columns Restaurant in Avon-by-the-Sea. The structure, built in the Seashore Colonial Revival style in the 1880s, had a wraparound porch, with white spindled balustrades, covered by green canvas awnings. Below them, on the sidewalks of Ocean Avenue, crowds strolled in casual beach attire. And, directly across the busy road, lay the beach and the Atlantic Ocean.

"How far did we walk?"

Jack scratched his chin. "Two or three miles. Why? Do you want to Uber back?"

"No way, I love the boardwalk. It's fun to people-watch, and we could use the exercise." She glanced around. "Nothing's changed, has it?"

"A few things. I'm bummed that Key Largo's gone, but at least D'Jais is still standing. Mostly it feels the same as when we were young, cruising those beach-bar happy hours, in surf shorts and sandals."

Connie held Jack's hand as they crossed Ocean Avenue and ascended the few gray Trex steps to the boardwalk. On the west side of the street, the shops and restaurants were backlit by the orange and red sky, as the sun set behind them. They walked south with the breeze coming at them from the ocean; the surf crashing into explosions of white foam. Lazy stragglers dotted the beach, oblivious to the approach of evening.

They crossed the Shark River Inlet and passed Lake Como and decided to sit on a bench just beyond The Breakers hotel. It was a beautiful evening, and Connie snuggled up to Jack, who put his arm around her and rested his cheek against her hair. They sat like that for a while.

Connie tilted her head back and looked into Jack's eyes. "You seem far away, deep in thought."

"Do I?" Jack squinted. "I'm sorry."

"Don't be." Connie looked away. "Do you still think about her?"

Jack didn't answer right away. He looked down at his lap. "Sure, sometimes. Why do you ask?"

"Oh, come on, Jack," Connie's eyes dropped to the sand, "last Sunday I took my clothes off and got in bed with you, and you know..." she shrugged her shoulders, "I mean... we didn't..."

"Connie," Jack took both of her hands into his, "you were intoxicated. You know I would never take advantage of you in that situation. But before you start thinking I'm the perfect gentleman... you fell asleep."

"I did?"

Jack's eyebrows peaked. "Yeah."

"Oh," she giggled, staring at the waves crashing onto the shore. "Sorry." A flock of seagulls squawked overhead, swooping down to the beach to collect morsels of food left behind by the beachgoers.

Jack reached over and put his finger on Connie's chin. He gently turned her face toward his and kissed her. She reached her hands under his arms and grabbed his shoulders.

She whispered into his ear. "I'm not intoxicated now."

He pulled her close. "Well, that's good, because I haven't stopped thinking about you since that night."

The marimba ringtone on Jack's phone sounded. They leaned back on the bench. Jack rolled his eyes, then pulled out his phone and answered it.

"Hello?"

"Jack." Erin's voice came through the speaker. "Where are you?"

"I'm in Spring Lake."

"What are you doing there? Are you by yourself?"

"No," he stood up and took a step forward, "I'm with Connie."

"Hmm, you two have been spending a lot of time together." She paused. "Anyway, I'm gonna have to burst your bubble. I need you back here on Monday."

Jack clenched his teeth and winced. "Are you kidding me?"

"Wish I was. Ready for round two? The dark lord strikes again."

Jack let out a sigh. "What's that jerk's problem?"

"He's got nothing, Jack. I'm gonna bury him. So, I need you at the courthouse, Monday at 10:30 a.m. Don't be late. And do not, under any circumstance, show up in that ridiculous outfit. Got it?"

"I'll be there."

"Without the outfit?"

"Yes," he shouted, then hung up the phone.

"That didn't sound good," Connie said. She stood up and put her hand on Jack's shoulder.

"I've got to be back in court on Monday."

"Don't worry, Jack. You have a great lawyer, and you have the truth on your side."

Jack nodded. "Yeah... nothing I can do about it."

Connie took his hand and hugged him. "Let's go back to the inn and relax in those rocking chairs on the porch, and later we can..." she kissed him on the cheek, then whispered in his ear, "you know..."

They walked back on the boardwalk and took a right on Salem Avenue. The Spring Lake Inn was a lovely three-story bed-and-breakfast. The exterior had red plank siding with white trim, capped with a Dutch gambrel roof. Striped canvas awnings hung down covering the porch.

Jack went inside and grabbed a bottle of iced tea and two glasses from the proprietor Andy, an affable gentleman with salt-and-pepper hair. He and his wife had owned the B&B for many years. It was one of Jack's favorite getaways. Jack rejoined Connie on the Victorian porch, where they sat in large wicker rockers, amidst flowering potted plants. The salty smell of the air wafted down with the breeze from the overhead ceiling fans, slowly rotating.

The conversation focused on memories from their youth at the shore, and of their friends' various exploits. The time passed comfortably as they sat and laughed together. Until Connie started fidgeting in her chair, holding her belly. She switched positions several times, which Jack noticed.

"Are you okay?" he asked.

"Yeah, I'm okay. My stomach is a little upset. Maybe all the olive oil, or the fish." The smile left her face, which had blanched to an ashen gray tone. She folded her arms across her abdomen.

"Are you sure?" Jack persisted.

"I don't feel good, Jack." She stood up. "Excuse me," she said as she assumed a hunched posture, and scurried through the doorway to the inn.

Jack followed, bringing in the glasses and bottle, placing them on the walnut piecrust table in the lobby. The decor was eclectic Victorian, with ornate woodwork and nautical motifs.

"Everything okay, Doc?" Andy asked. "Your girlfriend didn't look so good."

"She's got an upset stomach."

Andy reached behind the check-in desk and pulled out a bottle of Pepto-Bismol. "Maybe this will help."

Jack took the bottle. "Thank you. That's kind of you." He walked up the stairs to their room.

They were lodging in the suite called The Corner Room, whose walls were painted in soothing colors of taupe and sage with white moldings. The antique bed frame rested against a wall whose upper portion sloped inward, following the roofline. Rumpled on the mint green quilt lay Connie's black bikini from the beach earlier that day.

"Connie," Jack called out.

"In here," Connie responded from the bathroom.

"Andy gave us Pepto-Bismol if you need it."

"Thanks," she said, a subtle groan in her voice.

"Can I do anything?" Jack asked.

"No, thank you. I'm really sorry. I have a weak stomach. This happens sometimes when I eat out."

"Okay. Well, I'm here if you need me."

"Actually, Jack, this is embarrassing. Could I have a little privacy for an hour or so?" She let out a groan. "I'm so sorry I've wrecked our plans again."

"You didn't wreck anything. I guess I can take a walk over to the Parker House. A lot of our friends have places down here. Maybe I'll run into somebody." He turned to leave then paused. "I love you. Give me a call if you need anything."

"Thanks, I'm so sorry."

"Nothing to be sorry about."

***

Jack walked six blocks south down First Avenue and across Wreck Pond, to the corner of Beacon Street. The Parker House was an imposing green and white building, which rose two stories above the terrace. It was built in 1878, in the same architectural style as the Columns, only grander. As Jack approached, there were people milling about outside in upscale casual attire, holding cocktails and waiting for their tables.

From a grassy plateau at sidewalk level, white plank steps with a white wooden railing ascended up to the first-floor wraparound porch. Red and white flowers lined the breakaway wall under the porch. Jack walked up the stairs into the building, passing patrons dining on the terrace under slowly turning ceiling fans. Aromas of grilled peppercorn steaks and freshly caught seafood filled the air.

He passed through the building, and through Mediterranean-style archways to the bar area, which had a green and white checkered tile floor. He took a seat at the corner of the bar and ordered a Long Island Iced Tea. The Jimmy Buffett song *Margaritaville* played through the wall-mounted speakers.

Not long after he arrived, he saw his friend Jeff Howley, who had attended both grade school and high school with him.

"Jeff," Jack called to his friend.

Jeff Howley turned around, a grin stretched across his face. "J-a-c-k," he drew the name out in dramatic fashion, "long time, no see, buddy." They shook hands.

Howley was a rags-to-riches story. He'd parlayed a lucrative career in insurance into a fortune through the real estate boom of the 1980s, and now ran his own financial asset management company.

Jeff had an athletic build and ruddy complexion, with reddish-brown wavy hair. He would have been right at home in the Hamptons or Newport. With his infectious laugh, and effusive personality, he could sell ice to an Eskimo, and make the Eskimo feel like he got the better part of the deal.

"How are things, Jeff?"

"Couldn't be better, my friend. Life is grand."

"How's Iwonna?"

"She's fantastic. Taking it easy tonight. Went a little overboard on the sun today." He let out a cackling laugh, and grabbed Jack's shoulder. "I just came out for a cocktail... or twelve," he said, deepening his voice, "with Mathis. He's down here for the weekend." He leaned forward, speaking in a more serious tone. "I've been following the news. Unbelievable." He did a fist bump. "Everything okay?"

"I'm fine. Thanks for asking."

A few minutes later Mark Mathis entered the room. He looked over the heads of the crowd.

"Jeff, there you are," then he noticed Jack. He smiled as he approached. "Jack Monroe, as I live and breathe," he said, slapping Jack's chest with the back of his hand, "you're alive."

Mark was a slim, handsome fellow. One of Jack's medical school classmates, a dermatologist with perfect skin.

"Great to see you, Mark." They shook hands.

A tall woman with a floppy straw hat and dark sunglasses surreptitiously slipped onto the barstool next to Jack. She wore white J.Crew shorts and a sleeveless turquoise top which exposed a small portion of her firm abdomen. She sipped a tropical cocktail adorned with a cherry and a slice of pineapple. Jack didn't notice the woman as his back was to her. But Jeff and Mark both eyed the gorgeous blonde, with her long pale athletic legs which she had crossed, as she sat on the barstool.

The music changed speed as Eric Clapton's *Wonderful Tonight* started. The woman put her drink down, then leaned over, her lips near Jack's ear.

"Dance with me," she whispered.

Jack, caught off guard, spun his head around to face the woman. It took a split second because of her disguise, but through it, Jack recognized Special Agent Katie Creighton. In ditching the black suit for shore attire, her transformation was stunning. He turned back toward his friends. "Excuse me, fellas," he said as he got up to walk to the dance floor. Agent Creighton followed and put her arms around him. Jack reciprocated and they started swaying to the slow rhythm of Clapton's melody. Mathis stood with his hands on his hips, his mouth open. Howley looked at Jack with wide eyes and a smirk. He put his palms up, mouthing the words, "What the hell?"

"To what do I owe the pleasure, Agent Creighton?"

"You're being followed," she whispered.

"Yes, I know. But doesn't it defeat the purpose if you tell me?"

"Not by me," she huffed, putting her lips closer to his ear. "Well yes, by me... but by others."

"Who?"

She looked around the room, making sure nobody was listening. "Guys you don't want to meet. Irish mob."

Jack's face stiffened. His heart seemed to skip a beat. He put his mouth close to her ear. "What would the Irish mob want with me?"

"They may believe your ex-girlfriend is alive, and hope you might lead them to her."

"But I haven't seen Eileen Delaney in twenty-five years."

"Well, maybe they don't know that."

Jack swallowed hard. "Am I in danger?" Then panic seized him. He froze. "Wait, is my girlfriend in danger? She's at the Spring Lake Inn."

"We know, we've got a man there now. She's safe."

"What should I do?"

"Nothing. Relax. Act as if nothing is wrong and go about your business. We believe Ms. Delaney, if alive, may hold the key to an ongoing Bureau investigation out of Boston. Needless to say, if she were to contact you, we need to know immediately."

The song was ending. They stopped dancing momentarily, but then another slow song followed. It was Percy Sledge belting out *When a Man Loves a Woman*. Agent Creighton put her arms back around Jack and rested her head on his shoulder.

"Is there more?" Jack asked.

Katie Creighton slowly shook her head. "No."

Jack's eyebrows rose. He hesitated then replaced his hands on Creighton's back, and they slow danced quietly until the song ended.

"Thanks for the dance," she said, then kissed him on the cheek. "That's to bolster the ruse, for the benefit of your drooling friends." The kiss surprised Jack, with a jolt of static electricity. She whispered in his ear, "you'll be hearing from us soon." She stuffed a card in his front pocket, carefully pushing it all the way to the bottom, and made her way toward the door.

Jack walked back, pulled a few twenties out of his wallet, and dropped them on the granite bar top.

"Okay! What the hell just happened?" Jeff said.

"Man, he's still got it! The perpetual bachelor," Mark added, bobbing his head. "You've gotta love the Jersey shore."

Jack shrugged. "Gotta run, guys, I'll see you around." He followed Agent Creighton out, under the archway. He caught up to her, as she stood waiting on the terrace. She turned and faced him. "It's too bad you have a girlfriend waiting, Jack. It's a beautiful night for a walk on the beach." She reached up and straightened the collar on his shirt. "Let me know if that ever changes." She turned and walked down the stairs.

CHAPTER 33

Saturday, June 13, 2020

Seamus Callanan sat in a booth at J.J. Foley's Irish Pub in Boston's South End. He looked at his watch, then waved to the waitress with red hair and freckles as she glanced at his table.

"Another Guinness, Mr. Callanan?"

"No, young lady, I'll have a Jameson."

"Certainly, sir."

Derrick arrived, looked around the room, and spotted Callanan in the back. He squeezed past crowded tables and dropped into the dark wood booth across from Callanan. Lively Irish music played in the background amid raucous laughter and conversation.

"I've been waiting patiently, Derrick, for the names of the incompetent screwups who bollixed things at the quarry. Have you got them?"

"Aye, Seamus."

"Go on, then."

Derrick leaned forward and looked around the room. He spoke softly. "It was Sean O'Reilly and Patty McKellen."

"I'll need to make an example of them. I want you to arrange a meeting at our usual place of business. And have a boat ready. They'll not be needin' a change of clothing."

"There's a small problem, Seamus."

"Problem? I hate the word, Derrick."

"We can bring you Sean, alright, but McKellen is in the middle of a fifteen-year stint at MCI-Concord."

"I believe we have some men at Concord," Callanan said.

"We do."

"Well then, we don't have a problem, do we?" The waitress returned with the Jameson. Seamus took a sip. "I want this dealt with, Derrick. I'm sure you understand, I don't want to have to say it again."

"No, Seamus, I'll take care of it."

"And what about the ex-boyfriend in New Jersey? Do you think she'll contact him?"

"That's anyone's guess, Seamus. We've got people trailing him. The only sensitive issue is that his current girlfriend could pose a problem."

"There's that damned word again, Derrick. And why would that be?"

"He's dating the daughter of Jimmy Gigante, boss of the Collazzo family. Jersey Mafia."

"Tread carefully, Derrick. We don't need to be stirring up trouble with the Dagos."

***

Lars Johansson shuffled up the gravel shoulder of the country road with a slow, plodding gait. In one hand he held a dozen freshly cut white roses. The other hand held his daughter Lisa's arm to maintain his balance. There was a small upward gradient, making the trek difficult, and he panted as he walked. Sweat dripped from his brow.

Off in the distance, the majestic White Mountains kept their vigil under a presently overcast sky, while the lives of the people of New Hampshire played out beneath them. Lisa Johansson tried hard not to cry for the sake of her father. He'd been through enough and needed her to be strong, but her best effort failed. The quivering of her lips gradually increased in amplitude; her eyes grew red and irritated as the tears slowly fell, like drips from a leaky faucet. They approached the old stone stairway which ascended thirty feet to the western edge of the Madonna of the Mountain Cemetery.

Several generations of Johanssons shared this final secluded resting place. At the top of the stairs there was a clearing among the pines, and a moss-covered brick walkway, worn smooth by two and a half centuries of rain and snow.

"Watch your step, Dad," Lisa said, bracing her father's back with her palm. They slowly meandered down the path past the older thin granite slabs with semicircular tops and gothic engravings. Some fifty yards down the walk, they came upon a spot in the shade of a massive red maple. Below it lay a newer rectangular gravestone. Freshly turned soil, of reddish clay, sat in an oblong mound before the stone, a few inches above the surrounding grass.

The inscription on the stone read: **JOHANSSON**, in large capital letters. Underneath in smaller letters: **ANNA**, and the dates July 11, 1951 - June 7, 2020.

Lisa broke down in tears. "Why did she have to die, Dad? Why now?" She squatted in front of the grave, burying her face in her hands. "So close to learning the truth about what happened to Elsa." Her sobbing became louder, her chest heaving every few breaths.

The roles reversed as Lars bent and hugged his daughter. "Your mother went to her rest with hope, Lisa. Perhaps God wanted it that way. And now..." Lars choked up and started to cry, "now she's with Elsa in Heaven. And soon, Elsa's remains will be back here, with your mother, where they belong."

They both looked up when a large, barred owl, perched on a branch above them, began to make hooting sounds, its dark round eyes staring down at them.

***

MCI-Concord, the oldest prison in Massachusetts, was a dank, hopeless place holding some of the commonwealth's most dangerous and dysfunctional citizens. Patrick McKellen stayed out of trouble. He followed rules and tried not to make enemies. His behavior during his incarceration had earned him certain privileges, including a job working in the laundry facility in the basement, as opposed to some of the less desirable jobs assigned to inmates.

Aiden Gallagher and Connor Doyle were doomed from an early age. Aiden's father died when he was two years old. Connor wished he was so lucky. His father, a raging alcoholic and frequently unemployed longshoreman, beat him with clock-like regularity.

Both had turned to crime, starting with petty theft as youngsters, recruited by the Clan Kilkenny. Later, as they grew into teenagers and young adults, they put their sinewy muscles to use, beating the crap out of people who owed money to the loan sharks. One of the beatings got out of hand, and the debtor died. Unfortunately, the young man was the son of a prominent judge with political connections. Gallagher and Doyle were currently serving life without parole.

Gallagher dipped his mop into the bucket and dragged its wet strands across the floor. He pushed it back and forth, inching his way down the hall. He glanced up to see CO John Hoffman standing near the metal door leading to the stairway to the laundry. Hoffman looked at him and gave a subtle nod. Hoffman had been deeply in debt when Callanan first approached him and offered him cash for certain services. Over the years, this arrangement had proved mutually beneficial.

Gallagher looked back down the corridor and gave a faint whistle. Doyle popped his head around the corner and hustled down the hallway carrying his broom.

They waited for Hoffman to go into the guard room.

"Let's go," Gallagher said. He and Doyle scurried to the metal door. Gallagher turned the handle and smiled, as it opened. They crept down the dark stone stairwell, pushing away cobwebs, and stepping softly to avoid making noise.

At the bottom of the stairwell was a door with a window. Gallagher put his finger to his mouth. "Shhh," he whispered. He checked the doorknob, turning it ever so slightly to make sure it would open. They looked through the window and saw Patty folding laundry and putting the garments onto a wheeled cart. He was alone. They gently opened the door and waved to him. He looked back, confused. Gallagher, again, put his finger up to his mouth.

He whispered, "Patty, we're breaking out, are you with us?"

Patty looked around, and slowly walked over to where Doyle and Gallagher crouched behind a laundry cart.

"What are you talking about?"

"A hidden tunnel, into a ventilation shaft."

Patty shook his head. "No way. I've got four years left."

"Four years is a long time," Gallagher said, "your choice. We haven't got all day."

"If we're caught, they'll tack on five years." He shook his head. "No thanks, count me out."

As Patty McKellen turned to look around the room, Gallagher grabbed him from behind and covered his mouth with his hand. Doyle pulled out a four-inch steel shank and began repeatedly plunging it into Patty's abdomen. McKellen struggled fiercely, but with each rapid thrust of the blade, his fight became weaker. An ever-expanding bloodstain soaked the front of his khaki prison shirt. It started to drip onto the floor.

Gallagher whispered into McKellen's ear. "Easy now, Patty, nothing personal. You'll be home soon, out of this shithole." Patty's arms went limp. His eyes assumed a glassy, glazed look as the life drained out of them.

Doyle looked down and he was covered with blood. "Christ, what a fucking mess."

"Over there," Gallagher pointed to an empty laundry cart. They dumped McKellen into the cart and covered him with stacks of towels. They removed their own bloody clothes, washed their hands in the stainless-steel sink, and put fresh clothes on. They quietly slipped out the door they had entered.

***

The *Finnegan's Wake* bobbed up and down with the surf just outside Boston Harbor. Seamus Callanan sat in his leather captain's chair eating a pastrami sandwich. "How long before that sedative wears off, Derrick?"

"It should have done by now, Seamus." Seamus got up, hobbled to the refrigerator and grabbed a Guinness. He returned to his chair. Soon after, Sean O'Reilly started to groan, coughing and sputtering. Derrick leaned over and began smacking his face back and forth. "Wake up, Sean," he said.

Sean's eyes opened and he looked around, still groggy from the drug. "Where am I? What's happening?"

Seamus walked over as he took the last bite of his pastrami sandwich. "Twenty-five years ago, I sent you to New Jersey to dispose of the little bitch who sent me to prison. You said the job was done, but now we've come to find out that you killed the wrong girl."

Sean looked down and saw the shackles and the bucket of cement. He started to tug furiously at the zip tie around his wrists. "Please, Seamus! I'll find the girl. Please, give me a chance!"

"You know I can't do that, Sean. My authority, and ability to lead this organization, will come into question. You bollixed it. No second chances."

Seamus looked at Derrick. "Off with him."

Sean screamed at the top of his lungs, but in every direction lay nothing but ocean.

Derrick nodded. He grabbed Sean under his armpits and hoisted him up onto the gunwale and pushed him over the side. Sean remained horizontal, floating on his back and coughing up seawater.

Derrick slowly dragged the bucket of cement toward the side of the boat and hoisted it up to the gunwale where he balanced it with his hand. Sean started to weep spasmodically, begging for mercy. "Please, Seamus! I've got a little girl! She's just three years old!" He choked on the water between words. His tears mixed with the seawater. "Have mercy. I've got to walk her down the aisle one day."

"Oh please," Seamus spit the words out, "don't be pathetic. Kids are resilient. Your wife's a good looker, she'll remarry. Half a minute and you'll be out of your misery, and ours." He laughed. "Say hello to Richard Navagh." He looked at Derrick and nodded.

Derrick pushed the cement bucket over the side. It made a large splash. As it sank, the chain went taut. Sean's head shot upright above the surface of the water, with one final anguished scream, and then plunged downward, disappearing beneath the green and white foam.

CHAPTER 34

Monday, June 15, 2020

Judge Harlan Moody thumped his fingers on the mahogany bench. An espresso coffee from the Cafe Le Mans sat on a stone coaster bearing the Yale coat of arms. Picking up the cup to take a sip, he read the logo: *Lux et Veritas*, light and truth. It was dubious whether any light or truth was being dispensed by Gavin Schictman, yet he continued to babble on with his new theory about Dr. Monroe being a double murderer. Something about that didn't add up.

Judge Moody grimaced and looked at his watch. "Mr. Schictman, is there much more?"

"Not much, Your Honor, perhaps fifteen, twenty minutes."

"I'll allow it, but it seems that you have come up with an elaborate new theory, yet not much new in the way of evidence. Can we expect something? Anything?" The judge raised his hands.

"Yes, Your Honor. I was getting to that."

Schictman stood upright with his hands on his hips. "As we have learned, the girl discovered in the McKinley Quarry was New Hampshire runaway Elsa Johansson. Her path was traced, from when she was last seen by her parents, through several northeastern states, until she arrived in New Jersey. Archived bank records show a purchase on a credit card linked to her father's account, which was used in a convenience store."

The judge glanced at the defense table. Erin Monroe sat with her arms crossed, a disgusted frown upon her face. Jack Monroe sat next to her staring blankly. Moody felt sorry for the guy. He didn't appear the type that could murder anyone. But in his capacity as a judge, he'd been surprised at how many model citizens turned out to be sadistic animals.

"Allow me please," Schictman said as he geared up his MacBook to present an image on the LCD screen in the front of the courtroom.

Judge Moody scanned the courtroom. Seated in the back was Monroe's investigator, Mikolajczyk, who he knew to have a solid reputation. He was with the oriental guy, Wan or Wang, something like that. Gigante's daughter sat nearby. He still couldn't figure out that connection. A number of other observers were present. A woman sat off to the far left in the back wearing dark glasses and a French beret.

Schictman tapped his computer's trackpad and a map appeared on the screen, with a jagged red line drawn on it. "This is the path taken by Ms. Johansson, ascertained by reported sightings at the time. I will now show, superimposed on that map, the most direct route from the Gigantes' home on Lake Hopatcong, to Sea Girt. The path that Ms. Delaney would likely have taken that night, followed shortly thereafter by Jack Monroe."

Schictman tapped his trackpad again. A blue line traced down from the upper left in Western New Jersey southeastward toward the Jersey shore. The red line ended where it intersected the blue line.

Erin stood up. "Objection, Your Honor, speculation."

Schictman countered, "For the record, Your Honor, I said likely path, not definitive path."

"I'll allow it," Judge Moody said.

Schictman walked up to the LCD and put his finger near the point where the lines intersected. "This, we allege, is the singular location through which Eileen Delaney, Elsa Johansson, and Jack Monroe all passed that evening." He looked around the courtroom, arched his back, and thrust his finger in the air. "It is also the location of the convenience store where Elsa Johansson made her last purchase."

Erin Monroe leaned over and whispered something to her client.

Schictman strutted about in a circle, again raising his finger. "In summary, of those three individuals, Ms. Johansson is dead, Ms. Delaney, or Ms. McCarthy if you will, is presumed dead." He spun around, pointing his finger at Monroe. "And that leaves Jack Monroe."

There were a few gasps and whispered comments, then a hush descended over the courtroom. The woman with the French beret and dark glasses stood and walked around the benches toward the front of the courtroom. This drew the attention of the spectators. No one seemed to know what she was doing. The bailiff approached her from the other side. "You need to return to your seat, ma'am." He put his hand on her shoulder.

She twisted her torso, releasing his hand. "Let go of me," she said, turning to face the judge.

Judge Moody slammed down his gavel. "Order in the court. Please return to your seat, madam."

"Jack Monroe is innocent," she shouted.

"And who are you to make that determination?"

She turned her head and looked at Jack. Tears filled her eyes. She turned back toward Judge Moody. "Your Honor... I'm Eileen Delaney."

***

Gasps and groans filled the courtroom as faces registered shock and disbelief. Erin Monroe jumped out of her chair and strode, arms swinging aggressively, toward the bench. Jack Monroe sat with his mouth open, catatonic from the revelation. Tears filled his eyes as he stared at his ex-girlfriend for the first time in twenty-five years. She stared back. Her hair was light brown now, and the years had left their mark.

Schictman held his forehead, his newly hatched double murder theory dead in the water, like the vertical stern of the *Titanic*, awaiting its inevitable plunge.

The judge waved off the bailiff. "Let her be." He looked at Eileen. "Ms. Delaney, do you have any identification to verify this claim?"

Eileen shook her head. "No, sir. Not if you're looking for something that says Eileen Delaney, or Ellen McCarthy."

"I see..." Judge Moody reached down to a shelf where he had files pertinent to the case. He ruffled through a couple of folders and pulled out an eight-by-ten photo of a young Eileen Delaney. "Please step forward and remove your hat and glasses."

Eileen did as he asked.

Judge Moody looked at the photo, examining the almond-shaped green eyes atop high cheekbones, the soft nose, and the blond hair. He held the photo at arm's length, juxtaposed next to Eileen's face. The eyes were exactly the same. Her hair was brown, but near the part in her hair he could see a quarter-inch length of blond roots. She was much older, yet still an attractive woman.

Erin stepped forward and stared into the girl's face. "Eileen? Is that really you?"

Eileen wiped away her tears. "Hi, Erin." She nodded. "It's me." The two women hugged each other. Schictman folded his arms and threw his head back, blowing air through pursed lips.

The judge banged the gavel. He waited for the room to quiet. "In light of this development, I'd like to invite Ms. Delaney to take the stand and fill in some blanks for us, if there are no objections from Ms. Monroe or Mr. Schictman."

Both shook their heads.

Eileen turned and stared at Jack. His body appeared lifeless, as though just an inanimate pedestal supporting his head. His arms lay limp on the table with his hands folded. He smiled at her, half laughing, half crying.

Eileen took the stand. Schictman and Erin Monroe returned to their respective tables.

"Ms. Delaney," said Judge Moody, "perhaps you could begin by telling us what happened that night at the lake house."

"Certainly, Your Honor. But for it to make sense, I need to recount the events leading up to that night." She cleared her throat and began. "On March 15, 1991, I witnessed a murder in Boston, and testified to it in court. Afterwards, my family and I were put in the witness protection program and had been living in River Edge, New Jersey for two years under assumed identities. At that time, I met and fell in love with Jack Monroe." Jack, who was looking down at the table, looked up and their eyes met.

"I'd settled into my new identity. Then one day, I learned that the U.S. Marshal who had handled my case in Boston was found murdered. My parents and I assumed that Callanan's men had gotten to him, trying to learn my whereabouts. It would only be a matter of time before they came knocking at our door. I decided I had to run again, and my parents agreed. My father was a stubborn Irishman, and he said that he was done running and would take his chances. My mother felt the same way." The mention of her parents caused Eileen to choke up.

"It's alright, Ms. Delaney," Judge Moody said, "proceed at your own pace."

She continued. "The problem was that I loved Jack. I couldn't bear the thought of leaving and never seeing him again. So I tried to convince him to come with me. Of course it was crazy. He had no idea why I was leaving, or what I was running from, and I couldn't tell him. My parents and I maintained hope that our identities were still secret, that the U.S. Marshal hadn't given up the information. That last night at the party, I realized that I would always bring trouble to Jack's life, and that if I loved him, I had to let go."

Eileen started sobbing. "I'm sorry, Jack."

Tears welled in Jack's eyes as he listened.

"Do you need a break, Ms. Delaney?" the judge asked, giving her a moment.

Eileen shook her head. She regained her composure. "I'm alright, Your Honor." She readjusted her shawl. "And so, I hit him. It was the most difficult thing I ever had to do because what I really wanted to do was to kiss him, and to tell him how much I'd always love him."

Jack swallowed, his nose starting to run, and he had to sniff forcefully to stop it.

Connie Gigante looked at Jack, and at Eileen. The interaction between them, even at that distance, was palpable. The love was undeniably still there. She picked up her handbag and slipped out the back of the courtroom unnoticed.

"And then I left," Eileen continued. "I decided to go stay with my friend, Laura Stevens, in Sea Girt, but I never made it. Along the way I stopped for a girl who was hitchhiking along a desolate section of highway. I felt sorry for her. She was about my age and looked like she could be my sister, so I empathized with her. She told me that she'd run away from her home in New Hampshire. Elsa was her name.

"Anyway, we stopped at a convenience store for gas and soda. I went in to use the restroom. When I came out, I saw Elsa standing by my car. Then a couple of guys jumped out of a van, and shoved her into the car. I had given her the keys so she could sit in it, and put the air on."

Eileen started to cry again. "I wanted to call the police. But what could I tell them? I tried to rationalize with myself. I thought that they would figure out that they had the wrong girl at some point and let her go. All these years I had hoped that was the case, until a few weeks ago. I saw the news stories about my car being found in that quarry with a dead girl in it, and I knew." Eileen buried her face in her hands and wept.

Erin stood and raised her hand. "Your Honor, may I approach?"

"This is informal discovery, Ms. Monroe. You and Mr. Schictman may both ask Ms. Delaney any pertinent questions."

Erin walked up to the witness stand and put her hand over Eileen's hand. She gave Eileen a moment. "Eileen, do you have any idea how Elsa may have come to be wearing Jack's high school ring?"

Eileen looked up. "Yes, I do. She saw it sitting on the console of my car. I knew that I couldn't keep it. Every time I looked at it, it would remind me of Jack, so I told her she should take it. The gold content, and the gemstone, had value, and she needed money."

Schictman stood and cleared his throat. "I'm sorry, Ms. Delaney, for what you went through. But what happened next? How did you get out of there, and where have you been all this time?"

"I called my father to pick me up, and hid in the woods behind the building for about an hour, in case they came back. I told my father what had happened and he realized that I had to get out of there immediately. He called a friend who helped supply me with a new passport, money, and a plane ticket to Dublin. I didn't know if I could trust the Federal Marshals Service again after the breach that got their agent killed, and almost got me killed."

"Weren't you worried about your parents?" Erin asked.

"Of course. But my dad was a military man. Our house had been outfitted with steel doors and frames, and bulletproof glass on the first-floor windows. They'd spent a lot to make it safe. But sure, I worried about them all the time. They came to visit me in Dublin, always taking a circuitous route to avoid being followed. Until they died in a car crash some years ago. Then I was alone."

Eileen looked at the judge. "That's it, Your Honor. And when today's proceedings hit the news, I'll be on the run again."

The judge looked at her with heartfelt sympathy. "We've not asked your current identity, nor shall we. You may step down."

Eileen stepped down and walked back to her seat.

Erin rose and addressed the judge. "Your Honor, in light of Ms. Delaney's provocative testimony, I move for dismissal."

"Mr. Schictman?"

Schictman's head hung low, his skin sagged below his jawline. It was the face of defeat. He thought for a moment, then shook his head. "No objection, Your Honor."

Judge Moody slammed the gavel down. "Case is dismissed. Doctor Monroe, you are free to go."

"Thank you, Your Honor." Jack smiled and hugged Erin, lifting her off the floor. Mik and Henry joined them.

"Congratulations!" Mik said, patting Jack on the back. "I can't believe Eileen is here, risen from the dead."

"Eileen." Jack spun his head. "Where did she go?"

***

Jack scanned the back of the courtroom where Eileen had sat. The chair was empty. "She's gone." He sprinted to the door and out into the marble atrium. He looked in both directions, down the hallways. "Eileen," he yelled. His voice echoed unanswered through the marble halls.

Mik found Jack standing in the atrium. "This calls for a celebration," he said, "let's head over to the Yorkie, drinks are on me."

Jack stood with his arms folded, looking at nothing in particular. "How could she leave, Mik? We haven't seen each other in twenty-five years, and she doesn't want to talk to me?"

Mik put his hands on his hips. "I don't know, man. Look, what I do know is that she risked her life, and came out of hiding to save your ass. That took courage."

"She did, didn't she?" Jack calmed.

"And she's alive! That's the best news, right?" Mik grabbed Jack on both shoulders. "We can celebrate that as well."

Jack nodded, his eyes lighting up. "She's alive."

Erin and Henry joined them, elation on their faces.

"We're heading to the Yorkie," Mik said to them. "I called Sherlock, he's gonna join us."

"I'm in," Erin said.

"Where did Connie go?" Jack said. "I need to call her." He pulled out his iPhone and dialed the number. It rang six times and went to voicemail. Jack hung up. He forced a smile. "Okay, sure, the Yorkie."

✳✳✳

It was six o'clock when Jack's BMW rolled into his driveway. Despite the revelry at the Yorkie, Jack managed to moderate his drinking. He had a lot on his mind. Foremost, Eileen. Where was she? Was she still in the area, or had she fled, disappearing once again from his life? The memories of their days together had played in a continuous loop since he'd left the courthouse.

He sat in his car and called Connie. Again, it went to voicemail. It had to be difficult for her seeing Eileen reappear into their lives, just as things were heating up between them. He recalled the day in his office when Connie recounted how she had felt dumped. Jack felt awful about it. He could only imagine what she was thinking now.

Jack reached for the car door handle when his phone rang. On the second ring Leslie's photo appeared on the console screen. The phone continued to ring. Jack leaned back in his seat and put his hand up to his chin. On the seventh ring, it went to voicemail and Leslie's voice came through the speaker, its tone subdued.

"Hi, Jack. How are you? I, um, heard the good news and I'm happy for you. I just wanted to talk to you. Give me a call please, okay? I mean, if you want to."

Jack sat and stared at the console and Leslie's smiling photo. He pulled out his iPhone. His finger hovered over her number. He closed his eyes and let his muscles relax. After a few minutes, he refocused, shook his head, and locked his phone screen. He got out of his car and was walking around it to go to the front door when a black sedan pulled up in front of his house. The rear window opened and Jimmy Gigante's elbow rested on the car door. Jack walked over to the car.

"Mr. Gigante, what brings you here?"

Gigante extended his elbow until his hand, containing a manila envelope, pointed straight toward Jack.

Jack took the envelope. "What's this?"

"Resolution, Jack," Gigante's voice was flat and he looked tired, "long overdue." He closed the window and they drove away.

Jack looked around him. The neighborhood was quiet except for the sound of a gentle breeze ruffling the leaves on the trees. He opened the envelope and found a theater handbill from 1995, from the Teaneck Theater, advertising *The Bridges of Madison County*. He rolled it over in his hand and written on the back was a message: *Tonight 8:00 p.m., balcony, come alone.*

***

Jack didn't know what to expect as he drove from his home toward Cedar Lane. He'd considered the possibility that this could be some sort of trap. With everything that had happened recently he couldn't be sure of anything. He remembered Agent Creighton's warning about being followed. But he lived on a quiet street and when he left his home no other cars were on the road. Nevertheless, he kept vigilant. As his car descended the hill toward the business district, he passed BV Tuscany and remembered his recent dinner with Leslie. He wondered if he was being unfair for not answering her call, but shook it off. He would call her at some point, but he couldn't get past the fact that she had abandoned him when he needed her most. He wasn't angry, and held no animosity toward her. She did what she thought she had to do. But for their relationship, it was a deal breaker.

Jack started to feel the same sense of nostalgia that he had experienced on his recent drive down Cedar Lane. The sights and sounds and sensations of his childhood came vividly back to life, smothering out the present. Parking was limited near the theater, so he made a right on Beverly Avenue and parked behind the building.

Jack revisited the idea that this might be a trick by Callanan's men to lure him out. He shook his head, dismissing the thought. How could they have known about *The Bridges of Madison County*, or the Teaneck Theater? Furthermore, how would the note have gotten into Jimmy Gigante's hands? He considered that for a moment. How did it get into Gigante's hands?

Jack closed his eyes, laughing to himself about how stupid he was not to see it. It was Jimmy who helped Eileen get away after the party. While he was hiding Jack for those few days at his home in Sea Girt, he was simultaneously helping her escape to safety. It made perfect sense. Jimmy Gigante was best friends with Eileen's father. The puzzle pieces were coming together.

Jack approached the theater. The exterior bore the same art deco facade that he remembered from his childhood. It was dark, and the lights of the vintage storefronts created a nostalgic ambiance. Jack entered the lobby of the theater and immediately felt a tinge of sadness. Though the interior maintained its period art deco styling, it was tired and worn. A mustiness pervaded the space. It had lost the grandeur that it commanded in the mind's eye of his youth. Jack approached the ticket counter and was greeted by an enthusiastic young girl with glasses and shaggy brown hair.

"Can I help you, sir?" she asked.

"One ticket please."

She looked at him over the top of her glasses. "Umm, which movie, sir?"

"Oh," Jack looked at the listings, "which one is up in the balcony?"

The girl appeared confused. "Balcony? We don't really have a balcony, but there are two movies upstairs, and two downstairs."

Jack tried hard to remember where they sat that night of their first date. Jack pointed to the left staircase. "This side. What's up there?"

"That would be the re-release of *Jurassic Park*," she said. "That's probably your best bet."

Jack paid for the ticket. He climbed the stairs, with worn burgundy carpet, grabbing the iron railing as he went. He entered the dark theater where they had begun showing previews. A few scattered groups dotted the theater. Jack took a seat in the approximate location of his date twenty-seven years ago. He closed his eyes and tried to remember the details of that evening.

Twenty minutes later, a woman wearing jeans, a light blue sweatshirt with a hood, and dark glasses approached. She dropped quietly into the seat next to him.

His eyes remained closed, savoring a moment long in coming. A moment that had played out so many times in his dreams over the years. He was afraid that if he opened his eyes, he may find himself lying in his bed, in a puddle of sweat, awakening from one of those dreams.

His right hand, resting on the armrest, felt the warmth of her hand next to his. Slowly the pinky finger of her left hand wound over and around the pinky of his right hand, recreating the same gestures she had made at the fire pit the night they first met.

Jack swallowed, his throat feeling knotted. He slowly opened his eyes and let them drift downward. He watched her hand slip over the top of his own. A familiar hand, in size and shape and feeling; its fingers dropping between his.

"It's really you," he said softly, his voice choked with emotion.

"Yes."

"It's been a lifetime."

"Two," she said, "yours and mine."

"Two," he repeated, nodding.

She took her glasses off, slowly turning to face him. Her eyes still looked like emeralds shimmering in almond-shaped ponds. Small crow's feet now bordered them above each cheekbone. Her soft silky hair was blond again, peeking out from the sides of her hood.

Tears welled in Jack's eyes. "I'm sorry." He choked up, having difficulty forming the words. "I wish I had known what you'd been through. I would have gone with you."

She leaned close, her breath warm on his face. Her lips hovered near his, until slowly she kissed him, with a strangely beautiful familiarity that had not been diminished by the years. Her clean fresh scent, the taste of her mouth, and the chill of the tip of her nose against his cheek made those years evaporate in an instant.

He wrapped his arms tightly around her and pulled her in, her face still framed by the light blue fabric of the hoodie. They kissed passionately, as the crook of his elbow cradled her head, keeping them firmly locked together.

An image of Connie flashed through Jack's mind and he leaned back. A few days ago, Jack was falling in love with Connie. But now, the woman he'd always considered the love of his life was back in his life. He loved them both; but he'd spent his entire life pining for Eileen, and now here she was.

"This is surreal. When I thought you were..." the words trailed off.

He looked down. "It hit me really hard. The thought that I would never see you again. Even though I hadn't seen you in years, I felt that you were out there somewhere and that we'd meet again someday. But when the body was found in the quarry, the notion that I would be the sole keeper of our memories overwhelmed me with a feeling of loneliness."

He looked at her and smiled. "And now you're here, alive." He pulled her close again and kissed her. He rested his head on hers.

They hadn't noticed that the movie had started, nor the two men who had taken seats behind them a few rows back.

With dinosaurs and lush jungle scenery as the backdrop, Eileen recounted her story in detail. She told of her previous life as Ellen McCarthy, up to and including the fateful day at the warehouse that would change her life forever. Jack listened intently, caressing her hands when the memories became too painful.

Forty minutes passed. "I need to use the restroom," she said.

Jack nodded and stood so she could pass. As he sat back down, he glanced behind him and saw two men sitting together a few rows back. They looked at him, averting their gaze a little too quickly. One had short-cropped red hair with a mustache. A large scar on his right cheek pulled the skin taut, deforming the symmetry of his face. The other, more muscular with brown curly hair and deep-set eyes. There was something off about them.

Adult men didn't go to movies together. Unless they were... He looked at them again. No, definitely not. Not these two. Jack turned his focus to the movie, which until that point he'd not been following.

He glanced back over his shoulder. The redheaded guy had folded his arms, and Jack saw a tattoo of a shamrock on his left forearm. The other had a button-down shirt, and visible, where the top two buttons were open, hung a Celtic cross.

An electric shock ran down Jack's spine. He took a deep breath and let it out, trying to remain calm. He pulled out his phone and put it on his lap and typed out a message.

Stay calm. Don't make any rash movements. Two suspicious guys behind us. Irish. Don't look. Follow my lead when the movie ends.

Eileen returned from the restroom and sat down. She put her arm around Jack and smiled. He laid his phone on his lap with its light dimmed. He tapped her leg with his knee. She looked down at his phone. It took her a second to read it. The smile drained from her face. She inhaled deeply and let it out.

Jack spent the remainder of the movie plotting their escape. It would take luck for it to work. The pulse in Eileen's neck was visible, and pounding rapidly. As the movie ended and the credits rolled, they stood up, as if nothing was wrong, stretched, and walked down the stairs. The two men followed. Jack took Eileen's shaking hand, and they walked through the upper lobby and down the burgundy-carpeted stairway. Once they reached the first floor, instead of heading out the main entrance, they turned back and walked through the doors to the movie playing on the first floor.

Jack glanced over his shoulder. His eyes made contact with the one with the scarred face. He knew. Jack's heart thumped in his chest, his abdomen tensed.

As soon as they passed through the door and it shut, Jack pulled Eileen by the hand and started dashing down the aisle. This movie had more patrons than the one they'd just left, and people turned their heads to see what the commotion was. Along the way Jack grabbed a wide folding chair with the handicap logo stenciled on it. The two Irishmen had burst through the back door and were sprinting toward them.

As Jack and Eileen reached the emergency exit, Jack pushed open the door and threw the folding chair outside. Once he and Eileen were outside, he slammed the door, turned the folding chair upside down, and wedged it under the doorknob. He jammed the lower part forcefully against the concrete with his foot.

The doorknob turned. A loud percussive bang sounded, and the door heaved. From the other side they could hear sounds of the men kicking the door, cursing, but it held. The emergency door put them out the back close to where Jack's car was parked. They didn't have much time. It would only take a minute for the Irishmen to come around from the front.

"Run!" Jack said. "My car's over there." He pointed toward it. As they ran, Jack pulled the keys out of his pocket. The keys snagged on his clothing and sprang out of his hand. They bounced twice on the pavement, over a sewer grate.

"No! No!" he yelled. The keys slid through the hole in the grate, but the FOB was too wide to fall through. He snatched them up and pressed a button. The car's lights flashed and made a twirping sound as the doors unlocked. They jumped into his car, and Jack hit the start button. The 617-horsepower twin-turbo V8 engine roared to life. The car leapt forward, going from zero to 60 mph in seconds, through Teaneck's residential back streets.

When it was clear they'd evaded the Irishmen, Jack dropped his speed so as not to attract police attention, and drove down Queen Anne Road to the high school. He parked so he could formulate a plan. It wouldn't be safe to go home.

He thought, then remembered something. He pulled his wallet out of his pocket and rifled through it. He found

Agent Creighton's business card, on which she'd written her cell phone number back at the Parker House. He called it and she answered.

"Agent Creighton?" He spoke with urgency.

"Yes."

"It's Jack Monroe, I've got Eileen Delaney in my car. We're being followed by two Irishmen. They chased us out of a theater, but we got away. We don't know where to go."

"Jack, I'm with Agent Spath. Where are you?"

"Queen Anne Road at Teaneck High School."

"Okay, we just pulled up your location on GPS. We're not far from there. Just stay put. We'll come to you."

"Okay, please hurry."

Eileen took Jack's hand. "I'm sorry I got you involved, Jack. That's why I've stayed away all these years. I've thought about you so many times." She closed her eyes. "There's a worn, faded photo of you in your football uniform, which I keep on my bedroom nightstand. It reminds me of the only time in my life when I was happy."

"None of this is your fault, Eileen."

"Maybe it is. Maybe it would be best if I disappeared again. You could go back to your life and forget about me."

Jack took her by the shoulders. "Is that what you want? Because I've never stopped thinking about you. All these years."

She looked away, wiping a tear from her eye.

"Would you be happy?" he asked, his tone softer.

She looked up at him, slowly shaking her head.

He hugged her and her tears fell onto his neck, dripping down the front of his shirt. "The FBI will be here soon and we'll be safe." Night blanketed the town, the darkness broken by the lights from the high school, high above on the hill.

A green SUV screeched to a halt behind them. The doors popped open and the two Irishmen jumped out brandishing pistols. "Get out of the car," one of them shrieked. Jack looked in the mirror, grabbed Eileen's neck and yanked her head down to her knees.

"Stay down!" Jack yelled. He floored the gas pedal and the tires squealed as they spun, shooting loose gravel and road soot at the Irishmen's faces. When the tires grabbed hold of the pavement, the car launched forward, the G-force pinning them to their seats.

The rear window shattered as a bullet passed through the car, exiting low on the passenger side of the windshield. A spiderweb shatter pattern radiated outward from the hole. Two more bullets pinged as they hit the bumper.

The Irishmen got back in the SUV and began pursuit. Jack's BMW took a solid lead with its superior acceleration. He knew they couldn't keep up with him if he could get it to top speed. He envisioned Votee Park ahead as if it were a race track. He zoomed up the straightaway where Queen Anne Road ran along the east side of the park. In his mirror he saw the Irishmen's SUV and behind them, a black Lincoln Town Car with a blue flashing light in the windshield. Creighton and Spath.

Jack tapped the phone app button on his console display.

"Agent Creighton," he said to the Siri voice recognition software. The phone started dialing.

"Jack?" Agent Creighton's voice came through the speaker.

"Be careful. They're armed. They shot at us."

"Are you alright?"

"For now. We're gonna lap the park and get onto Route 4." Jack downshifted to make the turn onto Court Street. Another bullet crashed through the broken rear window.

"Agent Creighton?" There was silence. Jack looked for his phone. He had put it on the dashboard. The bullet had struck it.

Jack took the left turn hard and they lurched to the right. After a short drive down Court Street they reached Palisades Avenue on the west side of the park. Jack made the left and, with another long straightaway in front of them, floored the gas pedal. The car roared and shot down the road like a rocket.

The Irishmen's car trailed in the distance. "How did they find us, Jack?"

Jack hadn't had time to process that question. He clenched his fist. "Damn it! They must have tagged my car with a tracker."

"So, we can't outrun them?"

"We can outrun them, but they'll find us."

"What are we going to do?" Eileen said.

"I've got an idea," Jack said. "Call Jimmy Gigante on your phone. You've got his number?"

"Yes." Eileen pulled her phone out of her purse and dialed the number.

Agent Creighton rode shotgun in the passenger seat of the Lincoln, holding her handgun. Agent Spath was at the wheel, in close pursuit of the Irishmen's SUV. They took the turn from Court to Palisades much too fast and the car hit the curb, bouncing over the top across the railroad tracks. The car came to a stop on the tracks, the right front and left rear tires torn open.

"Are you alright?" Creighton asked.

Spath shook his head. "I'm good."

Creighton dialed Jack's number. There was no answer.

Jimmy answered on the third ring. "James Gigante."

Eileen's voice was frantic. "Mr. Gigante, it's Eileen. We're in trouble."

"Slow down, Eileen. What's going on?"

"I'm in Jack's car. We're being chased. They're shooting at us."

"Tell Jack to go to the Trinacria. Give us twenty minutes to assemble a team. Drive in circles if you have to. When you get here, leave the car in the parking lot and go around back, by the dock."

"Okay," Eileen said, "what's that name again?"

"It's my social club. Jack knows where it is."

"Got it."

***

It was 10:50 p.m. when Jack's car rolled into the driveway of the Trinacria. It was dark, the only light coming from the club itself and a few lamp posts around the perimeter. As they pulled in, Frank was waiting, holding a shotgun in one hand and waving for them to park. Two men stood nearby, each holding the upper torso of a department store manne- quin. On the roof, a fourth man holding a scoped hunting rifle watched the driveway behind them.

Jack and Eileen got out of the car. Frank waved for them to follow him around the back of the building. The other two men propped the mannequin torsos in the front seats of the BMW, topping them with hats and a blond wig for the one in the passenger seat.

"Follow me," Frank said.

As they rounded the back of the building, Jimmy Gigante stood waiting on the dock holding a pistol. "Jack, Eileen, no time for talk." He tilted his chin toward a single-engine Piper Cub seaplane floating at the end of the dock. "Get in."

"Thanks, Mr. Gigante," Jack said. They hustled down to the end of the dock. A blond-haired young man wearing black pants and a white shirt jumped out and opened the door for them. He was tall, yet still his uniform seemed too large for him. They climbed into the cramped and musty-smelling passenger compartment. The leather seats were cracked and worn.

A curtain separated where they sat from the cockpit, which was filled with buttons, dials, and LED lights. The blond kid climbed up into the pilot seat and turned toward them, smiling through thin lips. "Welcome aboard, my name's Nick." He put on a black and white captain's hat with yellow embroidery, then turned back toward the control panel and started fidgeting with the knobs and buttons. "Buckle up," he said, as the engine roared and the propeller started spinning.

Jack and Eileen looked at each other, their eyes wide. Jack turned his palms up and clenched his teeth.

"This is huge," the kid said over the drone of the engine, "one more hour and I'll reach my one thousandth hour of flying time."

"Oh, that's... wonderful," Eileen said, returning the same clenched-tooth look to Jack.

The pilot brought the plane around in a small circle and then pushed the throttle. The plane roared down the Hackensack River south toward Secaucus, and in a few minutes was airborne. The bright lights below shimmered in the night sky. As they gained altitude they could see the skyline of lower Manhattan to the east. It was cool inside the plane. Jack put his arm around Eileen as they snuggled to keep each other warm.

***

The Irishmen's SUV crept slowly down the drive to the Trinacria. They stopped halfway and proceeded on foot. Weeds poked through cracked pavement. They drew their guns.

"There they are, Shane." They crouched along the side of the building.

Shane scratched his chin. "They can't be armed, or they'd have returned fire earlier."

"What are they doing?" Connor asked.

"Just hiding, I suppose. They don't know we've got a tracker."

"Right. Let's go then." They jumped up and scurried toward the BMW, keeping low.

"Get out!" Shane yelled. But there was no movement in the car. Both had their guns pointed at the occupants. "Get the hell out," he repeated, but still there was no movement. They inched closer and looked through the windows.

"What the hell?" Connor said.

"Drop the guns!" Frank yelled in a booming voice.

They looked around and saw that they were surrounded by seven men. Five had shotguns pointed at them, and the others, handguns. They slowly bent down, placing their guns on the ground.

***

Connie lay in her bed, still wearing her clothes and shoes, under a thick comforter. Her mascara had bled all over her face and pillow. How could this be happening again? Her cheeks tugged at the corners of her mouth, as she choked back the tears. Jack loved her. She knew that. But he loved Eileen more. It was high school all over again.

She pored through the pages of her journal, which she had kept throughout her youth. Somewhere along the line, she'd stopped making entries and lost track of it. She'd recently found it buried in a dresser drawer, and reminisced while reading it; the good and the bad, and the ugly.

Her apartment suddenly felt cold and lonely, uninhabitable. She had already allowed herself the luxury of imagining a life with Jack. She'd pictured a perfect, beautiful wedding ceremony at Saint Matthew's Church. She would move into his home, and they would have beautiful children, and live happily ever after. She clutched her pillow in a fetal position. But now those dreams belonged to Eileen. She sobbed into the pillow. It was all for nothing.

***

Frank held the shotgun to Shane's back. "Hey, Bobby, get the trackers off the car and smash them."

"Sure, Frank," Bobby answered.

Frank nudged the barrel into Shane's shoulder. "You two, inside." He marched them into the building followed by four of his men. Once inside, they zip-tied the Irishmen's hands and feet and sat them at a table.

Jimmy walked over to the table eating the last bite of a cannoli. His mouth still full when he started talking. "I wanna know everything there is to know about Seamus Callanan."

Shane looked at Connor, then at Jimmy. "You'll get shite from us."

Gigante put his hands on his hips. "Well, that's unfortunate. Frank here is gonna take over. When he's through, I think you're gonna wish you would've talked to me." He grabbed a bottle of wine and a glass, then walked through the door to the dock.

Frank went to a cupboard and pulled out a bottle of Jameson and two glasses. He walked over and put them on the table, then pulled up a chair. He opened the bottle and held it over the glass. He looked at Shane.

"One finger, or two?

Shane let out a nervous laugh. "You think you can pry us with alcohol? Save it."

Frank stared at him with a blank expression. "The whiskey is for me." He looked behind Shane. "Tommy."

Tommy walked over to the table holding pruning shears.

Frank said, "I'll ask you one more time. One finger, or two."

The smile left Shane's face, his eyes opening wide as Tommy moved behind him with the shears. Tommy hooked the blade around Shane's thumb.

"Wait, wait, wait," Shane said, twisting his head to look over his shoulder.

"Tell him, Shane," Connor yelled out.

"Seamus will kill us both, don't say a fecking word, Connor."

Tommy flexed his biceps and rammed the two arms of the pruning shears together. Shane let out a bone-chilling scream as his thumb dropped to the floor. Frank took a sip of the whiskey. "Ahh, that's good." He closed his eyes and licked his lips. He looked around the room. "Who's got a pen? We've got nineteen fingers, and twenty toes left. Place your bets."

It was about 1:00 a.m. when Jimmy came back inside carrying the empty bottle of wine. He looked at the table. The two Irishmen were slumped over, faces down, silent. Most of their fingers had been reduced to bloody stumps. A couple of pasta bowls sat under their zip-tied hands to catch the blood.

Jimmy winced and gritted his teeth. "Jesus, Frank, my pasta bowls?"

"Sorry, Jimmy, it was all I could find."

Jimmy walked over and grabbed Connor by his hair, tilting his head back. His face was a purplish-blue color, and his dead eyes were bulging. Several loops of piano wire remained tied around his neck. "How did it go?"

"Good," Frank nodded, "good." He handed Jimmy a few pieces of note paper. "That's what we got out of them. I can't believe how long it took. I thought they'd cave sooner, but Tommy had 'em read." He pointed at Tommy. "He won the pool."

Tommy nodded with a satisfied look on his face.

Jimmy shook his head. "I want this mess cleaned up tonight. What projects do we have running?"

Joe piped up, "We got that parking ramp at the Meadowlands."

"Nah," Jimmy said, "too much traffic."

"What about that office project in Bayonne?" Frank said.

Jimmy pinched his chin and nodded. "That might work. Call up Carmine and tell him to get a mixer over there in an hour. Take Beans and Jags."

Jimmy clapped his hands. "Come on, guys, let's move it. Morning is coming. These spud-munchers aren't gonna move themselves."

CHAPTER 35

Tuesday, June 16, 2020

The lights of the Jersey Shore shone brightly against the blackness of the Atlantic Ocean, as the seaplane's pontoons splashed down off the coast of Manasquan. The pilot turned westward, taxiing through the Manasquan Inlet and up the river to the Brielle Yacht Club.

The marina was eerily silent as the plane approached the dock, the only sounds coming from the waves lapping against the wooden pilings and wind buffeting canvas sails and flags. The young pilot jumped from the cockpit, hooking two ropes to the fuselage, which he used to secure the plane to mooring cleats. He opened the passenger door and Jack and Eileen stepped onto the dock. Eileen folded her arms against the cool breeze.

"Now what?" Jack asked.

Nick pointed to a large sloop docked adjacent to where they stood. It had a black hull with a white stripe near the gunwale. The name on the back read *Joan's Ark*. "Mr. Gigante's boat. You'll be safe, but just in case..." He reached into his pocket and pulled out a black polymer handgun, turned it around, and handed it to Jack. "Mr. Gigante said to give you this. He'll contact you tomorrow."

Jack took the gun. *What's one more felony?* he thought.

He and Eileen walked down the dock and got onto the sailboat. They climbed below deck and turned on a lamp. Venturing forward into the master suite, they kicked their shoes off and lay down, thoroughly exhausted. Eileen put her arm around Jack and opened a button on his shirt.

Jack looked into her eyes. "I should be upfront, Eileen." He paused. "I'm dating someone."

"I've been gone a long time, Jack. I had no expectation that you'd be waiting for me." She smiled. "I half expected you to be married with three kids and a dog." She turned away, looking at the ceiling. "You don't owe me any explanation."

"It's Connie Gigante," Jack said.

Eileen nodded. "Connie's a good person. She was always nice to me."

Jack sat up. "I just thought of something. My phone is gone, and she's probably been trying to call me."

Eileen reached into her pocket and handed Jack her phone. He dialed Connie's number and after a few rings she answered, half asleep. "Hello. Who is it?"

"Connie, it's Jack."

"Jack?" The words came quickly. "Where are you? I've been calling you. Whose phone is that?"

Jack hesitated. "It's Eileen's," he said finally.

"Oh... I see," she said, her voice dropping off. "I should have seen that coming. I saw the way that you two looked at each other in the courtroom. Who am I kidding, Jack? I can't compete with that."

"No, Connie, it's not like that. I don't want to scare you, but tonight has been a living nightmare. Eileen asked me to meet to explain everything, but things went downhill fast. We were chased by two men. They shot at us! My phone was damaged, and your father helped us get away."

"Oh my God, Jack! Are you alright? Where are you?"

"I'd rather not say over the phone. Your dad can explain everything. In the meantime, I'd feel better if you'd stay at his place tonight."

"Okay, I'll go. Just be careful, Jack. I love you."

Jack looked at Eileen. He paused, then lowered his voice to a whisper. "I love you too." They hung up.

Eileen's eyes started to moisten. "My life has been a complete mess. All because of one horrible night. I lost everything. I lost my identity, I lost you, and now I've put you in danger."

Jack took her in his arms, cradling her. "It's not your fault."

"If only the jurors had believed me. They thought I was drunk and drugged, but I wasn't. I can't imagine why Amanda lied like that. It really hurt me. They must have threatened her; that's the only explanation. We witnessed a murder. I swear, I wasn't crazy. And if Callanan had been convicted of murder, he'd still be in prison. I wouldn't have to hide."

Jack pondered it. "I have an idea. I can't promise anything, but first thing in the morning, I'll call Mik and see if he'll send Henry back to Boston to dig around. Last Friday,

I learned that the FBI is investigating Callanan for narcotics trafficking again. In fact, they'd like to speak to you. But right now, we should get some rest."

Eileen laid her head on Jack's shoulder. She nudged his lips with her nose. He didn't pull away. He should have, but he didn't. Their cheeks flushed with the warmth of each other's breath. She slowly moved her lips to his, barely touching at first, then hesitated before pressing firmly. She cradled his head tightly in her hand and began kissing him, just as he had fantasized so many times in his dreams over the years. In that instant, all the lost time melted away.

***

It was 2 a.m. Frank drove the van. Billy Beans sat in the passenger seat and Kent Jagiello rode sandwiched between them. Fortunately, Jags was thin. Jagiello, a younger member of the organization, was tall and broad-shouldered with angular features and steely, aqua-blue eyes. The van slow rolled to a stop in front of the gate at the construction site. A sign read: PALERMO BROS. CONSTRUCTION, KEEP OUT!

Frank reached across Jagiello and handed Beans the keys. "Beans, get the lock."

Beans slid out of the van and unlocked the padlock on the gate. Behind them, a cement mixer with its barrel slowly rolling approached. It was dark and quiet. The moon hung low in the blue-black sky.

Frank looked in the rearview mirror. "There's Carmine, right on time." Beans jumped back in the van, and they drove to the nearest corner of the building's foundation. Large steel H-beams stood upright, like sequoias, rising out of a concrete base layer several feet below ground.

Frank did a U-turn and backed the van up to the foundation. They got out and opened the back doors. Inside were two carpet rolls, tied with piano wire.

"Let's go," Frank said. "It's late, I wanna go to bed."

Beans and Jagiello pulled the carpet rolls to the edge of the van's cargo space and let them drop to the ground with a thud. A police siren wailed on a nearby road. As it drew near, Frank pulled a handgun from his flank. They all stood still and silent until the siren retreated in the distance.

"Keep moving," Frank said. They pushed the carpet rolls off the ledge into the wood-framed hole. The rolls dropped onto the concrete base.

"Close the doors," Frank said. "I'll move the van so Carmine can get in here."

Jagiello stroked his wavy, light brown hair. "I don't know," he said, shaking his head side to side.

"What now?" Beans asked, putting his fists on his hips.

"I'm a little worried about the support."

Beans looked at him sideways. "What the hell are you talking about?"

Jags pointed to the base concrete layer below. "That's high-performance concrete. It'll take 8,000–10,000 psi of compression. You follow?"

"No. Not at all," Beans said, throwing his hands up. "Who gives a shit?" Carmine backed the cement mixer to the edge of the hole.

"These stiffs won't take 8,000 psi. I can tell you that." He put his hands in his pockets. "Engineers made calculations, and we're screwing them up."

Beans dropped his arms, a puzzled look on his face. "Will you please tell me how a *cafone* like you comes up with this shit?"

Jags put his thumb to his chest. "I'm a *cafone*?" He swatted his hand. "*Va fa'n culo*, Beans. You're the *cafone*. Some of us read, you know. You oughtta try it."

"It's a freaking tiny area," Beans said, stretching his arms out, "in a sea of concrete."

He started to think, folding his arms. "They must have built in some room for error."

Frank arrived back after moving the van. He motioned for Carmine to start pouring the concrete.

"Why couldn't we just dump 'em in the ocean?" Jags persisted.

"For God's sake, Jags," Beans threw his head back in frustration, "will you shut up already? Because Jugs said so, that's why. You're Jags, you're not Jugs. When you're the boss, you get to make the decisions. *Capisce?*"

Beans walked away, then turned around. "Besides, the ocean ain't so great either. You put a guy's feet in cement. A shark comes along and chews on his legs like a couple of buffalo wings." He waved his hand. "All of a sudden, you're having a nice day at the beach with your wife and kids, and a bloated corpse comes bobbing along like a turd in the kiddie pool."

Frank looked at them. "What the hell are you two *cidrules* blabbering about?"

Beans pointed at Jags. "This knucklehead is worried about the structural support of the building," he said mockingly, drawing the words out.

Frank looked around. "If it was a problem, half of the buildings in Hudson County would be falling down." He and Beans laughed as the concrete flowed down the chute, covering the two Irishmen.

***

Daylight filtered through the portholes. The sound of seagulls squawking cut through the soft hum of boat engines in the harbor. Jack rubbed his eyes and realized that he was alone in the cabin. He got up and crouched through the bulkhead door and saw Eileen sitting on the deck. She looked at him and smiled.

"I made coffee. The pot's full if you want some."

Jack poured himself a cup and climbed up to the deck, sitting down next to Eileen. A cool breeze blew across the teak planks. They looked on as some of the fishermen navigated their boats out of the harbor for an early start to the day.

"This is beautiful," Eileen said. "I wish we could stay here."

"It is beautiful." Jack nodded. Eileen put her arm around Jack's waist.

"Hey, can I use your phone again?" Jack asked.

Eileen handed Jack her phone. He Googled Verizon, locating a Verizon store in Sea Girt. Then he dialed Mik's number.

Mik was semi-conscious when he answered. "Hello?" he grunted.

"Mik, it's me."

"Jack, what time is it? Where are you?" Jack explained everything that had happened. He filled Mik in on what Agent Creighton had told him about the investigation in Boston.

"I have a nagging feeling that there's more to this story," Jack said.

"Jesus, Jack, this is getting serious. We poked a god-damned hornet's nest."

"Maybe so," Jack sighed. "Listen, I've got another favor to ask. Would you send Henry back to Boston? I'd like him to look into that murder that Eileen claims to have witnessed. I don't believe she imagined it."

"Sure, Jack," Mik said, "I'll call Henry. Meanwhile, for God's sake, just lay low."

Jack hung up the phone. Off the stern, fifty yards down the dock, he saw a suspicious-looking man approach. He was solidly built with curly black hair and a mustache. His hands were in his pant pockets under a loose-fitting sport jacket. Jack whispered for Eileen to go below deck and he followed her. He retrieved the handgun that the pilot had given him and tucked it into his waistband. The man approached the boat and stopped on the dock in front of it.

"Jack Monroe?" he asked.

Jack reached back and put his hand on the pistol grip, disengaging the thumb safety. "Who's asking?"

"Jimmy sent me."

Jack scanned the surroundings. "How can I be sure you're telling the truth?"

The man shrugged his shoulders. "I'm just doing what Jimmy asked."

Jack thought for a moment. "If Jimmy sent you, what's the password for the Trinacria?"

The man laughed. "Don't be a moron."

Jack jerked the gun out and pointed it at the man, who threw his hands up.

"Whoa! Whoa!"

"That's not it," Jack said, his hand and voice both trembling.

"*Non fare il citrullo*," the man said slowly. "It means... don't be a moron."

Jack bit down on his lip and leaned his head back. "Sorry about that." He reengaged the thumb safety and put the gun away.

"Jimmy wanted me to check on you guys, get you whatever you might need. He's got your car in his shop." The man climbed aboard the boat and handed Jack keys. "Here's a loaner in the meantime. It's the silver Camaro right over there." He pointed.

"Thank you..." Jack extended a hand.

"Vinny," he said, shaking Jack's hand.

"I'm Jack." He put his hand on Eileen's back. "This is Eileen. Tell Jimmy thank you." He looked at Eileen. "Let's go to Verizon. I'm gonna need a new phone. I'm pretty sure the bullet voided the AppleCare warranty."

***

Later that afternoon, they returned to the boat. Jack answered a call on his new phone. "Hello. Jack Monroe speaking."

"Jack, it's Katie Creighton, I've been trying to reach you all night."

"I'm sorry, Agent Creighton, they shot my phone. I just bought a new one."

Silence. "That's impressive."

Jack looked down at his phone. "I meant, incidentally."

"Right... You had Eileen Delaney in the car with you?"

"Yes, that's correct."

"Jack," his name came in a staccato blast through the phone, "I thought we agreed that if you located Ms. Delaney, you would inform us."

"To be honest, I didn't know I'd be with her. I got an anonymous request to meet at the Teaneck Theater. I suspected it was Eileen, but couldn't know for sure. Then we spotted the two Irishmen in the theater. We were lucky to get out of there alive."

"Are you both alright? We tracked your car to the Trinacria, but you were gone."

"We're fine. Thanks for your help last night. I'm starting to appreciate that tracker. I've never been shot at before."

"Thank God you're alright."

"I should be asking about you," Jack said. "We saw you miss the turn at the park, and spin out."

"Luckily no injuries, but it interrupted our pursuit. What happened to the men who were chasing you?"

"Good question. Mr. Gigante helped us escape."

"Yes, we talked to Mr. Gigante, after we called for a backup vehicle." He told us he provided you passage via seaplane, but wouldn't give us your location."

"Yes, that's right."

"He also told us the men chasing you never arrived there."

"He did?" Jack said, flustered. "That's strange."

"Yes," Agent Creighton dragged the words out, "very... strange."

"Hopefully we won't see them again, "Jack said.

"I'm acquainted with Mr. Gigante, Jack," Creighton responded with a sarcastic tone. "I suspect no one will ever see them again. But there will be others. Bet on it. We need to take you into protective custody. Where are you?"

"Actually, Agent Creighton, I feel safe where I am."

"Call me Katie, Jack. You're not a suspect any longer."

"Okay then, thank you, Katie. I'll get in touch with Brendan Mikolajczyk, and arrange to have him pick you up tomorrow, along with my sister, and we can meet."

"I don't like it. I still think we should bring you in right now."

"Let's just say that Ms. Delaney and I don't entirely trust the federal government; yourself, and Agent Spath, excluded of course."

"Fine, we'll do it your way. I'll wait to hear from you, and Jack... be careful."

They hung up.

***

Henry Wan jumped at the chance to return to Boston. His mouth watered thinking about the lobster rolls and clam chowder.

When he arrived, he got straight to work. His first task proved easier than he had envisioned. From knowing that Amanda Henderson attended St. Agnes Academy, he was able to find her childhood address. Using that, he found a marriage record, her current home address, and other pertinent information.

Henry took the tunnel to East Boston. Amanda lived in a modest brick rowhouse near the Bremen Street Park, tightly sandwiched between the neighboring homes. The street lacked sufficient trees for Henry's taste. He arrived around 4 p.m., hoping that he might catch her returning from work. This aspect of the job was tedious. Fortunately, there was a coffee shop nearby.

Henry used his time efficiently searching on his laptop for newspaper archives from the end of March 1991. He looked specifically for reports of murders. That yielded nothing useful. The few murders mentioned were of youthful offenders and drug related. One store clerk had been fatally shot during a robbery.

It was 4:40 p.m. when a woman got out of a white Honda CR-V and walked with purpose toward the rowhouse. She was slender, with shoulder length brown hair and a light-colored dress. She inserted her key in the door and went inside. Henry closed his computer and started to formulate a plan. As he stood up, the rowhouse door opened again, and the woman was being tugged by a golden doodle on a leash.

Henry followed her down the street, keeping his distance. When the dog stopped for a bowel movement, Henry stopped, pretending to tie his shoe. An observer may have wondered why it took so long to tie a shoe. Ask the dog. They turned a corner heading for the Bremen Street Park. Within the park, enclosed by a chain-link fence, was a dog recreation area. The woman put her dog inside, where several others were running and playing. She closed the gate and sat down on a nearby bench. Henry strolled up, plopping down on the other end of the bench.

"Good evening,"he said.

"Good evening," she replied.

"Amanda Henderson?"

The woman startled, snapping her head toward Henry. She pulled her purse up on her lap and looked around. "Yes. I mean... I was." She paused, then squinted. "I'm sorry, do I know you?"

"No," Henry smiled and waved his hand, "we have a mutual friend."

"Oh? Who might that be?"

"Ellen McCarthy."

Amanda's eyes froze. She chewed her lip and started fidgeting. "I haven't seen Ellen since we were kids."

"Yes, of course, the trial." Henry turned toward Amanda. "Ms. Henderson..."

She crossed her arms over her chest. "Barton. It's Barton now. I'm married."

"I'm sorry, Mrs. Barton," Henry rested his elbow on the back of the bench, "I know this is difficult. But not as difficult, I would imagine, as it's been for Ellen." Amanda's head sank. Her lips tightened. "Recently, someone tried to kill her. We presume that attempt was orchestrated by Seamus Callanan. We're looking for information that might help bring Callanan to justice."

Amanda looked around and she clenched her fists, tears welling in her eyes. "Look, I have two children. I can't help you. He threatened to kill my family. I did what I had to do. I'm very sorry about Ellen. I really am. She was my best friend. I've thought about her so many times over the years."

Henry looked down, putting his hands on his knees. "Eileen talked about what good friends you were." Amanda swallowed hard as Henry continued, "so, Ellen wasn't crazy, or drugged that night? She was telling the truth about what you both saw?"

Amanda sat silently, trembling. She covered her mouth with her fist, and with her other hand, wiped away tears. Henry waited. Finally, she nodded. She looked at Henry, desperation in her eyes. "I can't tell the police. He'll kill my family! I've been living with that guilt my entire life. You have to understand, Mr..."

"Wan, Henry Wan." Henry extended his hand and she took it. "Ellen knows. She's forgiven you."

Amanda smiled. She looked down at the ground, then back at Henry. "How is she doing?"

"She's safe for now." Henry looked around. A few of the other dog owners leaned against the fence, or strolled nearby. Nobody was paying attention to them. "We would never do anything to endanger you. Perhaps though, there was something, anything, that you can remember from that night, that might help us?"

Amanda shook her head, then leaned back. "It was noisy. There was thunder, and the rain pelting the metal roof. We were two floors above, scared for our lives. We couldn't hear much."

"Take your time," Henry said, "Try to picture yourself there, that night. Do you recall anything? Anything at all?"

Amanda closed her eyes and thought for a moment. "Yes." Her eyes popped open. She nodded. "Something about a boat. I heard the word boat."

"That's great, Amanda. Anything else?" Henry pressed.

She closed her eyes again. "Race. I heard the word race, I'm sure of it."

"Was it a boat race?" Henry asked.

Amanda shrugged. "I'm sorry, I don't know."

"That's fine, Amanda. This is helpful. Do you recall any details about the man who was shot, or the man in the chair opposite Callanan?"

Amanda winced and shook her head. The recollection of that event was clearly painful. "No. They were both very ordinary. Nothing special, except... I'm not sure."

"Except what, Mrs. Barton?"

"The guy who was shot may have had a limp. I noticed as he walked into the room, that he favored his right leg. I'm not sure why I would remember that." Henry made notes using his phone.

She looked around. "I'm sorry. My husband will be bringing my children home soon. I really must go."

Henry reached into his pocket for a business card. He handed it to her. "If there's anything else, please give me a call. This will remain strictly confidential. I promise you. Thank you for your time."

"Good luck, Mr. Wan. And please," she looked at him with sadness in her eyes, "tell Ellen I'm so sorry... more than she'll ever know."

Henry nodded. "I'll do that." He stood and left.

***

Back at the hotel, Henry relaxed in the restaurant, downing the last bite of a lobster roll. On his computer, he searched "boat race," cross-referencing it to March 1991. Several listings appeared. He found *The Head of the Charles* an annual rowing competition. Additionally, multiple races popped up involving sailboats and speedboats. None of the articles seemed relevant.

Perhaps, he thought, the words weren't used in conjunction with one another. So, he tried each word separately. He searched for incidents involving boats or boat accidents. There were a few, but one caught his eye. He read the newspaper clipping dated March 18, 1991:

Coast Guard search efforts continue for State Assemblyman Richard Navagh *who, days ago, rented a small cabin* *cruiser from a local marina. Alarm was raised by the boat's owner when the assemblyman failed to return. A flash thunderstorm and inclement weather prevailed at the time, and it is feared that the rough weather may have claimed the life of Mr. Navagh and his rental boat. The assemblyman was heavily favored to win the house seat in Massachusetts' 7th congressional district this November. When asked for comment, his opponent in the race, Mason Hollingsworth, expressed deep concern for the safety of the assemblyman, and hope for a successful outcome.*

Henry's eyes lit up when he saw the word race and the name Mason Hollingsworth. Hollingsworth was a sitting United States Senator from Massachusetts.

Henry recalled recent speculation by political pundits that Hollingworth was on the short list of vice-presidential contenders on the Democratic ticket. This warranted a deeper look.

Henry redirected his search efforts to Mason Hollingsworth. The first thing that appeared was fortuitous in its timeliness. Mason Hollingsworth was in Boston attending a fundraiser that very evening, at the Fairmont Copley Plaza. Henry lacked enthusiasm for a second stakeout in one day, nevertheless, this was an opportunity he couldn't squander.

At 7:30 p.m. Henry sat in his rental car, idling across the street from the entrance to the Fairmont Copley Plaza. He opened his brief case and pulled out the GPS tracker strapped to a large magnet. He also removed an 8x10 photo of Senator Hollingsworth, pulled from his official government website.

The Senator arrived late at 8:50 p.m., likely to the irritation of all the wealthy benefactors hoping to get a handshake, a photo, and promises of future favors. Henry checked the photo, verifying that it was Hollingsworth as he exited his limousine. Henry put his car into gear and drove across the street, following the limousine into the parking garage. When the driver parked, Henry chose a spot nearby, but not so close as to be obvious.

As Henry surmised, the driver had no intention of remaining in the parking garage all evening. He'd probably head directly to the cocktail lounge. It didn't really matter where he was going, the important thing was that he left the car. Once the elevator door closed, Henry grabbed a towel and walked to the Senator's limousine. He scanned the ceiling for security cameras and did not see any active cameras in the area. He dropped the towel on the ground and lay on it. He slid under the car and affixed the magnet and GPS device to the frame. It took less than thirty seconds, and he was on his way.

Back in his car, Henry accessed the internet using his iPhone. He opened the tracking software and brought up the map view. The limousine's location pinged with pinpoint accuracy. "Perfect," Henry said, rubbing his hands together. Then he drove out of the parking lot and found a spot to park on the street. Not an easy task, but he managed.

With time on his hands, Henry did a search on Richard Navagh. Mr. Navagh was a native of Boston from a wealthy family. He attended expensive prep schools and then the U.S. Naval Academy. Henry read page after page of biographical history, skimming where appropriate. Then something caught his eye. Mr. Navagh was awarded the Navy Cross for heroism during deployment to Lebanon in the early 1980s. He was credited with a daring rescue of seven fellow Marines under heavy enemy fire, during which he was shot twice in the leg.

Henry pulled out the notes he had scribbled down earlier after his meeting with Amanda Henderson. He scrolled through them to the entry that he was looking for. The man who was shot in the warehouse may have had a limp, Amanda had told him. Henry tapped his temple with his index finger, *interesting*. He pulled up archived photos of Richard Navagh from his days in the Massachusetts legislature, just prior to his disappearance, and saved them to his computer.

***

It was 11:30 p.m. and Henry was struggling to stay awake. He'd set his surveillance software to alarm when the subject's vehicle changed positions. The alarm went off. Henry drove his car to a spot near the exit ramp.

Soon thereafter, he saw the Senator's limousine exit the garage and followed it, staying back several car lengths to avoid detection. They meandered a few blocks through Back Bay, eventually heading east along the Charles River. Lights shimmered on the water from the buildings on the opposite side of the Charles. The traffic was still congested even at the late hour.

Twenty-five minutes later, the limousine came to a stop on the corner of Commercial and Hull Streets, and the Senator got out. Henry would have to follow him visually, since he was out of the car. Henry pulled past the limousine driving slowly along Hull Street, keeping the Senator within sight.

He watched as he entered the Copp's Hill Burying Ground, then lost sight of him, so he pulled around the corner onto Snow Hill Street and parked. The Senator stopped in front of an elevated tomb. The windows in Henry's car had a sufficient tint to make him inconspicuous. He picked up his digital SLR with a telephoto lens and watched as

Mason Hollingsworth stood in front of the gravesite. Why would he be visiting a gravesite at midnight, Henry pondered. A little creepy, if you asked him.

Soon, another man approached with a cane, limping, from the other direction and stood next to Hollingsworth. Was Navagh still alive? Henry zoomed the telephoto lens until he could clearly see the men's faces. He started clicking the shutter. The lens made electronic buzzing sounds as it found its focus and fired. He got several good shots and made a mental note of where they were standing. Henry slumped down in his seat.

Ten minutes later, the two men parted. Henry remained low in his seat until they had left. He got out of his car, climbed the cobblestone steps into the cemetery, making his way to where the men had been standing. Henry was knowledgeable about American history, so when he came upon the gravestone, he knew of its significance. He made an entry in his notebook and left.

CHAPTER 36

Wednesday, June 17, 2020

Callanan sat at a patio table outside a coffee shop in South Boston, nibbling on a scone. It was a quiet street, shaded by tall trees. Aromas of coffee and fresh baked goods filled the air as Derrick strolled to the table. He pulled up a chair.

"Have we heard anything from Shane or Connor?" Callanan asked, his mouth full.

Derrick shook his head. "Nothing. They don't answer their phones."

"I'll assume that's because they can't answer their phones, Derrick," Callanan said, his one good eye staring at the park across the street. "We may have underestimated our foes."

A gangly young waitress with an apron and a water bottle approached with a broad smile. "Can I get you a coffee, sir?"

"Please," Derrick responded.

They waited until the waitress left. "I think it's time we called in the Hebrew," Seamus said.

"G'way! Seamus. That wacko gives me the creeps. And he won't come cheap."

"I don't give a shit about the money, Derrick, I just want the job done." Callanan reached into his pocket and pulled out a piece of paper. He slipped it across the table to Derrick, who casually put his hand over it and slid it toward himself. He glanced around the patio at the other patrons, who were absorbed in their own conversations. He opened it up. Scribbled inside was the name Mikha'el Weinberg, and a phone number.

"You tell the Hebrew I'm aware he's a busy man, but this is important. I'd consider it a personal favor if he'd take care of it as soon as possible."

The waitress returned with Derrick's coffee. Derrick quickly folded up the paper and slurped down the coffee. He stood and nodded. "I'll get on it straightaway, Seamus."

Callanan looked at Derrick and nodded.

***

It was midday under an overcast sky when Mikolajczyk's SUV rolled into the parking lot of the FBI branch office in Newark. He sent a text to Agent Creighton to let her know he'd arrived. Moments later, a tall blond woman wearing teal blue shorts, a tank top, and a white floppy sun hat approached his car.

Mik's eyes seesawed like a schoolboy at a girl's volleyball match. "Is that babe the FBI agent?"

Erin looked at him from the back seat and rolled her eyes. "Oh, for God's sake."

Agent Creighton bent over, peering through the passenger-side window. "Brendan Mikolajczyk?"

"Yes," Mik said, his voice breaking higher than intended. He cleared his throat and deepened his voice. "Agent Creighton? I was expecting an old guy in a suit."

"Sorry to disappoint you." She pursed her lips. "No suit. You said we're going to the shore." She pointed at her clothing. "I'm undercover." She opened the door and got in.

"Not much cover," Mik mumbled to himself.

"Oh brother," Erin sighed. She pushed her hand between the front seats to shake Creighton's hand. "Erin Monroe," she said.

"Hello, Erin, nice to meet you." Creighton looked out the window. "So where are we going?"

"Jack asked us to keep that under wraps for now. It'll take forty-five minutes, but it's a pleasant drive." From behind his sunglasses, Mik glanced out of the corner of his eyes at Creighton's long bare legs. He looked straight ahead. A pleasant drive indeed.

It was going on one o'clock when the tires of Mik's SUV crunched their way through the sand- and seashell-covered parking lot at the Brielle Yacht Club. As they got out of the car, Connie Gigante pulled up next to them. She stepped out of her car, wearing white capri pants and a nautical striped top. She walked toward them.

"Connie, I didn't know you were coming," Erin said.

"Who's this?" Agent Creighton asked.

Mik made the introduction. "Agent Creighton, this is Connie Gigante, Jack's girlfriend." He turned to Connie. "Connie, Agent Creighton of the FBI."

Agent Creighton continued smiling, concealing her disappointment. "Oh... so you're Jack's girlfriend." She pulled down her sunglasses, looking over them at Connie. "Well, that explains a few things."

"Connie," Mik asked, "where does your dad keep his boat?"

"It's there, Mik." Connie pointed to the *Joan's Ark*. They walked along the dock to its slip. When they got to the boat, Connie jumped onto the deck, threw her arms around Jack, who had extended his hand to help her on, and pecked him on the cheek.

Eileen came out from the cabin and stood with her arms folded. Connie looked at her, then walked over and gave her a perfunctory hug. "Eileen, it's been a long time."

"Good to see you, Connie." Eileen forced a smile. "I've missed everybody."

Jack clapped his hands together. "Why don't we move below where it's cooler?" They all followed him and took seats in the cabin.

Jack sat on the port-side bench, with Eileen and Connie on either side of him. He smiled awkwardly at each. Mik sat across from them next to Agent Creighton, looking content with the seating arrangement. Erin stood.

Jack spoke first. "Mik, tell us what Henry found."

Mik leaned forward, clasping his hands. "First, I have to say, Henry earned his pay this week." Mik recounted the details of what Henry had told him the night before. He told them of Henry's suspicions regarding Hollingsworth's involvement in the disappearance of the state assemblyman, roughly coinciding with the time Eileen claimed to have witnessed the murder at the warehouse.

Agent Creighton's mouth dropped open as she put her hand on her forehead. "Good God, Mik. You're talking about a United States senator possibly being involved in a murder."

Mik looked around the cabin at their faces. "Oh, it gets better. Henry followed the senator to the Copp's Hill Burying Ground, where he rendezvoused with another individual."

Creighton folded her arms. "Do we know who he met?"

"Oh yeah," Mik said, smiling. "It was Seamus Callanan."

"I don't understand," Connie said. "What does all of this mean?"

Mik continued, gesturing toward Creighton. "Agent Creighton informed us on our ride down that the FBI is currently investigating Seamus Callanan for drug trafficking. But Callanan's assets were seized with his conviction in the 1990s. Callanan no longer has any commercial property on the Boston waterfront. That we know of."

Erin stepped forward. "What does this have to do with anything?"

"Well," Mik explained, "as it turns out, Mason Hollingsworth's grandfather made his fortune in the import/export business. Years ago, his company, Hollingsworth International, was transferred to his son, and more recently to his grandson, the senator."

Erin flashed a wry expression. "Are you suggesting that the senator is trafficking drugs through his family company?"

Agent Creighton nodded, taking it all in. "This is a lot to digest, Mik. I'm going to pass all of this on to the Boston office. But we're talking about a United States senator, for God's sake. This is going to need clearance from the top, from the Director himself."

"I understand," Mik said.

Creighton looked at Mik. "Where exactly was it that Hollingsworth met with Callanan? We could get surveillance on that location in case they meet there again."

"Henry said they met in front of a historical marker. Mathis?" Mik snapped his fingers, glancing at the ceiling. "Cotton, something like that."

"Do you mean Cotton Mather?" Erin asked.

Mik shot both index fingers at Erin. "That's it."

Erin shook her head.

"That's good, Mik," Agent Creighton said. "On the off chance that they might meet there again, we'll have our tech guys plant a bug."

Eileen listened quietly through the discussion, finally speaking up. "Mik, did Henry send you photos of these guys? The senator, and the state assemblyman?"

"Yes." Mik pulled his laptop out of its case and booted it up.

Eileen moved to the seat next to Mik. Mik pulled up a recent photo of Mason Hollingsworth from his official senatorial website.

Eileen tilted her head. "I've seen him in the news, but it doesn't ring any bells."

Mik pulled up a second photo. "This is a photo of Mason Hollingsworth from the early nineties, when he won his seat in Congress."

Eileen's mouth dropped open. She held her breath. "Oh my God!" Her eyes widened and she began to stutter. "That's the guy! He was the one sitting in the chair in the warehouse."

Mik opened a third photo. "What about this one? This is a photo of Massachusetts state assemblyman Richard

Navagh, prior to his disappearance." He turned the laptop screen toward Eileen.

The color drained from her face and her breathing became labored. She closed her eyes and turned away.

"Eileen?" Mik asked. "Have you seen this man?"

Eileen nodded. With tears in her eyes, she struggled to get the words out. "I'll never forget that face. That's the man I saw murdered in the warehouse." Creighton jumped up and pulled out her phone. The signal strength was only two bars. She climbed back up to the deck to get better reception and dialed a number. "Hello, this is Special Agent Katie Creighton. I need you to connect me to the Boston office... Thank you... Agent David Roche, please." She waited on hold for a moment, then he answered. "David, this is Katie Creighton from Newark. You better take a seat." Agent Creighton briefed him on everything they'd just discussed.

"Wow," was all he said, and then again, louder, "wow." There was a brief pause. "Sorry, I had to close the door. We'll get a bug on that Mather gravesite as soon as possible. Listen, I've got some disturbing news. Now, you better sit down. Have you ever heard of a guy named Mikha'el Weinberg? Ex-Mossad assassin. He started freelancing a few years back."

"No. Why do you ask?"

"We've intercepted chatter over tapped lines from Seamus Callanan talking to an associate. Apparently, they've recruited Weinberg to take out the girl you're protecting. Ellen McCarthy, or whatever she calls herself now. Are you in a secure location?"

Creighton looked around the harbor. "Yes... I think so... maybe."

"This guy is bad news, Katie. The Mossad trained him well. He's a stone-cold killer. A ghost. We have no idea where he is at the moment. He arrived under an assumed name at Newark Liberty, but our agents lost him."

"I understand. Can you send photos of this guy?"

"I'll send them now. Be careful, and for God's sake, watch your back. Do not engage this guy under any circumstance."

"Thank you."

Mik watched Creighton's body language as she hung up the phone. She paced back and forth with her palm on her hip. Mik stepped on the ladder to the deck. "Everything alright?"

She shook her head. "No."

She told Mik what Agent Roche had said. "That's not good," Mik responded. "Can I see the photo?"

Creighton pulled up the photos on her phone. Weinberg had a stocky build, with a closely cropped crew cut and neatly trimmed mustache and goatee. He had beady eyes, like two black peas, highlighted against his cadaver-like, blanched skin. They were dead, icy-cold eyes.

Mik clenched his teeth, tilting his head. "Handsome fellow."

They went below deck and informed the others.

Agent Creighton looked around the cabin. "I'm going to need you all to shut off location services on your cell phones right now. Does anyone here know how to sail this thing?"

"I do," Connie said, putting her hand up as if in school. "I've been sailing my whole life."

Jack said, "It's been a while, but I can help."

"I'd feel a lot better if we got this thing off the dock and out into open water," Creighton said. "At least until we can get further guidance on where this guy might be."

Creighton turned to Connie. "Connie, does your father keep any weapons on the boat?"

"I'm not sure. I don't think so."

Mik said, "I've got my Sig, 9mm, two magazines."

Jack chimed in. "We have the handgun that the seaplane pilot gave us."

Creighton looked at them. "With mine, that makes three handguns. That's gonna pale against whatever this guy's likely to bring. Our best hope is that he doesn't find us. Eileen and Mik, why don't you search below and see what you can find? Jack and Connie, get us the hell out of here."

Jack jumped onto the dock and detached the mooring lines from the metal cleats. He jumped back onto the boat and started the engine. They backed out of the slip and then steered for open water toward the Manasquan Inlet. Mik came back up the ladder.

"Find anything?" Agent Creighton asked.

"Yeah," Mik smirked, "a few boxes of commercial-grade fireworks. Anyone have a birthday they'd like to celebrate?"

"Those were left over from the Fourth of July last year," Connie said. "We never got down here to use them."

Mik looked at the others. "I hope we don't have any closet smokers on board."

The boat glided slowly through the harbor under the meager power of its electric engine until they had passed through the inlet. Connie started rattling off instructions, which the others followed. "Mik, would you please unzip the bag on the mainsail?"

"I can do that."

"Okay, Jack, take the wheel and steer us into the wind. Eileen, go with him. You're going to hold our course. I'll need Jack for the sail." Jack and Eileen did as she asked.

"Wind is from the southeast, Jack."

"Check."

"Okay, let's get the mainsail up." She pointed. "There's the halyard. Do you remember any of this?"

"Vaguely," Jack admitted.

Connie looked at Mik. "Mik, I need you to adjust the boom vang."

Mik looked at Katie and shrugged his shoulders. "Are we speaking English? What the hell is a boom vang?"

Katie Creighton shrugged.

"It's that cylindrical thing under the boom."

"Oh sure," Mik said, making the OK sign, "that clears it up."

Connie pointed to it. "Right there."

Jack cranked the winch, which made loud clicking sounds as the sail rose to the top of the mast, catching the wind and billowing outward. The boom swung around, nearly knocking Mik off the boat as he ducked for cover, and the boat started cruising effortlessly through the water.

Ten minutes later they had the jib up. The wind was strong and steady, and they scudded a southerly course toward Mantoloking and Beach Head. "Where are we going, Katie?" Connie asked.

"Nowhere, Connie. Let's just sail. As long as nobody knows where we are, we're safe." She sat down and put on her sunglasses. She tilted her head back, the sun warm on her cheeks as the wind blew her blond hair in fits.

Mik made his way over, sitting down next to her. "I could get used to this."

"Me too. I've never actually been on a sailboat before."

"Really? Well, as you might have guessed, I'm not exactly prepping for the America's Cup," Mik said. "Maybe when this is over, we could do it again sometime, for fun."

"Maybe," she lowered her glasses. "I'd like that."

They sailed down to Island Beach, past Seaside Heights, and slowly made their way back again. The sun was starting to set in the west and the sky boasted beautiful shades of pink and orange. The lights of the buildings on the shore illuminated the coast as dusk settled. Connie was taking her turn at the wheel. Jack and Eileen sat near the bow, catching the breeze.

"There is so much that I have missed," Eileen said, looking at Jack. "Tell me the truth, Jack. In all these years, have you thought about me?"

Jack exhaled a puff of air and looked down at the deck. "So many times."

"Have you ever imagined where we might be today if I hadn't had to leave?"

Jack nodded his head. "I've often thought about that. Maybe we'd be married with three kids and a dog, in a nice house in suburbia." He laughed. "Or," he clasped his hands together, dropping his eyes, "maybe our dating would have run its course, and we'd have gone off to different colleges, going our separate ways, like so many of our friends. I guess we'll never really know the answer."

Eileen folded her hands on her lap and looked down at them. "For what it's worth, regardless of what happens, I'll always look back on the summer of '95 as the best time of my life." She looked up and smiled at him. "It's part of a past that we shared, and always will be. Nothing can erase that."

Jack nodded. There was a lump in his throat and he wanted to speak, but the words wouldn't come. Before he could say anything, his eyes caught a glimpse of Connie holding a tequila cooler, with her head hung down, leaning against the side of the cabin. He didn't know how long she'd been standing there.

"Connie," Jack said, "join us."

Connie made her way over and sat down with them. She didn't look up when she spoke. "I want you guys to know," her lip quivered, "that if you still have a thing for each other," she choked up, "I won't stand in the way. I can't pretend that it doesn't hurt, because it does." She looked at Jack. "I've known that I loved Jack ever since we were kids. But when you love someone, that person's happiness should be the most important thing to you, even if it means losing them."

Eileen got up and hugged Connie. "Thank you, Connie. You're such an amazing person. The three of us have a lot to sort out, but I'm glad we're talking."

Jack looked at Connie, but she wouldn't make eye contact. It hurt him to see her like that. He had no idea what he could say to make her feel better, so he kept quiet.

"Maybe we should join the others," Eileen suggested.

Jack looked toward the back and saw Mik with his arm around Katie as they sat with their backs up against the cockpit. "Well, what do you know?" Jack said.

"Are those sharks?" Mik said, standing up and pointing out over the water.

"There are quite a few out there," Jack stood up. He could see at least four fins in the water, circling.

Connie waved her hand. "This area is full of sharks. There's a fish-packing plant nearby and they dump their scraps in the ocean. They aren't supposed to—it's illegal—

but they do it anyway. My father told me about it. He told me never to swim off the boat out here."

"Well, so much for my moonlight dip," Mik said. "Maybe we can make our way back to Manasquan and drop anchor there for the night."

"I like that idea," Katie said.

***

Special Agent Bob Hurley couldn't remember when he'd last gone to work in anything other than a black suit. Today, however, he wore denim overalls with an embroidered patch reading *Boston Department of Parks and Recreation*. He held one of those grip-operated grabbers for picking up litter.

There wasn't much litter in the Copp's Hill Burying Ground. Thankfully, most of the Bostonians and visitors still had respect, both for the dead and for the historic sites of the commonwealth.

His partner, Jim Healy, returned his broom to the utility vehicle after having swept some sand off the brick walk. The two men looked around. An eclectic assortment of people strolled the grounds, nobody paying any particular attention to them. Bob nodded at Jim, who picked up the small resin faux rock with the built-in microphone and transmitter. He placed it in the space next to the Mather gravesite, where they had earlier removed a similar-sized stone. He used a brush to whisk dirt against it so that it looked natural.

Bob walked some twenty yards down the path and adjusted his earpiece. He reached into his pocket and turned the volume up on the receiving unit, then tapped his hat twice. At the signal, Jim spoke with a volume slightly above a whisper. "Testing, one, two, three. Testing, one, two, three."

Bob turned around and gave him the thumbs up.

***

The sun had set over the homes and commercial establishments on the shore. Connie went down the ladder into the cabin and found Agent Creighton sitting on the bench. "Katie, is it okay if I call my dad and let him know what's happening?"

Creighton nodded. "Sure, Connie, just keep it short."

The phone rang twice and Jimmy Gigante picked up. "Connie, where are you?"

"I'm on the boat." She filled him in on everything they'd been told.

Gigante wasn't happy. His voice was agitated. "Where's Vinny?"

"Vinny?" Connie said, confused. "How would I know?"

"He was at our beach house in Sea Girt. I called him a while ago and asked him to go to the boat to check on you guys."

"Well, he's not with us."

"Damn it," Jimmy's voice shook the phone. "I'll find out what happened and call you back. Stay safe, and be careful." Jimmy hung up.

Connie sat down and looked at Creighton. "He said he sent one of his guys to check on us."

"How long ago?" Creighton asked.

"I'm not sure. He said he'll call back."

Creighton pinched her lower lip. "Connie, do you have any binoculars on board?"

"Yeah. They're in the cabinet next to you."

Creighton opened the cabinet and found the binoculars. She went up and sat on the deck and scanned the surrounding water. The others were gathered near the bow, engaged in conversation, as the boat rocked with the surf.

"It's peaceful out here," Erin said, "the complete opposite of D.C."

"The waves are hypnotizing," Mik added. "That smell of the ocean reminds me of being on the beach as a kid." He lay back on the deck and looked up at the night sky, brimming with stars.

It was about a half hour later when Connie's phone rang. When she answered, her father's voice was frantic. "Connie, thank God!"

"What's wrong?"

"Do not bring the boat in! Do you hear me?"

"What's going on, Dad?"

"It's Vinny," Gigante said, trying to catch his breath, "he's dead. We found him in the beach house garage, throat slit. Keep the boat out, and turn your lights off. Don't trust anybody. Okay? Nobody."

Connie's face blanched white. "Okay, where are you?"

"Hang tight. We're on the way."

Creighton saw the alarm in Connie's eyes. "What's wrong, Connie?"

She sat down, grabbing her abdomen. "I feel sick. My dad's employee, Vinny, was murdered!"

Connie's distress caught the attention of the others. Creighton looked around in every direction, searching for approaching boats. There were none. "Let's get out of here. Pull the anchor, Jack, and tell us what to do."

***

Mikha'el Weinberg stood behind the wheel of a cabin cruiser, the boat owner's shoes visible through the cabin hatch, where he lay motionless on the floor with an ice pick sticking out of his cervical spine. The stolen boat traversed the Manasquan Inlet at a slow speed as Weinberg searched for the distinctive, black-hulled *Joan's Ark*. A photo of the boat was taped to the bulkhead.

A group of young revelers partied on a yacht moored at the end of one of the piers. Weinberg maneuvered close to their boat and set his engine to idle. His expressionless face effortlessly morphed into one feigning congeniality as he glided close to their boat. They eyed him with curiosity as he approached, and turned the music down.

Weinberg suppressed his Israeli accent and replaced it with one of the many in his repertoire. In this iteration, it was a nondescript Midwestern voice.

"Howdy, folks. Sorry to bother you," he started with a smile. "I'm looking for a boat called *Joan's Ark*. There's been an emergency and I need to contact the owners." He held up the photo of the boat.

The two young men who were closest looked at the photo. "Oh yeah," one of them tapped his friend on the shoulder, "remember we passed them? They were heading south, I think. Yeah, south."

"Thank you, fellas, I appreciate your help. Enjoy your evening." As he turned his face away from them, the broad smile reverted to a frosty linear crease. He steered the boat toward the inlet and the darkness beyond.

Once through the inlet, he reached into the cabin and lifted his IWI Dan .338 from its carrying case. He took the magazine filled with Lapua Magnum cartridges and clicked it into the magwell. Then he took the Emtan Karmiel suppressor and screwed it onto the threaded barrel. He laid the rifle on the bench seat and headed south.

*****

The *Joan's Ark* sailed with a strong easterly wind prevailing. The boom angled far to starboard, with both sails held taut as the boat's hull sliced through the water. They blew past an anchored sailboat with lanterns fore and aft, and a commercial fishing trawler returning from a day at sea.

It was Mik's turn manning the binoculars, keeping watch off the stern, when a small cabin cruiser appeared in the distance heading in their direction. "Look there." He handed the binoculars to Creighton.

"A little late for a pleasure cruise," she said.

Mik shrugged. "Could be a couple out for a moonlight boat ride." He tilted his chin up to the oversized white moon above, which shimmered on the water's surface.

"Maybe," she sounded unconvinced. She put her hand on Mik's shoulder. "Keep an eye on that boat, Mik."

Connie stood in the cockpit, steering the boat, while Erin and Eileen sat below, reminiscing about their high school days. Erin apologized for how she'd treated Eileen in high school, unaware of her past. Jack sat on the deck above the cabin with the handgun tucked into his khakis. He looked at Connie and their eyes met. He smiled at her, but she looked away.

It was eerily quiet except for the sounds of the flags on the rigging snapping in the wind and the ocean sloshing against the side of the boat. Their conversations created a low background drone.

"That boat's gaining on us," Mik said, handing the binoculars back to Katie.

She took them and pressed them to her eyes. "Oh my God! I think it's him."

Mik's jaw dropped. "How can you tell that from here?"

"I have 20/10 vision."

"Why doesn't that surprise me?" Mik said. "Are you sure?"

There was a loud blast as a piece of the fiberglass hatch above the companionway shattered and flew off. "Yeah!" she gulped, "I'm sure!" She yelled, "Everyone get down!"

Connie dropped down to the deck. "We can't outrun a motorboat, Katie."

Katie dialed her phone and reported the situation to Agent Spath.

"Shit, Katie, it's gonna take time to scramble a helicopter, and the Coast Guard," Spath said. "Hang in there. I'm on it."

She hung up the phone and looked at Mik. "The choppy surf is skewing his shots, otherwise one of us would be dead already."

Jack dropped down and crawled up to them. "Our handguns aren't going to do us much good against that cannon." Mik looked out over the ocean's surface, glowing with the moonlight, and saw the shark fins. They were passing through the area Connie had mentioned earlier.

"Connie, get below deck!" Jack shouted. Connie crawled out of the cockpit and crouched down, dashing for the cabin. Another loud crack echoed as a piece of the aluminum railing flew off. Connie screamed in pain as her body spun around and she fell to the deck. Blood soaked her blouse.

Jack jumped up, scrambling to where Connie lay. "Connie!" He lifted her shirt and saw that the bullet had hit the fleshy part of her left arm near the shoulder. He grabbed her and pulled her down the ladder into the cabin.

Erin and Eileen had shocked looks on their faces. They backed up to make room. Erin grabbed onto Eileen. "Is it bad, Jack?"

He didn't answer.

Jack ripped off his shirt and balled it up, putting pressure on the wound. He kicked off his running shoe. "Eileen, pull the lace out, please." She did as he asked. Connie was crying and hyperventilating. Jack used the shoelace to tie a pressure dressing on her arm. Connie looked into his eyes with tears streaming down. Jack hugged her tightly, kissing her forehead. "You're going to be alright, Connie."

Eileen looked on, bowing her head. She crouched down and took Connie's hand.

"Do you promise?" Connie asked.

Jack felt a wave of déjà vu from the day of her surgery. "I promise," he said, repeating the same words. He looked over Connie's shoulder and saw the boxes of fireworks in the corner. An idea came to him.

Katie dropped into the cabin. "How bad is it?"

"Could be worse," Jack said. "It missed any major vessels. Please, stay with Connie. Everyone else, grab those boxes of fireworks and pass them up to me on the deck." Jack grabbed a box and retrieved a butane lighter from the drawer in the galley. "Keep your heads down."

Mik lay sprawled on the deck as Jack slithered up next to him. "Well, that's a long shot," Mik said, looking at the firework box.

"All we have to do is get a spark to land on the boat when it gets closer, and fire a few rounds into the hull, near the fuel tanks."

"Oh, is that all?" Mik said, breathing heavily, peeking at the boat coming toward them.

"Got any better idea?"

"Afraid not."

Jack grabbed the aluminum tube used for holding rolled nautical charts and emptied the contents. "We'll use this to launch the bottle rockets."

The motorboat was now about one hundred yards off their stern. Another bullet ripped a hole in the mainsail.

"Let's fire one," Mik said, "to gauge the distance."

"Okay," Jack said. He put the launch rod into the canister and aimed it toward the motorboat at a thirty-degree angle. He lit the fuse with the butane lighter. Two seconds later the propellant ignited, and there was a brilliant flash as the rocket took off, whistling through the air. It soared over the top of the motorboat and exploded into sparks above it.

"Too steep," Mik said. Another bullet ripped through the mainsail. "Take it down to fifteen degrees."

Jack loaded another bottle rocket into the canister, lowered the angle of incline, and lit the fuse. The second rocket followed a flatter path and crashed into the water in front of the boat.

Jack loaded up five of them. "Keep the same angle," Mik yelled. "He's gaining on us, so that should compensate for elevation. This better work."

Jack loaded the five launch rods into the canister and twisted the fuses together. "Mik, when I light the fuses, I want you to shoot at his hull. Aim toward the rear quarter. On three."

Mik pulled the slide on his semiautomatic handgun, loading the chamber.

Jack counted. "One... two... three."

Mik rolled over, rested his forearm on the gunwale, and started firing. Jack lit all five fuses. The propellant flashed and the rockets took off in near synchrony, whistling toward the target. Two fell into the water, one burst into colorful sparks just above the boat, and two hit it directly. Jack pulled the handgun from his waist and joined Mik in firing at the boat's hull. One of the bullets hit the mark and fuel started spraying out. A moment later a fire broke out on the deck. In thirty seconds, it was a raging inferno.

Weinberg dove into the water away from the flaming boat as it exploded, sending debris everywhere. They were far from shore, and a rip current was pulling everything out to sea. Sharks circled the periphery.

"Mik, can you drop the sails? Get Katie to help you."

"I'm right here," Katie said as she climbed the ladder to the deck.

Jack went down into the cabin and dropped to his knees next to Connie. He hugged her again. "How are you doing, Connie?" he asked.

"It hurts really bad," she winced, "but I'm okay."

"I've got to check it again." He started to untie the shoelace. "Erin, grab me a towel please, from the galley." Erin did as he asked. Jack took the bloody shirt off and redressed the wound with the towel and tied it on again. "It's not as bad as it looks, Connie," he said, holding her hand and kissing it.

Jack picked up the bloody shirt and climbed back up to the deck, teeth clenched, furious. Mik and Katie had the sails lowered. Jack jumped into the cockpit and started the motor. He turned the wheel hard to starboard and the boat puttered slowly, coming around. He turned all the running lights on.

"Mik, Katie. Keep your guns drawn, and watch the water. He may have a handgun. Be careful."

"I see him, Jack," Mik said. "Come around ninety degrees."

Jack maneuvered the boat into position. Katie and Mik kept their guns trained on Weinberg, who was floundering in the water as the waves swelled three to four feet.

"Don't leave me here," Weinberg yelled. "We can work something out."

Jack watched the sharks circling closer. "No deal," he yelled.

Weinberg spun his head, looking in horror at the fins gliding through the water. "Take me in! I'll abort the contract. I swear it." He started swimming toward the boat.

Jack, seething with anger, yanked the handgun out of his pocket and pointed it at Weinberg. "So help me God, I'll blow your goddamned head off! Not one inch closer." His hand shook. "You shot my girlfriend." Jack noticed Eileen standing beside him, arms folded, looking down at the deck.

Jack balled up the shirt that had been on Connie's arm. He glared at Weinberg, knowing that the blood would send the sharks into a feeding frenzy. "Right now, I'm wondering what to do with my girlfriend's blood-soaked shirt." Jack hesitated, then brought his arm back, like a baseball pitcher.

Eileen blocked his arm gently. "Don't, Jack. Don't be like him. It will eat you up." Her eyes glazed over and she looked away. "Trust me. I know."

He let it fall to the deck. "The police will be back for you," Jack yelled. "I've got to get my girlfriend to a hospital, you bastard." He jumped into the cockpit and started the engine.

Agent Creighton agreed. "We do need to get Connie to a hospital. She's still oozing."

"Mik, let's get the sails up, and get this thing back to Brielle," Jack said.

He turned to Creighton. "Katie, can you call ahead and have an ambulance waiting at the yacht club?"

She nodded and dialed her phone.

A few minutes later a bone-chilling scream echoed in the darkness behind them as Weinberg's torso glided horizontally across the moonlit water, trailing a wake, then plunged downward. The screams returned, through waterlogged gasps, when his head bobbed up, but abruptly stopped as he went under for the last time.

***

A crowd awaited their arrival at the yacht club. Jimmy Gigante stood on the dock with Jimmy Jr. and a couple of his men. Next to them were Agent Spath and a few agents wearing blue jackets with the large yellow FBI logo. Whirring blades of a Coast Guard helicopter made a *thwop-thwop-thwop* sound overhead, and an ambulance with emergency lights spinning waited to take Connie to the University Medical Center in Neptune.

Connie was helped off the boat by the EMTs and placed on a gurney. Gigante stood next to her and held her hand. "Look what they did to my baby girl," he said through tears, rage in his eyes. His jugulars were bulging. "Who did this, Jack? I'll fucking kill him."

Jack shrugged. "Too late, Mr. Gigante. You might say, he sleeps with the fishes." Jack tilted his head. "Well... technically, he sleeps in the fishes."

Gigante looked at Jack. "That'll work."

The FBI took Eileen into protective custody. Erin made plans with Mik to drive her back to her hotel. Agent Spath reached out to shake Mik's hand. "Mr. Mikolajczyk? Gerry Spath, FBI." Mik shook his hand. "Your investigator, Mr. Wan, came through for us." Katie Creighton walked over and joined them. Spath continued, "The Boston office just informed us that they've got a digital recording of Senator Hollingsworth and Seamus Callanan discussing their fentanyl trafficking operation. They also discussed Callanan hiring an assassin, Mikha'el Weinberg, also known as "The Hebrew," to kill Ellen McCarthy."

"Yeah, we just met," Mik said. "So, what happens now?"

"An FBI tactical team is executing a search warrant at the warehouses of Hollingsworth International. The senator and Mr. Callanan have been arrested."

Agent Spath continued, "Again, I can't say enough about Henry Wan. He's been talking to Amanda Henderson, who is now willing to recant her testimony which she gave at the original Callanan trial. It may not be necessary though. We've had a preliminary discussion with the senator about a plea bargain if he'll testify against Callanan and resign from the Senate effective immediately. Anyway, we'll talk tomorrow. Go home and get some rest. You earned it."

Jack said, "I'm going with Connie in the ambulance."

"We'll follow you, Jack," Jimmy Jr. said.

Mik looked at Katie. "It was a pleasure working with you." He reached out and shook her hand.

"Likewise," she said, her eyes darting around, waiting.

"Well, I guess..." Mik stumbled over the words. Katie stood with her hands folded, her lips tightly drawn.

"Oh, for God's sake," Erin squeezed between them. "Mik, you fool. Just tell her you'd like to see her again. Katie, Mik would like your phone number."

Katie smiled and pulled a card out of her pocket. She borrowed a pen from Agent Spath, wrote her phone number down, and handed it to Mik. "Thanks, Erin."

Jack got into the ambulance and sat next to Connie. He stroked her hair with his fingers. She reached up and held his hand. As the ambulance pulled away, the gathered crowd started to dissipate.

CHAPTER 37

Thursday, June 25, 2020

The John J. Moakley U.S. Courthouse in Boston is situated in the northernmost corner of the Seaport District, jutting out into Boston's Inner Harbor. Inside, the preliminary hearing was underway in the case of *United States vs. Seamus Callanan*, for murder, racketeering, and narcotics trafficking.

Eileen sat holding Amanda Henderson's hand. "I want to thank you, Amanda, for what you did. I've always hoped that the truth would come out someday."

"I'm sorry, Eileen. I never meant to hurt you. You were my best friend." Tears started to well up in Amanda's eyes. "I let you down, and then you were gone. Can you ever forgive me?"

"We were just stupid kids, Amanda. I never blamed you. Not once. And I've missed you too." She squeezed Amanda's hand. "I forgave you long ago."

Amanda shook her head. "I wish we'd never stepped foot in that building. For years, I had terrible nightmares, and I'd wake up drenched in sweat."

Eileen nodded. "I went through the same. I thought I could start a new life and leave it all behind. Ellen McCarthy died that day." She grabbed the back of her neck. "I lost everything, and became a stranger, even to myself. It was much harder than anyone might imagine, but eventually I found peace again." She looked down at her feet. "But they found me, and dragged me back into the nightmare."

Amanda turned toward Eileen. "How did we ever pick that building anyway?" She squeezed her hand. "It was so out of the way. I couldn't remember how we ended up there."

Jack's ears perked up. He was seated on the opposite side of Eileen, and he turned his head. Eileen looked down, her hands fidgeting in her lap. "Oh, who knows. It was a lifetime ago."

She was lying. It had been a long time since Jack and Eileen dated, but he could tell from the hand-wringing and the shifting eyes. Yet it didn't strike him as important. Jack's attention was drawn to the man walking into the courtroom.

U.S. Senator Mason Hollingsworth looked melancholy, with disheveled hair and a drooping posture. He shuffled slowly into the courtroom, accompanied by his lawyer. He took the stand and was sworn in. In exchange for his plea bargain, he told a long and sordid story.

"Yes, I paid Seamus Callanan to dissuade my opponent from remaining in the congressional race. I'm not proud of that." He held his forehead with both hands. "But I never intended for him to be killed. I swear to you." He turned to face the judge.

"By killing Navagh, Callanan made me an accomplice, and would wield that over me."

Jack felt a slight pang of sympathy for Hollingsworth. He wasn't guiltless by any stretch, yet he was one in a long line of people whose lives were destroyed by Seamus Callanan.

"As the director of MassPort, I provided Mr. Callanan cover for moving heroin through the port. I should have reported the murder and faced the consequences. I would regret not doing so for the rest of my life. But I was too much of a coward. I feared Callanan's wrath."

Eileen gripped her shoulders, tormented by the thoughts of how different her life would have been if he had found that courage.

Hollingsworth swallowed, biting his lip. "Callanan's stint in prison for drug trafficking gave me a reprieve. For years, I lived my life serving my constituents as best I could, hoping that by doing so, I could wipe the blood from my conscience."

"At that time, my father passed away." He paused to wipe a tear from his face. "I inherited the company, Hollingsworth International. When Callanan was paroled from prison, he blackmailed me to use the company to move the new drug of choice, fentanyl, through the Port of Boston."

Callanan sat at the defense table staring daggers at Hollingsworth. Both of his hands were balled into fists, his fingernails digging into the skin of his palms. Hollingsworth avoided looking at him.

Katie Creighton had told them that Hollingsworth's plea bargain was for a twenty-year sentence at a minimum-security federal prison. But for a man in his sixties, it was effectively a life sentence.

***

Diagonally across Northern Ave. was a high-rise building housing a draft house theater, along with other businesses and residential apartments. There were a lot of people busily moving through the building's public spaces, and nobody paid any particular attention to an older gentleman carrying a duffel bag. He was lean, with a thick beard and mustache, wearing a large-brimmed camo hat.

He took the elevator to the highest floor, keeping his gaze down to avoid the hidden security cameras. He knew exactly where he was going. He had rehearsed it several days before. From the highest residential floor, he ascended two flights of stairs to a door leading onto the roof.

He moved quickly to the northeastern side of the building, where he had a clear view of the main entrance to the courthouse and the red brick plaza outside. There he quickly rigged up some sheets, camouflaged to match the gray-white surface of the roof. There were dozens of large air-conditioning units scattered about the roof, providing additional cover.

He crawled into the makeshift tent he had created and opened his duffel bag. He removed his Vietnam War-era Remington M40 bolt-action rifle with its Redfield scope and loaded the internal box magazine. From the bag he removed a small pair of binoculars and then sat watching the door to the building. He started to feel jittery, a combination of nerves and his newly diagnosed Parkinson's disease. He reached into the pocket of his tactical pants and removed a metal flask containing Jack Daniel's, and took a long swig.

***

It was going on three o'clock when the hearing ended. Bail was denied, and Seamus Callanan was remanded into the custody of the federal marshals. Those in attendance were making their way out of the main entrance to the brick plaza outside. Amanda stood with Eileen. "So, what happens now?"

"I'm not sure," Eileen responded. "I have to be available to testify at the trial in three months."

"I've kept in touch with a few of our friends from St. Agnes Seminary," Amanda put her hand on Eileen's shoulder. "You remember Brigid and Isabelle?"

"Oh my God. Of course I do." A broad smile flashed across Eileen's face.

"They still live here in Boston. I see them often. They said they would love to see you. And Sandy is over in Cambridge. She teaches at Harvard."

"God, it would be great to see them all. I've missed Boston so much."

"So stick around for a few days. Stay with me. We can get together with the girls and maybe visit St. Agnes. We had a lot of good times there."

Eileen smiled and wiped a tear from her cheek. "I'd really like that."

Jack overheard the conversation. "You should do it, Eileen. It would be good for you."

"Yeah," she nodded. "I will. Thank you, Amanda. Give me a moment." She took Jack's hand and they walked a few steps away. "What about us, Jack?"

"What do you mean?"

"Well, I'll spend a few days here with my friends, but then I'll have to go back to Dublin. At least until I decide what to do with myself." She took both of his hands and looked into his eyes. "I want you to come with me. Ireland is a beautiful country. We can pick up where we left off. See where things go."

"Well," he folded his arms, "I am currently unemployed, so I guess I have the free time. It's tempting." Jack smiled and nodded his head. "Yeah... why not?" He hesitated, squinting. "Hey... do you realize? I don't even know your name."

She shook his hand and made an abbreviated curtsy. "Jack Monroe, pleased to meet you. My name is Maeve Hennessey, but I'll probably go back to being Ellen McCarthy."

"Wait," Jack scrunched his face, "did you copy the name of that Irish author?"

"Actually..." she stood with her hands folded in front of her, biting her lip.

"Oh my God." Jack brushed his hair back and smiled. "Seriously?"

Eileen nodded.

"That's crazy. I read your book, *Three Days in Cobh*. It was very good. I can't believe that I was reading a book written by you and had no clue."

"I have to give you the credit, Jack."

"Me? How?"

"I remembered your talk about wanting to be a writer. You made it sound interesting, so I thought, what the hell. At Trinity College in Dublin, I majored in English and creative writing. I struggled for a while, working as an editor at a publishing house. I wrote a few novels that fizzled, but then I finally had success landing a publisher."

Mik and Katie Creighton walked out of the courthouse and joined them. "Well, at least that lunatic is going to remain behind bars until his trial," Mik said.

"And forever after, God willing," Katie added. "The government's case is lock-tight. And with Hollingsworth's testimony, I think he's cooked."

"What have you guys got planned for the evening? Wanna grab dinner?" Jack asked.

Mik looked at Katie, then back at Jack. "Sorry, man, we've got tickets for a dinner cruise on the Boston Harbor. We thought it might be fun to try a boat ride without someone shooting at us." He put his arm around her waist and pulled her close. She leaned her head on his shoulder.

Jack threw his hands in the air. "I guess I'm on my own."

Mason Hollingsworth walked out of the courthouse accompanied by his lawyer and a federal marshal. He looked at them and then walked toward their group. Behind him, Seamus Callanan walked with his hands cuffed and chained to ankle shackles. He was flanked by two marshals.

Hollingsworth approached Eileen and Amanda. He bit his upper lip as he looked down at his shoes, then back at the girls. "For what it's worth," he said, "I can't begin to express how sorry I am for everything that I've done, and for how it has affected you both. I should have had the courage to do the right thing long ago, but I didn't."

Seamus Callanan was shuffling slowly across the brick plaza with venom in his eyes. He spat the words out. "Hollingsworth, you filthy coward!" the Irish brogue lacing his words. "You can run but you can't hide. You'll get what's coming, sooner than you think." He sneered at him and spat on the ground.

On the rooftop across the street, the man in the tactical pants and camo hat watched them come out of the building with his binoculars. He picked up his rifle and crouched down under the tent, placing the rifle's bipod on the concrete wall. He pulled back the bolt, loading the large round into the chamber, and peered through the reticles of his scope.

As he scanned the people standing on the plaza below, he adjusted the focus on the scope. He found Ellen McCarthy in his sights. The description was accurate. She was much older now, but he could see it. The blond hair, the eyes, everything about her. He'd already calculated the exact distance using the known geometry. He knew the height of the building and the horizontal distance to the plaza. He'd have to make an educated guess as to the wind speed and direction. First, he adjusted the elevation: click, click, click. Then he adjusted for windage: click, click, click.

He moved the scope to the right and found Mason Hollingsworth.

"And you," Seamus Callanan directed his gaze to Eileen. "You think you've gotten away with it, don't you?" He screamed at her, tugging and rattling the chains which kept him in check. "You know what you did, and I know what you did. And mark my words, you'll pay for it!" The federal marshal shoved him forward. "Keep moving."

Seamus Callanan continued shuffling with his shackles. A shot rang out, echoing off the tall buildings. A bullet struck the brick on the ground behind Callanan and ricocheted up, lodging in the wall of the building. Callanan's body convulsed. He looked down at the left side of his chest. His white shirt had an enlarging dark red stain. Blood oozed out through the gaps between the buttons. The marshals crouched down, drawing their handguns. Callanan looked at Hollingsworth, then at the girls. His eyes rolled back and his legs buckled. His body collapsed onto the ground.

On the rooftop across the street, Lars Johansson wept as he rolled onto his back, cradling his rifle. He looked up to the sky. "This is for you, Elsa. Rest in peace, peanut. And for you, Anna, for the years of sorrow he put you through. We'll all be together soon enough." He pulled up the sleeve on his left arm, revealing his tattoo. It read *Semper Fidelis, USMC.* He scratched at it, softly at first, then vigorously, causing the skin to bleed. "I'm going to have to get rid of this tattoo, Anna. I know how proud it made you, but I'm no longer worthy."

CHAPTER 38

Tuesday, June 30, 2020

The Yorkshire Inn was quiet, typical for a Tuesday night. They sat in a back-corner booth, surrounded by walnut paneling.

"So, what happened with that DA?" Mik asked Erin.

She finished chewing a piece of pretzel. "Well, I called in a favor from a friend at the DOJ." Erin strummed her fingers on the table. "They launched an investigation into Schictman's tenure as district attorney. The findings were alarming, to say the least."

"What'd they find?" Mik leaned forward.

"Officer Dudley agreed to a plea deal. He testified that Schictman paid him under the table to embellish evidence, to get convictions. The DOJ pressured the governor, whose fund-raising dinners I've attended on a few occasions." Erin smiled deviously as she raised her eyebrows, pushing her tongue into her cheek. "The governor suspended him pending the outcome of the investigation. Suffice it to say that his dream of becoming state attorney general is dead in the water." Erin covered her face. "Oops, sorry... bad choice of words."

Jack grimaced.

Mik smiled. "He'll lose his law license for sure." He turned to Erin. "Now that you're finished with the merger, Erin, when will you go back to DC?"

"Soon, but I've been considering a transfer to the New York office. I love DC, but my family and friends are here, and I miss this area. I didn't realize how much. Autumn is beautiful, and it's around the corner." Her eyes locked on Katie, holding Mik's hand under the table. She shrugged. "Maybe I'll have better luck finding a guy here."

Jack scratched his chin. "Do you still like riding your bicycle?"

"Sure," Erin responded. "Why do you ask?"

"Oh... no reason," Jack raised his eyebrows.

"What about you, Jack?" Katie asked. "What are your plans?"

"Not sure."

"Did you get your privileges back?"

"Yes," he put his hands behind his head. "They're begging me to come back, but then I remembered how they treated me. So, I'll let them stew for a while. Honestly, I'd already resigned myself to retiring from medicine."

"So that's it then?" Mik asked.

"Maybe not. I keep thinking about Connie and Andre Jackson, and the other people I've helped."

"That must be a good feeling," Katie said.

"Yeah," Jack nodded. "It is. So anyway, I thought maybe I'd go back part-time. And then with my free time... who knows? I could finally give writing a try. When I was a young kid, I read my first book, *Treasure Island*. Ever since, I was hooked, and I've always wanted to write one." Jack threw up his hands. "Call it a mid-life crisis."

"Maybe Eileen can help you. That's her line of work, isn't it?" Katie asked.

"Apparently so. I keep learning new things every day."

"So, you're really going to Dublin?" Mik asked.

"That's the immediate plan. At least for now."

Mik folded his hands and pressed his lips together. "Maybe I'm out of line here, but I have to say, I always thought that you'd end up with Connie. You guys seemed like the perfect couple. I mean, Eileen's great, don't get me wrong. What she has gone through is an epic tragedy." He patted Jack on the shoulder. "That's a really tough choice, man. I'm glad I don't have to make it."

Jack's smile faded. "I won't pretend that I don't have feelings for Connie. I do. But I've spent most of my life pining over Eileen, thinking about how our relationship was interrupted. I've always wondered what might have happened if she hadn't left, and now she's back. We have a second chance. That must be some sort of sign, right?"

They all nodded halfheartedly, averting their eyes. "I suppose so," Mik said.

***

Special Agent David Roche and his partner Ed Bolton walked up the brick stairway in Conway, New Hampshire, and knocked on the door. An older gentleman opened the door. He wore khakis and a long-sleeve shirt that hung off his emaciated frame. There was a sad, disconnected look in his eyes.

"Lars Johansson?" Agent Roche asked, holding up his FBI shield. "I'm Special Agent David Roche, and this is Agent Bolton. We'd like to have a word with you, if we may."

Lars Johansson opened the door and held it for the agents. "I've been expecting you fellows. Can I offer you a cup of coffee?" he asked.

They shook their heads. "No, thank you, Mr. Johansson, this won't take long." Agent Roche's eyes regarded the man sympathetically.

"I'm the one you're looking for." Lars Johansson lifted his finger and pointed to the corner of the room where a vintage scoped rifle stood against the pastel yellow wall. His eyes started to moisten. "If I could please just have a few minutes to close up the place and call my daughter to say goodbye, I'd be grateful to you."

Roche looked at Bolton and then back at Lars. "You're not going anywhere, Mr. Johansson. Please have a seat."

Lars flashed a curious look at both of them and tried to steady his tremor as he lowered himself into his easy chair. "I don't understand."

David Roche reached into his jacket pocket and pulled out a light blue ribbon attached to an anchor-and-star-shaped medallion. "We wanted to return this to you, sir." He got up and handed the medal to Lars.

"I still don't understand," he said.

"It wasn't hard finding you, Mr. Johansson. There are hundreds of people who wanted Seamus Callanan dead. But only one who was the recipient of the Congressional Medal of Honor. But I suppose you knew that too, and that's why you left it for us."

Lars held the medal in both hands. "I don't deserve it any longer. I've shamed myself and the Marine Corps."

"Nonsense." Bolton jumped in. "We know about your service, sir. You were the most decorated Marine sniper of the Vietnam War. A true American hero. You saved countless lives; my father may have been one of them. He was one of the evacuated wounded at Khe Sanh." Bolton rolled up his shirt sleeve, exposing a USMC tattoo on his upper arm. "That's why I joined. Because of my father, and men like you."

"Lars," Roche walked over and put his hand on his shoulder. He looked up at the portrait of Elsa on the wall. "You've suffered enough. More than any father ever should."

Roche walked back to his seat and faced Lars again. "You're a free man, Lars. Free to live out the rest of your life. The president has already issued a preemptive pardon and instructed the DOJ to table this investigation. It will be kept quiet. As far as the public is concerned, it is just another unsolved gang hit job."

Lars Johansson dropped his head. "I don't deserve your generosity, but I will use it to make the most of my remaining time with my children. Thank you both."

David Roche smiled. "If it's alright with you, I think we will take you up on that cup of coffee."

***

Jack and Eileen sat in a booth in the Sky Club lounge at JFK Airport. They sipped on the complimentary white wine and ate cheese and crackers.

"What's wrong, Jack?"

Jack shook his head. "Nothing, I'm fine."

She reached out and took his hand. "Jack, come on. Something's wrong. Tell me."

Jack looked into her eyes and hesitated. "What did Seamus Callanan mean when he said, 'you know what you did'?" Jack put both of his hands on hers. "It keeps going through my head. And then Amanda inferred that it was your idea to go to Callanan's warehouse."

Eileen swallowed. Her smile dissipated, and she leaned back in her chair. "I suppose I owe you that much."

She looked around the room, then down at the table. "When I was growing up, my parents owned a small pharmacy in South Boston. They had to pay the local mob protection money, whatever that means. In reality, it was extortion. Fifteen percent of their profits, stolen, just like they did to every other business in the neighborhood. If you didn't pay, they'd beat you or burn your business down, or worse."

She stopped. Her eyes were red, and she started sniffling.

"It's okay, Eileen," Jack said. "You don't owe me an explanation."

She took a drink of her wine. "My father got behind on his payments, and they beat him badly. Nearly killed him. I can't get the picture of his bruised face out of my head." A tear dripped slowly down her cheek.

"Callanan's nephew was one of his shakedown men. He was a skeevy, greasy son of a bitch. And he... took me aside one day and told me if I would perform certain... favors for him, he could give my father more time."

Jack squeezed her hands tightly. "I'm so sorry."

"And so, I agreed to meet him at his uncle's warehouse," Eileen continued. "We were on the third-floor landing. He had his pants down and then he started slapping me around. He said I'd better be good or he'd beat my father again. And then..." She paused.

Jack looked in her eyes, waiting. "And then... what?"

"I became enraged, not for myself, but for my family. I jabbed him with a syringe of ketamine which I had snuck out of the pharmacy. He jumped and the needle broke. Only half of it went in, so he didn't pass out, he just became dazed and disoriented. And then I pushed him."

"You pushed him? What do you mean?"

She looked into his eyes. "I pushed him really hard and he tumbled over the railing. He caught himself and was pulling himself back up. That's when I cracked him over the head with a ceramic lamp. He fell to the first floor and broke his neck, and I fled."

Jack stared at her. She was crying now, and a few people in the lounge noticed. They lowered their voices. "That's self-defense, Eileen. It wasn't your fault."

"Wasn't it? It was premeditated. I brought the drug. I intended to kill him. He was still alive and struggling to breathe. I went down to the first floor and stood over him as he suffocated. I grabbed his jaw and made sure he saw my face. Then I left. But in the confusion, I forgot that I'd brought my purse with me, with my identification."

"That's why I picked that place when I went back with Amanda. I didn't tell Amanda, but I needed to get my purse back before it was found. I guess Callanan must have found it before the police raided the warehouse. His nephew's death was reported as an accidental fall a few days earlier. I assume they pulled his pants up before the coroner arrived."

Eileen looked at Jack. "You hate me, don't you? I don't blame you. You must think I'm a terrible person."

"No. Not at all," Jack said, shaking his head. "I feel sad for everything that's happened to you."

"What is it then?"

"It's Connie. I feel terrible about Connie."

"I do too, Jack. It's like history repeating."

"How do you mean?"

"I remember when you guys were dating in high school. You were on the football team, handsome and popular. I decided that I wanted you for myself, just like the other girls. I thought that if I was with you, then I'd be popular too, and fit in. So, I decided to make a move. I'd heard Connie had saved up to buy you tickets to some workshop that you wanted to go to. It was expensive and she'd finally saved the money, so I figured I had to make my move before she did, or I'd lose my chance. I've always felt guilty about it. That was the night they had that summer party, and I met you sitting around the fire pit. Do you remember?"

Jack was still digesting what he'd just learned. "Yes... sure, I remember." And now he understood the look on Connie's face when she saw him holding hands with Eileen. "What sort of workshop?"

"It was something about writing. A creative-writing workshop. Something like that." She bit her lip. "I'm so sorry, Jack."

He started flashing back to all the times, over the years, that Connie had selflessly put his needs ahead of her own. He thought about how terrified and upset she got with him when he joked about committing suicide. He thought about how she was willing to stand aside to let him be with Eileen, as long as it meant he would be happy.

Jack looked at Eileen, and she knew. "I'm sorry, Eileen. I can't go with you."

She nodded. "You don't have to be sorry, Jack."

"You're a wonderful person, and I love you. I suppose I always will. And I'm sorry for all that you've had to go through." He took her hands into his. "Do you know how it is when a sequel to a movie comes out, and you want it to be better than the first movie, but it can't be? Because the first one was so perfect?"

She smiled at him with her almond eyes. "Our first 'movie' was perfect, Jack. But I know your heart is telling you that there's not going to be a sequel." She clasped her fingers. "I know you love Connie, Jack."

Jack nodded. He got up and moved to her side of the booth and hugged her tightly.

"If you ever get that first book written, give me a call," she whispered in his ear. "I have some clout with my publisher."

"Thank you," Jack paused, looking at her, "and what about you?"

"Well... there's a guy that I've dated casually for a year. He's a good man. When this thing erupted with your trial, and the premature reporting of my demise, I knew I had to do something. And I thought maybe, just maybe, there would be a spark left between us. And there was. I know we both felt it. And it was beautiful. But your heart already belonged to someone else. And this time, I don't want to mess that up, Jack. Connie is a great girl. I really like her. And I know how much she loves you."

Jack looked at his watch. "Your plane will be boarding soon. I guess it's time to say goodbye."

"Yes, it is," she nodded. "Can I ask one favor?"

"Sure, anything."

"Kiss me one last time. That's how I'd like to remember us."

Jack slowly leaned toward her. He put his lips to hers, and they kissed. For one brief moment in time, it was 1995 again.

***

Jack's mind was absorbed in thought. The drive home from the airport was a complete blur. He'd tried twice to call Connie, but she didn't pick up, so he drove to the Gigantes' home.

When he arrived, he was ushered in by the housekeeper into the lounge, where Jimmy Gigante was seated watching a baseball game. Joan joined them.

"Jack, what are you doing here?" she said. "We thought you were on your way to Ireland."

"My plans have changed, Mrs. Gigante. Do you know where Connie is? I need to talk to her."

The two of them looked at each other. Jimmy spoke first. "Jack, Connie was really down. She felt like she needed to get away and do some thinking."

"Away?" Jack asked. "Where did she go?"

Jimmy looked at Joan. She nodded. "I wanted to move my boat down to the Keys for the winter. Jimmy Jr.'s got a new girlfriend, and they were going to sail it down to Key West for me, today. Connie has a month off before school starts, so she decided to join them, to clear her mind and get a fresh start."

"Jimmy had a dentist appointment," Joan added. "They were going to leave after that. I think around three o'clock, or so."

Jack looked at his watch. Two o'clock. "It'll be close. I've got to go." He started to move toward the door. Then he stopped, looking back at Jimmy.

"Mr. Gigante, this may be bad timing, and somewhat old-fashioned, but I'd like to ask your permission to marry your daughter, if she'll have me."

Joan rushed over to Jack and hugged him, nearly knocking him off his feet. "Yes, yes, of course," she shouted.

Jimmy raised his palms. "Joan, please. He asked me. I'm the girl's father. Who's the boss here?"

"You are, dear," Joan said, rolling her eyes at Jack.

Jimmy smiled. "You heard the lady. Christ, Jack, you saved her life, how could I say no?"

"Twice," Joan said.

"What?"

"He saved her life twice. The brain tumor, and the gunshot."

Jimmy smacked himself on the head. "How could I forget? I must be losing my marbles. Go, Jack." He waved his hands. "You're gonna need that tricked-out engine of yours to catch her."

"Thank you," Jack said, running for the door. "Thank you both."

***

Jack arrived at the Brielle Yacht Club slightly after three o'clock. He parked and sprinted down to the dock where the Gigantes' slip was located. The *Joan's Ark* was gone. He stood next to the empty space, hands on his knees, catching his breath. He looked around the harbor and didn't see the boat.

Further down the dock there was a young guy with long blond hair in a short-legged wetsuit, getting onto a Jet Ski.

"Hey, man," Jack shouted as he ran over, waving at the guy, who appeared to be in his late teens. "Have you seen the sailboat that usually docks right over there?"

"Yeah, sure. They went out about twenty minutes ago. Probably just passing through the inlet."

"Could you take me to them?" Jack asked.

He laughed and shook his head. "Sorry, buddy, I'm not a taxi service."

Jack pulled out his wallet and looked inside. "I'll give you two hundred and fifty dollars."

The kid's eyes lit up. "Seriously?"

"Seriously."

He looked Jack up and down. "Are you gonna wear those clothes?"

Jack looked down at his khaki pants, Ralph Lauren shirt, and Cole Haan shoes. "That's all I've got."

"Okay, but you're gonna get soaked. The name's Chad."

"I'm Jack. I'll take my chances." Jack handed him the money.

"Hop on, man."

Jack got onto the back of the Jet Ski. Chad revved the engine and they took off.

Fifteen minutes later they were through the inlet, bouncing on the swelling surf. Jack saw the black hull of the *Joan's Ark* ahead, slicing through the water, its sails fully trimmed. "There they are," he shouted.

Chad headed for the sailboat, and within a few minutes they were along the starboard side of the boat. Jimmy and his girlfriend were out on deck. Jimmy held the wheel.

"Jimmy," Jack yelled, waving his arms.

Jimmy turned his head. "Jack, what the hell are you doing here?"

"Get close, Chad. They can't stop the boat. I'm going to have to jump."

"I can't get too close. I'll do my best." Chad had the Jet Ski within four feet of the boat between the bow and midsection. Jack crouched down, preparing to jump. "Thanks, Chad." He launched himself up and over the gunwale but fell short. He held tight to the rail while his body dragged in the water.

Jimmy rushed to the side. He reached over and grabbed Jack's belt, leaning his body backward to try to pull Jack up, as Jack tried to get purchase with his feet. His shoe fell into the water. Jimmy pulled harder, and Jack's body rolled over the gunwale onto the deck.

Connie had just come onto the deck from below. "Jack! Oh my God! What are you doing here?" She rushed over and knelt down beside him. "Are you crazy? What are you doing here? You're supposed to be in Ireland."

A girl with long brown hair and blue eyes looked down into Jack's face. Jimmy came up behind her. "Jack, this is Ava, my girlfriend. Ava, this is my friend, Jack."

Jack looked up at her upside-down face. A tattoo of a long stemmed rose spiraled around her left arm. "Pleased to meet you." She dropped her hand, and Jack shook it.

"Really, Jimmy?" Connie said. "Could you give us a minute?"

Jimmy shrugged. "We'll talk later, buddy." He and Ava went back to the cockpit. Connie knelt down next to him, running her fingers through his wet hair.

"You're supposed to be in Dublin, Jack."

"No, I'm not." He winced from the pain in his ribs. "I'm supposed to be here, with you. I realize that now. It's taken me twenty-seven years to figure it out." Jack grabbed Connie's shoulders. "I love you, Connie."

She turned her head. "I know... like a friend."

"No, not like that." He reached up and turned her face toward him, caressing her cheek. "I love you. I should have realized it long ago. I've been such an idiot. I want to spend the rest of my life making it up to you."

She looked into his eyes and started crying. "I've always loved you, Jack. From that first kiss on the hammock in Sea Girt."

He put his hands on either side of her head and pulled her down until their lips met. He was soaking wet and his entire body hurt, but he didn't care. He didn't want to let go, and he didn't.

***

It was nine o'clock and darkness blanketed the Atlantic Ocean. Low in the sky, an oversized moon hovered, its light dancing on the crests of the waves. They had decided to anchor for the night in a protected cove tucked along the coast of Maryland. Off the starboard side, the lights on the shore cast a colorful glow over the water's surface as the four sat on the deck, wearing sweatshirts, sipping wine. Jack had his arm around Connie, and her head rested on his neck. Across from them Ava sat with her back against Jimmy's side. A cool breeze blew from the east.

"Thanks for the clothes, Jimmy."

"No problem. Good thing we're the same size," he said.

Jimmy had been studying Jack and Connie, sensing that they needed a little privacy. He stood up, stretching his arms. "Come on, Ava. I'm pretty beat." Ava looked at Jimmy, as he gave her a quick head tilt, raising his eyebrows.

"Oh... yeah, me too," she said, exaggerating a yawn. "Good night, guys." They gathered up their things and went below to their cabin.

Connie spread out on the bench, laying her head on Jack's chest. "So... what about you and Eileen, Jack?" She rubbed his knee with her hand.

Jack rested his chin on Connie's head. There was an extended pause before he answered. "Eileen and I were two teenagers in love, Connie, for a fleeting moment in time. A very long time ago." He tightened his arms around her and kissed the top of her head.

"You know how you love peach pie?"

"Yeah, I do," she smiled. "You remembered."

"I remember a lot of things." He traced the skin on her cheek with his index finger.

"What's that got to do with anything?"

He went on, "So, if you decided to cut out sugar, and give up peach pie, you'd be okay with that, right?"

She twisted her head back to face him. "Do you think I'm fat, Jack? Am I fat?"

"No," Jack shook his head, "not at all. Just hear me out."

She thought for a second. "Yeah, sure... I suppose I'd be okay with that."

"But if someone said you can't have peach pie, ever again, and took it away from you, you'd crave it even more."

"Jack, if you're looking for dessert, we don't have any pie."

"No." Jack laughed. "I don't want dessert. I'm making an analogy. What I mean is that I spent my life consumed with Eileen's memory, because she was taken from me. And that loss affected my life, dooming other relationships. It blinded me to so many other good things in my life which I should have seen..." he swallowed, rubbing his cheek on the top of her head. "Like you."

Connie looked up into Jack's eyes. "It means a lot that you came back for me, Jack. I was sure I'd lost you again." Connie snuggled up against his chest.

"You'll never lose me again, Connie. That's a promise. When we get to Key West, we're going to go to that jewelry store on Duval Street. Then I'm going to take you to Mallory Pier at sunset and ask you an important question, and I'm hoping that you will say yes."

"You really suck at romantic analogies. Do you know that?"

Jack laughed. "Yeah, the pie thing sounded much better in my head."

She wrapped her arm around his neck and kissed him. "I think it's bedtime," she whispered.

"Are you tired?"

She looked at him coyly from the corner of her eye. "Not at all."

He kissed her and took her hand as they walked toward the cabin.

They stopped and faced each other.

"And this time, Jack, just to be perfectly clear, I'm not intoxicated."

Jack put his hands on her hips. "Duly noted."

EPILOGUE

September 26, 2021

Autumn splendor had peaked in the mountains of New Hampshire, with a brilliant palette of red, orange, yellow and green blanketing the hillsides. Connie walked slowly, caressing the baby bump in her abdomen, which had recently started to show. The smell of pine wafted over the tranquil footpath on the crisp mountain air. She walked down the moss-covered brick path through The Madonna of the Mountain Cemetery, coming to a stop in front of the Johanssons' gravesite, and placed a few cut flowers on top of the stone.

She stood silently, saying a prayer for the young girl buried below. When she had finished, she gathered her thoughts and spoke solemnly to the spirits unseen. "I can't begin to tell you how sorry I am," she said, as a tear rolled down her cheek, "I never meant to hurt you, or anyone."

Sometimes our actions have unintended consequences, which we have to live with, she thought. If only we could go back in time and change those things which we got so wrong.

Connie sat down under the maple tree next to the stone and leaned back against it. She reached into her bag and pulled out her journal and a pen. She scribbled the date and began to make an entry.

September 26, 2021

Jack is away on a two-week medical mission trip to Africa. He doesn't know that I am here in New Hampshire, and I suspect that's the way it will have to remain. I have finally come to pay my respects to Elsa Johansson. It's the least I can do. After all, I'm the reason that she's dead. May God forgive me. That day by the fire pit replays in a never-ending loop in my mind. I was so angry when Eileen stole Jack away from me. We were happy before she arrived. He loved me. It doesn't excuse what I did.

After all these years, my dad still doesn't know that the ventilation grill in his office carries sound up the shaft and through my bedroom closet. That came in handy many times when I was a teen. I knew all about Eileen's past through discussions I'd heard between my dad and her father. To this day, I still bear the shame of what I did. I was young and naive. I thought by sending an anonymous letter to Callanan, it would force Eileen into hiding again. They blamed that poor US Marshal, but he never talked. He never gave up her identity. The authorities got it all wrong. It was me. I knew that my dad would protect Eileen and not let them hurt her. Despite what she did, I didn't want her hurt. I figured she'd just have to change identities again and move on. Out of Jack's life, and mine. And I'd have Jack back, the way it was before. The way things were meant to be. I never envisioned the horrible chain of events that I would unleash by that one stupid act.

Connie put her hand on her abdomen and thought she felt the baby kick. She smiled, thinking how lucky she was. Despite all that had gone wrong, everything had come together for her in the end. Just as she had always dreamed it would. She continued writing.

> *The ultrasound showed that our baby was going to be a girl. I've given it a lot of thought, and I think I want to name her Elsa. It's such a beautiful name.*

From high above in the tree came a hooting sound. It startled her, and she looked up. There, perched on one of the branches, was a grayish-brown owl, its large round eyes staring down at her.

THE END

ACKNOWLEDGEMENTS

Writing this debut novel represents the culmination of a goal I have had for a very long time. Since I began reading books as a child, I imagined one day writing one myself. Unfortunately, the activities of life sometimes get in the way of our passions, and they are unnecessarily postponed. Well, not any longer. I hope this will be the first of many stories yet to weave and novels yet to write. I do it not for profit. I have a comfortable life already. Rather, my true intention is to entertain readers in the same way as I have been entertained over the years by so many of my favorite authors of fiction, such as Harlan Coben, Tess Gerritsen, Freida McFadden, and countless others. I hope in some small way I have accomplished that.

With that said, I'd like to thank those people who helped me bring this book to fruition. My editor and project manager Amy Savoy for putting it all together beautifully. Doris Smith for invaluable early assistance with developmental editing, which greatly improved the flow of the book. My query editors, Gina Denny and Alysha Welliver. I'd also like to give a nod of appreciation to several of my early beta readers who furnished much-needed encouragement and critique, including Leslie Krentz, Quentin Franklin, James Armstrong, Michael Weinberg, Meghan Roemer, Thomas Nebbia, Donna Carter, Cindy Grier Wolfe, Sherianne Simpson, Ronald Wall, and his wife LeslieAnne Dexter. Forgive me if I have inadvertently omitted anyone.

Lastly, I'd like to thank all the people in my life, present or past, who have encouraged and helped me along the way, including Leslie Krentz, my significant other, and our blended family: Erin Mason, Katie Nebbia, Nicholas Krentz, and Victoria Krentz, who have allowed me the time to toil away at my laptop. My parents Joan Ann Nebbia Wagner, Leo Weber, and stepfather George Wagner and wife Lori, stepmother Susan Weber, as well as my grandparents Patrick and Constance Nebbia, Cecil and Julius Weber, and siblings Thomas Nebbia, Steven Weber, Laura Lee Dietz, George Wagner, and Chris Wagner. My uncles Paul and Robert Weber, my in-laws Donna and John Carter, my ex-wife Robin Nebbia, newly acquired family members Ben Bolton, Brendan Mason, Carter Dewey, Lauren Falter, and their families. All of my great high school and college friends, especially Strube Cody Jackson, and Jack Howley. I have learned many varied and valuable things from each of these people.

And to Doctor Arnold Gold, MD, mentor and world-renowned pioneer of pediatric neurology and medical humanitarianism, who taught me how to use chopsticks.

And for you, the readers, who were kind enough to spend a few valuable hours of your lives reading my novel. I hope you enjoyed it.

The list wouldn't be complete without including all those individuals whose first or last names have been borrowed in naming the characters in this novel. Notwithstanding the standard disclaimer included on the copyright page — that the characters themselves are all purely fictitious and not meant to represent any real human being, which is technically true — but seriously, you know who you are. Consider it my way of letting you know that you have impacted my life in some meaningful way.

Thank you all.

ABOUT THE AUTHOR

STEPHAN PATRICK NEBBIA was born Patrick Conrad Weber, in Teaneck New Jersey. He attended the University of Notre Dame and Rutgers Medical School in Newark, NJ. He did his medical residency training at Emory, Vanderbilt and the University of Toronto and is a practicing, board-certified, pediatric anesthesiologist. This is his first full length work of fiction, and hopefully, the first of many. In his spare time, he enjoys skiing, snowboarding, golf, martial arts, writing, scuba diving and mostly spending time with his family.